The 13th Juror

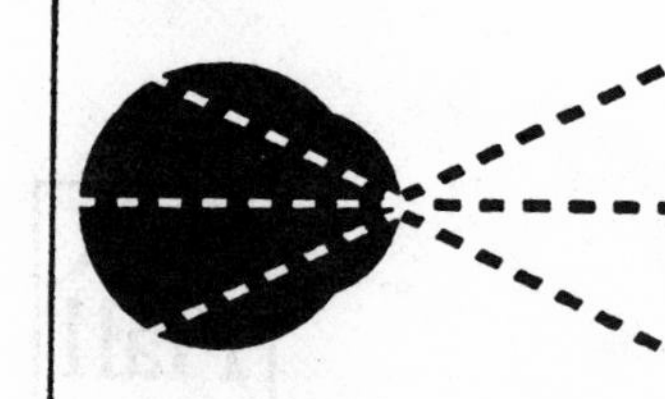

The 13th Juror

John T. Lescroart

G.K. Hall & Co.
Thorndike, Maine

Published in 1994 by arrangement with Donald I. Fine, Inc.

G.K. Hall Large Print Core Collection.

The text of this Large Print edition is unabridged. Other aspects of the book may vary from the original edition.

Set in 16 pt. News Plantin.

Printed in the United States on acid-free paper.

Library of Congress Cataloging in Publication Data

Lescroart, John T.
The 13th juror : a novel / by John T. Lescroart.
p. cm.
ISBN 0-8161-7448-2 (alk. paper : lg. print)
1. Large type books. I. Title.
[PS3562.E78A615 1994] 94-32218

To my brothers,
Michael
and Emmett

Acknowledgments

Many people have contributed their support and knowledge to this book. First among them is my wife — the rock of my life — Lisa Sawyer. Once again, Al Giannini has been a true friend and guide. Also in the San Francisco District Attorney's office, my gratitude to Laura Meyer, Mercedes Moreno, Candace Heisler and Diane Knoles, whose comments on battered women were insightful and ultimately inspiring.

I'd also like to thank San Francisco Coroner Dr. Boyd Stephens; bailiff Bruce McMurtry; Jim Costello; Frank at Zuka's, the real Lou the Greek's; Mike Hamilburg and Joanie Socola; Maureena Moore with Federal Express; Kelly Talbot; Steve Martini; Dick Herman; Kathryn and Mark Detzer; Peter Diedrich; Peter Bransten; my piscatorial pal Jackie Cantor for her unfailing sense of humor and support in all areas; and Arthur Ginsburg.

My editor (and publisher) Don Fine has done a yeoman's job nipping, tucking and tightening the sprawling manuscript into its final form, and I am extremely grateful for his unflagging efforts and support.

Finally, to some regular dinner partners — you know who you are — who have seriously lightened the load, and oh yes, to Don Matheson. Thanks.

We would give her more consideration, when we judge a woman, if we knew how difficult it is to be a woman.

— P. GERALDY

The fickleness of the women I love is only equaled by the infernal constancy of the women who love me.

— GEORGE BERNARD SHAW

PART ONE

Jennifer Witt rechecked the table. It looked perfect, but when you never knew what perfect was, it was hard to be sure. There were two new red candles — Larry had a problem with half-burnt candles, with guttered wicks — in gleaming silver candlesticks.

She had considered having one red candle and one green candle since it was getting to be Christmas time. But Larry didn't like a jumble of colors. The living room was done all in champagne — which wasn't the easiest to keep clean, especially with a seven-year-old — but she wasn't going to change it. She remembered when she'd bought the Van Gogh print (A PRINT, FOR CHRIST'S SAKE! YOU'D HANG A PRINT IN MY LIVING ROOM?) and the colors had really bothered Larry.

He liked things ordered, exact. He was a doctor. Lives depended on his judgment. He couldn't get clouded up with junk in his own home, he told her.

So she went with the red candlesticks.

And the china. He liked the china, but then he'd get upset that things were so formal in their own home. Couldn't she just relax and serve them something plain on the white Pottery Barn stuff? Maybe just hot dogs and beans? They didn't have to eat gourmet every night. She tried hard to please, but with Larry, you never knew.

One time he wasn't in the mood for hot dogs and beans, he'd had an especially hard day, he said, and felt like some adult food. And Matt had had a bad day at school and was whining, and one of the plates had a chip in the side.

She shook her head to clear the memory.

Tonight she was making up with him, or trying to, so she decided to go with the china. She could feel his dissatisfaction . . . it got worse every time before he blew up . . . and she was trying to keep the explosion off for a few more days if she could.

So she'd fixed his favorite — the special veal kidney chops that you had to go get at Little City Meats in North Beach. And the December asparagus from Petrini's at $4.99 a pound. And she'd gotten Matt down early to bed.

She looked at herself in the mirror, thinking it odd that so many men thought she was attractive. Her nose had a hook halfway down the ridge. Her skin, to her, looked almost translucent, almost like a death mask. You could see all the bone structure, and she was too thin. And her eyes, too light a blue for her olive skin. Deep-set, somehow foreign-looking, as though her ancestors had come from Sicily or Naples instead of Milano, as they had.

She leaned over and looked more closely. There was still a broken vein, but the eyeshadow masked the last of the yellowish bruise. As she waited for him to come home, checking and rechecking, she had been curling her lower lip into her teeth again. Thank God she'd noticed the speck of coral lipstick on her tooth, the slight smear that had run beyond the edge of her liner.

Quickly, listening for the front door, she stepped

out of her shoes and tiptoed over the hardwood floor — trying not to wake Matt — to the bathroom, where the light was better. Taking some Kleenex, she pressed her lips with it and reapplied the pencil, then the gloss. Larry liked the glossy wet look. Not too much, though. Too much looked cheap, like you were asking for it, he said.

She walked back to the front of the house. When she got to the champagne rug, she slipped her pumps back on.

Olympia Way, up by the Sutro Tower, was quiet. It was the shortest day of the year, the first day of winter, and the street lights had been on since she had gotten back from shopping at 5:00 P.M. *She checked her watch. It was 7:15.*

Dinner would be ready at exactly 7:20, which was when they always ate. Larry arrived from the clinic between 6:50 and 7:05 every day. Well, almost every day. When he got home he liked his two ounces of Scotch, Laphraoig, with one ice cube, while she finished putting dinner on the table.

7:18.

She wondered if she should turn off the oven. Would he still want his drink first? If so, what about the dinner? She could put it out on the table, but then it might be cold before he got around to it. Larry really hated it when his meal was cold.

Worse, he might think she was trying to hurry him. What he didn't need after a long day seeing patients was somebody in his home telling him to hurry up.

The asparagus was the problem.

What if Larry walked in the door in exactly one minute and wanted to go right to the table and the asparagus wasn't ready? It had to cook in the steamer for ninety seconds — if there was one thing Larry really couldn't abide it was soggy limp asparagus. Maybe, if he came in and sat right down she could dawdle over serving the rest of the meal and the asparagus would be perfect just at the right time. That's what she'd do.

It was a little risky but better than putting it on now, thinking he'd get home on time and want to sit down right away, and then having him be late and the asparagus be overcooked.

No sign of his Lexus coming up the street. No one was coming up the street. Where was he? Damn, she was biting her lower lip again.

7:20. She turned the heat off under the rice. At least that would be all right for a while if she kept it covered — each grain separate just the way Larry liked it.

She made sure the water was right at the boil and that there was enough in the steamer. Everything depended on the asparagus being ready to go as soon as Larry walked in the door. As soon as she heard him, even. If the water wasn't boiling, or if it ran out underneath, that would ruin everything.

By 8:15 she had taken the chops out of the oven, refilled the water in the steamer three times and added butter to the rice to keep it from sticking, but there wasn't any hope now. At 7:35, she had poured Larry's Scotch and added the ice cube, now melted long ago. At the hour she poured the diluted drink into the sink.

She heard the footsteps on the walk outside. God, she hoped he'd found a parking place nearby. Sometimes if you got home late there wasn't anywhere to park within blocks, and that always put him in a real bad mood.

The dinner could, maybe, be saved. She knew what she could do . . . she'd pour him the new Scotch now, with a new ice cube, greet him at the door and let him unwind for twenty minutes until the second round of rice was cooked. She could microwave the chops on low power and they probably wouldn't get too dry. The asparagus wouldn't be any problem.

She had the drink in her hand, ready for him, when he opened the door. He was tall and very handsome — with his cleft chin and his body still young at forty-one. He had all his hair, wavy and fashionably long. An Italian suit, colorful tie with a snow-white shirt — colors, he said, were okay in a tie, so long as they didn't clash. She put the drink in his hand, pecked his cheek, smiled up at him.

"Where have you been?"

God, she hadn't meant to say that. It had just come out, and right away she wished she could take it back.

"What do you mean, where have I been? Where do you think I've been?"

"Well, I mean, it's late. I thought . . . I was worried."

"You were worried. I like that." He seemed to notice the drink for the first time. "What's this?"

"It's your Scotch, Larry. Why don't you sit down, relax."

"What time is it? You know when I get home this late I don't like to drink before dinner. I'd like some food in my belly."

"I know but I thought . . ."

"Okay, you thought. You're trying. I appreciate it. But I'm starving. Let's just go and eat, all right?"

She stepped back, not too far, not as though she were retreating. "Dinner'll just be a few minutes, honey."

He stopped. "What do you mean, a few minutes? I walk in the door and there's no dinner? I work all day and I come home to no dinner?"

"Larry, there was dinner an hour ago. I didn't know you were going to be so late —"

"Oh, so it's late now. And somehow I've ruined dinner. Somehow it's my fault."

"No, Larry, it's not that. It just needs to be warmed up, it's all ready. Why don't you just have your drink? I'll call you in a couple of minutes."

She could use the old rice. Luckily she hadn't thrown it out. Maybe he wouldn't notice. And if she put the asparagus right in and micro'd the meat a little higher it should all be ready in five minutes, maybe less.

She saw his jaw tighten, his fists clenching shut. Opening, closing, opening, closing. She flinched backward, then, realizing it, gave him a quick smile. "Really," she said, "five minutes. It'll be no time. Promise. Enjoy your drink."

He looked down at the glass. "Don't tell me what to do, Jenn, all right? I've got patients all day giving me their opinions about things they know absolutely nothing about. All right?"

"Okay, Larry, okay. I'm sorry."

He shook his head. "And please stop saying you're sorry for everything."

"Okay." She started to repeat that she was sorry

and stopped herself just in time.

He was sipping his drink. His fists had stopped clenching. It looked like it was going to work.

Reprieve.

This time.

Maybe.

1

For forty-three workdays in a row Dismas Hardy had put on his suit and tie and made a point of coming downtown to the office that he had rented. The office was an interim step, not a commitment. He wasn't quite ready to go to work for a corporate law firm — not yet, at least, not without first seeing if he could work for himself and make a decent living doing something involving the law.

He was beginning to doubt if he could.

His landlord was David Freeman, another attorney who had hung up a shingle to make a go of it — except Freeman had done it. Sixty years old and crustier than San Francisco's famed sourdough bread, the old man had become a legend in the city. His shingle now was a burnished brass plate — *David Freeman & Associates* — riveted to the front of the Freeman Building, a gracious four-story structure on Sutter Street in the heart of the financial district.

Freeman and Hardy had met as adversaries in a murder case a year before. Before it was over, they had begun grudgingly to admire one another for the traits they shared — a certain relentless doggedness, a rogue streak regarding how the law game was played, a passion for details, a personal need for independence. The admiration had gradually turned to friendship.

Over the next months Freeman had courted Hardy, subtly, counseling him on the perils of life in the big corporate firms. Oh sure, the money was great but there was also the tedium of the paperwork, the burden of having to find forty billable hours week after week after week, the dependence on some partner you'd have to kiss up to (who was probably younger than Hardy's forty-one). You lived in a beehive and every decision you made — from where you indented the paragraphs in your briefs to what you were going to plead for your clients — was subject to some committee's approval. Did Hardy want all *that?*

Why didn't he give his real dream and instincts a chance? Freeman would let him rent an office upstairs, use the library, borrow his receptionist, pay a nominal rent, at least while he made up his mind.

So forty-three days ago Hardy had come in.

He had been in the courtroom at the Hall of Justice four times since. Three of these cases — two referred to him by David — had been DUIs, driving under the influence, where Hardy's involvement had been, at best, tangential. The clients wound up paying their fines and going home. In the fourth case, one of Hardy's acquaintances had a friend, Evan Peterson, with fifteen unpaid parking tickets. Pulled over for gliding through a stop sign, Peterson had been arrested on the spot on the outstanding warrant. Peterson had called for his friend who'd called Hardy and asked if he'd come down to the hall and walk him through the administrative maze, which Hardy had done.

Life on the cutting edge of the law.

It was the middle of the afternoon. At lunchtime he had gone home to see his wife, Frannie, and their two children, Rebecca and Vincent. After lunch, he had run four miles along the beach, through Golden Gate Park, back along the Avenues to his house on 34th. Then, giving in to his old Catholic guilt — what if a client was pounding on his door and he wasn't there? — he dressed in his suit again and drove back downtown.

Hardy had his feet up, reading. Looking up from the pages, he took a breath, trying to be philosophical about it, telling himself that today was the forty-third day of the rest of his life.

"Mr. Hardy."

Freeman's receptionist, Phyllis, stood at the door to his office. She was a rigid but, Hardy thought, potentially sweet woman in her mid-fifties, smiling hesitantly. Hardy took his feet off his desk, put down his copy of *A Year in Provence* — dreams, dreams — and motioned her in.

"You're not busy? I'm not interrupting you?"

He allowed as how he had a few moments he could spare.

"I just got a call from a woman named Jennifer Witt. Do you know who she is?"

Hardy's feet were suddenly on the floor. Phyllis stepped further into the office. "She was arrested this morning and wanted to talk to David but he's in court." Freeman was always in court. "And none of the associates is here."

Freeman had a small crew of young lawyers working for him and managed to keep them all busy.

"David want me to go down?" Hardy was already up.

"I buzzed him and he just called me back. They were having a recess. He's afraid Mrs. Witt will go to someone else if we don't get a representative down there in a hurry. He asked if you wouldn't mind . . ."

"Jennifer Witt?" Hardy repeated.

Phyllis nodded. "I think it's maybe a big one," she said.

Coverage of the crime itself had been all over the newspapers and television. It was the kind of grist that was the lifeblood of local news — Larry Witt, a doctor, and his seven-year-old son Matt had been shot to death in their home. The mother had been out exercising. A neighbor had heard shots and dialed 911. When the mother returned from jogging, a policeman had just arrived at the door and had told her to wait downstairs while he went up. He then discovered the carnage.

In the first couple of weeks news reports had advanced the theory that a professional hit man had, for some unknown reason, been hired to wipe out the Witt family. Mrs. Witt had allegedly seen a suspicious man — an Hispanic or African-American? — in the vicinity on the morning in question.

Jennifer Lee Witt, the wife, was hot copy on her own. Even the worst likenesses of her, two columns in the *Chronicle* or frozen as a teaser for the 6:00 P.M. news, crying or in apparent shock, revealed the photogenic face of a young woman just past innocence. The good shots tended to be so captivating that she almost appeared to be posing.

She was dressed in a yellow jumpsuit like all the other prisoners on the seventh floor. Though her blondish hair was cut short, the sides fell slightly forward, partially obscuring her face. She stared at the floor as she walked.

Through the wired glass window Dismas Hardy watched her approach the visitors' room, then turned back and sat at the table and waited until the guard could open the door and present her.

There was the sound of the key and Hardy stood.

"Mrs. Witt?"

"Mr. Freeman?" Tentatively, she had her hand out.

"No."

Disoriented, she now pulled in her hand and stepped backward. Hardy thought she looked about ready to break down. He spoke quickly. "I work with Mr. Freeman." Not strictly true. "He's stuck in court."

She didn't move. "What do you lawyers do, just pass people around? I called my husband's attorneys and they said they couldn't help me but David Freeman could. He's the best, they said."

"He's very good."

"So I agreed they could call him, fine, and next thing you know here *you* are. I'd never heard of Mr. Freeman. I've never heard of you. I can't believe I'm arrested. For Larry's murder, and my son Matt's for God's sake. They *can't* think I killed my little boy." At the mention of the son's name, her lip began to tremble. She turned away, hand to her face. "I am not going to cry."

Hardy nodded to the guard, who stepped out of the room and closed the door behind her. It was a small room, five-by-eight, with a pitted desk and three metal chairs taking up most of it. The window faced the office for the women's side of the jail. Two uniformed female guards moved in and out of the picture to their cluttered desks, up, out somewhere, then back in. The women's common tank was just around the corner. When the door had been open, noises exploded every minute or so. Clangs, sobs, voices. Now the door filtered most of the sound.

Hardy waited for Jennifer Witt's breathing to slow down. Finally she turned back to him. He was sitting with one leg over the corner of the table. "You can have Mr. Freeman if you'd like but he won't be available for a while. This is a grand-jury indictment. There is not going to be any bail."

"You mean I have to stay here? God . . . how long?" She was struggling with the effort to get words out. Suddenly she hung her head and sat down.

Hardy felt like an intruder. He let an eternal minute pass.

She took in a deep sigh as though she'd been holding her breath. "I'm sorry, it's my fault. I just didn't want to get in any more trouble and I thought I should have a lawyer."

"Okay." Hardy had come off the desk and went to sit across the table from her.

"Not that it matters."

"It might," Hardy said.

She wasn't going to fight about whether having a lawyer was a good thing or not. Wearily, she shook her head. "I keep thinking something's going to help, something's going to make it better."

Hardy started to say that the right representation could make all the difference. But her gaze was a blank. He wasn't getting through. "Mrs. Witt?"

She wasn't there. Or rather, as far as she was concerned, Hardy wasn't there. She shook her head from side to side. Eventually, a pendulum winding down, she stopped. "No," she said. "I mean Matt. My baby."

Hardy took in a breath himself and held it a moment. He, too, had lost a son. Over the years he had gotten better at keeping it out of the front of his mind. But he would never forget, never even approach forgetting.

Looking at this woman — frail now in the jail's jumpsuit — he found himself feeling a strong connection. It was unguarded and maybe unprofessional, but there'd be no harm in letting the legalities wait a few minutes. God knew, once they began they'd go on long enough. "How long has it been?" he asked.

She pulled at a strand of her hair. "I can't accept it." Her voice was hoarse now, her eyes distant. "Nothing seems real anymore, you know?" She gestured around the tiny airless room. "This place. I feel like I'm sleepwalking in a nightmare . . . I want to wake up . . . I want Matt back . . ."

She swallowed, seemed almost to gulp at the air. "God, I don't know. What can *you* do? What do you care?"

"I do care, Mrs. Witt."

She took that in without a blink, not a sigh, not a glance at him. Inside herself again.

Hardy looked down at his hands, linked on the table between them. Jennifer Witt wasn't worried about her lawyers and their games, about her bail and her baggy yellow jumpsuit. She'd lost her son and nobody was going to bring him back. She was right. Nothing Hardy could do would make that better.

There was a square of light from an outside window over one of the guard's desks. It had moved nearly a foot since Jennifer had been brought in.

She had begun to open up, to listen. The details of Hardy's proxy representation accepted for the moment, they were finally getting down to it. She didn't want to spend the rest of her life in jail, did she?

"Not for something I didn't do, Mr. Hardy."

"Okay. But let me ask you, what did you mean when you said you deserved it? Deserved *what?*"

In a reaction that struck Hardy as pathetic, she ducked away, as if she were going to be hit. "Nothing, anything . . . this . . ."

"What?"

"I shouldn't have let it happen. I wasn't there. Maybe if I'd been there . . ." She shook her head again.

"What *did* happen? Why do the police think

you did this?" Hardy wanted to hear her version. Never imagining he'd have any part in it, he'd followed the news of the crime casually as it appeared in the papers or on television, just another of the many stories of domestic woe that came and went to help sell soap or hamburgers or newspapers.

"I don't *know.* I don't understand. When they came to arrest me I asked them —"

"And what did they say?"

She shrugged, apparently mystified. "They got to talking about my rights, warned me about anything I said, that I could have a lawyer, that kind of thing."

"But you saw this was coming? You must have —"

She stopped him, interrupting with a dry noise that sounded bitter when it came out. "I haven't thought about *anything,* don't you understand that? I've been trying just to get through the days."

Hardy knew what she meant. She scraped a fingernail over the tabletop, staring at the yellowing strip of varnish that lifted and flaked away. Again, she swallowed — as though keeping herself from breaking down. But her voice — the tone of it — sounded almost matter-of-fact, if weary. He was sure the coloring was protective. Well, she would have to try to soften it if her case ever went to trial, if she ever testified. She would come across as too cool. Even cold.

But that, if at all, was a long way off.

"I was just getting used to the awfulness of it. I mean, okay, there might have been somebody who was robbing the house or had some problem with Larry — I don't know what. And Larry gets shot. Larry, Jesus . . . But *Matt* . . . ?"

She was losing the fight with her tears.

Hardy was with her. "The papers always said Matt must have been an accident, he walked in at a bad time, something like that."

She nodded. "*That's* what I've been thinking about, Mr. Hardy. If only he hadn't been there, if it had been a school day, if Matt hadn't walked in or said something or whatever it was he did . . . Or if I had stayed home, could I have protected him?" She bit her lip, hit the table with her small fist. "That's what I've been thinking about, not the goddamn *reasons* somebody might have thought it was me. And that's *all* I've been thinking about." A tear hit the table and she swiped at it with her hand. "Goddamn it," she said. "Goddamn it."

Again sounding tough.

"It's okay," Hardy said, meaning the language, the loss of control.

"Nothing's okay."

Hardy sat back in the hard chair. She was right. And he believed her.

Eventually she came up with something.

"I guess maybe they thought it was the insurance, but it wasn't —"

"How much insurance?"

"Well, Larry . . . he was a doctor, and you know . . . maybe you don't, but doctors are crazy about insurance. They have to be, with malpractice and all. Anyway, Larry was insured for two-and-a-half-million dollars."

Hardy took that in. "Double for violent or accidental death?"

Jennifer nodded. "Larry wanted to be sure that . . . if he died he could have the house paid off and give me and Matt security. It didn't seem too much when we got it and Larry could afford it. But now they think I killed" — she paused, fought it again — "killed for the money which is ridiculous. We had enough money. I mean, Larry made six figures."

"But you'd have more if he wasn't in the picture?" Testing. He felt he had to.

"Yes, but . . ." She reached out to touch his sleeve. "I guess that's the other thing. We were fighting."

She shrugged. Her mouth parted, closed again. "I'd been seeing a psychiatrist, and Larry . . . anyway, we'd had some fights but we hadn't even gotten to talking about a separation. Neither of us wanted that. We had Matt."

"How long had you been married?"

"Eight years."

Hardy had taken out his pad but mostly he was listening, waiting for a false note. Now he stopped her, realizing they'd been avoiding the main issue. "They didn't arrest you because you had a couple of fights with your husband, Mrs. Witt. There has to be something tying you more directly to the crime or there's no case. They tell you what that might be?"

She was biting down on her lower lip. "It must have been the gun, but the inspector asked me about that when they found it and I told them

I didn't know anything about it."

"What about the gun?"

"It was Larry's gun . . . he was shot with his own gun. But at first they didn't know it was our gun, it wasn't found in the house."

"I don't understand."

"We kept it in the headboard, but they found it like two weeks later. The inspector said somebody found it under a dumpster and it had my fingerprints on it. I told him of course it had my fingerprints on it, I pick it up to dust inside the headboard every couple of weeks."

Hardy let his silence answer.

She shook her head. "I'd been out jogging. We live, lived —" She made a fist and hit it on the table. "You know what I'm trying to say."

"You're doing fine," he said. "Just tell me what happened."

Jennifer stared at her hand, the balled up fist. She covered it with her other hand and brought it back toward her. "The house is on Twin Peaks, you know, pretty far up. It was morning, maybe nine-thirty or ten o'clock. Larry lets me . . . I mean I usually run three times a week. When I got home there was a police car in front of the house, and the man was standing by the front door, which I remember thinking was strange because if he had knocked why wouldn't Larry or Matt have opened it, right?"

"Right."

"But he was just *standing* there, so I opened the gate and asked if I could help him and he said he'd gotten a call about some shots. First some yelling and then some shots."

"Did you have a fight that morning? You and Larry?"

She seemed to duck again and Hardy found himself getting a little impatient with it. But her hand came back to his sleeve, tacitly asking for his indulgence. "How long had you been gone?" he asked.

"When? Oh, an hour. I had to be back within the hour." Seeing Hardy's reaction, she pushed on. "Larry worried if I wasn't home. He knew where I ran and how long it should take, so that . . . the hour thing . . . it was, like, a rule."

"Okay, let's go on. The policeman is waiting at your door."

"So I asked him if he'd knocked and he said yes but there wasn't any answer and I told him there had to be. I mean, I was sure Larry hadn't left. It was the week after Christmas, his first week off since last summer. Anyway, by now I'm starting to get worried. But maybe Larry's in the shower, or Matt is so they can't hear or something, right? But there's still no answer, so I take out my key and we go in and I'm calling 'Larry' and 'Matt' and I start to go upstairs, but this policeman tells me to wait and I go to the couch. Then he's at the top of the stairs saying 'Don't come up, stay right there now.' And I know. God, then I know."

Her mouth opened, closed, opened again. Finally she gave up the effort. She sat with her hands crossed in front of her, tears rolling off her cheeks and puddling on the table.

2

Hardy was not a popular man on the third floor of the Hall of Justice. The previous summer he had gotten caught in some political crossfire with Christopher Locke, his boss at the time, the District Attorney of the City and County of San Francisco. They had exchanged a rather unlawyerly bit of badinage, after which Hardy had quit, gone to the defense side and beaten the Assistant DA, who had stolen his case from him, and by extension Locke himself, in court.

Now whenever he had occasion to walk the once-familiar halls he felt crosshairs on his neck. Still, he owed it to himself and to David Freeman — and Freeman's client if it turned out that she stayed that way — to test the waters here.

At the end of the public hallway, he stopped at the double-glass reception window and asked for Art Drysdale, the Chief Assistant District Attorney, with whom he had always had a cordial, even friendly, relationship, although that too had been compromised by the events of the last year.

"Is that all she told you?" Drysdale had pushed himself back from his desk and stopped juggling his baseballs, but he held three of them in one enormous hand against his cheek. "I think she left out a little tiny bit."

"Art, I just spent an hour talking to her. She didn't kill her son."

Drysdale, more or less expecting this, nodded. "Maybe not on purpose."

"What does that mean?"

"It means let's say the kid got in the way."

"Of *what?*"

"Of Mrs. Witt killing her husband."

Hardy turned in a half-circle. "Please . . ."

Leaning forward, Drysdale said, "Please yourself, Diz, this indictment is rock solid. The kid was there and died while she was committing the crime of murdering her husband. As if you didn't know, that makes the son a Murder One, too. Just like if a bank robber shoots a guard by mistake. Sorry, but Murder One."

"Have you talked to her?"

"Oh sure. Everybody gets arrested, I run upstairs and protect their civil rights 'til they're processed. Then I hold their hand until bedtime and make sure they get tucked in. Give me a break, Diz."

Hardy knew Drysdale was right — of course there had been no reason for him to have talked to Jennifer Witt. But Hardy couldn't let it go. "She didn't even do it by mistake, Art."

Baseballs were getting juggled again, a bad sign. "That's why there are trials, my man. Figure out what really happened."

"But you've charged her."

Again, reluctantly, Drysdale stopped his routine. "Traditionally that precedes an arrest. You want, you can have a copy of the discovery on Larry

Witt and Matt Witt. Read it yourself."

"You want to tell me about it?"

Art Drysdale, his old mentor, the man who had hired him back to the DA's office a year before, said, "I'd like to, Diz, but it's not my case. I don't know much about it."

Baloney. Art Drysdale knew the nuts and bolts of every case of any import that got charged, especially any murder case. "It's Dean Powell's case. You know where his office is, don't you?"

In other words, bye-bye, and don't stop back on your way out. You're on the other side now. See you around.

Hardy decided he would rather not talk to Dean Powell, not yet. Instead, he went upstairs to homicide, hoping to run into Sergeant Inspector Abe Glitsky. Hardy and Abe had started out together as policemen walking a beat. While Hardy had gone on to law school, then to the DA's office, Abe had progressed through the SFPD for almost ten years until he made it to homicide, the place he called home. If Drysdale no longer was any kind of inside source, Hardy had no doubts about Abe, who was sitting at his desk, looking down at some papers and chewing ice out of a styrofoam cup.

Hardy walked through the open room of the Homicide Detail, poured himself a cup of old coffee, pulled up a chair and waited. After a moment or so, he sipped loudly. Abe looked up. Then back down with no change of expression. "The element of surprise," he said, "in the right hands, can be a powerful weapon."

Hardy sipped again, more loudly than before. Glitsky raised his head and chewed some ice with his mouth open. One of the homicide detectives walked by behind Hardy and stopped. "I'd give it to Glitsky on points," he said. "Those are real attractive sounds."

Hardy swallowed his coffee and brought the file up, laying it on the desk. "What do you know about Jennifer Witt?"

After a last look down at the papers in front of him, Abe closed the folder. "I wasn't doing anything."

Hardy smiled. "You've told me many times that nothing you do when you're in the office is important, isn't that a fact?"

Glitsky ran a finger around his expressive mouth, caressed the scar that ran top-to-bottom between his lips. "I like the way you say 'isn't that a fact?' instead of 'isn't that true?' like the rest of humanity would. It's very lawyerlike. Witt isn't my collar. You representing her? Of course, you are," Abe answered himself.

"Not completely true."

"Forty percent true?"

Hardy pretended to be thinking about the answer. "She's David Freeman's but he's in court. He asked me to go make her feel better."

"Which, of course, you did."

Hardy shrugged. "It's a modest talent."

Glitsky seemed to want to follow it up, find out how his friend got even this much involved with this particular client, but he resisted the temptation. He'd no doubt get it sometime. He took the folder over his desk and flipped some pages.

"Terrell made the arrest." He craned his neck, checking the room. "Terrell here?" he called out.

"Who's Terrell? Do I know him?"

"OFO," somebody answered.

"OFO?"

"Secret police code which I'm not allowed to reveal under penalty of death." He leaned forward, whispering. "Out fucking off." He went back to the report. "You've seen Terrell around. White guy, brown hair, mustache."

"Oh yeah, him. When I was at school, there was a guy like that."

Glitsky himself was half-Jewish, half-African-American. He stood six feet some, weighed two hundred something and had blue eyes surrounded by a light brown face.

"Terrell's okay," Glitsky said.

"But . . . ?"

"I didn't say anything. I said he was okay."

"I heard a 'but.' "

Abe chewed more ice, then spoke quietly. "If God's in the details, Wally and God aren't that close." He leaned back, spoke in a more conversational tone. "He's a big-picture guy, only here in homicide, what, a year? Gets an idea, a theory, a *vision* — I don't know — but it seems to keep him running."

"Isn't that what all you guys do?"

"No. What most of us do is talk to people, collect evidence, maybe some picture starts to form. Wally's a little heavy into motive, and motive only takes you so far. I mean, any victim worth a second look, there's five people with motive to have done him. Wally finds a couple of motives and starts digging around them rather than the other way round."

"So why's he still here?"

"He's been lucky. Twice he's hauled in perps with nothing — Frank wrote him up a reprimand, the second one was so sloppy — and both times, guess what, it turns out he was right. So what are you gonna do, bust him? It'll catch up to him."

Hardy tapped the file. "It might have here."

Abe glanced down, turned a few pages, shook his head. "Doubt it," he said. "Jennifer Witt was righteously arrested. See here? Police reports, witnesses, physical evidence. Plus, as you might have noticed, the public has been introduced to her. She seems like a swell person."

"I thought it might be helpful to talk to Terrell."

Glitsky raised an eyebrow. "I don't know if you remember, but if you're in a defense mode, my colleagues here won't tend to view you as an ally."

"Maybe you could vouch for me — you know, character, judgment, taste, generally refined nature. Sometimes everything doesn't make it to the file."

"You shock me." Closing the file, he pushed it back across the desk. "I'll see what I can do, but as always —"

Hardy beat him to it. "Don't hold my breath."

Glitsky nodded. "Words of sublime wisdom," he said.

Although Hardy was not yet legally entitled to it, Art Drysdale had done Hardy the favor of arranging for him to pick up the discovery on the

Witt murders, which was basically a copy of the DA's file on the case.

Drysdale, it turned out, had been half-wrong and half-right when he said that Jennifer Witt had left out a few tiny things. Right about leaving out some things, wrong about them being tiny.

They included the testimony of an eyewitness, Anthony Alvarez, a retired fireman with a drawerful of decorations. Sixty-four years old, he lived with his invalid wife directly across the street from the Witts and had heard two shots. If there had only been one, he might have thought it was a backfire and not even bothered to look. As it was, he didn't really suspect shots even after he heard them — it had been more of a curiosity, that kind of noise. He'd gone to the window and seen Jennifer Witt in front of the gate to her house, looking back toward her door. His initial thought was that she had stopped, was wondering about the noises herself. She stayed there a couple of seconds, then began running.

There was another witness, the next-door neighbor, Mrs. Barbieto, who'd also heard the shots and had been the one who had called the police. Larry and Jennifer Witt had been fighting for weeks, she said. Their son was an unhappy little thing. He cried all the time. The night before, that morning, "You should have heard them on Christmas" (three days before) — it seemed they nearly ruined the Barbietos' family dinner.

Hardy was taking a shotgun approach to his first reading of the file, and had turned right away to the tab marked "Civilian Witnesses." Apparently there were eyewitnesses. From a defense point of view, eyewitnesses were not particularly heartening.

He was sitting on the side of the steps outside the Hall of Justice at 7th and Bryant. The day was cool and sunny with a light breeze that would probably kick into a gale by five o'clock. Now, though, it was pleasant, even with the bus exhaust and the fast-food wrappers beginning to swirl on the steps.

He turned back to the arresting officer's report. Inspector Terrell had begun to suspect Jennifer after she had provided him with an inventory of items that might have been missing from her home and had omitted the murder weapon. She had carefully searched the house and reported nothing missing. This was before their gun had been found under the dumpster.

After that, Terrell had questioned Jennifer about this oversight and Jennifer had said she must have simply overlooked it, blocked it somehow. Hardy didn't remember this fact from any of the news reports, and it wasn't a good one to find now. He closed the file.

"Hardy."

He squinted up into the sun and stood up. A tall man, slightly older than Hardy himself, hovered over him in a light charcoal suit, his hand extended.

Hardy stood and took the hand.

"Just saw you sitting here, Diz. Rumor has it you're defending Jennifer Witt."

"You know rumors, Dean. They never get it quite right." He explained his stand-in status, helping out his landlord, the famous defense attorney David Freeman.

Dean Powell showed a mouthful of teeth. He had a glorious mane of white hair, ruddy skin and an impressive posture. Hardy hadn't wanted to go see Powell earlier and didn't feel particularly prepared to chat with him now. But here he was, smiling and talking.

"Art wanted to warn me early that you had the case. So I'd take it more seriously." Some more teeth to flavor the compliment. "But it's Freeman, huh?" His face clouded briefly. Powell might be nice to Hardy and stroke him about what a good job he'd do, but the mention of Freeman moved things up a big notch. Freeman didn't lose too often.

Powell motioned downward. "That her file?"

Hardy patted it. "It seems a little thin on motive for Matt's death — the boy's. I mentioned it to Art and he didn't seem to want to talk about it."

Powell's grin faded. "*I'll* talk to you about it. The motive was the husband's money. The boy got in the way. Period."

Hardy turned sideways out of the sun's glare. "You really believe that?"

"Do I *really* believe it? Tell you what, I think it's inherently believable."

"That's not what I asked you."

The Assistant DA ran his hand through the flowing hair. "Do I personally think she shot her boy in cold blood? To tell you the truth, I don't know. We've charged women with that particular crime four times in the last two years, so don't tell me it's just too heinous to even imagine a woman could do that."

Hardy persisted. "I'm saying *she,* Jennifer, didn't do it. I just spent some time with her upstairs."

"She was *sad,* was she?" Powell shook his head. "Remember Wanda Hayes, Diz?" He was referring to a highly publicized case from several months earlier. Hardy nodded, he remembered. "Well, Wanda was a real wreck, crying all the time. And she *admitted* that she killed two of her kids. She said she just kind of lost her temper one day, felt *real* sad about it."

"Okay, Dean, but —"

"But nothing, Diz. I'm not saying that Jennifer's plan was to kill her son. What she *did* do, and what we can prove, was that she planned to kill her husband and didn't take the time or whatever else to make sure her son was out of the way. Maybe she was just *careless.* I don't know and I don't care. The bottom line is the son's dead and she's going down for him, too."

The flash of anger spent, Powell suddenly exhaled, as though surprised at his show of emotion. He reined himself in. "Listen," he said, "I'm just on my way over to Lou's. You feel like a drink?"

Lou's was Lou the Greek's, the local watering hole for the cops and the DAs.

Hardy motioned to the file again, shaking his head. "Another time."

The Assistant DA's face tightened. Powell was said to be considering a run for State Attorney General in this year's special election and he had obviously been working on his public moves — this invitation for a drink had the ring of sincerity, for example — but it put Hardy on guard. Powell was saying that, as Hardy knew, one of the duties of the prosecutor was to provide full and free disclosure to the defense team. "You know, you might want to drop by Art's again. We don't want you to have any surprises."

Hardy squinted, moved to the side. This was unusual. "I just got the file an hour ago."

"Yes, well, Art and I discussed the case after you stopped by and we decided it would be better to lay it all out at the beginning. Like I said, we don't want any surprises."

"What surprises?"

Powell's face took on a serious expression. "You haven't seen the indictment yet. We charged Mrs. Witt with a third count of murder."

"What third murder?"

"Her first husband died of a suspected drug overdose nine years ago. Did you know that? I don't know how the media hasn't come up with this yet but I'm sure they will."

Hardy stood still as a pole. He wondered whether his once-upon-a-time friend Art Drysdale had deliberately given him only half of the discovery — there wasn't really any legal advantage in doing so, but Drysdale had been known to mess with defense lawyers just to keep them off balance. It was a good reminder for Hardy — he really *was* on the other side.

"In any event," Powell went on, "Inspector Terrell, the arresting officer? He's been pushing for exhumation and got it through with Strout." This was John Strout, the coroner. "It seems Mrs. Witt made a small bundle on that death, too. Something like seventy-five thousand dollars, which back then was a reasonable piece of change. Terrell found out she was dating a dentist when Ned — that was husband number one — bought it. Dating this dentist while they were still married? Bad form. Anyway, when Ned died it looked like an overdose — so the coroner ran the *A* scan, found coke and alcohol and ruled it an accidental overdose."

Hardy knew the medical examiner ran three levels of tests to scan for poisons in dead people. Level *C* included a lot more controlled substances — barbiturates, methamphetamines — then the check for volatiles — essentially alcohols — that turned up on a Level *A* scan, but it also cost a lot more to run, and when the apparent cause of death was found at the *A* level, unless there was an investigator's report indicating foul play, the coroner most often stopped there.

Hardy knew all this but he had to ask: "He didn't check for anything else?"

"Why would he? They found what they were looking for, coke and booze in an overdose situation . . . hell, you know. And Ned had 'em both, so the book got closed. But guess what?"

"I can't imagine." Hardy was feeling numb.

"Atropine."

"What?"

"Atropine. Jimson weed. Deadly nightshade."

"What about it?"

"Atropine is what killed him. We exhumed him on Terrell's hunch and there it was."

"So he OD'd on atropine."

Powell shook his head. "You don't just OD on atropine. Atropine doesn't make you high. It's not a recreational drug, but Ned was loaded with the stuff."

"That's not necessarily murder —"

"I think in connection with these latest two it is."

"She didn't do these either."

Powell favored Hardy with one of his world-weary looks, which said okay, that's a defense attorney's answer about his client, but between us two professionals we know the truth. What he said was: "Your Mrs. Witt's a black widow, Hardy. We're going for Murder One on these. A death sentence. This is a capital case."

3

You can't be serious . . ."

The color was gone from Jennifer's face. She simply hung her head, then after a beat shook herself, stood and walked over to the window in the visitor's room, through which she stared out into the guard's office. "Ned killed himself, maybe by mistake . . . But somebody else killed Larry and Matt. I swear to God . . . *I couldn't have killed my little boy.*"

Hardy noticed she didn't say the same about her husband. He sat with his shoulders hunched over, fingers locked together on the table in front of him. "Tell me about Anthony Alvarez," he said.

She combed her bangs back with her fingers, twice, still facing the window. "I don't know any Anthony Alvarez . . ."

Hardy kept his voice low. "The police report identifies him as your neighbor, lives across the street."

Now she turned. "Mr. Alvarez? Oh, that's *Anthony* Alvarez? I never knew his first name. What about him?"

"What about him is that he's a lot of the reason you're here." Hardy told her the gist of his testimony. While he talked she returned to the end of the table and sat again, kitty-corner to Hardy.

"But I didn't do that. I always start out by walking a couple of blocks to warm up. I wouldn't have just shut the gate and started out running. Not only wouldn't have, I *didn't*."

Hardy nodded. "Why do you think he says it was you? You have any words with him, anything like that?"

"I don't *believe* this." Jennifer inhaled, shook herself, let it out in a sigh. "Maybe in four years I've said a hundred words to the man. I don't think I'd recognize him if he wasn't standing near his house. Why is he doing this to me?"

"I don't know," Hardy said, "but for now I think we'd better concentrate on something that could help you. Was there anybody that might have seen you walking? Another neighbor?"

Jennifer shut her eyes, leaning back in her chair, revealing the curve of her body, the plane of her cheek. Hardy suddenly realized how attractive she was, even in the jail garb. Pouty lips, a strong nose. Bones well-limned.

"I passed a man," she said, eyes still closed. "An older guy, maybe black or Mexican, dark anyway."

"I read about him." Hardy sat forward now. "I don't think he's going to fly."

"What do you mean? I *did* see somebody. I think it was, I mean it could have been the person . . ."

Hardy was shaking his head. She reached a hand across the table to him. "No, no. No, listen. It was the week after Christmas, no traffic, no one around, and here's this man walking up the street, he's wearing this heavy trenchcoat, looking like he's checking house numbers. I almost stop and ask can I help him but I didn't want to be late so I keep going by." She stopped talking, staring at Hardy. "It really could have been *him,* the one . . . I mean, *somebody* had to do it . . ."

"Did you notice if this man had a gun?"

"No, but . . ."

"Did you stop and see him turn up your walkway?"

"No, I'd have —"

"Do you have any idea why somebody who didn't know Larry personally would want to kill him? Or your son?"

Her eyes stared into the space between them. "If you find a yes to any questions like these, Jennifer, then we can usefully talk about him again, but I'm afraid he isn't going to do us any good right now."

"But it might —"

"When it *does,*" Hardy said, "then we'll look at it. Okay? I promise."

Hardy reminded himself that he wasn't here to upset her. He had felt, though, he should tell her they were going capital. It was still going to be essentially Freeman's case but it wouldn't hurt to collect more impressions of Jennifer. "Let's go on to anything else about that morning, anybody else who might have seen you."

"But that man, he might have been . . ."

Hardy patted her hand, held it down on the table. "Let's move on, okay?"

She pulled her hand away. "You've got to believe me, I didn't *do* this. If it was that man . . ."

"*If* it was that man," he said. "There could have

been somebody, all right, he might even have shot Larry, but he also might be anybody — a neighbor, a tourist, a guy just taking a walk."

She glared at him. "He had his hands in his pockets, both hands. He might have been holding a gun."

Hardy almost said, Forgetting, of course, that your husband was killed with your own gun. He slowed himself down. "Let's stop. Look, we're not here to argue. We'll come back to the man later. For now we've got to leave him, he's not going to help us unless he lives near you and we can find him. Now I'm trying to find something to hang your defense on, and he's just not it."

Her face went all the way down to the table, within the circle of her arms. Her body was shaking as she rolled her forehead back and forth.

"Did you do anything unusual at all on your run? Anything you might already have told the police? Or forgotten to tell them?"

She stopped the rocking. As though struggling with its weight, she raised her head, sighing again. "They didn't ask any questions like this," she said. "I didn't think . . . I mean, I didn't know they thought I was a suspect. They misled me, they never asked any of this."

Hardy said quietly, "I'm asking now, all right? Let's try to get something."

Jennifer nodded, then recalled that she had stopped at the automatic teller at her bank on Haight Street. Which seemed odd to Hardy. "You left to go running and happened to have your ATM card with you?"

"What's so strange about that?" And she explained that most of her running outfits had Velcro pockets and as a matter of course she grabbed her house key and her change wallet — in which she kept her ATM card — whenever she left the house. She told Hardy that on that morning she had walked down her block, passed the man in the trenchcoat, started running for a couple of blocks, then stopped for cash — "It was the Monday after Christmas, we hadn't been to the bank for three days."

At least it was someplace to start.

In some ways Hardy's involvement with Jennifer Witt was easier to explain to the client than it was going to be to his wife.

After the successful conclusion of his first murder trial — defending former Superior Court Judge Andy Fowler — Hardy had been surprised to find himself something of a property in the small world that was San Francisco's legal community. Trial lawyers — men and women who were good on their feet in front of a jury — were, it seemed, in great demand. Even in the large corporate firms, the final outcome of all the work done by offices full of bean counters and number crunchers, library rats, technical brief writers and legal strategists, paralegals and lesser staff often came down on the shoulders of the person in the firm who could convincingly present it all in front of a judge or jury or both.

Since most corporate attorneys rarely if ever saw the inside of a courtroom, many firms hired trial lawyers the way baseball teams purchased designated hitters — the role was limited, but if it came up it was far preferable to having the pitcher come to the plate with the game on the line.

Because of the sensational nature of Judge Fowler's trial and of Hardy's own role as an unknown, underdog, first-time defense attorney, it seemed that Hardy had unwittingly been auditioning for half the firms in the Bay Area. When the verdict came down in his client's favor, his phone had started ringing.

Another event that had coincided with the end of Fowler's trial had been the birth of Hardy's and Frannie's son, Vincent. So for the first month Hardy had begged off many of the interviews, pleading his new fatherhood, Frannie's desire to have him at home for a while.

Now, three months later, he had visited eleven firms, riding elevators to plush offices in his only three-piece suit, going out to fine lunches with men and women with whom he felt no connection whatever — nice people, sure; smart, well-turned out, confident, financially secure, socially aware, all of the above. But no one to whom he was drawn as a human being.

Seven of the firms had offered him positions, with salaries ranging from a low of $83,000 to a high (Engle, Matthews & Jones) of $115,000. All of the offers put him well onto the partner track, crediting him with up to six years of previous service. This meant that within, at the most, another three years (and at the least, one), he would become a partner in any of the seven firms and could expect annual compensation in the realm of $300,000 to $500,000.

Frannie had brought an insurance settlement to

their marriage. Hardy, aside from the fees in the Fowler trial that had run to low six figures, owned a one-quarter interest in the Little Shamrock bar. Their house payment was under six-hundred dollars a month. So Frannie and Hardy were not hurting. Nevertheless, the kind of money the big firms were waving in his face was not pocket change, was even tempting.

Their house in the Avenues was already, with the addition of the two children, starting to feel pinched. They could see moving up; they'd even discussed it casually after Hardy had received the first couple of invitations. It had become more or less understood that Hardy would choose one of the firms, get a linear job, be an adult.

But he just hadn't been ready to commit to any of the firms — something better might come up, some people he felt better about being associated with. So in the interim he borrowed an empty office and paid a nominal rent in the building owned by David Freeman, which was where he had been, essentially twiddling his thumbs, when David Freeman himself had called up with the Jennifer Witt referral.

"It's probably going to be a fair amount of money," Hardy said.

"But it's another *case*. It's not a job."

"And I'm not even really on it. It's Freeman's case."

"But there's something here for you."

Hardy's hands, crossed in front of him at the table, came open. "Maybe. There might be."

Frannie was trying to understand, and he

couldn't blame her for being a little upset. He might argue to himself, and tell her that he wasn't really changing the basic plan they'd discussed, but they both knew that wasn't true. Working as a member of a defense team in one potentially lucrative case was not even remotely comparable to going to work as a senior associate in one of the city's prestige law firms, and Frannie wasn't being conned by it.

"It's a case that lasts a year, maybe two. Who knows, that could be as long as any of the jobs last, Frannie. Life's uncertain."

Frannie rolled her green eyes, as if she had to be told that.

Hardy pressed on. "Mrs. Witt is worth a couple of million dollars, maybe more . . ."

"Which the insurance company isn't going to release to her now that she's charged with the murders."

It was a point he had hoped she wouldn't raise. "Stranger things have happened." He tried a grin. "They might."

"Do me a favor, would you, Dismas? Find out? You owe *us* that much."

Dinner finished, both kids asleep, they were sitting across the dining room table from each other, finishing the last of their red wine with chocolate candies on the side — Frannie's latest culinary discovery that had addicted them both. A brace of nearly burned-out candles sputtered with fitful light.

Frannie sighed. "You don't want to work for anybody, do you?" She held up a hand, cutting off his response. "If you don't, that's okay, but we shouldn't talk about it as if you do."

"It's not that."

"I bet it is. You call all these people who've been interviewing you corporate rats. I think the phrase betrays a certain prejudice."

Hardy popped a chocolate, sipped some wine. "I really don't know what it is. This thing with Jennifer Witt just walked into my life this morning. What am I supposed to do? Freeman has asked me to help. He'll take over in the morning."

"But you are interested, aren't you?"

"No commitments," he said. "But yes, it's interesting. I looked at the file."

"You mean the file you couldn't get your nose out of, that you seem to have memorized?"

Hardy gave up. "Yeah, that file."

"And what if she did it?" Frannie was grabbing at straws and knew it.

Hardy sat back. "She still has the right to an attorney."

Frannie gave him a look. "What's that got to do with you?"

"I'm an attorney?"

They both laughed, the tension broken a little. One of the candles gave up the ghost, a wisp of smoke rising straight in the still room.

Frannie reached a hand across the table and took her husband's. "Look. You know I'm with you. I just want you to be sure you're doing something you'll be happy with. This isn't just one case, you know. If you take this one, that's what you're going to be doing, taking cases. Maybe defending people all the time."

Hardy had once been a cop, and on two separate

occasions he had worked in the District Attorney's office. Frannie was of the opinion that if anyone was born and bred to the prosecution, it was her husband. She had heard his tirades against and/or scornful dismissal of defense attorneys, the "ambulance chasers," the "pond scum" who took anybody for their fee up-front.

"It doesn't *have* to be sleazy," Hardy said.

Frannie smiled at him. "I just wonder if that's the life you want."

"The life I want is with you."

She squeezed his hand. "You know what I mean."

He knew what she meant. It worried him some, too. But he knew if David Freeman asked him to help with Jennifer Witt, in almost any capacity, and off the top of his head he could think of several, he was going to do it. Which meant he wasn't pursuing any of his job possibilities. Which, in turn, meant . . .

He didn't know.

The other candle went out. "Let's leave the dishes," he said.

4

San Francisco's Hall of Justice, located near — almost under — the 101 Freeway at the corner of 7th and Bryant, is a gray monolith of staggering impersonality. Its lower stories house various City and County departments, including police, coroner, the office of the District Attorney, and courtrooms and jury-selection waiting rooms. The jail on the sixth and seventh floors is administered by the San Francisco County Sheriff, as opposed to the City's police department. Behind the building, a new jail is slowly rising in what used to be a parking lot.

Hardy entered through the back entrance, was cleared through the metal detector and, deciding to bypass the slowest elevator in America, ascended to the third floor by the stairway and into the familiar bedlam that reigned in the wide high hallway.

Aside from the usual circus, this morning's sideshow featured a convention of perhaps twenty gypsies. Uniformed policemen were remonstrating with several women about their use of a Butagas container to heat their coffee in the hallway. Hardy first wondered how they had managed to get a portable gas container through the metal detectors, then watched for a while, fascinated as he often was by the raffish mélange one encountered almost daily between these institutional green walls.

It seemed to be a reasonable discussion — no one, yet, was raising any voices. But neither had the flame gone out under the coffeepot. While one woman tended to the argument, another was pouring liquid into small porcelain cups and passing it to some men, who put lumps of sugar into their mouths before they began sipping.

"They should just set up a TV camera and run this hall live." It was David Freeman, rumpled as usual in a cheap rack suit, looking like he hadn't slept in a week. "Probably pull a thirty share."

Hardy gestured around them. "You'd need a commentator to explain what's happening. Like here" — he pointed — "it's a little ambiguous."

Freeman considered it. "The host is a good idea. Maybe we could have the judges rotate, like they do the calendar. 'This week on calendar we've got Marian Braun, and here in the hallway, LADIES AND GENTLEMEN, LIVE, IT'S JUDGE OSCAR THOMASINO!' "

They started toward Department 22, the courtroom where Jennifer Witt was to be arraigned in an hour, which was all the time Freeman was going to take getting filled in on the case. No sense wasting it. "How's it look?" he asked.

"They're talking capital."

"Capital. Powell ought to go and stand in the witness row outside the gas chamber a few times, mellow him out a little."

"I think Powell might like it."

Freeman thought that was debatable. He had

witnessed six executions in several states — no sane person could like it and he did not think Powell was insane. Not even close.

"Well, they've got special circumstances two ways — multiple murders and killing for profit. You know they're alleging three counts?"

"Three?"

Like Hardy, Freeman was surprised to learn of the last count against Jennifer, murdering her first husband Ned Hollis nine years earlier. "That's digging pretty deep, wouldn't you say?"

"You better read the file."

They got to the twelve-foot solid wood double doors that led into Judge Oscar Thomasino's courtroom, Department 22.

"That bad?"

"At least they've got a case. It's not frivolous. But she says she didn't do it."

Freeman pushed his way through the doors. "Well, there's a first."

"Maybe she didn't."

"Maybe," Freeman agreed. "On the other hand, maybe not." In the high-ceilinged empty courtroom, even whispers echoed. Dismas Hardy and David Freeman sat in the last pew, a long, hard, cold bench of light-colored wood. Freeman, legs crossed, unlit cigar in his mouth, was starting to peruse the file, pulling papers and folders from Hardy's extra-wide briefcase.

"You're heartening to talk to. Anybody ever told you that?"

Freeman shrugged, scanning pages. "My clients love me. Why? I get them off. Do I think they're guilty? Do I care? Probably — to both questions. Most of the time."

"Most of the time you think they're guilty?"

Now Freeman looked up. "Most of the time they *are* guilty, Diz. Our job's to get them off, so that's what I try to do."

"Well," Hardy said, "I found myself very much wanting to believe her. She was torn up, crying, really a wreck."

"Over the loss, or over being caught?" Freeman marked his reading place with a finger. "I know, I know, I'm cruel and cynical. But tears fall for all kinds of reasons, not the least of which is self-pity, and when someone's sitting in jail, believe me, they get to feeling very sorry for themselves. It can seriously tear a person up, I've seen it happen." He went back to reading, turned a few pages, stopped.

"She's attractive, right?"

Hardy nodded.

"Young?"

"The file says twenty-eight."

"Twenty-eight's young, okay. Humor me on this one." Freeman himself was perhaps fifty-five. Hardy thought he didn't look a day over eighty. "Okay, so she's young and attractive and crying — of course, you want to believe her. And guess what? She *knows* you want to believe her. Whether or not she did these horrible things to her husbands, she's aware of the effect crying has on a normal red-blooded male such as yourself. And that effect is . . . you want to believe her, want to make her feel better. You want more than anything to get her to stop her crying, don't you?"

Freeman took the cigar from his mouth, spit out some leaf, reinserted it. "And while we're at it," he said, "tell me honestly. This is my personal public-opinion poll. She do it, or not?"

"I don't know. I'm leaning to not."

"None of it?"

"I don't know."

"What part of it don't you know?"

"The boy . . . Matt. And if she didn't kill him, the rest of it falls apart, doesn't it?"

"You don't think she killed her kid?"

"I don't see it."

"Why? And don't tell me you don't think she's the type."

"Well, two reasons," Hardy said. "One, she didn't just deny it; I thought she seemed genuinely stunned that anybody could think she'd done it. She didn't even want to talk about it, David. I mean, she acted like it was all a weird mistake that would get cleared up. As for killing her own son, how could *anybody* believe that?"

"Diz, Diz. Let's just, for argument's sake, say she did it. And if she did it, it was for the insurance money. We agree here? Good. Okay. This is a high-risk position, deciding to kill somebody. People do it all the time, but people who do it for money, they're a different breed. Jennifer Witt decides in cold blood to do this deed, she's sure as hell not going to admit it. She's taken a risk — already taken it — and she's going to get the whole banana or go down in flames. Believe it. Now, what's the other reason?"

Hardy had said there were two reasons he thought Jennifer might not have done it — Freeman had given an argument refuting the first and now wanted the second. "I just don't think she's the type?"

Freeman went back to reading. "I charge by the hour," he said, "and I don't charge enough."

Hardy accepted the reprimand in good humor. "Take out the son Matt and the case doesn't look very strong against her."

"We can't take out Matt. Matt was there, Diz. I wish to hell he hadn't been, but that's what we got. Powell's not going to let it go — it's what's putting our girl face-to-face with the gas chamber. It will influence a judge."

Hardy had had this discussion before. Even if Jennifer did kill her husband Larry, and Hardy was not convinced of that, he was at least certain that Matt's death had somehow been an accident, a random, tragic wild card. But now that card, like it or not, had been dealt to them. It was their hand and they had to play it. "I still think the right jury could walk her," he said.

"The right jury could walk Attila the Hun. But don't count on it in this case."

Freeman leaned forward, put an avuncular hand on Hardy's shoulder. For not the first time, Hardy marveled that Freeman was so successful and even downright likable. As always, he needed a shave. His lips were thick and purplish. His rheumy eyes had yellowish whites, the skin around them flecked with liver spots. He was handsome as a leprous warthog, if warthogs got leprosy. "The smart money doesn't put too much on the jury. If I go along with believing she's innocent, you know, I actually hurt her chances. You realize that?"

"How do you do that?"

Freeman looked around the empty room, making sure no one was eavesdropping. "It's a tightrope walk. You want to convince yourself that you're defending an innocent person — that much is all right, it's part of it. But if you actually start to *believe* that your client is innocent, you're going to assume that the jury's going to see what you see. You'll convince yourself that they want to believe you, your interpretations of the facts."

Hardy picked it up. "And those arguments, because you didn't have to make them to yourself, just aren't going to be as strong."

"See? Diz, I do believe you've got a knack for this business." Freeman moved his cigar around. "If the matter gets to a jury, your client's already in big trouble and it behooves you to take it as seriously as you can."

"I do take it seriously, David. You asked me if I think, gut level, that she did it. At the least, I'm saying I'm not sure the case is that strong —"

"That why they're going capital? That why Powell's got it, with his political ambitions? He maybe needs the practice in court? I doubt it."

Hardy couldn't help smiling. "You've got to learn how to express your feelings, David. It's going to eat you up someday, holding it all in."

Freeman nodded. "I know. I'm trying. They'd mind if I lit up in here, wouldn't they?"

Freeman was sitting under the international no-smoking symbol.

"I'd bet on it," Hardy said.

"I was assuming all along you'd be part of it,

to tell you the truth."

Hardy had not decided on a precise strategy to introduce the subject of his continued involvement in Jennifer Witt's defense, but as was so often the case with David Freeman, the question got preempted.

In California, all death penalty trials had two phases before the same jury — guilt and penalty. In practice, the lawyer in the guilt phase never stays on to do the penalty phase. Juries got cynical about a person when first they argued passionately that their client didn't do it and — once it was established that yes, they did, too — then turn around and say, in effect, Okay, so my client did it. I know I said it wasn't so, but I lied. But at least now let's talk about what a nice person my client is and why execution would be really too strong . . .

So, to avoid this appearance of inconsistency, there was also always a penalty-phase attorney, commonly called the "Keenan counsel," and it was this role Freeman had now asked Hardy to take should Jennifer be found guilty and it came to that. "Assuming, of course, that she can pay." He seemed serious when he said it.

Jennifer Witt had the right to counsel, but if she did not have the personal funds to cover the costs — and in a capital case they would be enormous — the court would appoint a public defender. And even if the public defender claimed some kind of conflict of interest, there was no guarantee that Freeman and Hardy would be appointed.

Freeman, of course, was a long-standing court-approved defense lawyer, but Hardy had not yet even applied for the list, and in any event, with this kind of case at stake, the other vultures would be circling. This looked like it was going to become a high-profile case — the very best advertisement in the business. But if Freeman and Hardy were going to defend Jennifer, she, personally, was going to have to pay them. No getting around it.

"And I'll tell you something else," Freeman said. "This is Private Practice 101. I don't care if your client is Mother Theresa, you get your money up-front." He seemed very serious. And it bothered Hardy.

The clerk entered from the front of the courtroom talking with the court reporter. They started setting up their work areas, organizing, talking in low voices. In the gallery, what looked to be some of the other attorneys had arrived — Freeman nodded to a few of them. Non-lawyers, perhaps relatives of defendants or victims, were beginning to straggle in.

This was Superior Court. People coming before the judge in this courtroom were not here for traffic tickets. Hardy left Freeman reading the file and stood, wandering up to the rail that separated the gallery from the principals.

The prosecutor Dean Powell tapped him on the shoulder. "I kind of expected you this morning."

"I thought I mentioned that David Freeman's got this one, Dean. There he is back there, doing calisthenics." Freeman was pulling on an ear, studying, oblivious to the world. "I'm mostly along for the ride."

"Freeman decide on a defense?"

"No, but Jennifer has. It's your favorite."

"Not guilty? No insanity? Justifiable, even?"

"Mrs. Witt says she did not do any of it."

Powell nodded, poker-faced. But Hardy had the sense that he was delighted. "Yes she did," he said.

Judge Oscar Thomasino, short brush-cut hair and swarthy complexion, had a no-nonsense demeanor in the courtroom over which he had presided for ten years. He had come in this morning with another of the surprises that marked life behind the rail.

"Before we begin today," he said, "is there someone in this courtroom driving a Green Chevy Lumina license number 1NCV722?"

An Hispanic male in his mid-twenties raised his hand and stood up in the third row of the gallery. Thomasino motioned him up through the bar rail. Reluctantly, the man complied, and the judge frowned down at him. "Did you happen to notice, sir, the large sign in the space you took outside that read Reserved for Presiding Judge?"

The young man bobbed and half-turned around, looking to the gallery for support. "Aw, come on, I'm in trouble now because I took your parking space?"

"Not precisely," Thomasino said, "although that's part of it. Your big problem is that the car is stolen." Thomasino directed the bailiff to take the man into custody. They would figure out what to do with him upstairs. The car had been towed to the City lot.

Hardy was still chuckling about it when they called Jennifer's line — her computer number. Hardy and Freeman then came through the bar rail. Dean Powell and a fresh-faced young assistant moved over from the jury box, and Jennifer Witt was brought out to the podium that faced the judge. Hardy thought that Jennifer, beaten down and deflated, looked very much like a defendant, but the jumpsuit could do that to Cindy Crawford. He introduced her to Freeman.

She took in her ragged attorney with something less than enthusiasm — a reaction he was accustomed to. She made a face at Hardy — this is my lawyer? — then faced the judge. As in all murder cases, the clerk read out the complete indictment.

"Jennifer Lee Witt, you are charged by indictment with three felony counts filed herein, to wit, violations of Section 187 of the Penal Code in that you did, in the City and County of San Francisco, State of California, on or about the 31st day of August, 1993, willfully, unlawfully, and with malice aforethought murder Edward Teller Hollis." The clerk read the special circumstances, going on to add the charges regarding Larry and Matt Witt. When he had finished, Thomasino nodded toward the podium and said he assumed by the presence of Messrs. Freeman and Hardy that Jennifer was represented by counsel. He asked Jennifer how she was going to plead.

"Not guilty, Your Honor."

Making a note on his printout, Thomasino looked over his reading glasses, which were slightly tinted and half-moon shaped. "Mr. Powell. The people seek to deny bail?"

Powell stood up. "We do, Your Honor. This is a special circumstances case. The allegations are multiple murders and murder for profit. The defendant has already killed —"

"Your Honor!" Freeman was not having any of this. To date, it was not established that Jennifer had killed anybody. That was, after all, what this was about.

The judge scowled down at the prosecutor. "Mr. Powell, please."

Powell put on a show of contrition, but wasted no time getting the needle in.

"I'm sorry, Your Honor. But this is a death penalty case. The law provides that this defendant should be held without bail. Further, the People believe there is substantial risk of flight."

Freeman came back matter-of-fact. "Your Honor, Mrs. Witt will surrender her passport. She has never been accused, much less convicted, of any crime. There is no basis in Mrs. Witt's history or in fact for the prosecution's contention that there is risk of flight. She has stayed in the City since December, and she must have had some inkling that she was under suspicion during that time. She did not resist arrest."

"All right, all right." Thomasino peered over his glasses. "Nevertheless, Mr. Freeman, at that time she was not yet charged with any crime, let alone three counts of capital murder. We've got a different situation now, wouldn't you agree?"

"Your Honor, Mrs. Witt did not commit these crimes and she is anxious to clear her name in court."

Thomasino almost smiled. "Yes. Well, she will get that opportunity, but I'm inclined to agree with the People that, facing the possibility of the death penalty she might at least be tempted to forgo that opportunity. And without any remaining ties to the community and no immediate family —"

"Your Honor!" Jennifer's voice was a surprise to everyone in the courtroom. Defendants were, after all, usually so intimidated by these proceedings, by being referred to in their own presence in the third person, that it rarely occurred to them that they could actually speak up themselves. Jennifer did. "I do have family here today."

Hardy turned around. In the second row a graying man who might have been Thomasino's brother was halfway to his feet. Another younger man looked as though he was thinking about getting up, too. Between the two sat a middle-aged woman.

Hardy also noticed something pass between Jennifer and a well-dressed bearded man a few rows farther back in the gallery. Who was he? And why didn't Jennifer make some kind of friendly gesture to her own father, brother, mother? She pointed them out to Thomasino in hopes that they might help her win bail, but she didn't so much as nod to any of them.

Thomasino recovered quickly. "All right, thank you. You folks back there, please be seated."

"If it please the court." Dean Powell was on his feet. "I'd like to ask Mrs. Witt about the last time she saw her family."

"Your Honor, please!" Hardy was sure that, like himself, Freeman had no idea what Powell was talking about, but he wasn't going to let such a request go unchallenged. They were a long way from trial here, and questioning the defendant was out of line.

"What are you getting at, Mr. Powell?"

"Your Honor, in the course of our investigation it's become clear that Mrs. Witt is not at all close to her family. In fact, they have been estranged —"

Freeman, from the hip, shot out. "And that's why they're here today, Dean?"

The gavel slapped down. "Mr. Freeman, you will address *all* your remarks to the court. Clear?"

"Of course, Your Honor, I'm sorry." Like most of Freeman's moves, this one was calculated. Get off a losing point, direct attention anywhere else, even if it got him a contempt warning. And taking Thomasino's reprimand gave him another few moments to think of something else. "But Mr. Powell should know better. Ms. Witt's family is *here* today, *obviously* supporting her. What more do we need?"

Thomasino waved him down, cradling his hands over his gavel. "Mrs. Witt, your family's presence here is noted, but it doesn't change the law. This is a no bail case."

"Your Honor . . ." Freeman, one last time.

But Thomasino had had enough. The gavel came up with a judicial glare. He tapped it gently, then intoned, "Bail is denied."

5

In the hallway outside of Department 22 the gypsies had disappeared but there was still the usual hum of voices echoing off the bare walls.

"How can they not let her get bail?" Jennifer's father, Phil DiStephano, was saying. He was in Freeman's face, not exactly belligerent but certainly not cordial.

"We could appeal," Freeman said, "but I warn you, we'll lose. And even if we won, the judge would set an outrageously high bail."

The attractive Mrs. DiStephano spoke up quietly from behind her husband. "How much, Mr. Freeman?"

Phil DiStephano turned on his wife. "It doesn't matter, Nancy. It's out of our league." From appearances, it seemed he was right. Regardless of what bail turned out to be, if in fact they won an appeal, the DiStephanos didn't look like they would be able to pay it.

Phil wore a plain black suit that showed no sign of having been recently pressed, a white shirt, ironed but not new, a thin tie. The mother's clothes, though not the rest of her, reminded Hardy of Pat Nixon during the Checkers Speech. She was attractive enough — still, some might say, even beautiful, like her daughter — but something in her bearing, in the pinch of her lips, conveyed that her life hadn't been easy. The son, perhaps twenty-three, wore jeans, work boots, longish hair, a tucked-in Pendleton, and an attitude.

A working-class family, and it surprised Hardy a little. Jennifer had never been portrayed in the media as anything less than upper class, and in Hardy's interviews yesterday she had come across — even in her prison garb and through her grief — as the comfortably off successful doctor's wife. Her family suggested different roots.

When Freeman went on to tell them they could expect bail of a million dollars, or more, if they got it at all, the son exploded. "Where the fuck she supposed to get that?"

"Tom!"

Freeman held up a calming hand. "Exactly, son. The point is they don't want her to get out. They think she'll take a long walk and disappear."

"I don't think she will. She has a very solid defense." The man who belonged to the new voice moved forward, hand out to Freeman. "Ken Lightner." As though the name explained something. He added, "I'm Jennifer's psychiatrist."

It was the other man Hardy had noticed in the gallery. Reasonably good-looking, somewhat burly even in his tailored suit, Lightner sported a well-trimmed red beard under a head of dark brown hair. It was a striking combination that Hardy thought might come out of a bottle.

"What's Jenny need a shrink for?" Tom DiStephano said.

Nancy DiStephano put a hand on her son's arm

as Lightner stepped in. "You must be Tom."

"No. I'm the Queen of England."

She stepped between them. "Don't be rude, Tom."

Hardy wondered if Tom DiStephano was in enough control of himself to be anything — even rude — on purpose. Whatever the source of his anger, it was pretty clearly eating him up. He looked about, around the hallway, as though searching for an exit, an escape. His mother still held onto his arm, but he shook it off and turned to Hardy. "Are you guys trying to get her off as crazy? Is that the deal? You think she's crazy?"

"No, not at all." Lightner seemed to be striving for an understanding tone, trying to include everybody.

But this was Freeman's show and he was not about to hand the lead away. "We haven't decided on a defense," he said. "Jennifer is innocent until she's proved guilty. I trust we're all in agreement here?"

It was a multi-layered tableau — anger, positioning, concern, grief, power. Brother Tom was at the center of it, perhaps slightly defused, but Hardy hoped nobody picked that moment to push him further. He would lose it.

Now, though, with no one to direct his anger toward, Tom stood there flexing his hands, feet flat on the floor, breathing hard. "Well," he paused, looking for an answer to something in the broad and echoing linoleum hallway, in the high ceilings. "Well, just shit."

"We'll all need to handle this," Lightner said. "This is a very trying situation and it's certainly okay to get angry, we all get angry . . ."

Hardy glanced at Freeman. All professions had their jargon. It probably passed for normal conversation in Lightner's set. But Nancy cared neither about anger or jargon. "They're not really going to ask for the . . ." she couldn't say death penalty . . . "for my daughter, are they?" She was close to tears, gripping her husband's hand.

Hardy thought he would take some of the focus away from Freeman, spread the pressure around. "We're a long way from even getting to a trial, Mrs. DiStephano, much less a verdict and a penalty. We don't have to worry about that yet —"

"We damn well better worry about it," Tom said. "We don't take care of it now, it's going to happen."

"Tom, you know something I don't?" Hardy said.

Now with a direction, Tom let it go. "Yeah, I know something. I know people like us don't get a fair trial, that's what I know. Not against them."

"Not against who? What people like you?"

"Poor people, working people, goddamn it. Against the people who have money."

"Jennifer's got some money, Tom," Phil said.

"It's not her money, Pop, and you know it. It's Larry's money. That's what this is all about, and the rest is all just bullshit! They want their money back."

"Who does?" Hardy asked.

"They're not letting her in. She just doesn't fit, does she? Just like we don't, like Larry cut us out. Except Jen tried to crash her way in, didn't she? Married her fancy doctor. Drove her fancy car. Tried to be one of them. And they don't forgive you for that, do they? They go get you for that . . ."

"Nobody's trying to get her, Tom —"

"Mom, you don't *see*. You buy their crap. That's what's kept us down —"

"Tom, stop it!" Phil stepped between his son and his wife but Tom now turned it on him. "Oh yeah, sure. And you'll take anything, Pop, won't you?"

It happened in an instant. Phil's hand flashed and rocked his son, hard, open-palmed, high on the cheek. The noise resounded in the hallway. "Don't you dare use that tone with me!"

The men were squared off, Nancy now between them. She had started crying. Tom backed up, glaring at his parents. "Aw, screw it," he said finally, turning, running off down the hallway.

His mother turned to the two attorneys. "I'm sorry for my son. He thinks the world . . ." She let it hang, tears in her eyes.

This was the moment. Defenses were down. Freeman figured he could use it. He went after Phil. "Did you see Jennifer often, Mr. DiStephano? I mean, do you visit each other?"

"Well, sure. She's my daughter, isn't she? We're all close, even Tom . . . he's just got a hot head. Like you said in there, it's why we're here today."

Freeman turned to Mrs. DiStephano.

She shook her head. "We haven't seen them in years."

Phil tried to put a face on it. "Hey, Larry was

a busy man. It wasn't that he didn't —"

Nancy cut him off. "Larry wouldn't let her. We never saw any of them. Never."

Hardy, Freeman and Lightner watched Jennifer's mother walk off stiffly, a step behind her husband. A young couple emerged from one of the doors behind them, hugging and laughing — maybe Thomasino had just given one of them a break.

Freeman, Mr. Small Talk, turned to the psychiatrist Lightner: "So what's her defense, Doctor?"

Relaxed, hands in pockets, Lightner didn't have to think about it. He nodded up the hall after Jennifer's parents. "Slightly dysfunctional, wouldn't you say? I'd kind of expect it."

"You'd kind of expect it," Hardy repeated. They started moving through the crowd, toward the elevators. Hardy and Freeman were going upstairs to see Jennifer, find out if they had a client.

Lightner was nodding. "You just saw an object lesson. It's generational, you know. Father batters mother and children. Children go on to batter their own —"

"Who's battering who?" Freeman asked.

Lightner stopped. "No, *no* . . . I mean, Larry, of course."

"Larry was battering Jennifer?" This was news to Hardy. Probably to Freeman. Perhaps not to Powell. In any event, Jennifer hadn't mentioned it.

Freeman was a step ahead of them. "If you're

talking burning bed, I think the boy is a problem there."

The "burning bed" had been gaining a good deal of momentum in legal circles as a valid defense for killing. When a spouse had been battered long enough, juries in several cases had decided that killing the abusive spouse was justified as a form of self-defense, even if the actual event took place during a period of relative calm, as for example when the abuser was asleep. This was far beyond the usual legal standard for self-defense, when the person being attacked was in imminent danger of being killed.

"Why is Matt a problem?" Lightner asked.

"Because battered wives don't kill their children," Freeman said. "If she was a battered wife."

"She *was*. And it might have been unintentional, if it happened while she was defending herself."

"That would be a tough sell to a jury," Freeman said.

"You think she did it?" Hardy asked abruptly.

For the first time, Lightner appeared to think carefully about an answer. "She had reason to," he said.

Hardy didn't like this. Another person, not even in the prosecution's loop, with the so-called informed opinion that his client "had reason" to kill her husband. "Because her husband abused her?"

"Not, of course, that having a reason means she did it," Lightner was quick to add.

Hardy squared around on the psychiatrist. "What exactly *are* you saying?"

"I'm certainly *not* saying she did it, Mr. Hardy.

I *am* saying you perhaps ought to read the literature. People become crazed in the situation Jennifer was in. Understandably so. I'm saying that *if* that happened to Jennifer, *if* she was as horribly abused as I suspect —"

"I thought you just said —"

"— then that should be a central part of her defense. And that's *all* I'm saying, Mr. Hardy."

Covering her both ways, Hardy thought.

The elevator arrived. "We're going up." Freeman dismissed him, then softened it. "Thanks for the input."

"You're very welcome. Please call on me any time." And Lightner disappeared behind the closing doors.

They were waiting for Jennifer to be brought into the women's visiting room. Freeman was going over more of the file; Hardy sat across the small table taking in the view through the window — a female guard filing papers in an ancient metal cabinet.

"You know" — he didn't turn around — "a man of your sensitivity and experience ought to be able to do this alone." Hardy had had to be talked into returning to the seventh floor. It was not a pleasant place.

"She hasn't met me yet." Freeman did not stop his reading.

"She just met you downstairs, remember? Department 22. Big room, judge in the front." Freeman raised his rheumy eyes. Hardy came around the table, hovering over him. "You know, one of my beliefs is that everybody should try to get some sleep every night."

"I get enough," Freeman growled.

"Beauty rest, then, you could use more beauty rest."

"Look." Changing tracks. "We may not be doing this at all. I want it, don't get me wrong, but if there's no fee . . . and then there's the fact that I wouldn't blame her at all if she dumped me right now on her own. Her reaction to me was something less than warm. To combat *that* eventuality I've asked you to accompany me — she seemed to relate to you for some unknown reason. Maybe you can at least buffer things at the beginning here. I explained this once."

"I know. I even understood it."

"What, then?"

"Just trying to lighten you up, David. We've already lost one downstairs. We want this case, we might want to slap on a little of the suave."

Freeman gave him a face. "I don't do suave." But he forced a weary grin. "That's why I need you."

They were getting through the first minutes. Jennifer, tight, said nothing while Freeman explained the bail situation — how there just wasn't much any attorney could do in a capital case such as hers. It was also a sales pitch of sorts — defense work might be Freeman's vocation, but it was also his livelihood, and he felt obliged to nail down the level of his involvement before he proceeded, but all she wanted now was for him to appeal the bail denial.

"You can't want me to *stay* in here?"

Hardy stood, back to the door, hands in his pockets. After a night in jail Jennifer's feelings about the relative importance of bail had only escalated, and understandably so.

Freeman folded his hands on the table in front of him, speaking very quietly. "Of course not, Mrs. Witt. But we have got realities to deal with, and I'm afraid one of them involves money."

"Money. It's always money, isn't it?"

For a moment Hardy thought she almost sounded like her brother.

Freeman spread his hands. In fact, he thought, it often was money. He felt obliged to lay it out for her now, however unpleasant it might be. "You might get a million-dollar bail on appeal. That's a hundred thousand to the bondsman. Plus the cost of the appeal. If you can't manage that you'll have to go with a public defender at trial."

Her glance — quick and frightened — went to the door. "Why not you and Mr. Hardy?"

Freeman's hands came back together. "Frankly, our retainer . . . it's *my* decision . . . is going to be two hundred thousand dollars, and anybody else would require as much. So if you can't raise the money you go with the public defender." In addition to believing it was better to be even brutally frank up front, Freeman also held the view that it was actually better for the client to show your tough side, on the theory that if you could be this difficult with your own, think how you'd eat up your enemies. He had long since stopped asking himself if this were a rationalization. He couldn't afford such thoughts, he told himself.

"But isn't a public defender just anyone?"

"No, they have to be approved by the court. And in capital cases there's a substantial level of competency."

"A level of competency," she muttered, shaking her head.

"I'm very sorry, but those are the facts of the matter —"

"But this is my *life!*"

"David." Hardy felt he had to break in here. All of what Freeman was saying might be important and even true, but the money wasn't the point for Hardy and he suspected that, at bottom, it wasn't really for Freeman either, though he put on a convincing act to the contrary.

Now the old man lifted his baggy eyes. "What?"

"Let's go outside a minute."

They left Jennifer sitting at the table in the tiny room. Outside, in the stark hallway, the jail noises now much louder, Hardy got to it. "How about we come back to the money later?"

"When?"

"Later."

"It's got to get settled, Diz. She doesn't want to change attorneys." He scratched at the lines around his right eye. "She doesn't have enough, then ethically we've got no business starting. I'm just trying to find out, get things clear."

"You're grilling her, is what you're doing."

Freeman waved that off. "Grill, schmill, we need to know and we need to know now." He patted Hardy's shoulder. "Look, I know, it's a good case. Hell, we could do it *pro bono* for advertising. But

I want to know what we're dealing with, and this is the time to find out. After that . . . well, I'll make it up to her." He inclined his head. "Let's go back in. I'll make it short and sweet. Promise."

Freeman sat across from Jennifer. "Mr. Hardy and I are sorry to have to put you through this, Jennifer, but we do need to know your financial situation. That will help clarify where we go from here."

The muscles in Jennifer's jaw were working, her face blank. "Well, I don't think money's a problem . . . the insurance, you know?"

Freeman was shaking his head. "No, Jennifer. They'll hold it until you're finished with this. If you're found guilty, they won't pay."

Hardy couldn't believe it, was she actually trying to smile? "But you'll keep them from finding me guilty."

Freeman shook his head. "I'm afraid I don't gamble with my own money, Jennifer." Hardy was thinking that his partner hadn't lied — he didn't do suave. "So let's leave that aside," Freeman was saying. "What else? I mean, besides the insurance."

They had lived in their house for five years, she said, but they had bought high, just as the market was slowing down. Equity was probably at seventy thousand, or a little less. Providing she could sell it. The house account was around twenty thousand. They had had some stocks, another sixty-five thousand. Furniture, some jewelry, two cars. Garage sale prices, Freeman figured.

"What happens if you get bail and . . . what

do they say? . . . jump it?" Jennifer asked. Then, at Freeman's glare, "I mean in theory."

"Don't even *think* about it. And don't let anybody hear you ask about it. In fact, don't talk to *anybody* here in jail about *anything?* That's good free advice. Now, if you jump — first, you lose the money you put up. *All* of it, and then they will catch you, believe me, they will. You'll never ever get a bondsman again. Finally, you've got the entire judiciary *A,* convinced you're guilty and Two —"

"B," Hardy interjected.

"And Two, prejudiced like hell against you. It's a bad, bad idea. Don't even think about it."

"Not that she's got any bail to jump anyway," Hardy reminded him.

"Do you guys rehearse this?" she asked.

Freeman was scribbling on his pad. He looked up. "Here's what I get — even if you don't do the bail appeal *and* if you sell your house and completely tap out, you're still short. We want to help you, but I'm afraid I'll have to tell the judge we're withdrawing —"

Jennifer faced them. "There's more," she said. "There's another account."

Freeman stopped gathering his papers. Hardy pulled a chair around and straddled it. "What do you mean, another account?" Freeman asked.

Jennifer looked down, swallowing. Obviously nervous. "Sometimes . . . I just didn't think Larry and I were going to make it, you know? And I thought, well, if I had to go out on my own, with Matt, I mean . . ." She looked from one man to the other. "I mean, I just felt I had better have something of my own for Matt and me. Just in case . . ."

"Just in case what?" Freeman was staring at her.

"Well, you know, like I said, in case it didn't work out. In case I had to get away or something —"

"Get away from *what?*" Freeman was remembering what the psychiatrist Lightner had said about abuse.

"Are you saying your husband beat you?" Hardy asked. "You never . . ."

Jennifer brought her hand up to her face, as though feeling for remembered bruises. "No, he didn't, not really, but, you know . . . still, if I really needed it . . ."

She stammered it out. She had been squirreling money away for some nine years. In spite of Larry's tight grip on everything, she had found ways to take "a little from here, some from there," pad about what she spent on Matt, toys, clothes, make-up, decorating, anything she could manage. The amounts had grown to almost a thousand a month, and she had learned to invest it in high-risk stocks so that the account now totaled close to three-hundred-thousand dollars, unencumbered and liquid.

"Well," said Freeman, allowing himself a smile, "if you still want us, Mrs. Witt, you've got us."

Hardy did not smile. Jennifer's revelation, however justifiable she might make it seem, still bothered him. He'd rather not have known, to tell the truth.

6

Tell me about Larry Witt."

Jennifer and Freeman sat across the table from one another. Hardy was a fly on the wall against the inside of the door. Freeman had produced a thermos of coffee from his briefcase, and three Styrofoam cups now steamed on the table.

"What do you want to know? About him and me?"

"I want to know everything." Freeman had his coat and one arm draped over the back of his chair. He slouched, his shirt was half untucked. "But I suppose we should start with how often he beat you up."

Jennifer blinked, then recovered. Her eyes widened, went to Freeman, then settled on Hardy. "I said we were fighting, not that Larry beat me."

Freeman put out his hand, back toward Hardy, keeping him from responding. He spoke soothingly. "But he did beat you?"

"I don't see why that would matter."

Freeman kept his voice low, persuasive. "It matters, Jennifer, because it gives you a defense. It gives the jury something they can hold onto." Hardy couldn't help noticing this was not what Freeman had told Dr. Lightner downstairs when he had characterized the battered-wife defense, given the death of Matt, as a hard sell to the jury. "In fact, though, he did beat you?"

She took a moment, the muscle in her jaw working. "*I didn't kill Larry,* Mr. Freeman. I don't care *what* reason you come up with why I might have, I *didn't* . . . What about Matt? My God, are they going to say I killed Matt too?"

"They're already saying that, Jennifer."

Her laugh was so brittle it broke. "And what's their reason? For me to do *that?* Have you thought about it? How are they saying I killed my son?"

Freeman kept his voice flat, quiet. "Matt's not what we're talking about, Jennifer. Right now we're talking about Larry."

"I don't *care* about Larry." Jennifer slapped the table. "*I didn't kill Matt.* Don't you understand that?" She looked up at Hardy.

He felt he had to answer her. "They're going to say that Matt just showed up by accident, that you panicked or he got in the way of you shooting Larry."

She closed her eyes, breathing heavily now. "But . . . but if it was an accident it's not first degree murder, is it? I mean, it didn't happen, but if they say it did, it's not the same as Larry . . ." Her face was deathly pale.

Hardy was tempted to explain it as Drysdale and Powell had put it to him. He resisted, but it worried him some that she had even asked, followed by a quick denial.

At the same time, as though he had just confirmed something to himself, Freeman nodded, straightened himself and sat forward, cradling his hands on the table. His voice, again, was carefully modulated, but it was a master's instrument, and this time, beneath the soothing tone, thrummed a hint of a threat. "I want you to be very clear on something here, Jennifer. *I* am not accusing you of anything. But you should know that I will neither believe nor disbelieve anything you tell me. Anything. Whether you did it or didn't do it. Why or why not."

"But I didn't —"

Freeman held up a flat palm. "You must believe me that if your husband, in fact, did hit you, the prosecution will hammer that point again and again as one motive for you to have killed him. Now, if *one time* you and Larry had a fight and he struck you, that isn't going to satisfy most juries that he gave you a reason to kill him. But if we can come back and show that this was a recurring event in your marriage, that you were living in a state of constant fear and stress, then at least we've countered their argument. Regardless of whether or not you killed him —"

Jennifer was shaking her head. "I didn't kill him, but if I did I was justified? Is that it?"

Hardy straightened up. He had been thinking the same thing, that you could not have it both ways. Reason or no reason, either she killed him or she didn't.

Jennifer understood and cared about this distinction. Good, Hardy thought. But then, he had to face another countering thought . . . an embezzler with a logical mind, capable of long-range planning and execution? Was Jennifer Witt the kind of person who might just get away with murder?

But Freeman wasn't backing away. "We're going to find *some* defense out of all of this, but we'd damn well better be prepared for all the arguments, and to just keep repeating I didn't do it will not, I'm afraid, be effective."

Hardy moved forward to the table. Jennifer's face was hard, her eyes angry. Tears threatened. Suddenly Freeman reached across the table and covered Jennifer's hands with his own. "Let's just talk, all right, Jennifer? Did Larry hit you?"

She nodded. "But it wasn't . . . I mean, there were a couple of times he got physical, but . . . I guess they were my fault —"

"How could it have been your fault?" Hardy said.

"Well, I messed up. I would just, I don't know, make a mistake and —"

"And your husband would beat you?" Freeman, who had heard it all from many clients, still sounded incredulous.

Jennifer balled a fist and pounded the table. Was that an act? Hardy couldn't figure it.

"Look, please, stop saying he beat me. Maybe he did hit me a couple of times but it wasn't like he . . . he beat me up. He'd get mad, yes. But he loved me and it just disappointed him that I didn't live up to what I should have."

"And then what?" Freeman said.

"And then what what?"

"What happened next, after Larry beat . . . hit . . . you?" He didn't add, for your own good. He waited. This was getting serious.

She hunched her head down again — the mannerism suggesting a cowed, beaten state of mind, and it was becoming almost familiar. "He felt terrible, I know. I couldn't believe I'd made him feel that way . . ."

"*You* made him feel that way? How did you do that?"

"By messing up. If I hadn't . . ."

"He wouldn't have hit you?"

"Yes. Do you see?"

Hardy and Freeman exchanged a look, then Freeman continued. "So Larry felt bad after he hit you?"

"Awful. Really. He did love me, you know. I can see what you're thinking, and it's just not true. He's the only one who knew the real me. Afterward he'd be so affectionate, bring me flowers the next day." Now something seemed to embarrass her. "Sometimes, those were the best times. Afterward, I mean."

"After he hit you?

"But it was only a couple of times, wasn't it? You just said that. And a couple is two. Might it have been three?" Freeman said.

She didn't cave. "No, no, it was two. I didn't mean sometimes, I mean both times." She nodded. It seemed they had hit the bottom of that well. But her reluctance to acknowledge the abuse was still hard to understand.

Freeman glanced at the folder on the table in front of him. "Let's talk about who did kill Larry if you didn't. I mean, *since* you didn't. Any ideas?"

She took a minute to change gears, then reached for the coffee. Her eyes were getting better. "He worked hard, he was a doctor."

"Yes, but did he have any enemies, anybody who might have it in for him?"

"Well, maybe his first wife . . . I mean, this sounds so ridiculous, I don't want to accuse his first wife or anything. I know she didn't kill him."

"How do you know that, Jennifer?"

"Well, I mean, she just wouldn't, not after all this time. It wouldn't have made any sense."

"Might it have earlier?"

Playing with the Styrofoam, picking at it, she shifted herself on the hard chair. "Well, you know, it was one of those situations where she worked while he went to medical school, and then he graduated and they just didn't get along. I guess she was pretty unhappy about it at the time."

"Did you figure in that?"

She let herself pout, which struck Hardy as somewhat affected. An act. Jennifer Witt was not easy to figure out.

Freeman prodded. "So Larry's ex-wife, what was her name?"

"Molly."

"And, I ask again, were you in the picture when she and Larry broke up?"

"Well, they were already having problems."

Which answered that.

"Did you mention Molly to the police?"

"No. I told you, she wouldn't have —"

"Just covering bases, Jennifer." Freeman jotted something on his pad, and Hardy came and sat back down. "Anybody else who didn't care for Larry? What about Tom?" Jennifer's hot-tempered younger brother had left an impression.

Again, that near jump, that blink, sitting up as though Freeman had slapped her. "What about Tom? How do you know about Tom?"

Freeman ignored the reaction. "What about him and Larry?"

She shrugged. "Larry and I never saw Tom a lot. He's got such a chip on his shoulder."

"Over money?"

"I don't know what it is exactly. Jealous of Larry, maybe."

At Freeman's look, she hastened to correct herself. "No, not that kind of jealous. Really, what do you think I am?"

Freeman leaned forward again. "I don't know, Jennifer, that's what I'm trying to figure out. You tell me how Tom was jealous. Jealous enough to kill Larry?"

The acting, if it was, suddenly stopped, and so did the fidgeting. "Tom is mad at his life, I think. He didn't have money, didn't go to college. He feels like he doesn't have a chance and never did, but that doesn't mean —"

"Like your father?"

"I guess that's what Tom's afraid of, that he'll wind up like Dad. Except my dad never wanted as much. Also, it was a lot easier to get a house in those days, even if you were blue collar, and the house was enough for Dad. But I think Tom saw it as . . . as a sort of prison. I did, too, in a way, but I got out."

"What does he do? Tom?"

"I don't think he does anything regularly. I know he drives a forklift sometimes. Does construction. Whatever he can find, I guess."

"And he resented Larry, and you, for having money?"

"We didn't have that much, but I suppose yes. And me for not having worked for it."

"But now you do?"

"What?"

"Have money. A good deal of money."

She bit her lip, perhaps not understanding Freeman's implication? Perhaps understanding it too well?

"What's that got to do with Tom?"

"Maybe he tried to borrow some and Larry wouldn't go for it. If Larry's gone, he's got a better chance, getting some from his sister alone."

She shook her head. "No."

Freeman made another note. Hardy decided he'd better check some alibis. Maybe Glitsky could poke around, too — Abe often said that going behind the department's back was just what was needed to spice up the otherwise routine life of the homicide investigator.

Freeman covered Jennifer's manicured hands with his own gnarled ones. "You know," he said, "I'm kinder and gentler than any prosecuting attorney will be. These aren't even the hard questions, Jennifer. These are in your favor. The prosecutor's won't be."

She half-turned, stretching the jumpsuit against her body, showing a fine profile. She smiled thinly — was she trying for effect? "That's really good to know," she said. "I can't wait for the hard ones."

"Okay." Freeman's hands came away and his smile was not friendly. "Since you can't wait, how about this? Were you having an affair?"

Jennifer's shock seemed a near-caricature. "What? When? With who?"

"Whenever. With anybody."

She drilled Freeman with direct-eye contact. "No. Of course not. Absolutely not."

"When?"

"When what?"

"When weren't you having an affair?"

But they had already done this. Jennifer withered the old lawyer with another look. "When did you stop beating your dog, right?"

Freeman, matter-of-fact. "Sometimes it works."

She lifted her coffee cup and drained it, grimacing at the cold dregs. "Sometimes it doesn't, Mr. Freeman."

Again Hardy found himself wishing she hadn't said something. Was she, perhaps unintentionally, telling them that if it had worked they would have gotten the truth? Or that she simply saw how the game was played and was telling the truth anyway?

Freeman began arranging his papers, putting them into the folder. "Well," he said, "I think we've got enough to get started. Let's digest this and meet again tomorrow."

"What time?" she asked.

Freeman shrugged. "At your convenience, Jennifer."

Now the fear showed through . . . of being left alone, of the ordeal facing her. "Early then, okay?"

Freeman gave her shoulder a pat. "Crack of dawn," he said.

7

At seven o'clock Hardy was nursing a Guinness, waiting for Frannie to arrive by cab at the Little Shamrock, the bar at 9th and Lincoln that he and Moses McGuire, his brother-in-law, owned. Wednesday, by sacred tradition, was the Hardys' date night.

Before Hardy had returned to the practice of law he had been the Shamrock's daytime bartender for a decade. Before that, he had been a young red hot with the District Attorney's office, married to a judge's daughter, starting out a family — Hardy and Jane Fowler and their boy Michael.

Michael was not supposed to be able to stand up at five months, so neither Jane nor Hardy paid close attention to whether or not the sides of the crib were pulled all the way or only halfway up. That oversight took the boy from them. He did manage to climb over the railing and fall onto his head. The fall killed him.

After Michael's death, Hardy's world gradually fell apart, within and without. Now, remarried to Frannie and with two new kids, he didn't feel like he was trying to recapture what he'd had — that was gone for good — but there was hope again, a future. A meaning? That wasn't Hardy's style, but not many days passed that he didn't reflect on how empty his life used to be, and how now it wasn't.

It wasn't clear to him where this fit into the professional turnaround he had taken in the last year, but there was some kind of a visceral bond that, he figured, had to be related. A year ago, for the first time in his life, he had found himself taking the defense side of a murder case because he'd become convinced that the defendant was innocent.

Several factors played into his hands during that trial — an inexperienced judge gave him unusual latitude in his arguments; an over-ambitious prosecutor brought a case that was not really locked up; Hardy, himself, had been angry enough at the DA's bureaucracy that his own motivation went into overdrive. For these reasons, plus the fact that it turned out someone else had done the murder, he had won. Now, after a lifetime during which he had sided with the People, he found himself, for the second time, a lawyer for the defense.

"No need to apologize," Moses McGuire said. "You've become a bleeding heart. It's okay. You're still in the family. We still like you."

Hardy checked his watch. "Where could Frannie be?"

Moses swirled his MaCallan, a fixture in the bar's gutter. "She's undoubtedly on her way, soon to arrive and save you from having to defend your basically untenable position against someone who's smarter than you."

"What's untenable?"

"Defense work." Moses held up a crooked finger. "Uh uh uh, you've said the same thing to yourself. More than once."

He found himself saying he wasn't sure Jennifer was guilty.

Moses snorted. "Again I quote from a reliable source who happens to be sitting across from me at this moment: 'If they get all the way to arrested, they did it.' "

Hardy smiled. "I was but a callow youth when I said that."

"And now you're mature?"

"Of course. I've married your sister, started a family, settled down. I'm a model citizen, and sometimes people get arrested when they didn't do it."

"How often?"

Hardy thought about it. "Twice, I think."

His case won, Moses nodded to himself, then walked the length of the bar, schmoozing with the eight paying customers. Wednesday night didn't get going until after nine, when they started the darts tournaments. Hardy drank stout.

Even if he, himself, a few years ago would have said he was on the wrong side, he no longer felt that he was. He could have told Moses he had seen what could happen with an overworked and undermanned police department, a DA's office hungry for "numbers" — convictions. Mistakes got made, simple venality or laziness or incompetence snuck in — maybe not often but often enough. And he was starting to think that that's what he was in it for — when the truth needed the hurlyburly showcase of a public trial to get its face out there, and sometimes that was the only way it did, he wanted to be a part of it. Balance of power. Man against machine, and that's what the bureaucracy of prosecution was. Abe Glitsky told him he had this tragic flaw of a fundamental need to continually restore order to a chaotic cosmos. Glitsky could get fancy. He wasn't sure he'd go that far, but, maybe there was something to it.

Hardy and Frannie sat with their feet in the recess under the table at a tiny place called Hiro's on Judah Street, a couple of blocks south of the Shamrock. Frannie was drinking tea and eating tempura, avoiding the sashimi and sake because she was still breast-feeding, but the platter of ahi, oni, quail eggs and gooey-duck in front of Hardy was nearly empty.

Frannie did not need a dim light to be attractive, but the candle's shadows flattered her wondrously. Hardy couldn't take his eyes from her face. She was holding his hand across the table, talking about Vinnie's day, about Rebecca's expanding vocabulary.

He let her ramble on, feeling that if the Big One — the earthquake all of California expected at any moment — came right then and swallowed them up into the earth, he would die happy.

"Also, besides 'thumbnail,' listen to this, she said her first three-syllable word — 'gravity.' "

"You want to tell me what context she used 'gravity' in?" The Beck — Rebecca — was fourteen months old. Up to this time she had shown almost no interest in physics.

"Her sippy cup fell off the table and she got all upset and I told her it was okay, it was just gravity, so she nods and stops crying immediately and repeats 'gravity.' Naturally then she wanted to experiment with it about two hundred more times."

"Of course. You wouldn't want to just let go of a concept like that. What if Newton had?"

"We didn't get into that. I just took the cup away."

Hardy pointed an accusatory finger. "Negative reinforcement, Fran. We've talked about this. If later in life she blanks on gravity, you'll have no one else to blame but yourself."

Frannie sipped at her tea. "I'm going to be able to live with that burden." Suddenly they'd talked about the kids enough — the moment was palpable. There were other items on the agenda. "So how was *your* day? Are you going to be working with David?"

To the tinkling background music, Hardy described his involvement with Jennifer Witt's case, the bail denial, everything — or almost everything. He did not bring up his nagging doubt that all was not completely as it seemed with his new client. He did, however, tell her about the existence of Jennifer's bank account. "So she's got the money to pay us." Then he tried to explain how she'd come by the money.

Frannie stopped sipping tea. "You're saying she . . . stole it? The money she's paying you with?"

"No. Not exactly stole it." Hardy pointed a finger. "I like that thing you do with your eyebrows. Scorn and rejection. It's good."

"She didn't *exactly* steal it? Please."

He gave up. "Okay, so she stole it. She had reasons. It doesn't mean she's a bad person." Trying for levity again, and again it soared like a tractor. "Anyway," he went on, "it's at least a year of work. Keeps my hand in. And if David gets her off, which he often does with his clients, it's a good deal all around."

"What if he doesn't?"

"Well, if he doesn't, it'll be my job to keep her out of the gas chamber."

Frannie, like most people, wasn't too clear on how capital trials were handled in California. Hardy explained that Freeman would conduct the first phase, the one that would determine Jennifer's guilt or innocence. When that was over, *if* Freeman lost, there would be a second phase, in effect a second trial, to determine one of two possible penalties — life in prison without the possibility of parole, or death.

Hardy was going to argue the second phase, if it came to that.

Frannie shook her head disbelieving . . . "You're kidding me. That's a good deal? That's my vision of hell."

Nope.

"It'll never get that far. Don't worry about it."

"Can we write this down? Dismas Hardy says it won't get this far. I shouldn't worry about it. I'd like a copy for my records."

Hardy carefully picked an oni with quail's egg from the plate in front of him and popped it, savoring the explosion of flavor. "I'll have my secretary run one for you. Look, Frannie, David's the best defense lawyer in the city. He's throwing me a bone, that's all it is. A big bone with meat on it."

"And what if she did it? Then what?"

Hardy shook his head. "She didn't kill her son."

"Somebody must think she did. I've heard you say that people don't get arrested unless they've done *something* . . ."

"I was wrong. Now I've seen the light."

Fiddling a minute with her glass, Frannie finally looked up. "This isn't all that funny, after all. I mean, isn't it true that there's a case to be made that she killed her son, even if it was by accident or whatever?"

He had to nod.

"And a good case that she killed her husband."

"Well, a grand-jury indictment isn't necessarily —"

But Frannie had heard this song and stopped him. "And what about her first husband?"

Hardy dismissed it with a wave. "That's just the DA's numbers game. They went back and literally dug that one up. They didn't charge it first time around, they aren't going to prove it now after ten years."

"More famous last words," Frannie said. "But what if? What if all of the above doesn't happen as you predict? Then what? Or worse, what if it turns out she really did do it, I mean killed both husbands *and* her child?"

Hardy didn't like these questions, mostly because he'd asked them so recently to himself. Jennifer's acting, posing, brains and plotting ability were not insignificant. He didn't, of course, want to argue mercy for someone who didn't deserve any, and on the off-chance that Jennifer was guilty of these things, she didn't deserve a break today or any other day.

But, turning into a good lawyer, he had at least developed an answer he hoped would work in a penalty phase. "If she killed her husband, I can argue that he beat her, which he apparently did."

"You know that?"

"I think so. Though she more or less denies it."

"Well, that's heartening. Very strong."

"Boy, this is fun."

"That's 'cause I'm a fun guy to be with. One minute, nothing's happening, then whammo, suddenly it's fun city." They were in their new Honda Accord — the jeep-like Suzuki Samurai a sacrifice to small children — cruising down Haight Street at ten o'clock at night. He took her hand. She gently removed it.

"Almost done," he said. It was an apology.

From Hiro's they had decided to go back to the Shamrock to spend some time with Moses. Frannie had been missing her brother, hadn't seen him in a week.

But first . . .

David Freeman did not like to use private investigators, preferring to do his legwork himself. And with his current trial taking much of his time, he had asked Hardy to check out a few details relating to Jennifer Witt.

So before they went down to the Shamrock, Hardy suggested that he and Frannie swing by the house Jennifer, Larry and Matt had lived in, just to get the feel of it. His copy of the folder was still in his car, so they looked up the address on Twin Peaks and it took them nearly twenty minutes to find it — Olympia Way. Then, since it was right on the way, Hardy said he might as well measure the distance from the house to Jennifer's bank, where she had taken money out of her ATM.

Unfortunately, there were four banks on the revitalized old hippy thoroughfare and all of them had ATMs. So Hardy was writing down mileages while Frannie commented on the good time they had been having for the past forty-five minutes.

The bank on Haight closest to the Witt house was just over a mile from their front door. The furthest, all the way down near the border of Golden Gate Park, was about two miles. Hardy had no idea if these facts would ever prove to be important, but felt more comfortable having them. He liked to operate under the general principle that facts made a difference, even if you didn't always know, precisely, what that difference was.

"Good. Now that we know that," Frannie exclaimed when he had written down the last numbers, "I'll be able to sleep tonight."

8

Hardy's own crack-of-dawn was literally that. The telephone next to his bed rang at five-forty as the thinnest line of pink began to show out his bedroom window. He got it on the first ring.

"This is Walter Terrell. Wake you up? Sorry. Abe Glitsky asked me to give you a call. What can I do for you?"

Hardy heard the young voice, noting the penchant some cops had for getting to you when you weren't ready for them. He bet that Terrell wasn't really that surprised that he'd woken him up, nor sorry. Five-forty was a little early for anybody except fishermen and most folks seemed to know that. Even Hardy's kids still slept.

But he had him now, and this might be the only time, so he swung out of bed and padded into the kitchen with the phone. "I thought we might be able to get together, talk a little about Jennifer Witt."

There was a pause. Perhaps Glitsky hadn't told Terrell exactly who Hardy was. Or his relationship to Jennifer. But one thing was sure — Terrell knew Hardy wasn't with the DA's office.

"You doing her defense?" Terrell asked finally.

"Keenan counsel." Hardy was pouring leftover

coffee into a mug and pushing buttons on the microwave. "Penalty phase."

"Yeah, I saw it was going capital. You guys got yourself a bitch. The case, I mean. The perp, too, actually."

Hardy bit back his automatic response of "alleged" perp. Hardy recalled when he had walked a beat — start saying "alleged" to cops about people they had arrested, pretty soon you'd find you weren't friends anymore. He wanted to keep Terrell on his side.

"Well, this perp's maybe got a decent defense, but she doesn't want to use it. I mean, it seems her husband had been beating her."

This evidently didn't change Terrell's world view. "So?"

"You knew that?"

Hardy almost thought he could hear a shrug. "Guys beat their wives, most of them don't get killed."

"What I'm saying" — Hardy pulled his coffee mug from the microwave, put in sugar, stirred — "is she could take the battered-wife defense and have a better chance of getting off, and yet she won't."

Terrell was silent. To him, these were legal shenanigans. His job was to deliver someone to the DA if there was evidence they'd committed a crime. What the DA's office did after that was not his problem. Finally he asked, "So what did you want to see me about? I assume you've read the file."

"Sure."

Terrell kept up the slow response. "The file's

the official record. I'm in it. Does it say anything about beating?"

"It said they were fighting." Hardy felt rudderless, struggling to get his brain moving.

"Well, there you go. Anything else? I got a big morning."

"Did you find anything on this hit man?"

The voice dripped scorn. "That's right, the hit man. City's crawling with them. No. I didn't mention him for the same reason I didn't mention the motorboat."

"What motorboat?"

"The one that wasn't there, just like the fucking hit man. There was a lot of things I didn't put in — space aliens, for example. If you read the report, the hit man's there in her statement. Hell, she's got to have something if it's her story somebody else did it. What's she gonna say?"

"It's so lame you'd think —"

"No. It's just lame, all right, but that doesn't mean she didn't make it up all the same. Perps make up dumb lies every day."

"But Mrs. Witt doesn't seem dumb, does she?"

"No," Terrell agreed, "no, I don't think she's dumb. At least it ain't an NHI — that's something, huh?"

NHI was shorthand for "No Humans Involved" — cases involving the scum of the earth — dope dealers, career criminals, sub-humans of all sorts.

Terrell was still on the line. "But you know, we sent people to a lot of doors and asked and nobody saw a thing except the FedEx truck at 9:30 and the neighbor who saw Jennifer after the shots. After the two shots."

"What about the driver of the FedEx truck?"

"This *is* all in the file. What about the FedEx guy? You think he's some kind of hit man took the driving job as cover for a day?"

"No, I —"

"Well, as we like to do, we checked him, too. He's been with them for a couple of years, probably still is."

"No, what I wondered is if he saw Mrs. Witt in the house when he made his delivery. What was he delivering, by the way?"

"It's the Monday after Christmas, what do you think? Probably a late Christmas present. You can ask him. Did he see Mrs. Witt? I don't know. The husband signed for whatever it was."

Hardy could keep following this road until Terrell hung up on him in about another six seconds. An overworked homicide investigator and a defense attorney was not a natural pair to begin with. But he recalled Glitsky's comment about Terrell's fondness for theories and figured it was his only shot to get the man if not on his side then away from active hostility. You never knew but when an investigator could tell you something important you couldn't otherwise discover. As Glitsky had noted, some things just didn't make the file.

Hardy began again. "One last thing if you don't mind. What clued you to the first husband?"

"Well, maybe it's 'cause, bein' a cop an' all, it's my job."

The fuse was getting critically short. Hardy had to come up with something or this guy was history. "Look, Terrell, I want to know what I need to know. I need some help, one cop to another." At the silence, Hardy continued. "I used to be a cop before I was a lawyer."

"Ah, that the Glitsky connection?"

Hardy admitted he had walked a beat with Abe Glitsky after Vietnam and before law school. He felt a little foolish trotting out the old résumé, but he knew what were likely to be buttons for police officers. Sometimes it helped to push them. "Anyway, this first husband, the guy was poisoned . . ."

"Ned. Yeah."

"So what was that story? I mean, how'd you figure it? A gun and poison don't exactly point to the same perp."

The line of pink over downtown had widened to a blue band under low clouds. The sun broke over the Oakland hills. The coffee, old and strong, was kicking in. From the nursery in the back of the house, Vincent let out his I'm-hungry cry, and there was the soft sound of Frannie's voice settling him against her.

Hardy had missed a few words but picked it up mid-thought.

". . . insurance in both cases. I just thought Ned was worth another look. Turns out it was pay dirt."

"And you think it was Jennifer?"

"That's what ties 'em. Ned *was* murdered. Then Larry and the kid. Her own kid. Shit, I say fry her."

Rebecca came running through the kitchen doorway in her teddy-bear nightgown, attaching herself to Hardy's leg and announcing her choice for the morning's breakfast menu — syrup, juice, applesauce, syrup, pancakes, syrup and maple syrup.

"Sorry," Hardy said into the phone, "it's the invasion of the two-year-olds. But I'd like to talk about how you got this. If it's righteous . . . I don't know. I'd just like to find out."

Flattery, the great motivator. Terrell said Hardy could pick a good time and they'd see if they could get together.

When he hung up, he asked his daughter if she wanted syrup with her pancakes. She said yes, she did, syrup was her favorite.

It was all in the file. Although Terrell told Hardy that they had sent out lots of people to question neighbors and other witnesses, he had interviewed the driver of the Federal Express truck himself two days after Larry Witt had been killed.

Frederico Rivera was the twenty-six-year-old Hispanic male who had delivered the package to the Witt house at 9:30 A.M. on Monday, December 28. He knew it was exactly 9:30 for several reasons. First, Larry Witt had signed his name, then looked at his watch and written in the time ("very precise uptight guy") next to the time (Fred) had already written on the delivery record — so they had two people corroborating 9:30. But Fred had also been listening to Holiday Madness on KFWB where they were giving away trips to Hawaii if you were the ninth caller after they played the Solid Gold Oldie of the Day, which this day was "Two Faces Have I," by Lou Christie. And they always played the Solid Gold Oldie at 10:30 sharp. Fred remembered all this because it was only two days ago and the DJ had made a big deal about how they only had EXACTLY ONE HOUR left — so it had to be 9:30 — just as he'd gotten back to the truck, and he had been trying to figure his route so he'd be close to a pay phone at that last critical moment.

Hardy, sitting at the dining room table with his copy of the report that he'd photocopied in Freeman's office the day before, yelled in to ask Frannie if she knew who had sung "Two Faces Have I" and she said it was before her time.

It was still shy of seven o'clock.

"I'm only twenty-seven, Dismas. Nobody my age knows that stuff."

"Fred Rivera does." He told her about Lou Christie, about "Two Faces Have I," one of the great classics of the pop era. He'd have to play it for her sometime if he could find it among his ancient 45s. She said she couldn't wait. He asked her if she'd ever heard the long version and then, smiling, went back to the file.

And discovered that none of Fred's or Larry's actions had been really necessary to pinpoint the time precisely — Federal Express uses computerized vans, and after each stop the driver entered the delivery information. Terrell had checked — he might have theories, but he was also thorough — and the log-in had been at 9:31, giving Fred a minute to finish up with Larry and get back to his van.

Fred Rivera did not see Jennifer in her house at 9:30, but given his preoccupation with the Solid Gold Oldie, Hardy thought it was unlikely he would have paid much attention even if she had been parading around naked behind Larry. Well, maybe then. Hardy wondered where Matt had been.

So Fred Rivera hadn't seen anybody. Neither had he witnessed any suspicious persons walking up or down the street — again, not that he was looking.

Mrs. Florence Barbieto called the police at 9:40, a "couple of minutes" after she heard the shots. The houses on Olympia, though large, were set almost on top of one another, no more than fifteen feet between structures. She had heard shots, then looked out her window to the house next door, thought about it for a while, walked over and rang the Witts' doorbell. When there was no answer, she went back home and called the police.

Hardy thought that sounded more like five minutes than a couple. Which meant that either the shots were fired at 9:38 or three or so minutes before then. Could such a small detail make any kind of difference? Maybe. Maybe not.

The facts were beginning their slow accretion. So were the possible interpretations.

9

Jennifer soon realized that she and the people here weren't so different. She had not expected that. They weren't so tough or scary as they'd seemed when she'd first been brought in. And they were beaten down, caged, for the most part docile. Just like her.

Not that it was a knitting bee. There was constant vulgarity, but she found that almost comforting — an acknowledgement of shared feeling, of being in this together. This was their language in their world and to hell with anybody who didn't like it.

Nobody seemed to care at all whether or not she was guilty of killing her husband. But when they heard about her son . . . well, it got real to them. She could tell, and she couldn't blame them. Everything, though, still seemed unreal to her.

The night before, after her older money-hungry lawyer had gone away with the nicer young one, she had cried on the top bunk of her cell for hours. At 3:00 P.M. they locked everybody back in the cells and had what they called count to make sure no one was missing. That took the better part of the hour, and then they brought the food.

By then Jennifer thought she was all cried out. Without really thinking about it, she took her tray and her plastic utensils and followed some of the other women out to the large common room, the tank. She set herself down at one of the tables under the television set.

She couldn't eat any of it — meatloaf, gravy, fake mashed potatoes, peas, three slices of bread. Larry would have thrown the plate across the room, especially with the gravy slopping over into the peas and the bread. She found herself crying again.

"You best eat up, honey. They's worse shit than this." It was a tall, almost stately black woman. "This your first time?"

Jennifer hadn't even been sure what she was talking about. First time she'd had meatloaf? First time she'd cried? She hung her head, shaking it from side to side. "I don't know, I just don't know . . ."

The woman, Clara, didn't pursue it. Whatever Jennifer didn't know, it was all right with her. She sat down next to her, even asked permission, and started to eat, saying she was in — again — for thieving. "What you in for?"

Jennifer put a fork into the meat and brought it to her mouth. There was no taste, good or bad. "They think I killed my husband."

Clara nodded, unimpressed. "Shit prob'ly deserved it, am I right? How bad he beat you up?"

"I didn't say that. He was a good man, a doctor, and I didn't kill him."

" 'Course you didn't." Clara went back to her plate. "Don't worry. Say he beat you, they let you go. You see. Get out of here, no problem. Things work out. Nothing to cry about."

Jennifer didn't mean it, but it came out. "I miss my son."

Clara put down her fork. "I know, I miss my baby too — Rodney just two, but he be some beauty. They don't give me more than a year, so I do five months and twenty days and Rodney stay with Else, my sister. She good to Rodney. Sometime he too much for me, so this be maybe some kind of vacation. For us both. May be that's God's plan."

Jennifer shook her head again. "My baby's gone," she said. "He's dead." She felt Clara stop eating next to her. She put a hand on Jennifer's shoulders, her black eyes liquid and soft. "Oh, child."

"They think I killed him too. It's crazy . . . They say he came in while Larry and I were fighting over the gun, or something like that. It's so stupid, *crazy* . . . And there's no bail."

Clara took her hand away. Her voice was hoarse and low. "I never heard of no bail."

Jennifer told her she'd heard of it now.

"You sure? They done the hearing? Yeah, 'course they have. Oh, honey, I'm so sorry. How old your boy?"

"Matt. He was seven. They tell me they're going to ask for the death penalty."

"For you? Well, you lucky there." The news seemed to pluck her up. Jennifer stared at her, uncomprehending, and Clara explained. "You the wrong color for that, girl. They don't give no gas to no white woman look like you."

At breakfast there was Clara and the other new white woman, Rhea (grand theft). And Mercedes (murder) and Rosie (aggravated assault) and Jennifer. All of the men and women on the seventh floor were either awaiting trial or, convicted, waiting for their trip to state prison or another facility.

Mercedes was going to trial in a couple of weeks and had been in jail for four months. She had finally stabbed her no good husband because he'd been running around on her. Rosie, who had beaten her boyfriend with a rolling pin, didn't have two thousand dollars for bail. Her trial was in six days and she was sure no jury would convict her.

Rhea was about Jennifer's age, size, hair color, but all the beauty had been used out of her. She was telling them how her husband had been pimping her out and they'd gotten lucky (or unlucky) with a john who'd lost his wallet with nearly a thousand dollars in it. "That's why they went for the grand theft."

"They always lookin'," Clara said.

"What's your bail?" Jennifer asked. She had been giving more thought to bail lately. If she had three-hundred-thousand dollars and could get out of jail for a third of that, she could take the other two-hundred-thousand and disappear for a long time. Forever. Why did she want to spend it on David Freeman, just give it to him? It didn't seem right somehow.

"Five thousand," Rhea answered. "So it's takin' Jimmy a day or two to get it together. It's cool. We talked about it."

"You mean your boyfriend, he'll bring in five thousand dollars and you'll just go home tonight or tomorrow and that's it?"

"This girl got no bail." Jennifer was Clara's story and she wanted to tell it. "No bail at all."

Rhea, ignoring Clara, seemed to smell something. Something with Jennifer. "You got no bail? Is that true? Don't you want out of here?"

"Amen to that," Mercedes said. "Everybody want out of here."

" 'Cept me." Rosie, who had nearly killed her boyfriend, was the youngest of them, a diminutive, sweet-faced Hispanic. "I stay in here as long as they let me."

"You want that?"

Rosie's black eyes shone at Jennifer. "I want to be where I don't get hit no more."

"Amen," Mercedes said. "Amen amen."

"I get out of here," Rosie continued, "next day somebody's going to be hitting me. Next time he hit me I think I keel that son-of-a-bitch. So here" — and her face brightened — "I'm safe. Nobody hit me. I can't hit nobody back. I stay a while here. I think."

One of the guards, with a tag on her chest that read "Jessup," was moving their way. The talking stopped.

She came over to them. "You ladies having a nice time? Sure sounds like it." She tapped the table gently with her nightstick, her mouth becoming a thin line, nearly invisible. "Finish it up, now. Let's eat up."

Jennifer heard her name called over the loudspeaker.

Freeman was not sitting. Nor was Hardy. Jennifer looked defiantly up at them both. Freeman, who had obviously been through this sort of thing many times before, spoke matter-of-factly. "Typically, a full-scale murder trial will run to between half-a-million and a million in legal fees, so yes, I'd say your retainer will be spent."

"Then what?"

"Then what what, Jennifer?"

"After it's gone."

"Then we go to the court and get paid by the state."

"Couldn't they still just pick a public defender then?"

Freeman nodded. "They could, but they won't. They don't want some new defense team coming in and spending a year getting up to speed. By that time we'll know the case inside out and the court will stay with us."

"How about if we just don't mention my . . . my secret account?"

Freeman was shaking his head, pacing. "Jennifer. Without your secret account there isn't any money to begin with, so the court *then* appoints whoever it wants, and you've already said you don't want that. You know, I'm afraid I don't really understand your problem here. You're going on trial for your life, Jennifer. And you're talking about money you'll never be able to spend if you don't have the best representation and, frankly, maybe even with it."

That'a'way, David, Hardy thought, sugarcoat it. He did understand that Freeman felt he had to give Jennifer a dose of reality, but her response made Hardy feel that he was going too far. Her head was going back down in that cowed way she had; she was blinking back new tears.

Freeman appeared unaffected by this display, but he did stop in front of her and speak more quietly. "Jennifer, look at me, okay. Look up. All right, now listen. We are going to do our best to get you off here. That's what I do — it's my specialty, you might say. And as soon as you're found innocent you collect some five-million-dollars insurance money. But if you're not found innocent . . . well, you don't get any of your money, insurance or secret account. Plus you could face the extreme penalty. So what's it going to be? You decide."

She swallowed hard and, for a moment, studied the table in front of her. "The only thing is, Mr. Freeman," she whispered, "isn't it true that if I retain you, I won't have enough money for bail?"

At first it didn't even register. A minute earlier Jennifer Witt had been rocked. Or seemed to have been. Now her eyes were clear, her head was up.

Freeman noticed, too. This lady was nobody's fool. Now, suddenly, there was a sense of gamesmanship in the tiny room. Hardy was outside of it, but Freeman sat down and leaned toward her. "Good," he said, "good."

"Good what?" She leaned away from him in her folding chair, an elbow going over the back of it.

Freeman ignored the direct question. "*If* we can get bail, which you remember has been denied already. You're thinking a hundred-thousand pays the bondsman and you can get out and jump, isn't that it?"

Jennifer, still sitting back, silently met his gaze.

"You think your house is worth a million dollars? I remind you that you didn't think it was yesterday. The three-hundred-thousand in your secret account won't do it. And neither will the insurance. You'll need at least a million that's relatively liquid. And no matter who represents you and what you pay them, this is reality. Bail is a waste of time. Even if you get it, you can't pay it."

"Which means I'm here until my trial is over?"

Freeman nodded. "I'm afraid that's what it means."

Jennifer took that in, pulled herself up to the table, and crossed her hands in front of her. After a minute, surprisingly, she began to smile. It was the first smile Hardy had seen from her, and it was quite lovely. "I'm going to have to think more about this."

Hardy started to interject, but Freeman put up a restraining hand. "Fine, Jennifer, fine. Shall we just withdraw as your attorneys now?"

"No! I don't want that. Can't I just have a little more time to be sure?"

"Jennifer, a retainer is needed. The court will need to know that you're represented at all times. If it's not me, as I've told you, they'll appoint somebody, and until your personal money's gone you'll have to pay them too."

"Could I pay some say twenty-five thousand now and the rest by Monday if I decided to go ahead — ?"

"As opposed to what? *Not* go ahead. Do you want to plead guilty? If, and it's a big if, the DA will deal, it will probably mean life without parole."

Again, Hardy couldn't read her. Her eyes were bright, alive. Scared, a brave front? Or . . .

"I don't know."

Now Hardy felt he had to say something. "Jennifer, pleading means you say you did it for a lesser penalty. You realize that?"

She nodded slowly.

"But you've been telling us — adamantly, as a matter of fact — that you didn't. Now which is it?"

"Diz, it doesn't matter," Freeman said. "Not now."

But Hardy had had enough of Freeman's "professionalism." He was starting to get involved in the facts, in belief or doubt, in his own motivations, and in Jennifer's personal story. He slammed the table top with a flat hand, raising his voice. "Damn it, David, it matters to me!" He went back to the client. "Now which is it, Jennifer? And whatever it is, let's stick with it."

Jennifer hung her head for a moment or two, then raised her eyes. "Maybe I don't think I can win. Wouldn't that be a good reason to plead?"

Freeman said "yes" at the same instant Hardy replied, "Not if you didn't do it."

"Well, I *didn't* do it."

Hardy straightened up. "All right, then."

As though they had decided it long ago, Freeman opened his briefcase and removed a piece of paper. "Okay, Jennifer, we're in business."

10

Hardy was at Lou the Greek's, finishing his coffee and calling it lunch, having long since given up hope that what he had ordered would become edible. Lou's wife was Chinese and she did the cooking — some of it delicious, all of it unique — but today's special of Sweet & Sour Dolmas just flat didn't sing.

In nearly two hours of discussion with Freeman and himself, Jennifer had not budged — she was innocent. They were not going to plead guilty even if they could. Which, in its own way, was good. At least it eliminated any ambiguity. Jennifer was sticking her attorneys with the classic passive, negative defense — at every turn, demonstrate the weakness of the prosecution's case; the burden of proof was on the prosecutor and Freeman's position was going to be that they had not met that burden. Period.

Except, of course, nothing was really that simple. As both Hardy and Freeman had tried to point out to Jennifer, the prosecution's case, on the face of it, was not so thin. They had physical evidence, putative motive, even eyewitnesses. This was not, they had argued, some high-handed political vendetta come home to roost. Nobody had been out to get Jennifer Witt — the evidence had persuaded the grand jury to indict her, and it well might persuade a jury to convict.

The charges involving her first husband Ned made it much worse. The evidence might be older, but the coincidence factor, if that's what it was, to say nothing of the presence of significant insurance money in both instances, would be daunting to overcome.

At the same time, though, Jennifer's position gave Freeman a strategy and Hardy a concrete direction. Given their client's demands, there was only one course, time-honored and true, that they could take. Find the holes, if not in the facts, then in the arguments interpreting them.

The fog had burned off but, lest San Francisco bask in sunny warmth, the wind had come up off the ocean. Hardy stood in the outside stairway four stories up the Hall of Justice, listening to it howl through the structure that one day would be the new jail just across the way.

Abe Glitsky opened the door and stepped outside. Papers swirled and dust eddied. He took it all in. "I've got a nice office not a hundred feet away. Remember?"

"Powell's in there."

Glitsky nodded. "All too true. He works in this building. Which, I might add, you don't. Exactly what are we doing here, Diz?"

"We're having a secret meeting, Abe. I wondered if you felt like taking a ride with me?"

Glitsky's hands were in the pockets of his parka. He pursed his lips and the scar through his lips burned white. "Middle of the week, middle of the day, sure, I'll just take off. Nobody'll miss me. I don't do anything anyway."

"Abe, I need you to prevent me from committing a felony, which if I do and get caught —"

"If you do and if you get caught —"

Hardy stopped him. "Please, Abe, this is a critical time for my life and career. If I commit this felony, and if I get caught, I'll lose my license, get disbarred, Frannie will probably divorce me, the kids will have to live knowing their father's a criminal. Even talking about it, my life flashes before my very eyes . . ."

"Your very eyes." Glitsky shook his head and the wind gusted.

"Come on," Hardy said. "Won't even take an hour."

"Why do I do these things?" Glitsky asked.

"I think you've got a deep-seated need to prove yourself. I worry about it sometimes. I really do. A guy your age."

"My age is your age."

"I know, but I'm younger. I look better, too. It's funny but it's true."

Glitsky chewed his cheek. "Sad."

They were in the lobby of the Bank of America at the corner of Haight and Cole. Hardy had given Jennifer's power of attorney to the vice-president, a young black woman named Isabel Reed who did not appear to have any problem with Glitsky's age or looks. She had been checking on the ATM withdrawal on the morning of December 28 and returned with the news that the account had been accessed at 9:43 A.M., and since they were talking about times anyway, she'd be getting off at 4:30 if there was anything else they needed to talk about . . .

Hardy said no, he thought that was about it, that she'd been a big help. He nudged Glitsky and they started to turn to go.

"I'm here every day," Ms. Reed offered, "if you need anything else."

"You know . . ." Hardy stopped, just now remembering. "There is something if you wouldn't mind. Abraham, you think we should calibrate this thing?"

This, as Hardy had explained to Glitsky on the way out here, was why he had to come along. Glitsky's badge got them access not just to Jennifer's account but to the whole automated system. While an obliging bank employee ran receipts out of the ATM, Hardy dialed POPCORN — the number provided by Pacific Bell that police used for the "official time" of emergency calls to 911 — and checked it against the bank's computerized clock on the ATM.

They found that there was a three-minute difference between the times — 2:11 at the bank and 2:14 from Pac Bell.

"Is that important?" Ms. Reed asked Abe. Hardy had ceased to exist altogether.

"It could be crucial," Glitsky admitted, "in this case. But you should have it checked in any event. Records aren't much good if they're not accurate."

Ms. Reed, nodding and attentive receiving this wisdom, thanked them both and gave Glitsky one of her cards. Then, clearly as an after-thought, she pulled one out for Hardy, too.

Outside, the gale blew and both men leaned into it. "*That's* why you do this," Hardy said through his clenched teeth. "Records aren't much good if they're not accurate."

Glitsky, happily married with three children, couldn't stop smiling, something he did perhaps twice a year.

Driving back downtown, Glitsky finally spoke. "I give up," he said. "What felony have I prevented by this astute police work?"

Hardy answered straight-faced, "Plan *B* was for me to dress up like a Ninja, break into the bank in the middle of the night and do the cross-check. Plan *B* wasn't very good. I didn't think it would work."

Glitsky shook his head, withholding comment.

Hardy did some figuring. When Mrs. Barbieto had called 911 at 9:40, it had been 9:37 at Haight and Cole. If Jennifer had left two minutes before the 911 call at 9:35, which was Mrs. Barbieto's testimony, she would have had to run 1.7 miles to the bank and access her ATM at 9:45, eight minutes later. She couldn't have done that. If, on the other hand, as Hardy surmised, it was more like five minutes between the shots and Mrs. Barbieto's call to emergency, Jennifer would have had eleven minutes, three plus eight, which was fast but, Hardy thought, doable.

Glitsky, not knowing why, had been right. Ms. Reed's ATM information could prove to be important, maybe even crucial.

He had to go upstairs to the jail again, because

although Jennifer had given him permission to enter her house, he had neglected to pick up the key, which the sheriff was keeping with the rest of her effects. Hardy needed Jennifer's signature so the sheriff would release the key to him.

"Mr. Hardy, is it?"

The hand was out and Hardy took it. It was a surprisingly weak grip for such a big man — Ken Lightner, Mr. Clairol with his brown hair and red beard, Jennifer's psychiatrist, was standing inside the bars by the elevator as the door opened.

"I was just visiting Jennifer. We've got to get her out of here. She doesn't belong in that . . . you are here to see her, aren't you?"

Hardy explained about the key. He didn't warm to this man but he could be polite.

"Actually," Lightner said as the elevator closed, "perhaps it's fortuitous that you're here. I was going to call you."

"If it's about Jennifer you should try David Freeman. He's her lawyer in this matter."

"Well, Freeman," Lightner paused, began again. "Jennifer seems to have a higher opinion of you."

Hardy shrugged. What was he supposed to say to that? He'd let Lightner figure out where he was going.

"I mean, you're representing her, too, aren't you?"

"I have to tell you that if either you or Jennifer thinks I'm anywhere near the trial lawyer that David Freeman is, you're both mistaken. David's a little abrasive, okay, but that's mostly just his style. He doesn't get beat too often, and that's where Jennifer's interests lie."

"What if she just likes . . . feels more comfortable with you?"

There wasn't much room in the area between the elevator door and the bars, but Hardy backed away a step. "This is not a comfortable situation, Doctor. I'm working with David, for David, I'm not that involved in Jennifer's defense on the guilt stage, and I'm a little confused about your role in all this. Did Jennifer ask you to talk to me?"

"Not directly, no. I'm not interested in offending you, Mr. Hardy, but my main concern is Jennifer. She's lost, upset, grief-stricken . . . she's very, very unhappy —"

"She's in jail, Doctor."

Lightner turned his head abruptly. Impatient. "No, no. I don't mean her situation now, here." He got a grip on himself, spoke more quietly. "Look, Mr. Hardy, she can't stay here. I don't think she'd survive a year, whatever it might be for the trial, in there. Have you seen . . . of course you have. You know what it's like. And Mr. Freeman tells her to forget about bail. Why? Is that in her best interest?"

Hardy was losing some of his own patience. "It's about reality, Doctor. I'd advise the same thing if I were the primary counsel representing Jennifer. I'm afraid she's not going to get bail. She's not getting out."

Lightner shook his head. "If she stays in jail I believe it's not unlikely that she will kill herself."

"You're talking to the wrong person. You should be talking to the judge . . . or the legislature. Besides, I think that's a little extreme. Jail's rough, no question, but I certainly didn't see any sign of suicidal depression this morning and I was with her for two hours."

"Would you know it if you saw it, Mr. Hardy?"

Hardy knew he had a point there, but the man was getting to him. "I think so. Now if you'll excuse me —"

"No, listen, listen *please.*"

Hardy waited.

"I'm sorry. Maybe we've gotten off on the wrong foot, but somebody's got to understand what's really happening here," Lightner said.

"And you know?"

"I know. I've been treating this woman for four years. I've had to prescribe anti-depressant drugs during crises. Jennifer is clinically depressed."

An obvious if ingenious thought occurred to Hardy. "Well, Doctor, if she's been depressed for four years, it isn't jail that's doing it to her." Hardy glanced at his watch. "Now I've really got to go. Sorry."

Lightner touched his arm and took a deep breath, as though making up his mind about a major decision. "Suppose I told you," he said, his voice low now, "that she may have actually done it. Don't you want to know *why?* It's what this is all about."

"You said you noticed it yourself . . . one minute she's so smart, almost playful, the next she's like a beaten victim — head down, uninvolved, at sea. She has no appetite, she's subject to extreme mood changes, lethargic to hyper-active. Nightmares ruin her sleep. All of these are classic signs of clinical depression."

Hardy had gone with Lightner to pick up the release — the reason he'd come up here in the first place — and they had ridden together down to the third floor, the DA's floor. Hardy, who used to be employed in the building, knew a few of the private spaces, and he brought Lightner now into the reporter's room just off the hall by the elevators.

Here, on a Thursday afternoon, there was peace. No reporters, no other people. A comfortable clutter amid recycled school desks and old pitted library tables.

But Hardy's main interest wasn't in Lightner's diagnosis of Jennifer. "It still doesn't mean she killed anybody."

Lightner was sitting forward on one of the tables next to the slatted window. "No, it doesn't of itself, but I'm telling you now . . . I'm afraid she did kill her husband."

"You're sure of that? She tell you?"

"No, but I know."

"And her boy?"

"I don't know how that happened. It could have been a mistake. She might have thought he was Larry."

"A seven-year-old boy? Her own son?"

"I said I don't know how that happened. The boy might have gotten between them, the gun went off, I don't know, some terrible accident."

Hardy didn't like to admit it, had in fact avoided this conclusion each time it had surfaced before now, but Lightner had a point. Everyday people got killed by mistake with firearms. You put a gun in the picture, you got the possibility of an accident. Hardy could invent half a dozen scenarios himself that might have resulted, accidentally, in Matt's death.

"Except she denies it," Hardy said. "But, for the sake of argument, *how* do you know? *Why?*"

Finally, an open question. Lightner pushed his well-tailored bulk back onto the table. Sunlight cut steeply through the motes by the one window, fell across the psychiatrist's face, highlighting reds in the handsome beard.

He sighed, his fists clenched. "The simple answer," he said, "is *to stop Larry from beating her.*"

Hardy was cramped into the seat of a one-piece, old-fashioned school desk, complete with built-in inkwell, around which he was running his finger, leaning back, legs stretched out straight in front of him, crossed at the ankles. "She says he didn't beat her. She says they fought like everybody else but —"

"Of course, she says that. But it's not true."

"It's not true," Hardy repeated. "How do I know it's not true?" He held up his round-the-inkwell hand. "No, I'm not starting in again. I'm asking if you've got any proof, any corroboration. Jennifer's admission? Anything? I presume you're telling me this to give her an out, an excuse that might clear her if she did it."

Lightner nodded. "Yes, but I'm on very tenuous ground here, Mr. Hardy. I know that. Well, I've persuaded myself, that I can tell you some of what I know, things you might find from other sources given enough time. But I'm afraid I can't tell you *how* I know it."

It took a moment before Hardy said, "Privilege."

There it was, that familiar double-edged sword. Lightner's head inclined a bit. "Without my input, there still should be records that point to it. She never said, but I believe she must have switched physicians. They're mandated to report."

He was right about that, Hardy knew. When the same person, a woman, say, or a child, visited a doctor with burns, contusions, abrasions, bruises, saying they fell off their bicycle, down the stairs, walked into a door, whatever — if it looked suspicious the physician by law had to notify somebody in law enforcement. There was compelling reason to suspect abuse.

Hardy asked the obvious question. "But you *knew* Jennifer was being beaten. Why didn't you report it?"

Lightner was still on his hands, an unhappy look on his face. "We're exempt from the mandate. She refused to let me. She was my patient. I was her psychiatrist. It was her right."

"So she changed her doctors so they wouldn't suspect. Or report it. Anything else?"

"Neighbors might know. How many times have they moved? Sometimes that's a clue."

Hardy pointed out that all this might be fine, but Jennifer herself was the most likely source of corroboration about whether she was a battered wife, and *she* was denying it. "You'll agree," he said, "this poses something of a problem for us."

"I see that, yes, of course."

"Well?"

"I just thought you had to know. As you said,

it's *got* to be her defense. It's *why* she did it."

Hardy tried to straighten up in the tiny chair. He put his elbows on the desk. "Dr. Lightner, I've got to remind you, she denies both the battery and that she killed anybody. We went over this again and again this morning and she isn't going to go with any battered-wife defense — not with Freeman, not with me, not with anybody. And this leads me to the question . . . Why in the world wouldn't she just admit to being battered? As you said, people are increasingly getting off on this defense these days. The precedents are in place. We told her that. So why, since it's got a good chance, maybe the best chance, to save her life, won't she agree to it?"

"She's embarrassed."

For a second, Hardy thought he'd heard wrong. "Say what?"

"She's embarrassed. She doesn't want anybody to know that she's the kind of person who could live with being beaten. Why wouldn't she just leave?"

"Exactly."

Now Lightner leaned forward, into it. "But don't you see? That's the problem. They can't leave! I know this might come across as socialized claptrap to you, but in some cultures, it's more socially acceptable than in others to take this kind of domestic abuse, but it's not among upper-class whites in our culture.

"Well, now she herself is upper class. She's made it and she's not going back."

"What if she's convicted? What's she got?"

"She's still got her self-image."

"And you're telling me that's more important than her life?"

"I don't think she's ever faced that."

Hardy realized that Lightner could be right. Stuffed into the tiny desk, his posture was getting to him. He wedged himself out, standing.

"So Jennifer won't admit she was beaten . . . battered, essentially because she's embarrassed."

"That's right. Embarrassed may be too weak a word. Mortified is better, that she was battered, almost ritually beaten and, unbelievably, maybe even to herself, stayed around to take it." Lightner slid off the table.

Hardy was rubbing his shoulder. "I don't mean to offend here, doctor, but is any of this psychobabble? I mean, how many of your conclusions, assuming I independently discover some facts, can I depend on?"

Lightner didn't appear offended. He nodded. Maybe he thought it was a good question. "All of them, I'd say."

11

In the waning daylight the Witt home was impressive. The previous night, when Hardy and Frannie had driven by, there had been a sense of solidity to Olympia Way, high up on Twin Peaks. Most of the street bordered the Midtown Terrace Playground. It had been quiet, almost ghostly. Working street lights cast their beams through the early spring foliage of the trees that overhung the street. Hedges seemed trimmed and full-grown.

In sunlight the feeling of sheltered enclave was even stronger. Hardy got out of his car and stood looking at Jennifer's home, two lots from the park, from the south side of the street. To the west, the Pacific glittered, and just north, Sutro Tower stretched its rusted arms to the sky. Hardy thought some of the two- and three-story houses could sit comfortably on Embassy Row — landscaped and majestic, these were the homes of people who might not miss three hundred thousand dollars if it disappeared slowly enough.

The Witts' hedge — at perhaps three feet — wasn't as tall as some of the others, though it was as well kept as any. A white picket fence fronted it. The gate to the fence was shut, but the hedge turned ninety degrees up both sides of the straight brick path to the front door.

Hardy had to remind himself that until two days ago Jennifer had lived here, coming and going, apparently unaware that the grand jury was deciding that there was sufficient evidence to indict her for murder. It was an unsettling thought.

But no more unsettling than when he turned the key. A dog from somewhere nearby barked and kept barking. Hardy stood waiting for its owner to come and quiet it down, check to see what had set it off. That didn't happen. In fact, nothing happened, and the barking continued. Hardy could have been a burglar with a sledge hammer instead of a lawyer with a key and no one — apparently — would have questioned him.

And this was the block that had produced two eyewitnesses for the time of the murder and more of the FedEx delivery truck? Hardy thought Terrell must be one persuasive interrogator.

Inside, after another minute, the barking stopped.

The house was white. The foyer was of white Italian marble with pink striations. Soft furnishings were modern and white, tables and racks were black cast-iron. Everything sat on light champagne wall-to-wall carpeting. On the walls Hardy recognized one of the Mapplethorpe's that had caused the stir, along with a print of Goya's *Mother Eating Her Child.* Up close, he studied a couple of other prints or originals that he wouldn't have hung in a locked darkroom, much less in the living room of a home with a child.

On his yellow pad he made a note to make sure

David Freeman kept the media out of here. He had to assume the stuff reflected Larry's tastes, not hers.

Downstairs everything was spotless, antiseptic. The kitchen — a black-and-white checkerboard tile and black-and-white fixtures — looked as though it had never been used. Copper pots gleamed from their hanging cast-iron rack over the island stove.

The silence hung heavily — Hardy found himself walking on the balls of his feet as he moved through the other downstairs rooms. The dining room with its black lacquer table and six chairs. A library with mostly medical books. No novels, a lot of history and biography. There was a tiny sitting room with a fireplace and a loveseat with a magazine stand end-table. But there were no magazines. A guest bedroom. Hardy pulled down the quilt on the bed, there was no sheet under it.

He stopped at the bottom of the stairs. Jennifer had been living here? There was no sign of life. He jotted another note to ask her if she had stayed somewhere else during the past months. And if so, where?

A month after he and Frannie had moved in together he had bought her one of those little tiles at the Ghirardelli Art Fair that read: A CLEAN HOUSE IS A SIGN OF A WASTED LIFE. That tile hung proudly in their kitchen. He didn't think he needed to search for where Jennifer kept hers.

Upstairs was more of the same. To the left was what must have been Matt's bedroom, the bed now made, toys neatly arranged. The evening sun was going down, bathing the room in an orange glow. Off this was a full bath, sea-horse stencils on the wall — minimal as it was, so far it was the only sign of any comfort in the house.

Hardy passed the stairway again, stopping to look down at the living and dining rooms below him. White. Black. Mirrors and metal and a growing dusk. Whatever else he had to do, he wanted to be done and out of here in a hurry.

The master bedroom was a surprise. The yellow police tape was still there, no longer in place across the door but lying on the rug. He stepped over it and walked to the middle of the room.

After the police department's technicians had finished with their forensics and the cleaners had repaired the damage, Hardy was suddenly certain that Jennifer had not set foot in this room. There were folded sheets and blankets on the bed's bare mattress, towels on the cabinet by the bathroom door, balls of dust in the corners.

He didn't know if he imagined the remains of the bloodstains — it was getting darker so he flipped on the overhead light. It went out with a pop. There were other lights on night tables on either side of the recessed headboard to the bed, and quickly — jumpy — he got to one of them and hit the button. That was better. He walked around the bed and turned on the second one. Leaning down, he checked the white rug, running his hand over what might have been a stain. As part of him had known, nothing came up, yet it strangely relieved him.

Hardy stood, more steady than he'd been. Turning on the adjoining bathroom's light, he looked in. Again, no sign that anyone had been in there since it had been cleaned. Turning off the lights by the bed, he stopped at the hallway door for a last glance into the shadowy room where the murders had occurred.

At the end of the hallway there was another door, the last room on the left. The overhead light, which stayed on this time, revealed an impersonal study with credenza, files, a short bookshelf filled with medical and business periodicals. The centerpiece of the room was a neatly organized black tabletop desk with a new leather-bound green blotter. Hardy sat at it.

Evidently no one had been in here either. The dust was thick on the tabletop. Hardy wondered if the police had inventoried this room, realizing there may have been no need to. Jennifer, he remembered, had provided the damning inventory, "forgetting" that the gun was missing.

(And, of course, if she hadn't ever gone back into that bedroom, she might have been able to assume it hadn't been missing. This could be vital. He had to ask her, and he scribbled some more.)

Sitting, the sun all but gone now through the louvered window over the desk, Hardy tried to imagine what living here must have been like. The degree of control and discipline everywhere palpable was, he thought, the kind of environment that could have produced internal, and external, paroxysms, convulsions. There just wasn't any place for release, even a gradual release. When emotions got too tightly wound here, they wouldn't unwind, they'd explode.

He had jotted his last notes on his yellow pad

on the desk blotter, and as he stared at the rim of the ocean he realized he'd been picking at the blotter with his left hand. In the upper left corner, under the triangle of leather, a scrap of paper protruded. He pulled it out.

It was a piece of lined paper from a pocket-sized spiral notebook. The side was frayed where it had been torn off, which seemed a little out of character for Larry Witt — those irregularities in the edge, Hardy was beginning to suppose, should have been intolerable to him. He would have cut them off with the precise little scissors on his Swiss Army knife.

He smiled scornfully at his imagination. There was something more immediate at hand — on the paper was the date "December 23" and the single word "No!!!" which, in addition to the three exclamation points, was underlined twice and circled. And under that was a telephone number with a 213 area code — downtown Los Angeles.

Hardy dialed the number.

"Law offices."

Naturally, he thought. He identified himself and asked to speak to the office manager. His watch read five-fifty on a Thursday night, but law firms never slept — there was no hesitation. The receptionist said that Ms. Klein would be right with him.

It wasn't immediate but soon enough. Either Ms. Klein had had an extremely bad day or she was someone Hardy wouldn't want to party with. "I'm sorry," she was saying, "the message wasn't very clear. You are?"

Hardy explained again — that he was representing a client in the Bay Area and among the papers in her house had been a document on which he'd found the phone number he'd called. He wondered what the connection might be. The firm was? He figured that he could play her game as well as anyone.

"Crane & Crane. And your client is?"

"Jennifer Witt."

Ms. Klein paused. "Well, the name isn't familiar to me." A tired laugh: "But that doesn't mean anything."

"How about the name Larry Witt? He was her husband. Maybe one of your attorneys would know? Your managing partner? Could I . . ."

Abruptly, her voice seemed to break. "No. No you can't!" Another pause, so long that Hardy thought she might have hung up.

"Ms. Klein?"

"Oh, oh I'm sorry, you'll have to excuse me, please, I'm just not myself. This past week . . . I shouldn't even be saying this . . ."

"Is everything all right?"

"No, Mr . . . Hardy, is it? No, everything is not all right."

"I'm sorry," Hardy said. The tension in these big corporate law firms must be as bad as the rumors, he thought. "I'll try back later."

"No, later won't do either. I mean . . ." Now a sob broke. "I'm so sorry, I mean, Mr. Simpson won't be back later. He's, he was the managing partner. He's dead. He was killed."

Mesmerized, Hardy listened as the facts trickled out. Mr. Simpson was Simpson Crane, lately managing partner of Crane & Crane. About a week ago he and his wife were gunned down at their home in Pacific Palisades. Simpson Crane had been an anti-labor attorney and he had been negotiating some contracts. The suspicion was, she said, that organized labor had hired someone to kill Crane, but the police didn't have many leads and said it was mostly a theory. Simpson's son, Todd, was now running the firm for the time being, but, as Hardy could imagine, it was a very difficult time.

By the time Hardy hung up it was full dark outside. He folded the sheet of paper and put it in his wallet. Leaving the light on in the study, he made his way into the hall and down the stairway, across the marble of the foyer and, blessedly, at last, outside.

"Jesus," he whispered.

Driving home, partly to escape the feeling of unease that had clung to him at the Witts', Hardy allowed himself to be disgusted that he had used the word "document" to describe the piece of spiral notebook paper that now resided in his wallet. He distinctly remembered the first time he'd come on the word "document" in his law studies. The verbiage, the pretension, the self-conscious importance — in short, everything about the definition struck him as so ludicrous, so plain stupid that he had memorized it (the alphabetical order made it easier), vowing never to become a lawyer who would use it:

> "Documents" is used herein in the broadest sense and includes all written, printed, typed, graphic or otherwise recorded matter,

however produced or reproduced, including non-identical copies, preliminary, intermediate, and final drafts, writings, records, and recordings of every kind and description, whether inscribed by hand or by mechanical, electronic, microfilm, photographic or other means, as well as phonic (such as tape recordings) or visual reproductions of all statements, conversations or events, and including without limitation, abstracts; address books; advertising material; agreements; analyses of any kind; appointment books; brochures; calendars; charts; circulars; computer cards; contracts; correspondence; data books; desk calendars; diagrams; diaries; directories; discs; drawings of any type; estimates; evaluations; financial statements or calculations; graphs; guidelines; house organs or publications; instructions; inter-office or intra-office communications; invoices; job descriptions; ledgers; letters; licenses; lists; manuals; maps; memoranda of any type; microfilm; minutes; movies; notebooks; notes; opinions; organization charts; pamphlets; permits; photographs; pictures; plans; projections; promotional materials; publications; purchase orders; schedules; specifications; standards; statistical analyses; stenographers' notebooks; studies of any kind; summaries, tabulations; tapes; telegrams; teletype messages; videotapes; vouchers; and working drawings, papers and files.

And a partridge in a pear tree.

And now this piece of paper with a date, a phone number and the word "No!!!" written on it had come out of his mouth, like water through a sieve, without an editing thought, as a "document."

It didn't thrill him.

Rhea, the woman who resembled Jennifer Witt, had been yelling and swearing into the telephone at her Jimmy for so long that, finally, when the guard had come in and taken the phone from her, hanging it up, she just shook her head and walked silently back to her cell. Jennifer, in the next cell, propped herself on an elbow on her cot.

"That didn't sound too good."

"That shit!" After the thirty-second break, Rhea was getting her vocabulary back. "That cocksucker Jimmy says I've got to wait another *few days*, maybe a *week* in here! Maybe a week! Shit! If he's fucking somebody else I'll kill the son of a bitch."

"What did he say?" Jennifer hoped her calm would be contagious. That language was all right when everybody was laughing, teasing, being together. But when you mixed anger in, it reminded her of too many other times — with Larry, with others, with what came next. Even hearing Rhea like this, she was getting cramps in her stomach. She curled her legs up, trying to get comfortable on the stained mattress, trying to keep the cramp from seizing. "About bail?"

"That shit!" Rhea picked up the plastic cup that held her plastic utensils and her disposable razor blade and her toothbrush and threw it against the bars.

"Rhea, stop! Please stop."

She did stop raving, stopped swearing. But when she did it left her standing at the edge of her cell, where she crumbled to the floor, crying quietly.

After a minute or two Jennifer uncurled herself from her cot and went to the side of her cell. "He couldn't get bail?"

Rhea shook her head quietly, back and forth. "He said it would be a couple of days at the most. Now he says without me his income is down and it's taking longer. How do you like that? Without me his income is down!" She lapsed again into quiet tears.

"How much would it take?" Jennifer asked.

The crying slowed, went to sniffles, stopped. "What?"

"How much did you say your bail was? Five thousand?"

She nodded. "Why?"

Jennifer sat on the floor, knees up, arms wrapped around them. She had already learned a lot about the working of the jail. Clara knew a lot, so did Mercedes. If you had the stomach and the money for it, if you were desperate enough, guards could be bribed, things could be done. It had happened before, many times.

"I don't know for sure," Jennifer said, "but maybe I can help him get it." She spoke as quietly as she could, venturing a glance over to

Rhea. If anyone else heard her, she wanted to be able to deny having said anything. But Rhea was listening, her mouth half open, disbelieving. "Of course you'd have to help me if you could."

12

Halfway out from Van Ness to the beach, Miz Carter's Mudhouse had been a landmark on California Street for half a century. The "mud" was coffee, sometimes thick as Turkish, and before espresso had caught on with the yuppies in the late seventies the Mudhouse was the best place for java in the western half of the city. Miz Carter's daughter, Louanne, still made her mud the old way, loose ground beans stirred into boiling water, then strained as it was poured. The stuff could jolt you right up.

Which Hardy needed. He and Frannie had been awakened no fewer than six times by their two young darlings doing their tag-team number, Rebecca with an ear infection and low-grade fever, Vincent wanting to be fed. It was fun, but all and all, the Hardys agreed they'd had better times.

Glitsky's description of Walter Terrell — white guy, brown hair, mustache — wasn't exactly on the money. He was swarthier, Mediterranean somehow, not like the guy Hardy had been thinking about from school. Hardy had put his briefcase on the table to identify himself, and Terrell came and slid in across from him.

He was younger than Hardy had expected,

maybe thirty-two or thereabouts. At forty-one, Hardy didn't feel old, but it was disconcerting that so many people he worked with were starting to be so much younger, and that he noticed it.

Terrell wore new Reeboks, a worn pair of Levi's and an ironed dress shirt with thin maroon stripes under his Member's Only jacket that fit him neatly. In spite of Glitsky's feelings about Terrell and his theories, the guy must have put together some kind of record if he'd already made Homicide.

After he'd had his coffee poured, Terrell took a sip and shuddered, adding sugar like there was no tomorrow. "What kind of name is Dismas?" He tried the mud again. He kept stirring.

Hardy explained for the thousandth time that Dismas had been the name of the good thief on Calvary. He did not mention that he was also the patron saint of murderers. "Only thing I can figure, my folks wanted to punish me for some reason. When I think they could have named me Bill, or Jack . . ."

Terrell's face cracked. "Yeah, I know, anything but Sue." Trying his coffee again, he finally put his spoon down. "This stuff's awesome," he said. "People drink this every day?"

"Every day."

"Awesome." He motioned to Hardy's briefcase. "So'd you check out Ned?" Hardy nodded. He'd gone over the coroner's exhumation report on Edward (Ned) Hollis last night after they'd put the kids down, further endearing him to his wife, who after a day with no adult company had more or less expected him to share the evening with her.

The smile and the aw-shucks manner weren't

entirely convincing. This was one smart cop. He could be as friendly as you please, but he wasn't going to be sandbagged by any smarty-pants defense attorney, even if he happened to be a friend of Abe Glitsky.

But Hardy merely nodded again. There was no battle to be won here. "I'm trying to get a handle on Ned, I suppose. Jennifer doesn't seem to have much to say about him. They found the atropine?"

Terrell pointed a finger at the briefcase. "That what it says?"

"Yeah, but so what?"

It was the first time Hardy had surprised him. "What do you mean, so what?"

"They find a concentration of atropine on the front of the right thigh? Which indicates it might have been injected?"

"Right."

"All right, we'll grant that, but what's to say Jennifer injected him?"

Terrell tried the coffee again, ignoring its awesomeness. "He didn't shoot himself up. Atropine doesn't make you high."

"Okay, but again, so what? Maybe he was trying to kill himself. Maybe he succeeded. What I'm asking is if there's anything I'm missing here, because I don't see why this got charged as a murder."

Terrell was visibly holding himself back. His face was becoming flushed. "This got charged as a murder 'cause it *was* a murder. Your Jennifer aced him for the seventy-five grand."

Hardy tried to keep it loose. "I'm not saying she didn't. I'm just wondering what proof . . .

if you've got any proof that she was the one who gave Ned the shot? I mean, how do you even know she was in the room?"

"She was in the room. She got him tanked up on booze and coke 'til he passed out, then she bonked him with the needle. Now he's dead, the coroner finds lethal coca-ethylene and forgets about scanning for whatever else might have killed him, like the atropine." He stabbed a finger on the table. "That's what happened, Mr. Hardy. You can bet on it."

Getting back to "Mr. Hardy" wasn't a good sign, and it wasn't Hardy's intention to alienate the inspector. "I'm not saying it didn't. The DA bought it — they charged it. But it seems to me they had to have more."

On the defense now, but softening slightly, Terrell the new homicide cop was anxious to show he'd done it right. "There was more, they did get more. I got 'em Harlan Poole, didn't I?"

"Her lover, the dentist? How'd you get to him?"

"I saw his name in a couple of statements Jennifer made in Ned's file. So I went and talked to him." Eager to explain his technique, Terrell leaned forward across the table. "The thing about this police work is sometimes, you know, you got to have some intuition. I mean, sometimes you just *know* what went down, right? So you go on that, tweak things a little, and you get somewhere."

"And you tweaked Poole?"

Terrell obviously enjoyed the memory. "Wasn't much of a tweak. The guy's successful, maybe forty-something, wife and three kids. I told him if he cooperated, told us what he knew, we'd try to keep a low profile on him. Guy cracked like a nut."

"And said what?"

"Said he missed the atropine one day after Jennifer had been in the office for a little late night nookie. Evidently they did it in or on — that wasn't too clear — the chair." Terrell broke a grin. "I get the feeling the guy and his wife don't do it much that way anymore. Anyway, he didn't put it together until hubby Ned turned up dead, and then he figured Jennifer had done it and it scared the piss out of him, so gradually, he says, he dumped her."

"Because he thought she'd killed Ned?"

"Yeah, because she killed Ned."

Hardy sat back. To grab some time, he lifted his cup and knocked back the dregs, making a face. There was a crucial something missing here. "Let me get this straight," he said. "When Ned turned up dead, Poole concluded that Jennifer had killed him, is that right?"

Terrell nodded.

"Well, isn't that a bit of a leap? I mean, he must have had some kind of hint this was on her mind — something? Right?"

"Sure. She'd talked about it."

"Talked about killing Ned?" Hardy shook his head. "If Poole got scared off afterward, why didn't he see it coming and dump her before?"

Terrell was engaged now, thinking it through, elbows on the table. "I guess he didn't see it coming. She didn't talk about it as a plan or anything. I think afterward he just put it together."

"But why? Why would it even enter his mind?"

"Because she'd talked about leaving him, about wouldn't it be wonderful if he died, the insurance, all that."

"Leaving him and wishing he'd die aren't the same as actually killing him."

"Okay, but she'd tried to leave him before — a couple of times — and he'd come after her and beat the shit out of her."

Bingo. "Ned beat her, too? Is there any proof of that?"

"You mean did she report it, anything like that? Get serious."

This was good stuff, and possibly true, but Hardy was more than half-certain that all of it was inadmissible because it was hearsay, and twice removed hearsay at that — Dr. Poole saying that Jennifer had told him that Ned had beaten her. Nevertheless, it was a psychological bombshell. If it was true that Jennifer had killed Ned because he was beating her — to stop him and to get the insurance she could figure she was entitled to — who wouldn't believe she had done the same with Larry?

Because the argument was compelling, the temptation to compare the circumstances surrounding the deaths of Larry and Ned would be overwhelming, and Hardy found himself hoping that Powell and the prosecution would get caught up in the symmetry and pursue it. Because it gave her a sympathetic motive in both cases.

But he didn't mention this to Terrell. Instead, he told him he thought what he had was pretty good.

Friends now, or at least amicable adversaries, they stood by the counter waiting for their change, making small talk, Hardy asking if Terrell had ever noticed the funny coincidences that seemed to happen all the time when you got deep into a case.

"Yeah, I know," Terrell said, "it's weird. Couple of months ago, I'm still in burglary, I get a call out in the Mission and I go down there and I'm checking out a broken window when another window across the alley opens up and some guy yells, 'Hey Wally!' I look up and it's some guy I played ball with in high school. Amazing. But you're right. It happens all the time."

Hardy told him about the death of Simpson Crane in Los Angeles. "Is that strange or what? Here I'm at a murder victim's house, I find a phone number and call it, and I get another murder victim."

That stopped Terrell by the door. Maybe he just wasn't primed yet to go out into the swirling fog, but Hardy didn't think that was it. "How'd you say this guy — Crane? — how'd he get it?"

"They think it was some union job, a professional hit. Just like Jennifer says with Larry. Hell of a coincidence, huh?"

Terrell shook his head, almost as though he were trying to clear it, shake this rogue thought out completely. "No, Larry wasn't no hit. There wasn't any hit man. Jennifer did Larry."

Hardy didn't want to smile when he set the hook. Give this man a theory, Glitsky had said. "Still, you've got to admit, it's interesting."

Terrell tried to shrug it off. "Sure, but like I

said, this shit happens all the time."

"You're right." Hardy pushed the door open, steeling himself against the cold. "You're right, it does."

A seven-year-old Matthew Witt smiled up in full color and perfect focus. Whoever had taken the school photos had done a good job, capturing the personality behind the impish face. Whatever constrictions had worked on Matt in his sterile home, they apparently hadn't defeated him. There was a real smile in the eyes, some kidlike sense of jauntiness — maybe he'd just said something smart to the photographer and was proud of himself. But it wasn't a wise-ass look — it was friendly, open. A nice little boy aiming to please.

David Freeman was in the shower in his apartment and Hardy slumped deep in an ancient red leather chair near one of the living room windows, trying and failing to tear himself away from Matt. There were lots of other pictures in the folder that he held on his lap, and he had already gone through quite a few when he got to the boy.

He had black hair, neatly combed and parted except for a cowlick. He was wearing a green-and-white-striped T-shirt with a soft collar, up on one side and down on the other like puppies' ears. There was a gap between his two front teeth. Freckles across the bridge of his nose. Long eyelashes. The beginning of a dimple. The laughing eyes were a deep green.

Hardy sat back, pulling at the skin on his face, staring without seeing anything out the window into the fog. He didn't know how much time had gone by when he felt a hand on his shoulder.

"There's nothing we can do about that."

Freeman, in a frayed terrycloth bathrobe, gave Hardy's shoulder another gentle shake. He was, at times surprisingly, perhaps sympathetic — the tone said so — but ultimately pragmatic. If you couldn't affect anything, if you couldn't act, then by Freeman's definition there was nothing to be done. Hardy didn't agree — it might not produce any tangible result but he thought you could at least grieve.

Barefoot, unshaven, his wet hair in a gray-and-brown mess, Freeman walked across his living room to the breakfast nook, where on a shining mahogany table he had spread his own working papers, legal pads, binders, boxes of cassette tapes. Currently working a trial, planning for a new one, cleaning up the loose ends and appeals of trials gone by — was this what Hardy's life was going to become? He got a glimpse of it from Frannie's perspective and wondered if by getting involved with David and Jennifer he was making a mistake.

Then he looked down at Matt. God . . . if Jennifer had killed him, even by accident, even if he'd just gotten in the way . . .

But what if it wasn't that, what if Jennifer were telling the truth? Then someone else was out there. Someone who needed to die and was walking around, letting Jennifer go through this hell, leaving Matt unavenged.

Hardy did believe in vengeance — in severe, purposeful vengeance. It was what had drawn him into police work, then into the prosecution business in the first place. But, and in this way he knew he *was* becoming a lawyer, he now believed that before the vengeance he — personally — had to eliminate any reasonable doubt.

And this was what drove him now — not to sell his soul as a mouthpiece for some prosecution or defense posture, for some legal opinion, not to argue because he could prevail, but to uncover the truth of the matter, however it came out.

He put Matt's picture face down and went to the next one.

Freeman lived on the corner of Taylor and Pine, one steep block down from the peak of Nob Hill, a floor above one of the oldest and best French restaurants in the City. Freeman kept his own personal wine cellar in the restaurant and averaged perhaps ten meals there every month.

His own apartment was modest in size and conveniences — two bedrooms, living room, kitchen with eating nook. In spite of his income, the place resisted any nod to modern technology. Freeman still used a rotary wall-mounted telephone in the kitchen, and whenever he played his classical music, which was the only kind he listened to, it was on long-playing 33⅓ rpm records that he'd bought with his then brand new stereo system in the early sixties. The couches and chairs in the living room were comfortable, cracked old red leather; the coffee and end tables were of some dark wood with lion's claw feet. The lamps all had shades, and most of them were three-way.

His current trial had been continued — put on hold — until the following Monday because the prosecuting attorney had a toothache and needed to see the dentist. So he'd left a message at Sutter Street that Hardy should come up — it was only a six-block walk — to discuss some Jennifer Witt matters before the weekend.

The crime-scene shots had been in the file, of course, and Hardy knew there were people who turned to look at them first, before they did any reading. He wasn't one of them.

There were twenty-seven pictures of the room where the murders had been committed as the photo team had found it, although many were shots of essentially the same thing from a slightly different perspective. These photographs were, as usual, competently done. By design, they didn't strive for artful composition, but the focus was perfect, the color sharp, the angles inclusive.

There were also eight shots each of Larry and Matt, of the bodies and their wounds on the autopsy table.

Hardy and Freeman, separately, had gone through them all one by one. It was quiet work.

When they finished they spread out an even dozen of the crime-scene photos for a closer inspection together.

Both father and son had been shot one time each with a .38 caliber automatic. The bullets, in common with the five that had been discovered in the clip later, had hollow points, common enough among people who had bought their weapons for home defense. Sometimes the argument went, you only got one shot off, and that shot needed to do as much damage as possible.

By this criteria, the bullets had done their job. Larry had been shot through the heart. The slug, at that close range, had exited through his back, and the core of the original bullet had imbedded itself in the drywall. There was a close-up of that section of wall, and Hardy was surprised he had missed it completely while he'd been there, but then, he had not by that time been in his most objective state of mind.

The force of the shot had apparently knocked Larry backward onto the end of the bed, where he had rolled off onto the floor. He had come to rest on his right side, his life gone before he had hit the carpet, judging from the fact that there was no smearing of the bloodstains beneath him.

Neither Hardy nor Freeman wanted to view the pictures of Matt, who had been hit in the head. He evidently had been standing by the bathroom door. Last night, the bathroom had seemed antiseptic, but in these pictures the bathroom mirror was a shattered spider web, the walls dotted with red.

Putting the pictures aside, they moved on to the ATM, the discussion Hardy had had with Lightner, his tour of the Witt home, the Crane coincidence and Terrell's view of the Ned Hollis murder. Freeman, pacing the kitchen in his bathrobe, took it all in. He did not seem displeased. When Hardy had finished he acknowledged that he had been busy. "This isn't as bad as it looked yesterday. Of course, it may look worse tomorrow."

"I'm glad you said that last part. You wouldn't want it to look better two days in a row."

Freeman ignored him. "Still, our work is cut out for us. I had Phyllis wire the money over to our account, by the way. The initial retainer. It went through."

"Did you think it wouldn't?"

"Tell you the truth, like many other things about Jennifer, I just wasn't sure."

Hardy decided he wouldn't push it. "I thought I'd go talk to Jennifer again this morning, get some kind of line on Larry's work and her family that they never visited. I also want to find out about the last couple of months. That house showed no sign of anybody living there. I'd like to know if she ever went into the murder room after they cleaned it out."

"None of that's going to be her defense."

Hardy was packing the reports away into his thick briefcase. He was going to do what he was going to do, and didn't want to argue about it. "No, I know. But it might give you something to point at in your histrionic way. Keep the jury juggling the possibilities."

"The possibilities?"

"Of who else might have killed Larry."

Freeman nodded. "Yes, but we don't have to prove, or even show, that somebody else killed Larry. Mr. Powell's got to prove that Jennifer did."

"If she never went into the bedroom to take the inventory, it eliminates one of their major contentions."

"Only if we can prove it. We can assert it, but you can't prove a negative, and the assertion gets us nothing."

"It might get us some doubt. You get enough doubts . . ."

Freeman was wearing his dour face. "Well," he said, "we're a long way from trial. Whatever we find out might be useful at this stage. Certainly this Terrell thing, that was helpful. If Powell falls for it."

Hardy snapped the briefcase shut. "He's already charged the murder. He won't back out now. He's committed."

Freeman wasn't so confident about that. Not yet. "He must have something else. That's what I'd like to find out. He must know he can't win on what he's shown us so far." . . . He stared for a moment out his kitchen window. "In any event, we'll know soon enough. Meanwhile, I'll take a look at what they've actually given us. And don't misunderstand, your idea isn't bad — I've used it before myself — the old 'soddit' defense."

"Some Other Dude Did It?"

Freeman nodded. "That's the one. Find some other dudes to point at."

Hardy stood up, grateful to be moving again. "You know, it is possible she's telling a lot of the truth."

"Oh, I'm sure she is." Freeman scratched his stubble. "It's really very difficult not to let at least some truth out even if you're trying to dissemble." Freeman paused, added straight-faced, "I said *if* . . ."

13

So Larry also worked at an abortion clinic. So what?" Glitsky was barely listening, leaning back in the car seat next to Hardy. They were going home. "Hey, guess what?" he said. "It's Friday night. The week's over."

But Hardy wasn't letting it go. "So how many deaths and threats do we have so far this year against abortion-clinic workers?"

Glitsky kept his eyes closed. "I don't know. You tell me."

"Okay, I will. I happened to check this afternoon. Four in the city since December."

Glitsky opened his eyes. Homicides were his territory, and this fact surprised him. "Deaths?"

"Deaths and threats, combined."

"How many deaths, Hardy?"

"One."

Glitsky grunted, closed his eyes again.

"And Larry Witt would make two."

"It would if he'd been killed by a disgruntled anti-abortion activist instead of his wife."

Hardy kept driving west. The fog had lifted and the wind had stilled and it was a lovely Friday night, a postcard sunset coloring the sky before them. "You don't see it, huh?"

"Not if I'm on a jury. 'Course I'm a cop so I don't think like a juror, but what are you going to point at? You need something besides 'Ladies and Gentlemen, did you know that Dr. Witt performed abortions on Wednesdays and Saturdays?' You know how mad that makes some people? What are they supposed to do with that? You don't have anybody."

"Okay, how about Tom? The brother?"

Hardy had interviewed Tom after he saw Jennifer in the morning. Tom had, obviously, hated Larry. He wasn't particularly fond of Jennifer, either. He had no idea where he'd been the morning of December 28 — he hadn't been working so he was probably hanging at his apartment. He had never tried to borrow any money from either Jennifer or Larry. "Or Matt either," he'd volunteered with a sneer.

The only information Tom had provided, and Hardy had no immediate use for it, was that his father would hit his mother regularly. Hardy had, of course, already seen Phil slap Tom — finding confirmation that he'd also struck Nancy wasn't exactly a revelation, except that it did verify what Lightner had said about the culture of battery getting passed down from generation to generation.

Hardy was still looking for "other dudes" that Freeman might be able to use, people who had an opportunity, also a motive, to have killed Larry Witt, trying them out on Glitsky, and Tom was next up — after the "hit man" that had killed Simpson Crane in Los Angeles, then the anonymous disgruntled anti-abortion activist.

"So what about Tom?" Hardy was pushing.

Even he didn't give Tom more than about two points out of ten.

Glitsky roused himself. "Okay, let me get this out of the way and then can we talk about something else? First," as he ticked his fingers, "he *didn't* ask Jennifer and Larry for a loan, right? Right. So where's your motive? The guy's got no record and there's no immediate catalyst — everybody agrees these people haven't set eyes on each other in a year or so. You expect me to believe he wakes up one morning and says, 'Hey, I think I'll go kill my brother-in-law.' Second, no prints anywhere — in the house, on the gun. You'll kill your case introducing any of this."

Hardy squinted into the sun. "The problem is, this leaves my client."

Glitsky was matter-of-fact. "Which could, of course, be why she got herself indicted."

The previous Monday Hardy and his brother-in-law Moses had gone salmon fishing off the Marin Coast. They'd caught two each. That night, at Moses' apartment, they'd roasted one for dinner. A second — the sixteen-pounder they were going to have that night — they'd put in some of Moses' nearly patented home-made teriyaki sauce to marinate. The other two they filleted, rubbed with rock salt, sugar and cognac, packed with some peppercorns and brown sugar, wrapped in foil and weighted down with bricks in Hardy's refrigerator. They intended to eat gravlax until they didn't want to anymore or died, whichever came first.

Frannie was leaning against the kitchen counter,

drinking club soda in a wine glass. Pico Morales, the curator of the Steinhart Aquarium and one of Hardy's long-time friends, stood with his arm around his wife Angela eating hors d'oeuvres. The as yet unmarried couple, Moses and his girlfriend Susan Weiss, were nuzzling each other by the back doorway.

Hardy came in with Abe and introductions went around. He crossed the room and kissed his wife, who turned her face just far enough away from him to deliver the message.

She was still unhappy.

Hardy knew why, and even, to some extent, understood it. This week had featured himself in an abrupt career-path detour and it would be a while before the kinks got resolved. So he didn't really blame Frannie — on the other hand, he was fairly exhausted himself from last night's lack of sleep, then a full day of Jennifer Witt. And to top it off, they'd planned this party to eat the salmon before they had to freeze it — Pico and Angela, Moses and Susan, Glitsky and his wife, Flo.

So he pretended not to notice Frannie's slight, lifted the foil covering from the glass container on the counter and made a face. "Not salmon again." He sighed. "I guess I'll just have a hot dog."

Hardy loved salmon beyond reason — he took a knife and cut himself a thin slice. "All of you youngsters watching this at home, don't try this yourself." He put the raw slice into his mouth, chewing contentedly. "You know, one of the first labor laws ever enacted prevented employers in Scotland from feeding salmon to their workers seven days a week."

Susan Weiss couldn't believe that. "Is that true? That was a real law?"

"Laws are this man's life," Frannie said.

Perhaps she meant it playfully, and none of the other women seemed to take it wrong, but Glitsky gave Hardy a look that was interrupted by the doorbell — it would be Flo.

Hardy went with Abe to answer it.

Moses was regaling everyone — for Susan's benefit — about the time Hardy had saved his life in Vietnam. Embarrassed, Hardy was trying to put a face on it.

"Come on — this guy is shot in the legs and I'm fifteen feet away."

"And things hopping pretty good all around us, am I right?" Moses was exploding mortars and tracer rounds all around him in the air.

"What am I supposed to do, let you lie there? So I pop up, grab him, drag his sorry ass back in the hole. Whole thing took ten seconds."

"He left out getting hit himself."

"Believe me, that wasn't planned. And P.S. — twenty years later, the shoulder's still a pain."

Moses grinned. "My legs, though, are fine."

When the telephone rang, Hardy was going to let the answering machine get it, but he recognized David Freeman's voice and got up, excusing himself.

"Sorry to interrupt your dinner," Freeman began, "but this is not good news."

Hardy waited.

"There was a woman named Rhea Thompson brought in the same day Jennifer got arrested." Freeman's voice was hoarse, guttural. He cleared his throat. "Her bail was five grand and she made it today and walked out of here with her pimp."

"Okay."

"Okay yourself. Rhea's about five-four, one-twenty-five, blond hair, blue eyes. Sound familiar? The answer's yes."

Hardy waited. "So what happened?"

"So somehow Jennifer's picture got on Rhea's housing card."

The housing, the Field Arrest card, was the bailiff's ID of choice on the seventh floor. You looked at the picture, you eyeballed the person, they either matched or they didn't. Both Rhea and Jennifer had only been two days in jail — they weren't yet known on sight to many of the guards. Especially the swing-shift guards.

"What are you saying, David?"

"I'm saying our client only paid us through Monday because she wasn't planning on sticking around after that. Our little darling has flown the coop."

"Jennifer escaped? From the seventh floor? You've got to be kidding."

Freeman sighed. "Would that I were, my son. Would that I were."

PART TWO

Larry granted her forty-five minutes for the run, which was a reasonable length of time. He was a reasonable man, she tried to tell herself. He just didn't want her getting hurt — if she fell while she was running and there wasn't any time limit, she could be lying somewhere, suffering, at the mercy of strangers, and Larry wouldn't know. He'd have no reason to suspect that something could be wrong. This way, if she was late, he'd know — he could be there to help her.

He loved her. Yes, that was the reason for all the limits.

Taking Matt to his private school, Laguna Honda, twelve blocks away, was a half-hour, and that allowed for traffic on some days, though not any talking to the other mothers. That way, and it made sense, she couldn't get into trouble saying too much the way some women did. The Witts were who they were in the community because no one had anything bad on them and Larry wasn't going to let anything threaten that — he was protecting all of them that way. Not just her.

For shopping, just so long as she called him before she left and then again as soon as she got back . . . before she'd even unpacked the bags . . . he could be flexible. And she was good at shopping. She could get down to the big Petrini's on Ocean Avenue — they carried everything — and load up a cart and get back home in under an hour.

Sometimes she cheated. But that was because she was, at her very heart, a bad person. A rebellious person. Larry knew she would cheat, and he gave her rules so that she wouldn't have time and wouldn't be tempted. But she still got around the rules, even though she knew they were good for her. That was just who she was.

Larry loved her in spite of that, in spite of knowing who she really was. She didn't blame him, really, if once in a while he lashed out at her. If it were her she'd probably have killed someone like herself long ago. Sometimes she wanted to kill herself but that wouldn't be fair to Matt, or to Larry either.

It was like the time she tried to get away, to take Matt with her. What was that if it wasn't just a cry for help? And Larry heard her — she'd never even told Ken Lightner about that. Who else would have cared enough to come after her, to take the days off from his practice, to follow her all the way to Los Angeles? She didn't blame Larry when he said that if she tried that again he'd kill her. She couldn't leave him. He needed her, he loved her. He didn't mean that he'd actually kill her. In fact, after they'd come home that time he didn't even hit her for a couple of months. Ned had almost killed her when she'd done the same thing with him. But Larry seemed so happy to have her back.

And he was right about her family, too. They proved on that first visit or two that they didn't like Larry, or her either anymore. They were just jealous. Larry said he felt bad about that but it was one of those things you really couldn't do anything about. You didn't change people, she should know that. And she knew she wasn't going to change her mother and father. And especially not Tom. Nothing was going to change Tom — he was just plain nasty and mean.

Well, there wasn't any reason to put up with that. She and Larry hadn't asked for that, not from any of them. They'd given her family every chance in the world, and they just stayed who they were. They thought Larry hated them and had poisoned her toward them. But that wasn't true. Maybe she'd seen things a little more clearly after Larry had helped her with the connections, helped her hear the between-the-lines insults about her "airs" or their "culture." No, they were, sad to say, just jealous people like they'd always been, and there wasn't any reason to see them and get everyone upset.

The things with the banking and with Ken . . . Dr. Lightner . . . she was just scared. She'd always been scared. Life was scary. People changed or the life you were in suddenly went sour and sometimes you couldn't see it coming or do anything about it, but she wanted to understand it a little more so she'd gone — okay, sneaked off — to Ken. And he knew more about her than Larry — knew about Ned, in fact — and he still cared about her. She believed that, that Ken really cared. She wasn't just a patient with him. Of course, now . . .

Well, she didn't have to think too much about that. That was just another thing.

And the bank. It wasn't that Larry wouldn't give her the money if she'd asked. But it was hard getting surprises for him if she had to tell him what she was spending the money on. Well, at least that was how it had started. The account. It was easy asking the checker at Petrini's to just ring up an extra twenty dollars in cash, then fifty, then two hundred. Shopping was her job and Larry didn't check the receipts.

She opened accounts as Mrs. Ned Hollis, using her dead husband's social security number and was careful to see that all the taxes were paid. That had been a close one the first year. And then after that she got the post office box and the form got sent there, and it hadn't ever been a problem.

Besides, you never did know. What if Larry somehow lost all his money? Or really got sued for malpractice like he was always talking about? Then she could imagine his surprise and happiness when she told him she had all this extra money that had saved them. She'd been doing it to save them all, the family.

She thought about it sometimes, why she'd gone away that time. Besides the call for help, she'd wanted to protect her face and Larry had started to hit her face.

For a while Ken had made her see it differently — she thought that might have been it. For a while he'd had her believing that Larry hadn't been good for her, that she was her own power and all she had to do was, as he put it, assert it, walk away from Larry and take Matt with her. California law, he said, would give her custody.

But Ken didn't know — how could he know? She just felt . . . worthless without Larry. And the beatings . . . it wasn't Larry, it was her. Couldn't she bring the beatings on? By behaving badly? Oh, the beatings hurt, but they also were what made her feel she was in control of something. Larry gave her that, didn't he? Well, didn't he?

It was like the time she was planning the party for Matt's fifth birthday. Larry was even letting them have kids come over from Matt's class, which he normally didn't like because — it wasn't their fault but kids just had no respect for property. Larry said the way to avoid things getting ruined was you didn't let kids get the opportunity. If something got ruined because of a kid, it was the parents' fault — you could bet on that. Like supposing you let a bull loose in a china shop — well, who's going to blame the bull? Is it the bull's fault? Of course not, Larry said.

Anyway, back to the party. Telling Ken about it when he asked if she was worried Larry would ruin the party by getting mad when the kids were there. She had said, "Look, this isn't an out-of-control situation, Ken. You're always talking about control. Well, I'm in control here." And she'd been right because she knew that Larry had been getting the really tense way he got before he exploded. So three days before — it was a Wednesday and the party was Saturday — she had dinner late, and Matt wasn't ready for bed when Larry got home so he had to help with that after a long tiring day with patients. And then she'd worn this cheap K-mart robe that she knew he hated. And when he complained she said something back at him, so she'd brought it on and he hit her pretty bad a few times.

But then — the good part — he was all fine for the party, and there wasn't any scene, and she'd controlled . . . another Ken word . . . when it would all happen. So to say that as long as she stayed with Larry she didn't have any power — well, Ken just didn't see it, or maybe couldn't understand it.

But okay, the hitting was getting worse. More fre-

quent. That was a problem. It wasn't as easy to cover — she'd have the bruises on her face now, instead of just her stomach and her legs like before. Lately, more and more, it had been on the face, and that really did bother her. Her face was who she was.

When she'd been a girl she stared at her face in the mirror for hours, getting the expressions right, the way she looked when she said certain things. Now they were all second nature — the sort of pout and the frown and the quick smile.

So Larry hitting her face — that had to stop. It really had to. Last time it had gotten to that, that was when she'd gone away, run away, if she were being honest, and Larry had come and gotten her. He'd do that again, no doubt about it. He'd even said he'd kill her if she tried.

Like, he said, if she were with another man —same thing, he'd kill her.

Would he really? Maybe he would. He was strong, he did get out of control. An accident could happen. A bad accident. So she had to do something — talk to him, maybe, right afterward. That's when he listened the best. She'd just tell him he had to stop hitting her face.

Ken was right about this one — here she wasn't in control. She even hated Larry now, sometimes. Really hated him and knew it, admitted it to herself. That part was scary.

Or if it ever spilled over onto Matt. If Matt was there while Larry got crazy. She wouldn't let Larry hit Matt, even if he just got in the way, between them or something. If he did that, if that happened . . .

Whatever happened to her, come right down to it,

she deserved it. Why else would it happen? But Matt was different. He didn't bring things on. He was a trusting and honest little boy. She wouldn't ever let Larry hurt him.

Except how could she stop him? That was the question — if it ever started, how could she stop him?

14

On Saturday, July 10, Hardy was bouncing six-month-old Vincent on his knee, singing to him at near the top of his lungs. He was forty feet above the ground, perched on the three-foot parapet that surrounded the roof of Moses McGuire's apartment house.

Moses was taking it easy lately. When he finally gave up on the idea that Hardy was going to get tired of the law and come back to bartending at the Shamrock he hired a new guy, Alan Blanchard, to take over Hardy's old shifts, and this gave him lots of time to pursue his other interests, which for several months now could be summarized by two words: Susan Weiss.

It was early afternoon, the sun shone in a blue sky, there was a slight warm breeze from the east, and Susan was sitting next to Hardy on the parapet. She was an intense dark-haired cellist with the San Francisco Symphony. She wore her hair pulled back in a ponytail and looked about Frannie's age, although she was eight years older. She wore a tank top, shorts and sandals.

Moses was with his sister at the Weber turning ribs. Hardy passed his boy to Susan, who started cooing into his face. Frannie took it all in. Her glance finally came to rest on Susan. "Don't let her hold too many babies. That's how it starts."

Moses tugged at his bottle of Sam Adams. "How she looks is how it starts," he said, "then the other things happen."

"Well, the other things can produce babies. I have it on good authority."

Uncharacteristically, Moses took a moment to answer. "I tell you, Fran, she makes me think about it."

This didn't make Frannie unhappy — she liked Susan and had to admit she was lovely, although Moses was in his mid-forties. But she had to know. "Are you serious?"

Moses trotted out his usual bartender answer: "No, I'm Alpha Centauri — Sirius is the Dog Star."

Frannie basted his arm with some barbecue sauce, then looked gravely at her big brother. "This isn't an engagement party, is it?"

"It's not even a party." Moses was licking the sauce off. "It's just a lunch."

Hardy and Susan stood. Susan was holding Vincent to her, rocking him as she walked. Frannie heard her humming tonelessly. "I warned you," she said quietly to Moses.

"Of what?" Hardy had his arm around his wife.

"You weren't supposed to hear that. I wasn't even talking to you."

Hardy kissed her ear. "Well, which was it?"

Moses butted in. "She thinks Susan's going to want a baby of her own just because she's holding one."

Susan nodded. "She may be right." She held

Vincent away from her, making a face at him that he rewarded with a beaming grin. "Oh God, is he a doll or what? I could see getting used to the idea of having someone like this little guy." She put her shoulder against Moses, leaning into him. "Isn't he cute?"

Baleful, McGuire put his arm around her. He appeared to be studying the baby. He shook his head. "No, he looks like Hardy. Now Rebecca, my niece, she's cute. She resembles my sister, who in turn looks like me."

During this witty exchange, Hardy stood up to take the opportunity to kiss his wife, but Moses stopped them. "Uh, uh. No tongues."

"What do you mean, no tongues? Daddy and Mommy have tongues." It was Rebecca, over to join the party. She looked up at the adults, worried about where their tongues had gone.

"Uncle Moses is being silly," Hardy said. "Bad. Bad. Bad Uncle Moses."

McGuire squatted down. "In most societies, Beck, the uncle is revered above all other relatives. The psychic damage your father is trying to do to you by this display is incalculable should you take any of his nonsense to heart." He smiled sweetly at her, gave her a kiss.

"I still think this guy's cute," Susan said. "Do you mind if I hold him a little longer?"

Frannie gave her brother a knowing look, said it was okay with her, as long as she wanted.

There was a little beeping sound.

"What's that?" Moses asked. "Don't tell me an actual relative of mine has a beeper?"

Hardy already had it out. "Another family secret

bites the dust. Besides, stop calling me a relative. Frannie's your relative." He was squinting at the number.

"Just let it go," Frannie said. "Call them Monday. We're having a party."

"This isn't a party," Moses repeated. "It's a lunch."

"It's Glitsky. It's Saturday. It's got to be important."

"Dismas, just let it go . . ."

"Take me a minute." He was moving to the door on the roof. "I just have to see what it's about."

"Good-bye," Frannie said.

"I'll be right back. Promise."

Hardy got there first, as he had the time before. Unlike the time before, though, Freeman was on his way over. It was still light out, hot and now strangely still on the women's side of the jail. Saturday, late afternoon.

He was struggling to hold his temper. They had frisked him at the door. Normally, to get in the jail, he showed his bar card and the guard, whom he'd seen many times, would buzz him in. This afternoon, though, to see Jennifer, he'd gotten patted down and now they were making him wait in the hot and airless room.

Two female guards walked with her this time, and she wore a red, not a yellow jumpsuit. She also had leg chains and handcuffs attached to a metal band around her waist. Her hair had been cut, hacked off unevenly so that an inch or two remained all around.

Her face was blotched, her lips cracked, both eyes with purplish bruises.

Hardy — jeans and a T-shirt — stood up, and she nearly fell against him, reaching up until her hands were stopped by the chains. She was sobbing.

"What the *hell* . . . !" Hardy began.

One of the guards peeled her off him and got her seated in the chair. "Cut the act, sweetie."

"You get your hands off my client." The guard glared. The second one had her nightstick out. "Both of you can back off. Now!"

These women weren't going to be intimidated by a lawyer in blue jeans. But it also availed them nothing to harass Jennifer in his presence, so — grudgingly, gradually — they withdrew.

When the door had closed, Hardy leaned forward. "They didn't do this, did they?"

She shook her head no.

"Then who . . ."

"Down there," she mumbled, her head down. This wasn't the cowed look she'd shown earlier, Hardy thought, but real fear. Something had obviously happened to her.

Glitsky's call had filled him in on some of it — Terrell flying down to Costa Rica and handling the details of her extradition. They were coming in to SFO. Hardy and Freeman might want to be at the jail pretty soon after that.

"What happened?"

Slowly she raised her head. Unlike many of the inmates here, her eyes were not empty. They were full of pain. Again, she shook her head from side to side, tears streaming over her cheeks. "Everything," she said. "They did everything."

He got back to their dark house in the Avenues at 11:45 P.M. He stopped in the kitchen and opened the refrigerator. The tropical fish tank gurgled from his bedroom. He sat at the kitchen table, sipping his beer.

"It was an engagement party." Still dressed in her sundress, hair tousled from sleep, Frannie leaned against the doorpost. "It wasn't just a lunch. Of course, you missed it, so it doesn't matter."

"Frannie, don't —"

"No, of course not. Don't bother Dismas. His work is more important than any old family stuff."

"I didn't say that. I don't think that."

"Sure you don't."

He drank some more beer. "You want to sit down and talk about it? Or you just want to bitch at me?"

"I think just bitch at you."

He steadied the beer on the table, looked across at her. Life wasn't as simple as Frannie sometimes wanted to think. She tended to lose sight that there were some things going on in the world beyond two little kids and Moses' love life. "You're losing perspective," he told her.

"*I'm* losing perspective. That's good. That's really good."

"Thank you," he said. "But you know, this isn't really a good time for me. I don't feel like getting bitched at. I'm out trying to make a living so you can stay here and have the life of Reilly and I'm sorry as hell that sometimes I've got to do things that aren't on anybody's schedule.

Things happen. *Shit* happens, Frannie, and I'm supposed to deal with it."

"Oh, poor thing."

He stared at her. This had just escalated into a stupid fight. Retreat. He picked up his beer, took a slow sip, then stood and walked back down the long hallway to the living room.

She didn't follow him. Fine. He grabbed one of the throw pillows and tucked it under his head on the couch, where he would spend the night.

15

On July 11, the luckiest day of the year, Hardy woke up in the living room with a sore back. He looked at his watch and saw that it wasn't yet six. The house was quiet, the light subdued.

He opened the front door and picked up the Sunday paper. Then, walking in his socks to the kitchen, he took out the black cast-iron pan he'd had since college, put it over one of the burners and laid in a pound of bacon.

He moved economically, the kinks in his back easing as he crossed the kitchen, quietly opening cupboards, getting the coffee going, mixing up some waffle batter (the Beck loved waffles). The bacon started sizzling, the smell coming up.

He sat at the kitchen table with a cup of coffee.

For the last four months, while Jennifer was an escapee, he'd been working out of the office in David Freeman's building and, truth be told, he wasn't having the best time of his life. He'd gotten several hand-off cases from David or his associates. Perhaps half a dozen he'd gone down and pleaded out. The other two — a disputed DUI and a shoplifting were, in the snail's pace way of these things, moving toward a trial sometime during the century.

Worse, though, was the feeling that he was simply spinning his wheels, going through the motions. It was similar to being with the DA's office, where you dealt with petty malfeasances and moved them along through the bureaucracy — except here he was often, from his point of view, on the wrong side.

The other problem, and it loomed large, was that he had gotten himself qualified by the court for the list of approved lawyers available for appointment, and a month ago Leo Chomorro, who had been the presiding judge in his ex-father-in-law Andy Fowler's case, had tabbed Hardy as one of three defense attorneys for a Penal Code Section 187 — murder.

Where things went south was that Hardy studied the file and decided he'd be good and damned if he was going to spend six months trying to convince a jury that Leon Richman had not in fact sat in his Ford Escort with the other two defendants and fired approximately ten shotgun loads each into Damon Lapierre, who just happened to be cohabiting with Leon's ex-girlfriend.

Aside from the fact that Leon had already been convicted of manslaughter once and been acquitted of murder once, two sawed-offs and one regulation shotgun had been found in the trunk of the Escort. Shell casings were under the seat. Leon had bragged to lots of his friends that they wouldn't be seeing Damon anymore. And four patrons of the Woodshack saw Leon and the other two defendants leave the drinking hole with the less-than-cooperative victim on the night of the murder.

In short, Leon did it, and Hardy wasn't going

to help get him off. Period.

This hadn't sat well with Chomorro. Did Hardy want to be on the appointment list or didn't he? If he didn't, why was he wasting everybody's time?

Hardy had almost said that he had no interest in defending guilty people but stopped himself before saying it. Those words would have given him immediate status in the Hall as a legendary horse's ass. Instead he'd mumbled something to Chomorro about a conflict of schedules and the moment had passed. But Hardy knew it would come again, and he knew he'd feel the same way, do the same thing. It wasn't a comforting thing to think.

Rebecca, appearing silently at his elbow, interrupted his thoughts. "Hi, Daddy. Why are you up so early?"

He put his arm around his adopted girl — the natural child of Frannie and her first husband Eddie Cochran. Eddie had been killed on the day Frannie had found out she was carrying Rebecca.

Hardy pulled her closer to him. He couldn't imagine that a blood tie would make any difference. Rebecca was his daughter. He lifted her onto his lap and she snuggled into him for six seconds before she started squirming, which was close to a world's record. "Why are *you* up so early?" he asked.

This was a serious question, carefully pondered. "Daddy, you know I always get up early."

"And that's why you did today?"

The Beck nodded. "Mommy's still sleeping," she whispered. This, apparently, was confidential information.

"Let's let her, okay. We'll have a little special time, just you and me together. How about some waffles?"

"Maple syrup?"

Hardy tugged gently at her hair, kissed the top of her head. "Okay, maple syrup head, maple syrup."

Frannie and Hardy sat on a crumb-strewn blanket in the shade of the overhanging addition to their house that they had built when they'd discovered Vincent was on the way. The lawn was deep and narrow, flanked by four-story apartments, but to the east, over their redwood fence, on this clear day they had a view all the way to downtown — the Transamerica Pyramid, Coit Tower, the Bay Bridge, the East Bay hills. It was a fine backyard for the six times a year it was warm enough to use.

Rebecca, preoccupied, was building something in her turtle sandbox. Vincent slept in the porta-crib they had brought down for the occasion.

They had kept from acknowledging the fight all morning, then through the lunch with the kids. Now, in the long slow slide of the warm afternoon, it lay heavily between them. Hardy stared across the distance. Frannie picked at the crumbs.

Finally she reached over and put her hand on his leg. "I just didn't think it was fair to Moses."

Hardy covered his wife's hand, relief flooding through him. "I love you, you know."

"I know."

"I didn't know about Moses and Susan. As he kept saying, it was just a lunch."

Frannie was silent. Then: "He wanted to surprise us. I think it kind of hurt him."

"I'll call him, tell him it worked. I'm pretty surprised. They're really getting married?"

Frannie nodded. "September."

"And having kids, all that?"

"That's what they said." She moved over against him. "I was just upset."

Hardy let out a long breath. "What do you want me to do in that situation? Of course I care about your family, but sometimes —"

"No, don't start that again, please. That's what you said last night. Every time the job calls, you don't have to drop everything and run."

"I haven't been doing that. At least not for the last four months. Not really since Andy Fowler."

"But now here's another murder trial and it starts again."

Hardy took a beat. He wasn't going to let this escalate again. Fights with Frannie made him physically sick. "Murder trials *are* serious, Frannie. Murder trials are not like too many other things. This is not just a job. This is, after all, somebody's life, and you get to know them and then they call and need your help, what do you want me to do? What do you think I should do?"

With her free hand Frannie picked at some more crumbs, brushed the blanket. "Do you really think I've got the life of Reilly here, raising the kids, not working?"

"Is that an answer to 'What do you think I should do?' "

She was still looking down, smoothing the blanket. "No. I think that's an entirely different question."

"Okay, I'll do yours first. I'll give you the short answer. The short answer is no."

He felt her shoulders give. "The long answer is we think the kids should have a parent at home as long as we can afford it, and we can, so you're it as long as you want to be."

"I *do* want to be."

He squeezed her hand. "No problem. If you get tired of it, we'll do something different, okay? Maybe I'll stay home."

Frannie gave him a look.

"Hey, it could happen. The point is, sometimes I've got to do things when I've got to do them, not when it's convenient. Yesterday was one of those times. You think I'd rather go down to jail on a Saturday afternoon than hang out and eat ribs with you and the Mose?"

"No."

"Correct, I wouldn't."

"But you're going to stick with this one, aren't you? Jennifer Witt? Even though she ran away, escaped. Even if she did it?"

"She's facing the death penalty, Fran. I don't blame her for running away, although I don't think it was very smart. Juries do make mistakes, if they make one here it's pretty terminal. She might be mixed up — hell, she *is* mixed up, but she's a real person, not just a case."

"Maybe that's what I'm worried about, Dismas — that she's a real mixed-up person who might have killed two men she's involved with. Plus her baby. Maybe I'm even worried about her finding some reason to kill you."

He put his arm around his wife. "Clients don't kill their lawyers, Fran."

This was not a brilliant riposte. Just a week before, a madman who'd been dissatisfied with his lawyers had walked into the offices of one of the City's big firms in the middle of the afternoon and started blowing people away.

Frannie gave him the eye. "For a minute I thought I heard you say that clients don't kill their lawyers."

"Not often enough to worry about."

In the sandbox, out in the sun, Rebecca had started destroying the castle she'd built, kicking, zooming in like a kamikaze. One of the apartments in the building on the right had opened a window and turned up the stereo — Bonnie Raitt was telling the neighborhood that she'd found love right in the nick of time.

Hardy told Frannie he felt the same way.

16

Why would you take a plea now?"

Freeman brought in Hardy with the questioning look. After Jennifer's jailbreak they had both expected the DA to take an even harder line on Jennifer, and now Dean Powell had contacted Freeman and hinted at a willingness to take a plea to Murder One — no death penalty.

Powell spread his arms, expansive and at ease. "Hell, you know, David, we're *always* ready to talk." He pointed a finger, underscoring the point. "You guys remember that — my door's open."

"My client says she didn't do it." Freeman was flipping through a Sports Illustrated, barely paying attention. Powell's office was the usual fifteen-foot-square cubicle — two metal desks, file cabinets, a window welded shut with a charming view of the new jail going up thirty feet away.

Powell's officemate, Paul Bargen, had stepped out for coffee so there would be privacy, to say nothing of room, for three people. "If she offers to plead guilty to life without, of course I'll have to take it to the boss, but I think it's fair to say we'd take such an offer seriously. I heard," Powell went on, "that your client recovered from her amnesia down there in Costa Rica and now wants to throw herself on the mercy of the court."

"I don't think that's it." Hardy had originally taken the second chair in front of Bargen's desk, but one of the legs was shorter than the others and it listed uncomfortably, so now he was standing. "I just don't think that's it."

Powell shrugged. "I'd ask her again, just to be sure."

Freeman had stopped at an ad for a woman's swimsuit — he lifted the page toward Hardy, spoke to Powell. "I thought you wanted a trial. By the way, I'm voting for you."

Substantiating the rumors, Powell had recently declared his candidacy for State Attorney General, and he now broke out his toothy grin. For a moment Hardy thought he was going to jump up and try to shake both of their hands. "Well, that just delights the hell out of me, David. I can't tell you." He glanced over at Hardy, who kept his arms folded, his face impassive, leaning against one of the file cabinets.

Freeman flipped another page, seemed to be studying an editorial that had Barry Bonds in the headline. He didn't look up. "And you don't want a capital trial? Seems to me it would be pretty good copy."

"That's always true, David, but frankly I don't think I need it. To be perfectly honest, I'd rather use the time to campaign."

Hardy couldn't help noticing that Powell said "frankly" and "to be perfectly honest" in two consecutive sentences. Powell was lying about something — he obviously didn't think the verdict for Jennifer was all that foreordained.

But Freeman wasn't showing any cards for free. He scratched a stubbly cheek, turned a page of the magazine, sighed. "It's up to my client." Finally, Freeman put down his reading and made eye contact. "What the hell did they do to her, anyway, Dean? She claims she was raped in jail down there."

"I truly hope she wasn't, David, but she shouldn't have broken out of here. That was her choice, her risk . . ."

"I'd think you might, out of a little human sympathy for what she's been through — maybe, without a plea, at least drop the death penalty."

Powell showed no surprise. Strategically, this wasn't a bad move for Freeman — his client had been abused, perhaps raped. Freeman knew he had seen her, and Jennifer Witt was, at this moment, an object of some pity. But all this got processed in the time it took Powell to blink twice. "I have no sympathy for what she's been through," he said. "She's brought it all on herself."

"She asked for it, huh, getting raped?"

If Powell said anything like that, under any circumstances, he could forget his election chances. "That's not what I said, David, and you know it."

Freeman, of course, did know it. Hardy, not for the first time, was glad he was in the same corner as Freeman. The threat that he might repeat Powell's words in some public forum — that Jennifer had asked for getting raped — might break the deadlock. Hardy half-expected Powell to cave, drop the death penalty request, and offer a plea for Murder One, maybe even with the possibility of parole. If Jennifer took that, there would be no penalty phase and Hardy would be out of a job. He waited.

But Powell didn't get to where he was — the Senior Homicide Assistant District Attorney — by wimping out. He smiled in the face of this veiled threat. "My heart just doesn't go out to multiple murderers, and anything that happened to her outside of this jail, or this country, well" — he spread his hands — "that's completely out of our control."

"I'll be investigating what happened in Costa Rica."

"I would, too. I'd expect you to. Let me know if I can help you. That kind of conduct is unconscionable."

Back to posturing and politics. Hardy picked the Sports Illustrated from Freeman's lap, opened it at random. Whatever else was going to be said here, he didn't need to hear it.

The Yerba Buena Medical Group owned a square block of buildings that housed their professional offices half a mile from San Francisco County General Hospital.

Hardy got there a little after eleven. It shocked him — there was actually a free parking lot provided for guests, doctors and patients. Downtown, in North Beach, in Golden Gate Park, throughout San Francisco, lot parking was running four dollars an hour with a two-hour minimum. Street parking could not be found — people had been shot over twelve feet of curb space.

Following the signs through a landscaped maze of shrubbery and vine, Hardy stopped at a redwood kiosk inside of which was a glass-covered granite pedestal, the directory of offices including a you-are-here arrow. More than forty doctors practiced here. Larry Witt's name was gone, probably long gone. It had been over six months since he had been killed — Hardy reflected that the wheels of justice had not yet turned one degree, which was about normal for half a year. And it didn't look like things were going to speed up.

Jennifer's flight hadn't predisposed anyone in the Hall to do her any favors. She was in lockdown, with visiting and phone privileges drastically reduced. She said even her food was worse, if that were possible. It wasn't necessarily on the books, but in practice Freeman and Hardy were finding out that breaking jail constituted a pretty solid waiver of a lot of your rights. Freeman had been told that "due to bureaucratic complexities" over the extradition, Jennifer couldn't even get a preliminary trial-setting date for another week.

The good weather was continuing, and the air conditioning in the business office felt good. Hardy found himself impressed with this whole operation. His vision of the world of HMO health care — especially here in the city — was bleak. Anonymous doctors and nurses dispensing care to people they didn't know in perhaps antiseptic but non-personal surroundings.

YBMG's reception office had light green tinted windows all around. The couches were covered with soft cushions and cheerful fabric —swirls of yellows and oranges and reds and blues. A Berber rug — not the ubiquitous yellowing tile Hardy always expected — kept it quiet as Hardy walked to the desk. He had no appointment so he would have to wait, but Mr. Singh would try to be with him shortly.

More Sports Illustrated, the same issue Powell had had in his office. Forget July 11 — today, July 12, was his lucky day. He considered buying himself an extra lottery ticket.

Ali Singh had answered Hardy's first questions competently enough, but had his tiny hands crossed on his empty desk, as though this would prevent him from tapping his fingers or twirling a pencil or otherwise betraying his nerves. Dressed in a white button-down shirt, thin brown tie, new electric sportscoat, he was nodding, acquiescent. "Of course, you see, the police have already been here. They have asked these things."

Hardy leaned forward. "I've reviewed everything they've subpoenaed, Mr. Singh — his office files, the interviews. I was wondering more about the personal things, how he got along with the other doctors, nurses, that kind of thing."

"Well, that is . . . I don't know. I didn't really know Dr. Witt personally, as you say. You see, we have a lot of doctors here. They don't work together too often. It's not like a Kaiser operation, as you can see."

"So you didn't know him at all?"

"Well, of course, you see, we talked about administrative things, his help and so on. But he had his work. I have my work." Singh raised his eyebrows, unclasped his hands for a split second, put them back together.

"But no problem?"

Singh smiled. "There are at times problems with everyone. Doctors have egos, you know. They want things one way, their way, and I have to try to standardize, so of course sometimes there is conflict. But nothing so serious."

"With Dr. Witt?"

"I liked Dr. Witt. Occasionally we would spar over cost issues, how we did things."

"And how would you do things? How would it affect him more than anyone else?"

"It didn't. That was always my point. But the Group . . ." he gestured around, taking in the whole complex, "the Group had plans, has *plans*. You see, we have nice buildings here, pleasant, wouldn't you say?"

Hardy nodded.

"And this is not by accident, you see. It is the Group's, the Board's, philosophy."

"To have a nice environment?"

"Just so, you see? But this, of course — the landscaping, the furnishings, even the rent here — this takes money from the fund, and —"

"And Dr. Witt thought that *that* money should go to the doctors?"

Now Singh beamed at Hardy's understanding. "Ah, you do see. Just so, it is just so." Unclasping his hands, Singh finally sat back in his chair. "Dr. Witt liked to feel he had a say in these things, in many matters." He waved a hand. "This is not a criticism, he was not alone in this. He had a need to know, to feel that he was somehow in charge with his business, of where the Group was going."

This certainly comported closely with Jennifer's

analysis, with Lightner's opinion, with the FedEx man's report. Larry Witt had been a control freak. "So where was the Group going?"

"Is," Singh amended. "The Group is converting to a for-profit organization. We have been not-for-profit long enough. The Board feels to compete in this health market we need to attract capital. To do that we must be . . . attractive, and sad to say, part of that is the physical setting. You would think the quality of the care is the thing, but that is not business." Singh sighed. "It's reality, and the members — the doctors — were asked to take a short-term loss, no raises, that kind of thing, you see."

Hardy saw. Times were tight everywhere, but especially in health care and especially in California. The move, on the face of it, made sense in the long term, but he also understood why there might be resistance in the short term — no raises, less money, bite the bullet, wait wait wait. From all he'd heard, waiting and deferring weren't Larry Witt's strong suits.

"Did Dr. Witt fight with anyone about this? Get mad, lose his temper?"

"Dr. Witt? Oh good God, no. He never lost his temper. You can ask anyone here — he was always courteous, always reasonable, even if he wasn't backing down. Nothing here was to get mad about — minor differences among professionals. Dr. Witt had no enemies here. He was liked, looked up to."

"But somebody killed him. Could he have been having an affair with a nurse, with one of the doctors' wives . . . ?"

Singh was shaking his head, an amused look on his face. Thoroughly at ease now, he leaned forward. "It was no one here, believe me, Mr. Hardy. I think it must be his wife, you see?"

"This," Freeman said, "is called a cover-your-ass affidavit. And this," he lifted his other hand, "is a check for two hundred thousand dollars."

Hardy was in his office, feet up on his desk, thinking about where he was going to mount his dart board. He had been here in Freeman's building for nearly five months and during that time, what with feeling he should put in some regular hours and his growing family responsibilities, he realized his dart game had gone to hell.

He had pegged a round of darts into the drywall and Freeman's mouth hung slightly when he saw them there.

"I'll patch the holes and cover it with my board." Then, switching topics, "If I were her, I think I would have spent more in Costa Rica."

Freeman crossed to Hardy's open window, a view of buildings across the way and, four flights down, the after-lunch show on Sutter Street. "I think she was in a hurry when she left," he said.

"That could have been it."

"Also, she told me the bank wouldn't give her more than ten grand. In cash. On no notice. So she took that and ran, figured she'd wire for the rest or something, which was a bad idea."

"That how they found her?" Hardy asked.

Freeman nodded. "Looks like. But the good news is she's with us all the way, no more wait-'til-Monday-and-I'll-decide-then bullshit."

Hardy sat up, feet to the floor, rolled his shoulders. "I don't know. I feel pretty bad for her, David."

Freeman turned from the window and fixed Hardy with a look. He seemed short on sympathy for Jennifer Witt. "Why don't you go interview her again, like I did for two hours this morning?"

Hardy leaned back in his chair, hands crossed behind his head. "Tell me."

"She won't plead. She won't admit her husband was beating her. She won't talk about her escape, who helped her out — maybe get a little slack on that, at least something to deal with. But no, not our girl. She just didn't do it. The end."

Hardy pointed. "So what's the affidavit?"

"This?" Freeman went to Hardy's couch and sat down. "This is Jennifer's signed statement that I have advised her that her best defense is BWS . . ."

"Battered . . . ?"

"Yeah, yeah, battered-woman syndrome, and that she —"

"But you don't believe . . ."

"Yeah, I do. Now. She's gonna go down for the murders so I'm thinking about how to get into mitigation as early as I can. I tried to drive that home and what do I get?"

"Not much?"

Freeman shook his head. He'd never understand lay people. "Exactly. Squat. She didn't do it, she's not pleading." He reached inside his wrinkled jacket and pulled out a cigar, jamming it into his mouth. "I tried to tell her it doesn't matter if she did it. I can get her off on BWS." He shook his head again, stood and walked back to the window.

"Maybe it matters to her?"

"Well, of course." Freeman was patting his pockets, found a pack of matches, stepped back from the window and lit up, putting the cigar into the flare.

"You know," Hardy said, "you ought to wave the cigar gently back and forth an inch above the top of the flame. And don't inhale while you're lighting up."

Freeman glared at him through the thick blue smoke. "But I'll be goddamned if I'm going to let her get an appeal on my misrepresentation. If I know she's been beaten and I don't bring it up, it's reversible and I'm not letting her or anyone else pull that on me. Hence, my son, this affidavit."

"Do you know she'd been abused?"

"Does she admit it? No. But it doesn't matter. It's a defense. It can get her off, damn it. Or at least give her the best chance of getting off."

"It's also admitting she did it."

17

Mrs. Nancy DiStephano could not see Hardy while she was working but he could meet her afterward if he wanted, if he thought it might help Jennifer.

Since he was passing by with time to kill anyway, Hardy had dropped in at the office of curator Pico Morales in the basement of the Steinhart Aquarium and told him he was getting fat, he ought to get out more, take a walk, exercise. Pico contended he wasn't getting fat — he was actually in good shape except for his hyper-extended stomach. Nevertheless, he got up.

They were strolling along the paths in Golden Gate Park's Japanese Tea Garden, across the concert grounds from the aquarium, less than two hundred yards (as the crow flew) from the Little Shamrock. There was serenity here when it wasn't crowded, and it wasn't now. Huge koi swam lazily in the artificial streams, the water trickling and gurgling over moss-covered rocks and small waterfalls. The still-warm sunlight came dappled through the cypresses.

Pico had been listening to Hardy talking about the ATM and didn't think it was very clear. "So Larry Witt was alive at 9:30, right? You know that? What time were the shots?"

"Let's say between 9:35 and 9:40."

"And who told you about this difference between 911 times and the bank times?"

"Nobody. I went down with Abe and —"

"So this DA — what's his name? — you're telling me he doesn't know? What about the cops?" Pico walked on a few steps before he noticed that Hardy had stopped. He turned back to him. "What?"

"I am really stupid."

Pico nodded. "Now we're getting somewhere."

Hardy ran it down out loud to hear how it sounded. "No, listen. You're right, forget 911 time, Jennifer's at the bank at 9:43, right? Larry's definitely alive at 9:30. Take away two or three minutes for Larry to walk back upstairs, call it 9:35 or even later when he gets shot. Jennifer is at the ATM at 9:43, *not* 9:46 — eight, not eleven minutes later."

Pico was shaking his head. "See? All this worrying about the truth. If the DA doesn't know about the three minutes . . ."

"I'm not sure the DA even knows about the stop at the ATM."

Pico spread his hands. "Well, there you go. You win."

"No *way* could she have made it 1.7 miles in a maximum of eight minutes, even if it's all downhill."

"I believe you," Pico said. "Being faster than a speeding bullet myself, I could have done it, but your average bipedal human . . ."

Nancy DiStephano stood him up.

He was meeting her at five-fifteen outside the real estate office where she worked as a secretary. The office was on Kirkham near 19th Avenue and it was closed up when Hardy arrived. He double-checked the address, the time, the cross-streets. No Nancy.

After fifteen minutes he called it a day, debated with himself whether he should go by the Shamrock and apologize in person to Moses, decided not, got in his car and headed home.

"I want to meet her."

"Who?"

"You know who. I would just like to meet her." Frannie's red hair hung long and shiny, shimmering in the evening sun. They were walking along Clement Street — Hardy with Vincent on his back in a pack, Rebecca running ahead, stopping at driveways, alleys and corners the way she had been taught. Frannie caught Hardy with a sideways look. "You said she was a person, not a case, remember? It would just make me more comfortable. Rebecca!"

"Out of the street!"

Rebecca had dropped a toe over the curb. She pulled it back, turned around smiling. "Just teasing."

"That is nothing to tease about," Hardy said. "The street is dangerous. We hold hands crossing the street."

Rebecca knew this. She gave her mother a conspiratorial glance and slipped her tiny hand inside

Hardy's. "I don't think it's a good idea," he said.
"What?"
"Mommy and Daddy are talking, honey."
"We can talk about it later, Dismas."
"No. Now's fine. We ought to be able to have a small discussion without being interrupted, don't you think? And I don't think it's a good idea. I don't even know if you'd be allowed to. Or if Jennifer would want to see you."
"Who's Jennifer?"
Hardy let go of the Beck's hand. "You can run ahead now."
"But who's Jennifer? Do I know her?"
"Jennifer's one of Daddy's clients, sweetie."
"Doesn't she like you?"
"She doesn't know me. I want to meet her."
"Hey." Hardy, the referee, making hand signals. "Time out, all right? This is our discussion. Beck, enough, I mean it."
"You don't have to yell at her."
Hardy was trying to keep his voice under control. "I'm not yelling at her. I'm trying to teach her not to interrupt. This is a useful social skill." Vincent, suddenly startled, let out an anguished cry.
"Great," Hardy said. "This is just great."
Rebecca, arms outreached, mouth open, broke down. She clung to Frannie's legs, wailing.

"Here's an idea. Let's give them to Moses and Susan for two weeks." Hardy drank gin about twice a year and figured this was the night for it. Bombay Sapphire on the rocks with two olives.
They had gotten the children down to bed. It

was still light outside, not yet eight o'clock, and still warm. They were sitting together on the front steps, waiting for the pizza to arrive, holding hands, the door open behind them so they could hear if anyone called. Or — more likely — cried.

"I don't think two weeks is enough." Frannie was having a glass of white wine. The children's crying jag had lasted nearly an hour. "If they really want to get the flavor."

"Moses lives close." Hardy was running with it. "We could visit them all the time." He sipped at the cold gin, so smooth it almost wasn't there.

"Speaking of visits . . ."

Hardy shook his head. Jennifer again. "I don't know, Fran. I don't see what good it would do, what the point of it is."

"It would just set my mind at ease. That's doing some good."

"You don't really think she'd try to get at me, do you? I mean, we went through the same thing with Andy Fowler."

"I *knew* Andy, Dismas, or at least who he was. A judge, your ex-father-in-law. Plus you got him off. This woman . . ." she shivered, brought her glass to her lips — "all I know about her is what I've read, which is she's a money-hungry, cold-blooded, drop-dead beautiful —"

"She's not *that* pretty — she's nowhere near as pretty as you."

Frannie leaned into him, mocking the flattery. "Well, then, she's the most photogenic not pretty woman on earth. But what she isn't, to me, is a real person, somebody I shouldn't be afraid of, worried about."

"What if she won't see you?"

"Then she won't see me."

She was right. If Jennifer wouldn't agree to see Frannie that would be the end of it. The gin that almost wasn't there was telling Hardy's body that oh yes, it was, too — the evening had taken on a soft edge, a benign glow. He told her he'd ask, see what he could do. It was a small enough request. If it made Frannie feel better . . .

How could it hurt?

When he had tried to contact Nancy DiStephano earlier in the day asking her to call him back for an appointment, Hardy had not known what his schedule would be like so he had given her his home phone number as well as the one in his office.

She called at a little after nine, her voice a whisper, hoarse, nearly inaudible. "Mr. Hardy?" She told him where she was, would he please come and see her now? There might not be another chance. When he told Frannie he was going, she did not do cartwheels.

Ulloa Street was dark.

Hardy had had his one martini, switched to cranberry juice, and the earlier glow had dissipated with the warmth. The DiStephanos' house was in the 4500 block, two blocks from the cold Pacific. He pulled up in front of the number.

She was wrapped in a jacket, wearing jeans but barefoot, sitting in the dim porch light on her stoop. When Hardy got out of his car, she walked unsteadily down the cement walk that bisected the lawn, meeting him halfway. She touched Hardy's sleeve, then immediately pulled her hand away as if it were burned. "He won't hear us here. Not that he would anyway. Thank God he's passed out."

She was shaking. Hardy wondered if she were drunk. "Who's passed out?"

"Phil, of course." She laughed, low, nervously. "Who do you think? Listen, I'm sorry about tonight, our appointment." She wasn't slurring. "I thought we might . . . but Phil . . ."

Hardy waved it off. His eyes were adjusting — a sliver of moon gave a little light. There was a lot of Jennifer in her face — haunted but still attractive. It was unnerving.

She stepped in place, foot to foot, seemingly unaware of it. "But I thought it might somehow help my girl."

"It might. I don't know. Are you all right?"

She leaned again in an unnatural way, gripping her side. "Maybe we should sit down?"

Without waiting for him, she went back to the entryway. It wasn't a full porch — more a jutting, covered portico enclosed by a low stucco wall. She leaned up against one of the posts.

"Mrs. DiStephano?"

She held out her hand for him to be still, breathing her way through whatever pain she was enduring. When she could handle it, she tried to straighten herself and half-turned back to him. Her eyes were wet but seemed way beyond tears.

Summoning something — the effort was palpable — she pulled herself straight, then turned all the way to face him head-on. Raising her head, she inhaled deeply, making her decision, and pulled open the jacket she'd been wrapped in. Under it, she was naked.

Her body — her breasts, her ribs, her stomach — was bruised and welted in half a dozen places. He stood transfixed, two feet away from her, feeling his body begin to pulse in anger. Fist-sized blotches, splashes of broken capillaries, the rake of handprints over torn skin. He stepped toward her, grabbed the sides of the jacket and gently pulled it closed around her. Lightner had been right about Jennifer's abusive father . . .

She leaned back against the portico's post and let herself slump to the tiles, hugging her arms to herself.

"I told Phil, I told him it was for Jennifer, it might help Jennifer. I wasn't sneaking out. He said how come you didn't try to talk to *him*."

Hardy held his head in his hands. This was twisted beyond his imagining. "Jennifer suggested I talk to you. If she would have said him, I would have agreed."

"I know that. I told him that, or tried to."

"I didn't mean to put you in this."

She touched his arm again. "No, no, it's not you. This is just what happens."

Hardy raised his eyes. "You should get out of this. You've got to report this."

Nancy DiStephano shook her head. She was still hugging herself, still moving her body to ease the shifting pains. Her look said Hardy didn't know what he was talking about. "Where would I go?

What would I do?"

"Go anywhere," he said. "Do anything. But don't live with this."

She kept shaking her head. "But Phil would never let me. Never. He wouldn't even let me see you."

"You could move away."

"I've tried that, but you know, I always come back. It's a tough world out there, Mr. Hardy. Here at least I know somebody cares about me —"

"Someone who cares about you wouldn't do this to you."

"It's not so very often. I understand, he's mostly afraid he'll lose me. I tell him no but he's so jealous . . . I wouldn't have called you, maybe shouldn't have, but if it could help Jennifer . . ."

"Did Phil ever do this to her?"

"Jennifer? No. He wouldn't ever lay a hand on her. I think if he did I would have left him and he knew it. He couldn't stand me to leave him. No, all this" — she gestured downward — "this is all between me and him. It has nothing to do with Jennifer."

Hardy stared at the ground, at the sliver of moon — this woman defending the man who had just beaten her. "He's so jealous . . ."

He tried to clear his head. "So what now, Nancy?"

She shrugged. "I didn't even mean for you to know about this. It's nothing."

"Okay, it's nothing."

"You wanted to talk about Jennifer, if this

hadn't happened . . . I suppose I shouldn't have told Phil and just snuck out to see you. It's really my fault."

The reprise, the repetition, the denial. "It's really your fault. That's it, huh?" Was it the same for Jennifer?

Nancy nodded, apparently grateful that he seemed to understand. "So we can forget this and just talk about what you wanted before. Can't we just do that?"

Hardy tried. He sucked a lungful of the now-chilled night and tried to organize himself enough to talk to her about Tom. He couldn't.

18

As he sometimes did, Abe Glitsky arrived unannounced at the front door. When Frannie opened it for him, he stepped back and whistled. "My, my, my." Frannie was wearing a blue skirt and a plain white blouse, low pumps, nylons. She had touched her cheekbones with subtle highlights they scarcely needed. Her eyes were malachite set into the alabaster of her skin. The red hair, softly styled, fell to just below her shoulders. "Whatever it is," he said, "you'll do."

Frannie curtsied, smiling. "You don't think it's too much?"

"You panning for gold? Playing soccer? Mud-wrestling?"

Frannie looked serious. "No, I'm meeting somebody."

"I think for meeting somebody you're on safe ground."

They were walking to the kitchen. It was a smallish railroad-style Victorian house — one long hallway with openings to the living and dining rooms off it to the right, a bathroom to the left. In the back the house opened up into a pod of rooms — airy skylit kitchen, Hardy and Frannie's bedroom with another bath, Rebecca's room

(Hardy's old office) off that to one side, Vincent's nursery to the rear.

Hardy was coming out of the bedroom, a mug of steaming coffee in his hand. He was wearing the slacks to one of his better suits, a white shirt, a silk Italian tie.

Glitsky stopped in the kitchen doorway. "I must have the wrong house. Where are the kids?"

"We're taking a day off," Frannie said. "Their grandmother came and got them. I'll be back in a minute. You want some tea?" Frannie disappeared into the back room.

Glitsky was getting the hot water. "Who are you meeting?"

Hardy was still shaken by Nancy DiStephano. He'd told Frannie about it when he'd gotten home, then sat up alone in the living room, not able to sleep for a long time.

And now here was Abe, dropping in, wanting to know who Frannie was meeting. Abe wouldn't approve of Frannie going to get acquainted with Jennifer Witt. If you were smart and in any aspect of law enforcement, you didn't mix your job and your family life. The problem was that Hardy didn't feel like getting into a defense of why he was going along with Frannie's idea when he knew it wasn't a smart one. "I thought I'd drop Frannie off downtown and later we'd go someplace nice for lunch. What brings you around?"

It slid right by — Glitsky wasn't in his investigator mode, when very little got past him. "I've got to go see this couple about a gun they left laying around for their kid to find and play with." He tightened his lips, the scar shone white. He didn't need to say more — Abe was in homicide and homicide meant that somebody wasn't alive anymore. "It's out this way so I thought I'd stop by here and liven up your morning. You back with Jennifer Witt?"

Frannie and the three of them talked for twenty minutes while Glitsky finished his tea, Hardy and Frannie another cup of coffee. Hardy never mentioned the three-minute difference in times between the ATM machine and 911. By this time, he was convinced that it was evidence in a murder investigation, and if he revealed that it could be part of the defense's case Abe the policeman would be bound to report it to the prosecution.

"But who are you?" Jennifer, in her red jumpsuit, looked through the Plexiglas window in the public-visiting area at the women's jail.

Frannie was no longer sure about this. The woman across from her was certainly no threat to anyone at this moment. Nearly anorectic, with bruises on her face, her hair chopped at different lengths, her eyes skittish. Here was a woman, Frannie thought, who doesn't trust a living soul.

"I'm . . ." Frannie, her mouth dry, tried to swallow. "I'm with Mr. Hardy."

"I know. You've already said that. That's why I came out here. But then how come we're not in the visiting room?"

Frannie didn't know — she thought they were in the visitors' room. She didn't know that this long counter with folding chairs, Plexiglas windows, the telephones to talk through, wasn't where Hardy and Jennifer had their interviews. "I'm . . .

I guess it's just I'm not an attorney, so this isn't official or anything." Suddenly she understood why Hardy hadn't come with her to introduce the two of them. What could he have said? "Hi, my wife just wanted to come down and check you out to make herself feel better. She was a little worried you'd get out of jail someday and try to kill me."

She felt like a fool and she felt angry.

Dismas had humored her to teach her a lesson — a cruel one that he might have argued her out of.

But then she realized that she wouldn't have let him do that. She could be as strong and bull-headed as anyone. She had decided she was going to meet with Jennifer and, by God, she wasn't going to back down — that had been her position and now she was stuck with it.

Jennifer waited, her eyes now fixed on Frannie. Pained eyes. Frannie suddenly thought of the son Matt. What if this woman hadn't killed anybody? She had lost her son? And then got raped and beat up in a Costa Rican jail?

"I know this is unusual," she said. "I'm Mr. Hardy's wife. Frannie. He's told me what's happened to you and I just wondered if I could do anything to make things easier?"

The city-run Mission Hills Clinic was about midway between the Hall of Justice and the Yerba Buena Medical Group cluster on Mission Street but not particularly close to any hills.

Hardy stood across the busy thoroughfare and watched for nearly ten minutes. Judging from the signs people carried, there were, he decided, two separate picket lines — one protesting the abortions that took place here, the other comprised of public-health workers who were being laid off due to cutbacks in the City budget. The groups orbited in their own spheres, which warily circled each other, moving from one front door of the building to the next one and then back again. The dance almost appeared choreographed.

In the months Jennifer had been at large, Hardy had remained subliminally aware of the ongoing escalation of the anti-abortion activists. Since he'd had his discussion with Glitsky, a City worker in the Sunset Clinic had died when she'd had the bad fortune to be working after hours. Probably the people who'd left the bomb hadn't intended anyone to be there when it exploded, just trying to make a point, they'd say. The unlucky worker wasn't any less dead for the good intentions.

A doctor and a nurse had had their homes vandalized — windows broken, threats tied to rocks or tagged — graffiti'd — on stucco. There had been at least six reports of muggings of public-health workers after they had finished their shifts, although no one was saying whether these were typical late-night random acts of violence or related to the clinics.

Larry Witt had done volunteer work here, performing — Jennifer guessed — between two and five abortions per week. It was something Jennifer said he believed in — people shouldn't have unwanted babies, the biggest problem the earth faced was overcrowding, a child born to poverty and neglect would most likely stay there.

It was tragic and Hardy believed all of it, but the moral dilemma of when life started and — beyond that — the value of human life itself, wasn't going to go away soon for an Irish *ex*-Catholic. He strongly believed that people ought to be able to choose, but he also didn't particularly approve of abortion on demand as a form of birth control. At the very least, he thought, people ought to make a decent effort to remember what they forgot last night. But people should also make a decent effort to remember not to shoot each other, and that didn't seem to be happening with any great frequency, either.

He crossed the street, feeling overdressed in his suit. There wasn't another coat and tie on the block. The people in the picket lines — male and female — wore jeans and T-shirts, 49er and Giants jackets, running shoes, boots and Birkenstocks. Timing his approach, he crossed both lines and entered the building without incident.

Inside, the clinic was along the lines of what he'd expected and not seen at YBMG — yellowing tile, glaring fluorescence, that old hospital smell.

In the main office lobby he waited in a line for twenty-five minutes and got sent to talk to the secretary to the clinic administrator. When she returned from her break and discovered that Hardy wanted to talk about abortion records, she told him he could have called and found out that they released no records whatsoever, and no information on what might be within them. As Hardy surely could understand, these files were completely confidential.

Frustrated, and with another hour until he was

supposed to pick up Frannie, he paused outside in the cavernous main lobby, then followed the signs down a long echoing hallway to OB-GYN.

There were eight young women in the room. All seemed to be under twenty-years-old, a couple closer to fifteen. Two sat next to — maybe — their boyfriends, holding hands. One, crying, was flanked by her parents. Five sat alone, empty chairs between them — popping gum, flipping through magazines, listening to Walkman. Bored and unconcerned? Scared and withdrawn? It was hard to tell which.

The receptionist at the window was a cheerful and cooperative young black man with a neatly trimmed beard and Afro. He wore a white smock with a Gay Pride tag that said "Sam." Hardy handed him a card, introducing himself, asking if Sam might direct him to someone who could tell him a little about Dr. Witt.

"You can ask me. I remember him pretty well. Too bad what happened."

Hardy agreed, saying that's what he was trying to get clear on.

"I thought his wife did it."

"That's what they're saying."

"You think she didn't?"

"She says she didn't, so I'm just turning over rocks — maybe find a snake."

"Here? At the clinic?"

"Seems like there's a lot of angry people out there on the sidewalk."

Sam waved that off. "The pro-lifers? No, forget them. Those people *live* there on the street."

"People have been killed, Sam, beat up leaving

work at these clinics."

Sam kept up a confident smile. "What about grocery checkers or bus drivers? They get beat up, too. Welcome to life in the big city."

Hardy tried another tack. "All right, maybe it was personal. Someone on the staff? I don't know. Maybe Dr. Witt had a run-in with somebody?"

"No way, no way. This isn't a social club here. These volunteer docs come in and put in their time and leave. And Witt more than most. Nobody's billing anybody here — no reason to hang out." He gestured at the waiting area behind Hardy, lowering his voice. "This is not fun city west."

Hardy recognized the gospel when he heard it. He pointed at his card lying on the window ledge between them. "If you do think of something personal — anything at all — would you mind giving me a call?"

Hardy watched his wife walk from the back of the restaurant, noticed the heads at the bar turning. One of the problems he had had when he was starting to fall in love with her had been her looks — they were too good. He knew it was easy to get fooled by a pretty face. It had happened to him before.

And even though he had known Frannie since she was a young girl — Moses' kid sister — once he started connecting with her, letting himself really *see* her, he made himself put on the brakes. Not for too long, but enough to persuade himself that at least most of what he loved about her wasn't on the outside. He had to admit, though, that even after three years, a lot of it still was.

The waiter was there, holding her chair out for her. The little amenities.

"What are you smiling at?"

"I'm shallow. I have no depth. I wonder if our relationship is purely physical."

Frannie daintily popped a bite of calamari into her mouth. They were by the window at Mooses', looking out through the sunshine onto Washington Square. "Well, some of it, anyway."

They hadn't discussed it, but they had both felt they needed to go someplace nice — light, upscale, carefree — to wash away the tastes of their mornings.

She reached across the table and touched a finger to Hardy's cheek, trailing it along his jawline. Picking up her glass, she swirled the Chardonnay, staring into it. "Wine two days in a row. You think Vincent will be all right?" Their son was living on breastmilk and a few squashed bananas.

Hardy told her he didn't think Vincent would notice. It wasn't as if she was out pounding herself into the ground with alcohol.

"I know. Sometimes I just worry." She put the glass down, scratched at the tablecloth. But she wasn't really worried about Vincent — it was something else and Hardy was fairly certain he knew what it was.

"Pretty bad?"

She nodded. "You look around here, and you see all these people being so happy, and then back there, in the jail . . . it kind of makes you wonder what's the real world."

Hardy covered her hand with his own.

"I mean, how isolated are we?" she asked.

The waiter lifted the empty plate from the middle of the table. He removed some non-existent crumbs from the starched linen tablecloth with a small rolling hand-brush. Someone began playing classical music — expertly — at the piano by the bar.

19

By Friday Hardy felt that he'd covered a lot of territory and uncovered very little. Freeman had been his usual unenthusiastic self about the ATM, although he did admit — grudgingly — that it might be helpful at some point.

Freeman's attitude made Hardy decide that there was a real disadvantage in believing your client was guilty. He was trying to keep his own mind open. He had verified Lightner's opinion — about the battery passing through generations —with several other published and unpublished authorities. Their explanations were all consistent — Jennifer had seen her mother beaten at home. Her mother took it and took it, possibly without complaint to the children. So that behavior became Jennifer's expectation of married life — if it wasn't there, things just wouldn't feel right. Intimacy couldn't begin.

So, Hardy thought, Larry had been beating Jennifer. Without a doubt, so had her first husband Ned. According to Lightner's theory she would have had a difficult time marrying either of them if they hadn't gotten at least a little tough with her during courtship — they wouldn't have felt like husband material.

Whether or not it could be proved in a court of law, Terrell's scenario of Jennifer injecting Ned with atropine was plausible. And — Hardy had to believe — if she killed Ned, it was a possibility that she killed Larry, too.

Next was, if Jennifer *did* kill both men, at least she had a good reason, though Hardy had a hard time with *any* kind of premeditated murder. Jennifer, on her part, still hadn't budged an inch on her denial of abuse, which continued to infuriate David Freeman, signed affidavit or no.

Freeman was afraid he would lose and that the decision would be upheld on appeal. But he was hamstrung — he couldn't bring up BWS at all. If he did he was all but admitting that Jennifer did it and even process of saying why, in spite of all her denials.

Hardy had finally located brother Tom at a construction site near the Panhandle of Golden Gate Park. Struck out during the day, Hardy returned to the site after work hours wearing dirty jeans and carrying two six-packs of Mickey's Big Mouth and got him to talk for twenty minutes.

Hardy verified what the mother, Nancy, had said — Jennifer and Larry did not visit the family since a few months after the wedding. Tom had been seventeen at the time. Hardy could see that it had hurt the boy back then, although now the man covered it with bluster.

The last time Tom himself had seen the Witts had been Christmas Eve. No one had mentioned that before and Hardy asked why not.

Tom had shrugged it off. Why would anybody care? He'd gone by his parents' home during the afternoon, had a few beers, and his mother had started moaning about Jennifer and the grandchild she never saw. She'd bought Matt this great present and he wasn't even going to come over to see it.

Tom had gotten pissed off. He drove his motorcycle over to Olympia, intending — he said — to kick a little ass, but by the time he got there, he figured there wouldn't be any point. He wasn't going to change them. He'd dropped off his own Christmas present — a whiffle ball and bat — with his nephew, said Merry Christmas to his sister, told her she really ought to go by their parents so Matt could get his present from his grandmother, then left.

And, he added — no surprise, they didn't come.

But here, Hardy thought, might have been the catalyst Glitsky had been talking about. Out of the blue, Tom might not wake up one morning and say, "I think I'll go kill my brother-in-law," but he sure as hell might do it three days after being snubbed during the holidays, touching off years of resentment.

Walter Terrell sat in with them while they went through the physical evidence, and stood over them in the evidence lockup while Hardy and Freeman checked off the computer list with the items that came out of the bags.

There was Larry's blood-stained shirt. All the other clothes. The stuff that had been in pockets — Larry had a comb, a small Swiss Army knife, keys, some coins including a quarter painted with red nail polish.

"Larry hung out in bars?" This didn't fit Hardy's profile so far.

Terrell shook his head. "No sign of it."

"That's a bar quarter." Freeman and Terrell both looked at him blankly. "For the juke box," he explained. "You paint your quarters red, you feed the box, you don't get charged when they come collect."

Freeman was unimpressed. "So he went out for a drink on Christmas Eve. Maybe. I've had quarters like that turn up in my pocket. Means nothing."

But pickings had been so slim that Hardy wanted to keep grabbing. "Two days before he gets killed, *anything* he did means something."

Freeman didn't respond. He had already moved the pile of coins to the side, going on to what looked like a bag full of trash. "What's this stuff?" Forensics had picked the room clean and bagged whatever might have interest — in this case the contents of the bedroom wastebasket — used Kleenexes, used Christmas ribbon and wrapping paper, the kind of plastic bag they wrapped shirts in at the dry-cleaners. "This is evidence?"

Terrell pushed another bag toward Freeman, answered wearily. "You know the drill, sir. It's here if you want to use it. It's your decision what's important."

Freeman pulled the bag nearer and slid the gun out onto the table. He picked it up, checked its serial number against the prosecution's proposed exhibit list, smelled the barrel. He checked the fingerprint report and his eyebrows went up. "They didn't find her prints on the gun?"

"The clip." This wasn't any surprise to Terrell. He pulled another bag and pushed it to them. "She wiped the gun."

"*Somebody* wiped the gun." Freeman gave him the bad eye.

And Terrell shrugged. "If you say so." It was getting late on a Friday afternoon, and the room in the basement of the Hall of Justice didn't have the best ventilation.

Freeman tipped up the bag, expecting the clip to fall out. Instead they were all looking at another gun. "What the hell is this? Where's this on the list!?"

Terrell read from the list. "Bag 37. Dumpster contents. Want to see the egg cartons we found with it?"

"Yeah, but what the hell is it?" Freeman repeated. "Why is it here?"

Terrell was holding up his hands. "It was there. Now it's here. How should I know?"

"But it's a gun."

Terrell reached over and picked it up. He put on his official voice. "Sir! Please, calm down."

"I'm calm enough!" Freeman sat back in his chair. "All right, son, I'm calm."

Terrell explained. "It's a toy gun. It's a good toy gun, but it's plastic. See? That's all. As far as I know it's got nothing to do with the evidence in this case."

"Then why is it here?" Hardy could play the straight man if it came to it. The questions were obvious enough.

"It's here because they found it in the same dumpster as the other gun, the murder weapon.

I thought at the time it might be worth holding onto."

"The same dumpster?"

Terrell nodded. "They both clunked out onto the street. Guy who found 'em, when he saw the real gun, gave us a call."

"The garbage man?" Hardy asked.

"Right."

"How does this connect?" Freeman was still sitting back, trying to get a take on it.

"It doesn't, that's what I'm trying to tell you. I just had a theory and thought I'd run with it. You never know."

Hardy knew this was Terrell's MO. "What was your theory?"

"I don't know. The perp comes in with this gun — looks real, doesn't it? — maybe he's doing a burglary, keeps it to threaten people. He gets to the bedroom, sees the real gun, gets surprised by Larry and the boy, panics, *boom boom.* This was before I fingered Jennifer."

"Did they print that gun, the toy?"

"Sure. Nothing, though. Anyway, I figured they *had* to be connected, right? But I was wrong. Besides, the guy tells me guns are the number-one toy you find in the garbage sector."

"Garbage sector . . . ?"

"His words. Parents don't want their kids to grow up violent, so some relative sends them a gun for Christmas or something, they toss it. Second is Barbie dolls. You believe that? Who'd throw away a Barbie doll, brand new?"

"Can we stick to the gun?" Freeman was leaning forward now, interested.

Terrell shrugged. "Hey, you want it, you can have it. Here, check it out."

He handed it to Freeman, who gave it the once over, then passed it to Hardy. "What do you think?"

"It's a toy gun in a dumpster."

Freeman mulled it a few more seconds. "Anything else in this dumpster you bagged that isn't connected to anything, Wally? You want to waste more of our time." Freeman was picking at the bags, lifting them, dropping them. "We got trash, we got toy guns . . ." He shook his head. "Christ. How 'bout we get to see the clip?"

Afterward, Hardy went up to homicide and finagled Glitsky into a stop at Lou the Greek's. Freeman had gone to wherever it was he went on Friday nights — Jennifer was calendared for Monday morning and Hardy thought he was probably up to some behind-the-scenes shenanigans with somebody.

Now Hardy was trying to convince Abe that Hawaii was where the Glitskys ought to go for vacation, Glitsky saying that Hardy must be out of touch with what policemen made nowadays if he thought Abe, Flo and their three children could spend fourteen days at a Kampgrounds of America site, much less soaking up rays on Maui. He concluded by saying he thought they'd probably go to Santa Cruz for the weekend, maybe the Russian River, spend the rest of vacation painting the apartment. "If we can afford the paint."

"Things a little tight?"

Glitsky chewed the ice from his tea. "Things

were a little tight before my voluntary five percent pay cut."

"You got that?"

"Everybody who makes over fifty grand. And now, after a mere nineteen years on the force, when I have finally graduated to that lofty height, they whack me for getting there."

Abe swirled his glass in its condensation on the table, stared at the window. "Just the other day I was saying to Flo — 'Hey, hon, why don't I volunteer to work two hours free every week next year?' She thought it was a great idea since we don't need any money to live anyway." He drank some tea. "You know what I did? I went in to Frank" — this was Frank Batiste, Glitsky's lieutenant — "and asked him for a $2,001 pay cut, save the city some money."

"And what'd Frank say?"

"He said he wouldn't — it wouldn't look cooperative. I tell him I'm making $52,000 — take away the five percent, I'm down to $49,400. My two grand and a buck idea puts me at $49,999. All things considered, I'd rather have the extra $500."

"I would have done it."

Glitsky shook his head. "No, you wouldn't. You know why? Because the difference is fifty bucks a month, which after taxes is maybe thirty-five — call it two burgers a week. And for that you get a rep for being difficult. After nineteen years! And guess what happens to difficult guys? Here's a hint, eighty-five didn't get to take their voluntary cut — they got pinked."

"Eighty-five?" The number was higher than

Hardy would have thought. How could the city lay off cops? This was almost five percent of the force. "Eighty-five?"

"Sure. What do we need cops for?"

"Or health workers." Hardy mentioned the picket lines at the Mission Hills Clinic.

"But guess what? The mayor's still got his driver. You wouldn't want the mayor driving his own car around, would you? What would people say? How would it look?"

Hardy drank some beer. "Well, at least he's got his priorities straight. If it were me, I'd definitely do the same thing — lay off the police and keep my driver."

"I'm going to look into setting up my own security business," Glitsky said. His eye caught something behind Hardy. "And here comes my first recruit."

Terrell slid in beside him, across from Hardy. "First recruit for what?"

"Glitsky Home Security. Armed response in minutes."

Terrell took a pull from one of the bottles of Bud he'd brought over. "We get to shoot people, no Miranda? Catch 'em and put 'em down?"

"Yep. And get paid for it."

Terrell was bobbing his head. "I like it. I'm in." He had another swig, focused on Hardy. "Your partner might be famous, but whew!"

"That's why he's famous — he's that way." He looked at Glitsky. "Freeman."

"What way?" Glitsky asked.

"What way?" Hardy repeated mildly to Terrell. "You can speak freely to Inspector Glitsky."

"I got an idea bagged that might or might not be evidence and the guy goes ballistic on me. I tell him he can use it or not. Hey, I had a theory that might have worked — so? It didn't, big deal."

Lou's was getting crowded, louder. Hardy elbowed his way to the bar and bought another round. When he returned, Terrell was in the middle of something that sounded familiar.

". . . the Crane thing was at least worth looking into, but it turned out to be nothing, too."

"What did?" Hardy slid in, passed the round — two more bottles for Terrell, another iced tea for Glitsky.

"I was just telling Glitsky about that other thing, the guy in LA you called from the Witt house."

"Crane. The guy who was murdered."

"Yeah, Crane. Just talking about how theories sometimes pay off, sometimes not."

"Most times not." No argument, just stating a fact, Abe was already chewing the ice in his fresh drink.

It drove Hardy crazy, but he preferred not to change the subject if Terrell had discovered a link with Simpson Crane and was going to talk about it. But he couldn't resist the urge to get in a dig. "Why'd you follow that up? You've already got yourself a suspect."

Terrell didn't take any offense. Instead, he smiled disarmingly. "Hey, I love my work. You called it — it was one of those coincidences. You check it out, what do you lose? You can't tie up a murder too tight, am I right or not?"

On this everyone was in accord. Hardy sipped his beer, taking his time, not wanting to betray any particular interest. "So what'd you find?"

"Pretty much what you told me. No connection to Witt."

"Well, there must have been some — the number was stuck on his desk."

"I mean, sure, yeah, that. But I'm talking the actual hit, they know who did it, or think they do."

"So who?"

"Some local muscle down in LA." Terrell was into his story, a bottle of beer in each hand, from which he drank alternately and steadily. "This guy Crane was the premier union buster of the nineties — cleared like a half a mil a year making sure all the little people kept getting fucked. They try to organize, he gets 'em fired, figures out a way to make it stick. Time to renegotiate, he's got everybody scared they're going to lose their jobs, so they cave. They say the President wanted him for Secretary of Labor but couldn't pay him enough."

"He work for San Francisco?" Glitsky asked, joking. "I think they must be using somebody like him."

Terrell shook his head. "Well, nobody's using *him,* that's for sure."

"What happened?"

"Well, he'd already killed a couple of unions — meat packers, janitors, like that — small-time stuff, and then he thought he'd take on the machinists."

"And somebody important didn't like it."

"That's the theory." Terrell held up his empty beer bottles. "Are these things twelve ounces?"

He started to get up. "Anyway, they did it right — hired some pro, no paper trail, no indictment. My round this time."

He was on his way to the bar.

"No more for me," Glitsky called after him. He was still chewing his ice. "You're a sly dog. He's following your leads and doesn't even know it."

Hardy kept a straight face. "You heard him — he loves his work." He brought his beer up. "It is interesting, though, don't you think? Two murders and two hit men?"

Glitsky was shaking his head. "I count three murders and one hit man — Larry Witt, their kid, this guy Crane."

"Actually, you want to get technical, there were four murders — Crane's wife."

This didn't slow Abe down very much. "You have anything connecting any hit man to Larry Witt?"

No answer.

Glitsky got out of his booth, slapped Hardy lightly on the cheek, told him to have a good weekend.

20

The Master Calendar for Superior Court was called on Monday mornings at 9:30. It was July 19 and Jennifer's name appeared first on the computer printout tacked up beside the double doors in the hallway outside Department 22.

Since her extradition from Costa Rica and subsequent return to San Francisco had been reported in the *Chronicle* and on television, the media was on hand when Freeman and Hardy entered the courtroom a little after nine.

Hardy knew that David Freeman had no love for most reporters but was careful not to let them see it — they could be helpful in a trial with political overtones. Candidate Dean Powell wasn't going to let a photo opportunity pass without getting whatever possible mileage out of it, so the two attorneys — one on either side of the courtroom — were now chatting amiably with reporters.

Powell was coming across as considerably more sincere than he had four months ago — perhaps he'd gotten some coaching. The hand gestures didn't seem as rehearsed. He moved a step closer to his own personal knot of reporters. "Look," he lowered his voice, speaking from the heart, "I'm in favor of the death penalty. And we've got special circumstances here that, if proven, warrant the death penalty — hell, that cry out for it. Show me a little remorse, an admission of guilt, even a cry for mercy, the District Attorney can be responsive to that. Defendants aren't numbers to me — they're people, living and breathing human beings. This trial isn't a part of my campaign to Get Tough, California." He leaned a leg casually over the corner of the table on the prosecution side of the courtroom. "This is a gamble by the defendant — she thought she could commit murder for money and get away with it. She was wrong. Terribly wrong. I am not bloodthirsty, but if she is found guilty, we're going to ask for the extreme penalty. That's justice, and she'll have brought it on herself."

Freeman had his own group. "This is, unfortunately, all too typical of the ways things get done. The very fact that all you folks are here shows how out of line it is already. Nobody's talking about the weight of evidence, which is light — *fatally* light. It never would have gotten this far except it's likely to keep some names in the newspaper more than they would be otherwise. I doubt it will even get to trial after I file my motion to dismiss."

"You don't think it'll get to trial?" This was from a woman with a microphone.

Freeman shook his head. "I doubt it."

Another hand, another microphone. "But the grand jury indicted her."

Freeman smiled. "The grand jury tends to indict whomever the District Attorney asks it to."

"But she escaped from jail, didn't she? She ran away."

"She's resourceful *and* she's innocent, and she doesn't trust a system that's already gotten it this wrong. I think in her place I would've broken out, too, if I could have figured out how to do it."

Powell was standing now, a hand in a pocket, smiling his smile. Freeman, serious and indignant at the system's injustice, was warming up for when the judge came in. Everybody had an agenda.

Hardy walked back up the middle aisle and out into the hallway. They still had twenty minutes.

Looking through some papers, his briefcase beside him, Ken Lightner was sitting on the wooden bench in the hall across from Department 22. Hardy sat next to him. "I want to apologize to you. It seems you were right."

Lightner put the papers down. "About what? Not that I wouldn't take just about anything right now."

"About Jennifer's mother, her father beating her."

The psychiatrist nodded, shuffling his papers. This, obviously, was old news to him.

"You're disappointed?"

"I thought you might have found something a little closer to home, something with Jennifer herself."

Hardy shook his head. "Jennifer isn't giving anything away. Especially after this escape fiasco. Freeman's pulling out his hair, what he's got left."

"I'm pulling out mine, too. She's made me stop

talking about it, which given where she is tends to limit our conversations. How are we not supposed to talk about it?"

"What, exactly?"

"The truth. Larry beating her. *Abusing* her. Her defense. What she's going through. To say nothing of all this madness over the last months. How is she supposed to deal with all that?" Lightner pushed his hair back with his fingers.

"You've seen her, then?"

"I've seen her. I try to visit her almost every day."

"That must cut some hell into your practice."

Hardy hadn't meant to be accusatory, but Lightner's back went right up. "I take care of my patients, Mr. Hardy. I care about them. I try to be there for them when they need me. As I assume you do with your clients."

Hardy took the rebuke. Lightner had a point. Sometimes you didn't punch the clock. "You want to accept a second apology in five minutes? That didn't come out the way it was supposed to."

Lightner shrugged it off. "It's all right. I'm under a good deal of stress myself. I don't mean to snap back at everybody but I don't know what to do about this, about Jennifer. Her irrational guilts, her self-destructiveness . . . it's making me question my own judgment, whether I can do her any good."

"What do you think would help her?"

"I don't know right now. I don't know. The problem is I can't get her to talk about, even acknowledge, her real problem."

"So what *have* you been talking about every day?"

Lightner's expression said he knew how it must sound under the circumstances. "We talk about her self-esteem, Mr. Hardy. How she's finally growing up, taking responsibility for herself. About her future."

"Her future?"

"I know, I know, we don't have to go into it." Lightner had put his papers down, was rubbing his hands together. He raised his eyes to Hardy. "But that's what she wants to talk about. How she's finally getting things straight. She says she knows she can probably get out of this altogether by blaming Larry but she's just not going to do it. It wasn't his fault."

"Beating on her wasn't his fault? What about her saying she didn't do it, and a defense of battered woman syndrome would be an admission?"

Lightner nodded. "Yes, I'm afraid so. Things like that are deeply ingrained." He stood up, taking his briefcase, asking where the men's room was, if he had time before Calendar came on.

He had disappeared around the corner before Hardy realized that he had left a couple of his papers on the bench. Glancing down at Jennifer Witt's name, highlighted in yellow, Hardy picked them up.

This first page was an initial patient's sign-in form from Lightner's practice, filled in four years before, giving an overview of medical history, previous physicians, allergies, surgical background and so on. Hardy thought a minute, folded the paper, and put it in his inside coat pocket.

Jennifer in her red jumpsuit, handcuffs and leg irons, was the first computer number, or "line," called.

Something was up. Judge Oscar Thomasino wasn't interested in the computer printout on his desk before him — his eyes followed Jennifer as she limped from the bailiff's entrance on the judge's left until she got to the podium in the center of the courtroom where she stood flanked by her two personal bailiffs.

Freeman was waiting for her, though there was a near-tangible air of friction between them. Jennifer glanced behind Freeman's back to where Hardy sat at the defense table. She nodded to him, her eyes grateful, or at least welcoming, though he couldn't say why that should be so — he hadn't seen her in a week.

He also wasn't exactly sure why he'd come today — this was the second arraignment for Jennifer and she certainly wasn't going to change her plea. Maybe, he'd told Frannie lightly, he missed being in a courtroom. Now he wondered if there hadn't been a germ of truth there.

This was supposed to be a more or less pro forma administrative procedure that would determine the date that Jennifer's trial would start or, more precisely, when it would relocate to its eventual Department. Once the presiding trial judge and the courtroom were assigned, which would be at another calendaring Monday like this one, the trial itself might not start for another six months to a year.

But Thomasino started things off with a curve

ball from the bench. Judges had different techniques to combat the routine. Hardy was beginning to understand that Thomasino liked to start the day with a little drama before wading into the sea of paperwork. "Mr. Freeman, is your client all right?" He was taking her in — pale, thin, hair hacked off unevenly.

Dean Powell, who had hardly been paying attention, stood up. "Your Honor, we will stipulate that Mrs. Witt may have been badly treated during her incarceration in Costa Rica. She —"

Thomasino used his gavel. Everyone in the courtroom jumped. "The court addressed its remarks to Mr. Freeman," he said mildly. "If I remember, he could speak for himself last time we did this." His face was stern, but there was something near-playful behind it. "Mr. Freeman?"

With the door open it was Freeman's nature to stick his foot in. "Your Honor, my client has been badly beaten. She needs medical attention. She is so intimidated by what she's gone through that she's afraid to say anything. Certainly her civil rights have been violated. The People have given up this case by their handling of the entire extradition process."

"Didn't this alleged beating take place in Costa Rica?"

"They were our proceedings. It would not have happened if we hadn't —"

Thomasino's spark of humor vanished. "It wouldn't have happened if your client had not broken out of our jail here and fled the country."

"Nevertheless, Your Honor —"

"Nevertheless, Mr. Freeman, I've got a full

docket and I think the air conditioner's starting to act up. You mind if we get on with it?" Evidently Freeman did mind — his retort was on the way when Thomasino leaned out of his chair. "Give it a rest, David." Freeman, confidently, patted Jennifer's arm. She had no reaction.

Thomasino was back at his printout writing himself a note. "I assume, given the . . . interruptions to this point, that everybody's ready to proceed. Is that the case, Mr. Powell?"

"It is, Your Honor."

"Mr. Freeman?"

Freeman had another problem here. Normally in a potential death-penalty case the defense would delay and delay and then try to delay some more. But he had discussed this with Jennifer and, as usual, she hadn't agreed with his decision or strategy.

Powell wanted the trial to begin quickly, and to conclude before the election in November. As a matter of principle, Freeman hated to agree to anything the prosecution wanted, but Jennifer had tied his hands. She was in jail and she wasn't getting out until she was found not guilty. Not unreasonably from her viewpoint, she wanted the trial to begin as soon as possible.

Freeman had told her it wasn't at all certain that she would be cleared. She was up for three counts of capital murder, and he knew that the DA would not frivolously charge anything that serious. He also knew that her case, as presented by the prosecution, would feature the kind of motive and presumed callousness that persuaded juries to convict — murder for insurance money.

He wanted Hardy to have time to find "some other dudes." He wanted time to think, to plot, to devise. He wanted time for *something* else to happen, for Powell to be elected and a new prosecutor, without Powell's agenda, to be appointed.

"Mr. Freeman?" Thomasino reported. "Are you ready to proceed?"

Freeman had no choice. "We are, Your Honor."

Thomasino looked surprised and he was. He had never seen a capital case actually ready to be set for trial at the first setting date. "All right then." And the trial was calendared for Monday, August 13, in Department 25.

"It's you I'm trusting on this, you know, not him."

Before leaving the building after the hearing, Hardy had decided to go on up and share a few impressions with Jennifer. He also had a list of questions written on a legal pad in his briefcase. Now they sat, knee to knee, in the tiny interview room by the guard's station. Jennifer was expressing her displeasure with David Freeman.

"He's a slob and he doesn't believe anything about me — not even that they raped me down there."

Hardy pulled his chair back. He wasn't sure how their knees had gotten so close and he didn't want to be misinterpreted. "That's the thing about the pros in this law business, Jennifer, and it's why David's so good. It's not personal. If you getting raped would help your case in any way, he'd jump on it with both feet. But, unfortunately, it doesn't. I mean, it happened because you escaped."

"If I get off I'm going to go back down there, find that guard and kill him. I swear to God."

Instinctively, Hardy looked up at the bare yellow walls, fairly secure in the knowledge that this room wasn't tapped. He hoped. Leaning forward, he unconsciously lowered his voice. "It would be a good idea to keep the death threats to a minimum for the next few months, okay?"

She smiled. "It's what you call a figure of speech."

"I know. But sometimes the sense-of-humor thing around here gets a little fuzzy."

"I'll watch it." Jennifer stared a minute through the glass to the empty guard station. "I like your wife."

Hardy nodded, somehow wishing this hadn't come up, knowing that it had to. Maybe, in fact, it was another reason why he'd felt he needed another visit, to reassure himself that the connection between Jennifer and Frannie was unimportant. "She said you had a nice talk."

Jennifer shrugged. "We did. It was. Just mostly girl stuff but I haven't talked to anybody like I was a normal person in so long . . ."

"I thought Dr. Lightner talked to you every day here."

He saw her processing his knowledge of that information. It wasn't clear what she made of it. "Well, sure . . . Ken."

"I mean, doesn't he talk to you like a normal person?"

Out of any context, she smiled. Hardy thought

he'd like to videotape an interview with her and analyze when these random smiles appeared, but he was almost afraid of what he'd find. "Ken doesn't count," she said. "Besides, I don't think anybody's normal for him. Normal doesn't have any meaning. It's one of those psychological buzzwords."

Hardy had already heard enough jargon to know what she was saying, but she had left open an avenue for questions. "What about down in Costa Rica? Didn't you meet anybody down there?"

Her eyes shifted to him, then away. "No. I didn't think it would be a good idea."

"So what did you do?"

Again the empty guard station seemed to grab her attention. She spoke into the window. "The first few days I just stayed in the hotel. Then I went to the beach, I read a few books."

Hardy could probe this by asking her which ones but it wasn't his intention to interrogate her. Like her rape, anything that had happened to her in Costa Rica wasn't going to have much effect on what she'd done or didn't do last December.

"Did I tell you I'd seen your mother?" he said.

"You'd said you were going to. How was she?"

"She wasn't good, Jennifer. Your father had beat her up." He didn't think she needed to hear any details. The vision of her mother's battered body was still coming back to him.

Jennifer looked down at the table, a thumbnail to her mouth.

"I understand this thing — this beating — it passes down through generations in families," he said.

Her eyes came up, pained. "We've been through all this." And, she was saying, we're not going into it again. She became brisk, businesslike, and bizarrely, almost cheerful. "Anything else? You said you had some questions."

Hardy took his pad from his briefcase. Last night he had reviewed the notes from his visit to Jennifer's house, his questions.

Yes, she had stayed in the house in the months between the murders and her arrest, except she hadn't been able to make herself go upstairs. She had gone into their bedroom once to get her clothes and some personal items, and the experience had been so upsetting she hadn't been able to make herself go back in.

"So how did you do the inventory for Terrell?"

"Well, that's why I messed it up," she said. "Nothing was gone from downstairs, they hadn't taken my jewelry. I didn't even think about the gun." She held up a hand. "I know. A big mistake."

She might at other times not be telling the truth, Hardy thought, but this, he decided, wasn't one of them.

"Might there have been another gun?" Hardy asked.

"What other gun? Where?"

"I don't know. Anywhere. Maybe Matt had a gun? A toy?"

She shook her head. "No. We wouldn't let him own one. It was something Larry and I agreed on. When he was an intern he said he saw too many accidents."

"So no gun?"

"No gun. Why do you ask that?"

"Trick question. The dog that barked in the nighttime."

This time she sighed. "This can make a girl tired, Mr. Hardy."

"Just one more, a straight one. Okay?"

She nodded.

"Crane & Crane?"

Her face skewed up. "I don't know. Chess and checkers? Is this a quiz or something?"

"It's a law firm. Have you ever heard of it?"

"Why?"

"You tell me first."

She shook her head again. "It's not familiar, no. Now why?"

Hardy was putting his notes away. "Larry might have called them about something."

Jennifer gave it another minute. The female guards came back to their station. They passed a bag of Fritos back and forth.

"I don't know what it could be," Jennifer said. "Just some more nothing."

21

Hardy was feeling better about his office — the dart board was in place, moved in and nailed up over the weekend. It was early afternoon and he was getting back into the groove, throwing some "20 Down," trying to hit all the numbers on the board in descending order, ending with a bull's-eye. In his glory days Hardy had often done it in under ten rounds — thirty darts — and his all-time record was twenty-four. Now he'd already thrown eight rounds and was hung up on "11," which was normally his easiest shot, his "in and out" number in a wide range of money games.

Freeman entered without knocking. Hardy missed again.

"This is not billable," Freeman said.

"I'm thinking," Hardy replied. "Thinking counts."

The older man closed the door, then walked over and sat on a corner of Hardy's desk. "I'm thinking, too. I'm thinking that we get a trial in two months so Dean Powell can get free ink in time to get elected, and I can't object because my client won't let me."

Hardy pegged another dart, finally hitting the "11." He held a last dart and threw it randomly

— or thought it was random until it smacked into the middle of the "10." He was getting it back.

"And then," Freeman was continuing, "I come in to check on the progress made by my hand-chosen ace investigator and he is throwing darts. Am I the only one that feels some pressure here? I think that's a fair question. Two months for a capital case. It's unheard of."

"It's been five months since the original arraignment."

"So what? Who knew she was going to get found in Costa Rica? Does Thomasino think we were preparing for trial all that time? Whose side are you on, anyway?"

"As always, I'm on the side of justice and truth, but it's not going to trial in two months. It's just beginning jury selection."

Freeman, of course, knew this, but Jennifer's trial was going to begin more quickly than he wanted it to and there wasn't anything he could do about it. Hands jammed into his pockets, he stood near the window and studied buildings across the street. "I need a lever. Christ, Diz, I need *something*."

"Just this morning didn't I hear you tell some reporters that this thing was such a turkey it wouldn't even make it to trial?"

"You could write a book on what I've told reporters. You'd be surprised."

"I doubt it."

"I've had it work. Some rookie Assistant DA reads in the papers that I've got this blockbuster secret evidence that'll blow the trial wide open and next day I'm down at the Hall pleading a manslaughter on what should have been a righteous Murder Two. But in this case . . ." He trailed off, shaking his head. "In this case, we've got Jennifer and Jennifer's weapon and Jennifer's presumed motives. We're very much going to need somebody else to point at."

"The famous other dude." Hardy came around his desk and flipped through some pages of his yellow pad. "That's all I've been doing, David. The problem is, there hasn't been what you'd call a run on them. In the meantime, maybe it'll ease your mind to know I'm not just shooting darts to pass the time. I have an appointment on another matter. Actually the appointment was for about fifteen minutes ago, but Mr. Frankl is late."

At the window, Freeman half-turned. "Who's Frankl?"

"My DUI. Wants to go to trial."

"The guy with the 1.6?" In California, a blood alcohol level of .08 got you convicted for drunk driving. If that fact was undisputed you were guilty.

Hardy nodded. "He says he's thought up a defense."

"To a DUI? I'd like to hear it. It could make us rich."

The telephone buzzed on Hardy's desk. "That's him now. I'll keep you informed."

Freeman was at the door, going out, when Hardy picked it up. But it wasn't Mr. Frankl. It was Sam Bronkman from the Mission Hills Clinic and he had just remembered something personal regarding Larry Witt that Hardy might be interested in.

Late in the day Hardy parked in the long shadow of the Mission Hills Clinic. The evening breeze whipped at his jacket as he got out of his car and prepared to cross the picket lines again. Same people, same building, same wind.

There was no one in the darkened waiting room at OB-GYN, and the blinds behind the window at the reception area had been pulled. Hardy felt all his muscles go tight, almost turned to walk out, then made himself knock on the glass. He was here. Might as well make sure.

There was a slit in the blinds and they blinked open. Sam smiled, waved, pointed at the door to the inner offices and closed the blinds down again. Hardy crossed the room.

The door cracked and Sam's head appeared, a turtle poking out of its shell. Grabbing Hardy's arm, he pulled him through. "All clear," he said. "You wouldn't believe. We close at four-thirty. People come here at five, expect to waltz right in. Keep the desk open and you're here all night."

Sam, chattering, led the way to an employee's lounge — plastic yellow chairs, white metal tables, vending machines, a microwave. It was an inside room with no windows, and it was empty. They sat at one of the tables.

"I should have remembered when you were here last time, especially when you mentioned the personal stuff, but" — Sam snapped his fingers in the air — "the brain, sometimes it goes on hold. One minute you're there, the next" — the hands described a mushroom cloud — "*woosh,* nobody home."

"That's all right, Sam. I really appreciate you calling, whenever you remembered, and you did remember something?"

Sam nodded elaborately. "Over the weekend. Did you read that article about that senator who wouldn't let his daughter have the abortion? Well, anyway . . . I was at Jason's — he's my friend, Jason — and I was reading it and suddenly, it was like, I don't know, a vision or something, just" — again the hands fluttered — "*whammo,* there it was."

Hardy smiled. "There *what* was, Sam?"

"Dr. Witt. The same thing."

"Dr. Witt had a daughter?"

"No. No way." Sam reached over and slapped Hardy's arm. "No, listen, the personal thing, the connection, is this — there was this girl, Melissa Roman, whose parents told her she couldn't have an abortion, forbade it, you know." He rolled his eyes. "Smart, right? These people, I'll never understand . . ." A deep sigh. "Anyway, she tried one on herself — an abortion — and it didn't turn out so good."

"What happened?"

"What else?" The hands again, including the universe. "She winds up here. Dr. Witt's the pro with female plumbing and he's a volunteer. He calls for an ambulance right away. But before it even gets here she's dead."

"The parents blamed Witt?"

Sam nodded. "You got to. They're not going to blame themselves, right? So they need somebody and Melissa's already dead — kind of unfair to take it out on her, wouldn't you say? — so they pick Witt. They decide he's somehow responsible for the abortion that killed their daughter."

The logic of that couldn't stand much scrutiny, but Hardy supposed it rang true for the bereaved Romans. Hardy was leaning forward now. "How'd they pick on him? When did all this happen?"

Sam nodded, pleased with himself. "I looked that up today. It was right before Thanksgiving of last year."

"Which was a month before Witt was killed."

"Right."

"What did they do? Threaten to sue him? What?"

Sam's palms were up again, laying out the whole truth. "I don't know everything. I know Roman came down twice — we had to get security the second time. Then, right after that, Dr. Witt said he might just quit volunteering, it was too much. Somebody broke his car windows and he was sure it was Roman."

"Did he report that?"

"I don't know."

This was something Hardy could legitimately bring up to Terrell, or even Glitsky. Here was a crime that happened to a murder victim within a month of his death.

If Larry had reported it.

"The other stuff," Sam was saying, "if Roman was suing him or the clinic, I don't know. I haven't heard about that, but I'll tell you something . . ."

Hardy waited.

"How about this? If you're planning to kill somebody, you don't also sue him, do you? Maybe that's why I never heard of anything. Otherwise, why wouldn't he just sue the clinic?"

Interesting question.

His house was empty when he got home and he felt the emptiness trying to settle on him, heavy and cold as the city's familiar fog.

He had lived the better part of ten years alone in this house before he had gotten together with Frannie, and the associations weren't all good — he missed almost nothing from that lost decade. The house, back then, had been smaller (without the nursery), darker (without the skylights), colder. Just plain colder somehow.

He would get home from bartending or a ball game and go to his office in the back, which was now Rebecca's pastel bedroom. He'd take a bottled Guinness from the refrigerator and sit at his desk in the light from his green banker's lamp and read, or shoot darts, or clean his (now unused) pipes, or whittle something. He'd light a coal fire in the grate.

Everything he did he had done all by himself, even when he was with other people. He hadn't thought he was lonely. He wasn't lonely, he was just alone. And, he now knew, there was a difference.

Frannie hadn't mentioned going out and he'd talked to her after he'd seen Jennifer in the morning. It was possible she'd gone to the market, although they'd just spent a domestic weekend, including a trip to the grocery store on Saturday.

He didn't know where they were and, against any kind of sense, it worried him. On the drive home he'd been thinking about Jennifer and Larry and the Romans and the medical background sheet Lightner had — intentionally? — left for him to pick up.

All those thoughts were now gone. He looked down and out the window in Vincent's room, wondering if, even with the July evening chill, they might be in the backyard. They weren't. He fed the tropical fish in his bedroom, looked at his watch, started to call the Shamrock and decided not, checked the time again. He didn't know. There was no note.

He wasn't going to sit around waiting, letting the old emptiness fill him up. It was something he'd put behind him, and its sudden reappearance spooked him. Were the kids all right? Had Frannie run out quickly to the emergency room, not even having time to jot something on a pad? He walked from the kitchen to the front door down the hallway and back through the inside rooms, telling himself he wasn't looking for drops of blood on the floor.

In his bedroom he shucked his suit and put on shorts, a sweatshirt, tennis shoes. He had a four-mile circle he ran from his house, out to the beach, across Golden Gate Park, along Lincoln back to the Shamrock at 9th Avenue, then home. It took him about forty-five minutes.

He looked at his watch. He'd be home by seven. He wrote a note and left it on the kitchen table under a salt shaker. At least Frannie would know where he'd gone.

In the kitchen, Frannie greeted him with a kiss.

She was stirring her white clam spaghetti sauce and humming. Rebecca was pouring water from a watering can, getting almost half of it into the different-sized pans she'd arranged on the floor. Vincent was in his baby seat next to her. The windows were steamed with the boiling water. The sun was still up. In his house there was nothing empty or spooky or sinister.

Hardy went in to shower, berating himself for his paranoia, wondering how he got to be so old.

22

On Wednesday at a little after noon there was the sound of something being thrown, clattering against bars onto the floor in the jail behind where Jennifer sat on the bench in the visitors' area. Startled, Frannie nearly left her chair. Sitting back down, she forced a smile. "I hate that kind of noise. I always jump a mile."

"It doesn't really bother me anymore. I guess I'm used to it." Jennifer looked down at her hands. "Larry used to throw things sometimes, so by the time I heard the noise it meant most of it was over."

"What do you mean?"

"You know, the tension, waiting for him to blow up. It was almost a relief when it came."

Frannie put her hand on the Plexiglas. Jennifer put hers up against it. It had developed between them, some kind of signal, a touch by proxy. This was their third meeting. The hands remained in place. Frannie stared at the hands, at her wedding ring. Her face paled.

"Are you all right?" Jennifer asked.

"I'm fine. Sometimes just . . ."

"What?"

"I'm sorry. Moment of weakness. It's nothing."

Then smiled again, weakly. "I don't know what it is."

"You look sad."

Frannie nodded. "That's what it feels like. Like all at once things have sort of stopped" — she searched for the right word — "resonating, I'd say."

"Maybe it's just the postpartums. They can go on six months, you know, sometimes longer. After Matt," she paused, surprised by the name, from out of nowhere. A deep breath, pushing on, "after Matt, first there was euphoria, then this black hole that didn't want to go away."

Frannie shrugged. "Maybe. I don't know. I don't feel like it's that." She brought her hand back down to her lap. "I wanted to tell you — you know, my first husband was killed too?"

Frannie then told Jennifer about it, about twenty-five-year-old Eddie Cochran — Frannie's husband and Hardy's friend. Hardy had helped expose the murderer, and five months later they — Hardy and Frannie — had gotten involved, married.

Frannie told her about some bad moments since they'd gotten together. Guilt perhaps. Timing questions. But this, Frannie's sadness, seemed to strike a deeper chord somehow.

"Everything's been so kind of rushed, you know?"

Jennifer listened, rapt, her eyes glistening. Another woman had problems, had sadnesses. It was some comfort to know she wasn't so alone.

"It's just first there was Eddie, then Dismas and me. Then all of a sudden I'm married again and

Rebecca is being born. Next, before I've really given any thought to those changes, I'm pregnant again and having Vincent. And now . . . now I've stopped for a minute and I look back and it's like I've been running like a crazy person, as though I'm maybe running from something. Does this make any sense?"

Jennifer nodded. "Yes. Sometimes I think the trick is to just keep running so you don't have to stop and think about it. Once you stop, then . . ."

Taking a long moment, Frannie leaned forward, her elbows on the table. "Today I was sitting rocking, feeding Vincent, and all at once I'm crying. Really sobbing. Now why would that come over me when I look at my life and I'm fine? I'm happy day to day, Dismas and I are good. I love the kids. I don't get it."

"You miss your first husband, Eddie?"

"A little. But I'm used to him being gone. I know he's not coming back. It's not that. It's more that I haven't sorted things. Haven't even thought about it, and here I am in a marriage with two kids and this is my life and sometimes I don't even know how I got here."

Jennifer scratched at the pitted counter on her side of the glass. "Talk about not knowing how you got somewhere."

Frannie forced a smile. "Look at me, talking to you *here*. I've got no business doing any complaining, seeing where you are."

"It's okay," Jennifer said. "It's okay. I won't be here forever. Either way — at least I'm out of this place."

"I don't know how you're handling it."

Jennifer took a minute, swallowed, then forced her own smile. "It isn't like I've got much choice . . . He treats you right, does he? He doesn't hurt you?"

The segue here was unclear. "Who?"

"Your husband."

"Dismas?" Frannie shifted her weight on the hard wooden chair. "No, I mean *yes,* he treats me very right. He'd never hurt me. He loves me."

Jennifer gave her a look that seemed to ask what that had to do with it. But she said, "Did Eddie?"

"Hurt me? No, never."

Jennifer leaned back in the chair, ran both hands through her cropped hair. "It must be me," she said. "I've always believed it was me."

"What was you? What?"

Jennifer sat forward now, hunched. Slowly she lifted her hand and placed it against the glass. Frannie brought up hers, almost imagining she could feel the heat from Jennifer's skin. "Why they always hit me."

On the third floor, Dean Powell was listening to another Assistant DA analyze the merits of an aggravated assault.

The people who worked at the Hall of Justice spoke in a kind of code. San Francisco had a well-deserved reputation as the most politically correct of cities, and you could get yourself fired or worse if you labored for the City and inadvertently happened to use a word that had not been officially sanctioned — or had been officially proscribed — by some group or other.

The members of the police department and the District Attorney's office were among the most sensitive to irregularities in this area, and so had developed the most sophisticated code for use among themselves. Visitors could spend half a day in the Hall, people chatting all around, and be a hundred-and-eighty degrees off on what they thought they had heard.

Dean Powell, running for State Attorney General, still had to function as a prosecutor, and especially between now and November he was careful not to use too much of the code himself. Nevertheless, he didn't need a translator.

"If you ask me," Tony Feeney was telling him, "we got a stone BDI here. Professional women, some dispute over funding. Both of them Canadians. In my opinion, she'll go sideways like she has the three other times."

Feeney was another Assistant District Attorney, in Powell's office getting the more experienced man's take on whether he should even bother charging Mr. Duncan J. Dunlap for aggravated assault on his live-in girlfriend Byna Lewes — a "professional woman."

BDI was the code for a case in which the defendant believed and usually loudly proclaimed to police that the woman he had just savagely beaten or killed had brought the attack on herself. BDI stood for Bitch Deserved It. In this case Dunlap thought Lewes was holding out on him and might be about to choose another pimp. Feeney thought Lewes would "go sideways," which meant she'd refuse to testify or, even better, change her testimony on the stand. And, by the way, both parties were African-Americans, called "Canadians" by members of law enforcement to avoid offending anyone in earshot.

Byna Lewes had promised to testify against Mr. Dunlap on the three previous occasions when he'd beaten her, and each time she had relented, saying he was truly sorry (this time) and he really loved her. He just needed some help. Maybe the City could help pay for his counseling.

Powell crossed his hands behind his head. "You ever wonder why we keep doing this?"

Feeney had no response. He sat across from Powell, hoping he'd be remembered if Powell got lucky and took up residence in Sacramento.

"How badly was she hurt?" Feeney opened the folder, starting to take out the pictures. But Powell held out a hand, palm up. "Just describe it, Tony. How bad?"

The Polaroids had been taken by the arresting officer in Byna's hospital room shortly after the attack, before she'd been bandaged. Her left eye was swollen shut, her nose looked broken, there was blood in her hair and over her ear. Feeney went to the police report and saw she'd also had her arm dislocated. "Not bad," he said, about average.

"We charging it?"

Powell was getting to the meat of the issue. If Byna — the victim — would cooperate in the case against Mr. Dunlap, then he would be charged and the matter would proceed. If, on the other hand, the victim chose not to assist the prosecution, would not appear and testify — which in these cases was very common — then the case would fall apart.

"Well, it's a little iffy, is the problem. On picture night here" — Feeney gestured to the file — "Ms. Lewes had had enough, she was coming down as soon as she got out of the hospital and filing charges and put that bad man away."

"So what happened? He come see her?"

"He would have, but he was in jail at the time. But naturally, the minute he's out on bail, he buys her roses, candy, says he's sorry. Only this time she's not sure she believes him, but she's so afraid of him she doesn't want to testify."

"Logical. Good reasoning."

Feeney held up one finger. *"But,"* he said, "she says if we give her a subpoena she'll testify."

"What a citizen! This is a beautiful story. And you're asking me what I'd do?"

"I know what you'd do, Dean. I'm just wondering how you'd explain it. We got a third offense, we've got a witness who says she'll testify. How do you just drop it?"

"You don't drop it, Tony. You file it, hold her hand every day, and try not to feel too bad when she doesn't show up for the trial."

David Freeman's office was up one flight of ornate, scroll-banistered stairs in the front corner of the old building on Sutter Street. Below him, the ground floor was comprised of the comfortable reception area, a conference room that faced a brick and ivy inner courtyard and a small law library. Four years before, Freeman had redecorated and put in a lot of glass down below, giving the place an open feel.

At the head of the stairs, outside Freeman's lair, Phyllis Wells kept the howlers at bay, the howlers being their own code name for associate attorneys.

Phyllis had been with David for thirty-two years and in that time had seen associates come and go — enter the practice as eager law school graduates hoping to ride the coattails of the brilliant David Freeman to fame and glory, carve a reputation in the city and perhaps beyond, become a partner in a reasonable six or seven years. Most didn't last two.

Not one had hung on to become a partner. They worked their twelve-hour days and nights and weekends and wrote briefs and even got trial experience and then moved on, either to their own practices, to one of the big downtown firms or out of the law altogether.

The reason: David Freeman did not want partners. Not for nothing had he named his firm David Freeman & Associates. It wasn't about to change.

He didn't like to delegate. No, Phyllis knew it was more than that. He was incapable of delegating. Which was why, she thought, this situation with Dismas Hardy was a little unusual — Hardy was doing work that Freeman had always done himself. Freeman even seemed relatively pleased with Hardy's results. This was so out of character that it worried Phyllis. She wondered if David were sick. If he would tell her if he was.

Not that she had anything against Hardy. There was a good feeling around him. He was nice-looking in a craggy way, not too lean. Sometimes maybe a bit too quick with the humorous phrase for her taste, but God knew she'd seen enough humorless attorneys pass through these halls. It was refreshing to have one who seemed not to take himself *so* seriously.

Freeman had instructed her to let Hardy come in when he needed to talk, confer, even visit. Of course, technically he wasn't an associate, not one of the howlers. He wasn't even "of counsel." He just rented a room.

He came and went rather haphazardly and was beginning to show some sign of trusting her, which, of course, he could do, although she'd been somewhat resentful at the beginning when David had suggested he share her as his own secretary. But that had been working out, too. He was up on the fourth floor, connected to her by intercom that he rarely used.

Still, it was a change giving him information before she'd cleared it with David. Now her boss — Freeman would always be her boss — was at trial and here was Dismas Hardy, casually asking how Jennifer got referred to the firm. She had thought he already knew. Well, it wasn't a big issue — he had just come up the stairs from somewhere, snapped his fingers and came back, stopping at her desk.

Jennifer Witt was David's client, there was no mistake about that, even though she remembered it was near Hardy's first month or so in the office when she'd buzzed him after she'd beeped David in court and he'd told her to get Hardy down there to meet Jennifer in jail. But if Phyllis had learned anything in thirty-two years in this business, it was that information was the coin of the realm, and its dissemination — almost always — was strictly need-to-know.

"It just occurred to me," Hardy was saying, "that here I've been learning all I can about this woman and I don't even know how we got involved with her. I mean, she thought I was David when I first met her, so she didn't know him either, am I right?"

Phyllis smiled, adjusting her glasses. "Didn't you ask her?"

He leaned comfortably against the partition separating her desk from the open hallway. "If I recall, she said something about her husband's lawyers, but I didn't know who they were."

"She couldn't tell you?"

"She could if I went over to the Hall, paid four dollars for a parking space, rode the slowest elevator in America up seven flights, got patted down and admitted by the guard into the women's jail, waited fifteen minutes for them to get Jennifer, and then asked her." He knew he was charming her and, more strangely, she knew it and didn't mind. Now he grinned openly. "You're stonewalling me, Phyllis. I can tell."

The referral had come from Donna Bellows, a member of the firm of Goldberg Mullen & Roake. Hardy called her from his office, two flights up from Phyllis.

It was the middle of the week, the middle of the afternoon, and he got right through. Introducing himself, he was struck by the immediate chill that came over the deeply pitched voice.

"Perhaps it wasn't clear at the time, Mr. Hardy, but not only doesn't this firm take many criminal cases, I personally didn't want anything to do with Mrs. Witt, so I'm not inclined to be of much help. I'm sorry."

"Did you know her? Personally?" He had to keep her talking or she was gone, and he did have something he wanted to get to.

"I never met the woman. I never want to. Now I'm sorry, but if you'll excuse —"

"Please, if I might — one quick question. Can you tell me anything about Crane & Crane? Any connection to Dr. Witt?"

Silence, the decision being made. Hardy knew that he and Ms. Bellows weren't adversaries in any real sense. She might have felt a loyalty — or more than that — to her client Larry Witt, but good lawyers at least tried to observe the professional courtesies with one another. Hardy was counting on that. He heard her sigh, going ahead with this distasteful discussion.

"All right, I'm sorry, Mr. Hardy. I liked Larry Witt. I read the papers and I'm afraid I believe that his wife killed him and their boy."

"From what you've read in the papers?"

"That, yes, and some other things."

"What other things?"

Another pause, considering, rejecting? "Let's get back to the one question, shall we?"

Though there might be a wide vein of information here, Hardy knew he'd have to let it go if he wanted to find out about Crane & Crane. He'd spent the better part of a frustrating yesterday and all of this morning chasing down the chimeras of "other dudes" — Melissa Roman's parents, Witt's first wife Molly, a Dr. Heffler from

Dr. Lightner's form. He had not so much as spoken to any of them. Now he had Donna Bellows on the telephone and he'd take whatever she was willing to give.

"Crane & Crane. Some connection to Larry."

"That name is familiar in the sense that I believe I've heard it, that's all."

"It's a Los Angeles law firm."

"That may be it. You say Larry and — ?"

"I don't know. He called them a few days before he died."

"Before he was killed, you mean. He didn't just die. He was killed." He listened to her breathe for a moment. "I was Larry's financial advisor. With respect to Crane, he may have mentioned them in some context. This would have been about six months ago? Whatever it was, if anything, it couldn't have been too important. I really don't remember, but I can check."

"Would you mind?"

"Frankly, I do mind, Mr. Hardy. I don't like my clients being shot to death. It really bothers me. And I don't want to help their killers get free. But I'll look into it. I said I would and I will."

Hardy thanked her.

"I'll call you," she said, and hung up.

"Date night" was a free-form event. The traditional and sacred Wednesday ritual had taken them — before the children had been born — as far afield as Los Angeles or Reno or Santa Fe on the spur of the moment. Date nights had been known to continue for several days, Hardy calling into the Shamrock to have his shifts covered while he and Frannie gambled or perused art galleries or decided to take the ferry out of Long Beach over to Santa Catalina, the island of romance.

Tonight they were on another ferry chugging across the bay to Sausalito. Out near Alcatraz the water was choppy, the wind high, the sun lost in a bank of fog that was rolling over and around the Golden Gate Bridge. The temperature was in the fifties.

"Ah, summertime." Frannie watched Dismas suck the bracing air. They stood at the front rail on the upper deck, blown and sprayed. "Nothing like the middle of July to get rid of the winter blahs."

Frannie leaned into the rail, holding onto it with both hands. "Maybe that's it," she said. "The winter blahs." She looked up at her husband, her smile as lost as the sunlight. He put an arm around her, bringing her inside his heavy coat, and she leaned into him.

"You all right?"

She considered whether she should tell him, how much she should tell him. She felt like she was sneaking out, cheating on him. But she didn't want to get into it, not just now. It would become a discussion, the theme for the night, and she didn't need that. She didn't need to clear everything with Dismas. She loved him, but she had her own life, her own feelings.

For Frannie, seeing Jennifer Witt was somehow bringing things to the surface and that, she felt, was good. Once she recognized what she was dealing with, she'd be better equipped to handle things. Questioning how you felt wasn't necessarily threatening to her and Dismas, or to the kids. She loved them all — her husband and her children. It wasn't that.

It was what she'd started to say to Jennifer — that there was just so much that she hadn't been able to take time for. She was losing sight of who she was, of who Francine Rose McGuire Cochran (and now Hardy) had turned into and how it had all happened. And how she felt about it.

Was she just some adjunct to whatever man she was with, the bearer of their babies? She didn't really feel that with Dismas. She hadn't felt that way with Eddie. She and Eddie had been living an adventure. Eddie had been about to start graduate school when he'd been killed. They'd been saving money for everything, discovering new places, each other.

Then, suddenly, no warning, and Eddie was gone. And there was Dismas. Not in Eddie's old space, but close to it. And now, two years — five minutes? — later, she was a stay-at-home mother, with no money worries, where Dismas already knew all the good restaurants and the great places, where Dismas had already made the discoveries and so many of the decisions.

Like living in his old house — which, of course, they'd decided to do together. It made so much more sense. And she did love the house. But that wasn't it — the point was that even though she'd changed it to her tastes — brightened it up, painted, rearranged, added a room — it was still his house, Dismas' house, not really their house.

All of their friends, too, were his friends and their wives. Abe, Flo, Pico, Angela. Even Moses

— her own brother — even Moses had been Hardy's friend long before she'd been in the picture. Not that she didn't like these people — she did, but she hadn't found them on her own.

What about her old friends? The people she and Eddie had known? Didn't they count? Why weren't they part of her new life anymore? Was it the kids, or Dismas, or herself?

She knew Dismas wouldn't approve of the extra visits to Jennifer. The original idea had been simply to set her mind at ease about the kind of person Jennifer was.

But now something else was happening, and it was important, tapping into a vein of her own that hadn't been mined in a couple of years. Maybe by talking about things with Jennifer — why she continued to let both of her husbands beat her, for example — Frannie could help her change, see the way things were supposed to work. It seemed worthwhile, even if Dismas didn't know about it.

She was sure he had some secrets from her. You didn't have to tell your spouse every thought and word and deed in your life.

And seeing Jennifer was doing her some good. She was Frannie's own friend, confidant, and Dismas didn't need to know about it. She could choose her own friends, make decisions for herself in her own life. Later, she'd tell him. Maybe after he and Freeman got Jennifer off. After the trial.

She was her own person, but somehow she'd let the predictable in her daily life devalue her. She even found herself wondering whether Dismas would keep loving her, why he loved her in the first place, all the while telling herself she deserved to be loved. You're a great girl. Wonderful, sensitive, cool — if you don't love yourself how can you love anybody else? How can anybody love you?

The ferry had entered the lee of Sausalito and the chop had flattened. Dismas tightened his arm around her. "Hello?"

It really didn't have anything to do with loving him. She loved him, his face and his body and the easy way he did things. It was just that she needed a little more of herself in her life.

"I'm here." She kissed his cheek.

23

Molly."

Freeman's living room on Friday morning, and Hardy was sitting back in one of the leather chairs, Freeman in his maroon bathrobe checking off answers, making notes in pencil at the kitchen table.

"Molly wasn't here in December. She hadn't even heard he'd died, or she's even a better actress than our client."

"How'd she take it?"

"I think it would depress me if the news of my death was greeted so warmly."

Freeman raised his bushy eyebrows, a question.

Hardy continued. "She hated his guts, even after lo these many years. He used to beat her, too."

Again the eyebrows went up. "But he didn't beat Jennifer."

Hardy kept a straight face. "That's our defense, right? He didn't beat her. So she says."

"Never laid a hand on her."

Hardy had finally spoken to Larry Witt's first wife, Molly. She was now a guidance counselor living and working in Fargo, North Dakota. She had not remarried and had not seen or heard from Dr. Witt in five years. "I guess we could have somebody double-check, see if she was in North

Dakota over Christmas, but I'd bet she was. The news of Larry's death absolutely made her day."

Freeman put down his pencil, staring out the window. "Let's stop a minute, Diz. What kind of son-of-a-bitch was this guy?"

Crossing his legs, sitting back, Hardy took a minute. "By all accounts, he was a model citizen, total professional, concerned father, great provider. He just happened to beat his wives."

"You really believe that?"

"You don't?"

"I don't know why Jennifer couldn't cop to it. Even if the legislature doesn't go for it, there's a good chance a jury would walk her, and no chance she'd get the death penalty. Powell wouldn't even ask."

Freeman was referring, Hardy knew, to the fact that the California Assembly had recently failed to pass an amendment that would have codified Battered-Woman Syndrome as a legitimate mitigation for murder. Since the courts were often accepting it anyway, the precedent was established and it was a moot question, but the legislature's action — or lack of it — was a definite setback for proponents of the defense. "I simply can't understand her resistance to it."

Hardy could go through all of Lightner's explanations, but it all came back to Jennifer's contention that if she admitted Larry beat her, then she had a reason to kill him that a jury might well convict on.

"But that's just it," Freeman continued, "they'd be just as likely — hell, more likely — to let her go!" He stood up, stretched, sat back down. "But you believe he did beat her?"

"Yes, absolutely. He was a control freak. She got out of line, he whacked her around."

"And she really felt she couldn't leave? She had to stay there and take it?"

"That's the profile, David. It's sad but it's true. He'd track her down if she left. He'd take the kid. He'd kill her if she tried. All of the above."

"So she killed him first. It worked with Ned, it ought to fly with Larry, right?"

Hardy shrugged. "She says not."

"Well." The pencil beat a tattoo on the table. "I must say, in all my years doing this, I haven't seen too many cases this pure. I'd like to watch her play poker, see if she bluffs."

"Maybe she's a Vulcan."

"What's that mean?"

It amazed Hardy. Was it possible that David Freeman had never seen "Star Trek," didn't know that Vulcans never bluff? Looking around the apartment, he realized it was probably so. There was no sign of a television. "Never mind, David. It's a long story. You want to keep going here?"

The tattooing stopped. "We'd better."

From Freeman's apartment, Hardy walked up the street a block and treated himself to lunch, alone, at the Stanford Court — he wanted an hour to think.

There had been no police report on the alleged break-in of Larry Witt's car by Melissa Roman's parents or anybody else. Dr. Witt hadn't reported it, a fact which hadn't surprised Abe Glitsky, who had explained that the populace was beginning to understand that there was no such thing as a non-violent crime in San Francisco anymore.

There were bad things that happened, sure — like Larry's car — but if those things didn't physically hurt people, the police tended not to get involved. They weren't about to break out the troops tracking down a culprit who had lifted a five-hundred-dollar CD player from a car — they didn't have the manpower — any more than they would investigate a pine cone falling from a tree and breaking your windshield. Practically speaking it just couldn't be a police matter. Hardy loved it — vandalism as a *force majeure.*

He was having salmon again. Grilled with a light wasabe glaze. A glass of Hafner Chardonnay.

He was worried about Frannie.

Something was going on with her and she wasn't telling him about it. Maybe it was his continued involvement with Jennifer. She shouldn't have expected that one visit was going to change anything. And obviously, going to the jail had been a trauma.

He hated to see her unhappy. Maybe he was spending too much time running around for David, looking for a plausible "other dude." The inherent cynicism in it all was getting to him. David seemed to care almost nothing for the guilt or innocence of Jennifer, just whether he could get his client off. That was what he did for a living, he said. Was he really that cold? Was there a deeper concern behind the so-called professionalism? Hardy couldn't tell, couldn't really read David that well. And he suspected that that was just the way David wanted it. No black or white for Hardy in this case. Not with Jennifer, not with his colleague

David, not with anything, which could wear a person down.

The waiter appeared now and asked if the food was satisfactory. Monsieur had not touched the plate. If he would like to order something else, of course . . .

Well, for today at least, Hardy decided he would not be looking for "other dudes." The crux of the matter in court was whether proof existed that Jennifer was a battered woman. Once that was established, the question of her culpability could be debated. Providing Jennifer cooperated.

Anyway, Hardy couldn't let Freeman shake his belief in some objective truth, in the facts. Something specific did happen, in a certain way and at a certain time. If he had any pretensions of seeing justice done, the first step was to uncover those facts.

He had Ken Lightner's assertions. He had seen the bruises on Jennifer's mother. He had the first wife's, Molly's, admission that Larry Witt had beaten her. He even had Jennifer's acknowledgment that she and Larry had been in "a few fights."

This was ammunition but it wasn't a smoking gun.

Dr. Saul Heffler was one of the doctors from Ken Lightner's list that Lightner had "accidentally" left on the bench for Hardy to find and pick up. Heffler had a practice in a one-story office building on Arguello, halfway from downtown to Hardy's house. The doctor and the lawyer had played a serious game of phone tag during the week and it was time to put an end to that, even if it meant sitting a while in a waiting room.

The gods smiled and a parking spot opened directly in front of the address as Hardy pulled up. He took this as a good omen.

Inside, the receptionist was blessedly free of bureaucratic baggage and informed Hardy that the doctor could probably block out some time in about an hour. Would that be all right?

Hardy walked up to Clement Street, drank a cup of iced espresso at an outside table to ward off the post wine-for-lunch slump, then bought some earrings for Frannie from a sidewalk vendor.

He loved lower Clement Street, had loved it through its incarnations, first as a Russian enclave with piroshki and antique shops, then as an upscale — though not *too* upscale — Haight Street with its hippies, haze of incense, and coffeeshops, to now, a bustling Oriental bazaar with tea-smoked ducks hanging in windows and the slightly off yet somehow appealing commingled smells of cooked meat, raw seafood and garbage.

Strolling in the bright sunlight, enjoying the smells and the breeze, he bought a newly steamed pork bao and chewed it happily. There was a bright turquoise children's kimono in a window and he went inside the tiny store, buying it for Rebecca along with a tiny silk shirt for his boy.

He'd make this up to Frannie. Things were going to change. He wasn't sure how, but he wasn't going to let anything — not David, Jennifer, frustration, fear or silence — get between them and keep them apart.

Three minutes after he was back inside Heffler's

office and the receptionist told him he could go right in.

Heffler's small but well-lit office had three diplomas and about six hundred mounted fishing flies on the walls. The man was in his mid-fifties with a full head of pepper-and-salt hair, a flat unlined face — a hint of Navajo? — over a lanky, gangling frame. He smiled easily.

Hardy explained the situation. He was, after all, working for Jennifer's defense. He wondered if the doctor would help him verify some background. He showed Heffler Jennifer's signed release allowing her doctor to discuss her medical history. (Hardy had told Jennifer he needed her medical records in connection with what had happened to her in Costa Rica.) He'd be glad to help, the doctor said. What did Hardy want to know? Hardy told him.

"This was four years ago? Five? I can't say I remember her offhand. I'll have Joanie pull the file. We keep the archives in the storeroom. Take two minutes."

They waited, talking fishing. Heffler was leaving the next morning for a six-day wilderness trip to Alaska, going after the huge salmon that ran up there, maybe some Arctic char. Hardy held a hand over his stomach. "Don't say salmon to me. I think I'm hitting my limit."

Joanie came in, handed over the file and left. Heffler opened it and flipped some pages, his face closing down. "You want to believe people. You wonder how much of this you really see."

"You got something?"

"I don't know what you call something. Maybe I should have seen this, suspected something. I don't know."

Hardy waited. Heffler read some more, then closed the file. "She was my patient for seven months, came in without a referral, said she'd just moved here from Florida. First time I saw her she had fallen down the steps in her new house."

"The first time?"

Heffler nodded. He opened the file again. "Three months later she broke her arm skiing. She thought it was just a sprain until she got home, otherwise she would have gotten it set up at Squaw Valley." He turned up a page, scanning. "This one," he said, "maybe I really should have seen this one."

"What's that?"

"Three months after the arm — pretty regular, isn't it — she comes in with this fluke accident. She was cleaning out a closet and the shelf came off, loaded with stuff, slammed down against her back. Her urine had blood in it." He wasn't looking up. "Contusions and bruises over her kidneys, all the way across her back." He closed the file again. "I must have asked her, I can't imagine I didn't."

"And she just said no, simple as that?"

"And got herself another doctor." He took in a deep breath, let it out as a sigh. "I'm ready for a vacation," he said.

"You see a lot of this?"

"A lot? Some, I guess. I see some accidents. People hurt themselves. I can't go to the police every time someone breaks their arm, comes in with a black eye. I wouldn't have a practice left." He picked up the file, opened it, flicked impatiently at the pages. "Here's something."

Stuck to the back of the folder was a yellow post-it pad, and on it was a name and address. "I don't know why this is here."

He buzzed Joanie again and she came back. "Oh, that's just my note to myself when I get a request for records."

Heffler leaned forward, still frowning. "So this might have been the next physician this patient went to."

Joanie was as bright and cheerful as Heffler had been before this had begun. "It might be. I'd assume so, wouldn't you?"

"I told her I wouldn't treat her unless she let me inform the police. She ought to get some counseling. I saw her the one time and I knew right away."

Hardy was sitting in the waiting room of Dr. Helena Zamora's office. Now it was closing time. A tightly strung woman about Hardy's age, Zamora let him in but politely told him she had a dinner appointment in forty-five minutes and could spare him no more than ten. He outlined what he had learned at Dr. Heffler's and what he was trying to find.

"She came in," Dr. Zamora said, "with a large round bruise under one of her breasts and some cock-and-bull about tripping against a knob at the top of her bannister. I got suspicious, checked her sign-in form, sent for her records. Then I called her and never heard from her again."

She pulled her glasses up and balanced them

on the top of her forehead. "Common story, too common. Does that help you?"

Hardy said it did and thanked her.

Dr. Zamora took her glasses all the way off. "She finally killed the animal that was doing this, did she?"

"She's charged with it."

"Good for her."

From a phone booth in a gas station at 19th and Kirkham, Hardy called Jennifer at the jail.

In San Francisco it is a myth that prisoners get one phone call. The common areas in the jail have pay telephones on the walls and whenever the inmates want to, they can use them. There had even been significant calling-card fraud that had been traced to both floors of the jail, a thriving black market in phone numbers and the "pins" that go with them.

"Jennifer. Hardy. I've got a quick question. Have you ever lived in Florida?"

There was a longish wait. "This is not a trick question, Jennifer. Have you ever lived in Florida, that's all?"

"No, why?"

"No reason. Just checking something. Talk to you later."

So this Friday afternoon he had caught Jennifer in five lies — the fall down the stairs, the arm broken while she skied, the shelf accident, the knob on the top of the bannister, the state with Epcot and the Everglades. Lies, yes, except four of them were, apparently, to protect her husband.

Sick yes, but mitigation, at least . . .

Frannie was on top of him, lying long against him, moving like a calm ocean. His arms surrounded her. The covers had been kicked onto the floor at the foot of the bed. She was wearing her new earrings and Hardy took one of them into his mouth.

"Careful," she said.

"Careful yourself."

"I'm being careful."

"You're going a little too fast. This will slow you down some."

She bit into his shoulder. "I'm going to go a lot faster before I'm through."

"Promises, promises."

"Let go then. You'll see."

24

I knew this girl in high school," Moses said, "Rachelle Manning. We were in math together and I thought she was okay so I asked her out to some dance or something and she said sure."

They were queued up in a long line at Candlestick Park, having already missed half an inning when the last-place Padres had scored four runs off the first-place Giants, waiting to buy two beers each for a mere four bucks a cup before they closed the stand for the day after the seventh inning.

It was the conceit of Giants' management that people who had a beer after the seventh inning would more likely drive under the influence than those other puritan souls who had had two beers early in the game and then stopped.

Frannie had already designated herself the driver, and Moses had had seven so far, and now was feeling every one of them. "So listen," he continued loudly, "word gets around and guys are coming up, putting rubbers in my pockets, patting me on the back, one of the big guys, telling me they've done it with Rachelle in their cars and in her parents' bed and behind the student union and under the goddamn principal's desk on the weekend."

The guy behind them in line tapped McGuire on the shoulder. "I did it under the stands during a basketball game once. Best sex I ever had."

Hardy and Moses told him they thought that must have been great. They moved up a step. Hardy signaled maybe McGuire should tone it down.

"Anyway, I figured it had to be some kind of joke. I mean, Rachelle Manning is not a slut. She's not putting out for the football team. This is a sweet young thing — nice clothes, nice family, clean hair."

"Hair's important." Hardy moved closer to the beer vendor. The stands erupted with more noise, action on the field they were missing. "I was always a hair guy myself."

"So I take her out, I'm a little nervous, thinking . . . you *know* what I'm thinking. We're not out of her driveway and her hand is on me, I swear to God."

"I loved high school. I could do high school again."

"Turned out to be a hell of a night. I don't think we hit the dance. If we did, I don't remember it."

They finally got their beers and started moving back to the stands.

"It's a truly moving story, Mose, but was there a moral here I missed? I thought we were talking about Jennifer Witt."

"Of course we were talking about Jennifer Witt. You're a lawyer and she's your case, so that's what we talk about, and talk about, and talk about. But" — Moses drank a third of his beer — "and I reiterate, *but* there's some people — and I hate to say this but women seem better at it than men, you just can't tell anything. This is how Rachelle relates to the fascinating and mysterious Mrs. Witt. Looking at her back then, you would never have had a clue. Talking to her, you'd never know. I mean, I would have bet the horse that this girl was a stone virgin."

"Maybe she was."

Moses couldn't help grinning. "She definitely wasn't the next morning. I have it on the highest authority."

"What?" Susan said. They were back to their seats, ten rows back on the first base side. Great seats.

Moses got himself seated and didn't miss a beat. "Just talking about Jennifer Witt, about how some women lie."

Frannie had her beer and poured some into Moses' lap. "Oh, sorry, dear brother." She made a show of brushing it off. "If I'm not mistaken, men lie too."

"Okay, everybody lies at one time or another, but my point to Diz was that there are some women, and I just say women because in my own private experience I haven't run across this in that many men, who seem to embody conflicting personality traits — I mean they seem to be two completely different people, and still they walk around and act normal and you'd never know."

Frannie leaned over and spoke to Susan. "There's still time. You're not married yet. You can get out of this."

Moses had a Ph.D. in philosophy that he liked

to say he'd outgrown. He had not outgrown his love of talk, however. The words flowed, and sometimes Hardy thought he even thought about them before they came out, although this didn't appear to be one of those times. "Frannie, I'm not saying you or Susan. Look at all the literature on it — *The Two Faces of Eve, Sybil*, all of them."

"All two of them."

"It's well-documented. You don't have to get so riled up about it. Women just hide things better. They're taught to as kids. Let's face it, if they're liars, they're better liars. It's a compliment!"

"I think I'll cut him off here," Susan said. She lifted what was left of his last beer and held it on her lap. "I still love you but you're getting close. Jesus. Women lie better. It's a *compliment?*"

"Who's winning?" Hardy asked, trying to end it here, but Frannie wasn't having it.

"What about men who beat their wives, Moses? You think you can tell just by looking at them? You think that's not living some monstrous lie?"

Moses thought a minute. "I think you could tell somehow, if you got to know them."

Hardy entered. "Yeah, like if you got married to one and he beat you, then you'd know."

"This isn't funny." Frannie turned on her husband. "Don't make a joke of it, Dismas."

"I'm *not* making a joke out of it, Frannie. I'm on your side here, okay? What's your problem?"

"My problem? It's not my problem! My brother says all women are liars and I don't accept that and that's *my* problem?"

"I didn't say all women. I said —"

"I know what you said. What I'm saying is this

isn't *my . . . god . . . damn problem.*"

Suddenly Frannie was on her feet, half-falling over her brother and Susan, getting to the aisle, running up out of the stands. Hardy looked helplessly after her. Susan got up and followed.

Moses was shaking his head. "What did I say?"

It was after six when, exhausted, they finally found a parking space around the corner, unloaded the sleeping kids from the car seats and carried them — one each — a half-block to the picket fence that bordered their lawn.

Phil and Tom DiStephano were sitting on their front steps. They stood up together, both in denim and T-shirts.

Hardy swore under his breath. He opened the gate and stepped in front of Frannie. "This isn't a good time, guys," he said. Rebecca shifted, loose and gangling, in his arms, and he bolstered her up.

"You hiding behind some babies and a girl?" Phil had been drinking. A lot. His eyes were out of focus — he was having trouble keeping his balance.

Hardy kept his voice low. "I'm not hiding behind anything. How'd you find out where I live?"

"That's for you to know, asshole." Tom, the son, had talked to his dad, got his attitude adjusted. When Hardy had gone down with the six-pack and interviewed him last time he'd been surly but gradually somewhat cooperative. Now — never mind the profanity — his body language said it all. He was ready for a fight, blocking the path.

Hardy gave them both a weary, practiced smile.

"Let's move on, guys. All the way off the property. We're going in."

Neither man moved. "You come over to my home and molest my wife? You think you're getting away with that?" Phil said.

"Put down your kid, asshole." Tom's little mantra of "asshole" was getting under Hardy's skin. He half-turned back to where Frannie stood, as though rooted to the ground, holding Vincent. He was about to herd them all back to the car, drive down to the Safeway on Clement and call the police. Was about to.

"Takes a brave man to hide behind his kid," Phil said.

"You men get *out* of here!" Frannie's momentary shock had worn off. She started to step around Hardy but he held out a hand, stopping her. "We're going inside," he said. "Follow me."

He tried to get Rebecca to stir, to put her down, have her somehow be protected behind him, but she was dead weight in his arms. He turned back. "I'm real impressed with a guy who beats his wife. Takes guts. A real man."

"You put down your kid I'll show you a real man."

"You and your son Tom here. Two on one. That's about your speed, isn't it, Phil?"

"What's your speed, asshole?"

Hardy squared away on Tom. "That's for *you* to figure out." He paused, considered, decided against anything, moving forward. "Get out of my way. Right now. Anybody here gets touched you're going to wish you weren't born."

"Oooh, tough guy!"

Hardy the Vulcan nodded. "If that's what it takes," and started walking, Frannie a step behind him. First Phil, then Tom, stepped aside onto the lawn. As soon as they were past them, Hardy moved sideways and let Frannie go by, covering her back. With macho desperadoes like these, he knew a rock wasn't out of the question.

Her hands were shaking and she had some trouble with the door so he stepped in, turned the key and pushed it open. Before he entered himself, he turned around. "The next time I look out here, you guys had better be gone. Go sleep it off before you get into real trouble."

Phil pointed a finger at him. "You go near my wife again, Hardy . . ."

Frannie got sick — all day out in the sun, the outburst at the ballpark, the tension out front. Hardy tended to her, ran her a cool bath and did all the kid stuff, getting them down before he tucked Frannie in. It was still light outside.

He went to his chair in the living room, put on some classical music — was Freeman getting to him? — and started reading the paperback of *A Brief History of Time*, recommended by both Moses and Abe, separately. Black holes, the Big Bang, String Theory, maybe even God.

But he couldn't concentrate.

Or rather he couldn't get the confrontation out of his mind. He was racing, the adrenalin pumped and nowhere to go. How *had* they found where he lived. He'd given Nancy his home telephone number, a mistake. He knew that a reverse listing, even of an unlisted number, was as close as the nearest phone-company employee, and PacBell was probably the biggest employer in the state. Stupid.

He considered options, several illegal — going back out to Phil's house with a handgun, make the point a little more strongly that he didn't want them coming around anymore. Go back without the gun. Call the police, report Phil's battery of his wife? Report tonight's disturbance and threat? But he remembered Glitsky's words — random mischief just wasn't a crime, wasn't a police matter in San Francisco anymore.

He wondered what Phil had done — might be doing — to Nancy when he got home with his own unspent load of adrenalin. After Tom left, then what?

He picked up the telephone and got the number for Park Station. It might be a dead night, some red-hot young patrol person wanting to make some bones, do a little more than the minimum. Nothing ventured . . . it might do a little good.

"I'm not giving a name," Hardy said, "and this is not an emergency, but you might want to send a car . . ."

At the Shamrock it wasn't dead but it was slow. Sunday night. The new man — Hardy's replacement — was behind the bar. The juke was going steadily, not too loud — the Shamrock's usual mix of mostly old rock and roll and Irish folksongs. Since the day two years before when Moses had finally removed and ceremoniously smashed the '45 of "The Unicorn" — "green alligators and long-necked geese, some hump-back camels and chimpanzees" — Hardy didn't think there was a loser in the box.

On his second Guinness, Hardy was in a game of "301" with one of the locals named Ronnie. Ronnie was one side or the other of thirty, a piano player in a band that had the night off. He also illustrated children's books. Ronnie was a class act, evidently talented, certainly a match for Hardy at darts. He also possessed a deal of gray matter.

"My problem with it," he was saying, pegging his own customs at the board, "is I have a hard time imagining some brother or father letting their own sister, or daughter — specially daughter — get executed for a murder they committed."

"She's a long way from executed. If she gets off the worst of it is they put her through a very bad time."

"A murder trial is some serious bad time."

"Try living with these guys."

Ronnie retrieved his round — two twenties and a five — drew a line through the "182" on the chalkboard and without a pause, without even seeming to look at the board, scribbled in "137." Even dumb dart throwers got good at subtraction — and Ronnie was a computer.

Hardy stepped to the line. "Could be just bad luck. They didn't know she was even going to be charged. So now they're just waiting to see what happens."

Triple twenty, a good start. He took a sip of the stout.

"You know," Ronnie said, "I just thought of something — what if one of them was trying to kill her, too — I mean kill all of them — and she just didn't happen to be home?"

Hardy stopped, his dart poised.

Ronnie was into it. "Do you know who's the beneficiary if the whole family's wiped out at once?" Hardy's dart sailed, a second triple-twenty. Three in a row — a "180" round — was worth a free drink in any bar in the city. "Give me a break," Ronnie said. Then: "Did he have any other family? The husband? Who might have inherited anything?"

"I don't know," Hardy said. "It's a good question."

He threw the third dart, which kissed the flights of the other two but landed a millimeter above them in the "20" but outside the triple ring.

"Not a bad round," Ronnie said.

"Not bad."

25

That man was the devil."

Penny Roman, mother of Melissa, who had died from the botched abortion attempt, believed it. She was not old but somehow conveyed age — her hair was frosted to a flat glaze, her make-up heavy. She wore a calico print grannie dress with a frilly collar that had probably been designed for a teenager and the effect, as she walked in her flip-flops, carrying a tray with coffee and mugs, was nearly-grotesque.

"Now, Pen." Her husband Cecil sported a clipped graying mustache, a pencil in his ear, over-the-counter reading glasses, green slacks. "He might have been in the hands of the devil, doing the work of the devil . . ."

"He was the devil."

Cecil shrugged at Hardy. "It's been very hard. You can't imagine."

"I'm sorry."

He was almost sorrier that he'd come out here, by Mission Dolores, to the thousand-square-foot house with the feeling of doors and windows that never opened. Jesus and Mary peered down from three framed prints in the small room where they all sat, cramped and airless, Hardy and Cecil on the chintz-covered sofa and Penny on the front half of a wing-back chair. An oversized, ornately framed picture of their daughter Melissa smiled at Hardy from the end table. Cecil wheeled up a little metal portable stand for the coffee tray and their cups.

The Romans were an unturned stone that he had discussed with Freeman, who had upbraided him for his scruples about whether or not the Romans had actually ever even dreamed of hurting Larry Witt. The question was: Could he point at them? Could they, however tangentially, deflect the prosecution's case?

He also didn't love the idea that he was here on this Tuesday morning under false pretenses, keeping the appointment he had made with them yesterday after telling them he was a policeman. If Terrell or Glitsky couldn't or wouldn't do it . . .

When he had been an Assistant District Attorney Hardy had gone shopping one day in South San Francisco at the badge store. Badges were neither sanctioned nor forbidden by the office — everyone realized that sometimes they came in handy, especially with people whose English might not be perfect and who were used to looking at badges, who knew essentially what they meant even if some of the nuances were missing.

So he had been Officer Hardy on the phone, and now he had a badge. They had let him right in.

"This is just routine, especially after this much time. We keep trying to catch up. Someday, maybe." Hardy smiled ingratiatingly, sipped his coffee and opened the manila folder he had brought with him. The folder did not contain a police report on the reported vandalism to Dr. Witt's car. Instead, Hardy had borrowed for the morning his own copy of the police report on his client Mr. Frankl — the man who had thought — erroneously as it had turned out — that he had a defense for DUI. The Romans did not notice the deception.

"What does he say about us?"

Cecil was trying to see something he recognized in the folder. Hardy moved it away. "Frankly, he accuses you of breaking into his car, stealing his radio . . ."

"That's ridiculous!" Penny spilled coffee over into her saucer. "He's a liar, too."

"He's not anything anymore, mam. He's dead."

"Yes, I know that. Of course." Her lips tightened, trying to hold it in and failing. "And I'm glad he is."

"Now, Pen." Cecil reached his left hand across the table and laid it on his wife's knee. "We have to be Christians here. Hate the sin but love the sinner."

"I can't, I can't do it."

Cecil patted the knee absently. His attention back at Hardy, his hand stayed where it was and it made him sit crookedly. "Dr. Witt was a sinner, Officer. But that doesn't mean we broke into his car." He gestured around the room. "Do we look like the . . . like we steal radios out of cars? Why would we? What would it prove? Would it bring our daughter back?"

Hardy was beginning to think it was pretty likely

that, in fact, they hadn't broken into Dr. Witt's car. If anyone had. He jotted a reminder to ask Jennifer.

"You say Dr. Witt was a sinner, though. Did you know him personally?"

Hardy saw the tendons of Cecil's left hand rise up. He was squeezing his wife's knee hard. There was no reaction from her — Cecil's calm was chilling. "Dr. Witt was an abortionist, Officer. He killed our daughter."

They went through it, as Hardy knew they would have to. Penny began to cry, silently, unmoving. To them both, it was a seamless tale of evil's cause and effect — their daughter's unfortunate lust, her sin, not accepting God's will and bringing to fruit the life she had created, allowing Witt to turn the blade on her baby, finally casting her lot with the abortionists, the killers and — as Cecil and Penny had known would happen — they wound up killing her.

Hardy closed the folder.

"He deserved what he got." Penny couldn't hold herself in any longer. Cecil's hand tightened again. "We read about it in the papers, naturally. The Lord takes care of His own."

"I think someone else took care of Dr. Witt," Hardy said.

"He wasn't the Lord's, Officer. He was the devil. He was the last instrument of Melissa's torture. We never even saw his car. I don't know what kind of car he had." Penny began crying. "We didn't know anything about him. Now he's coming back from the dead to punish us some more."

Hardy was standing up, wanting out of there. "No, mam, he's not. He's not going to punish you. I'm closing his file and we're going to forget all about it. I believe you."

Gradually, the fire went out. Penny sat back, deflated, managing a weak "thank you."

Cecil walked with him to the door, took a couple of steps outside. It was another clear morning, with a light breeze. The Sutro Tower sparkled in the sun a mile away. Cecil stared at it for a long moment. "It does get meted out, you know. Punishment."

"We hope so." Hardy the cop, playing the role.

"I'm talking about him, about Dr. Witt."

Hardy waited.

"You know, after he killed Melissa, before he was killed himself, I knew he was living up there in his fine house, making all kinds of money, profiting from his sins . . ."

Hardy wondered if Cecil knew that Witt had volunteered for his work at the Mission Hills Clinic. But this wasn't the time to tell him.

"And I know that's the way in this world. Sinners prosper. But once in a while we see proof. We see some justice here in this world. It gets meted out."

"Yes, sir." They shook hands.

It wasn't until he was back downtown, parking at Sutter Street, that he realized what Cecil had said. Penny may have believed she knew — they knew — nothing about Dr. Witt, but Cecil obviously knew he lived in a fine house up by Sutro Tower. And he had known that before he'd read about it in the papers.

Hardy talked to Jennifer and learned that Larry's car had been vandalized but he hadn't reported it to the police. What were the police going to do about it? He'd simply gotten it fixed, bought a new radio. That's what you did. Insurance had covered it.

Larry had been an only child and his parents had died long ago. The Witt family had been alone in the world and they felt like it. That was why, she said, Larry was so protective, wouldn't let her go out on her own, wanted to know where she was all the time — so he could be sure she was all right, that the family was safe.

She and Larry had agreed that they didn't want Phil and Nancy to be Matt's guardians. So Larry had asked one of his cousins — Laurie something who lived down in Orange County — if she'd take the responsibility if it ever came down to that.

But all that notwithstanding, Jennifer's family — as closest next of kin — in fact would have inherited if Jennifer had been killed along with Larry and Matt.

Still, after all that, and though he'd be happy if it turned out that Tom or Phil or even the Romans had had a hand in Larry Witt's murder, Hardy didn't really believe any of them had. He was reaching.

After his day with her physicians, his gut told him that Jennifer was probably guilty of what she'd been charged with. He'd just about come around to believing, as Freeman did, that she had killed first-husband Ned and second-husband Larry to stop them from beating her. And somehow, tragically, by mistake, Matt had gotten in the way.

Frannie put her hand up against the Plexiglas and Jennifer did the same. They stared at one another for a long moment. Frannie hadn't really planned to visit Jennifer again. She'd left the kids with Erin, intended to go shopping.

Maybe it had been the scene with Jennifer's father and brother, maybe she just wanted reassurance that they weren't really so dangerous. Maybe she felt a little guilty, starting something with Jennifer she wasn't prepared to follow through on. She wasn't sure — it was complicated, but the fact was that she was here now.

Jennifer broke the silence. "You don't look so good. Are you all right?"

Slowly at first, then gradually building into a torrent of words, surprising herself, Frannie told about her fight with her brother Moses, the trouble with Dismas that seemed to be getting a life of its own, her guilt over leaving her children — again — with Erin Cochran, Rebecca's grandmother. Only at the end did she get to Phil and Tom DiStephano and their threat last night.

"My father and brother came to your house? Why did they do that?"

"I think to beat up Dismas. Maybe just threaten him. They were pretty drunk, I think. But it scared me to death."

Jennifer's eyes went to the hands pressed together on either side of the glass. "Those idiots. It never ends." She let out a long breath. "What were they threatening him about?"

"Something about molesting your mother. Dismas told me he'd gone and seen her —"

"I know. And my father had beaten her up. He told me that, too."

Silence.

Frannie was scared. She'd been frightened all morning, jumping at little noises, when the telephone rang, imagining the rooms and their house violated, the door broken down, the windows shattered. Angry, or embarrassed, or both, she'd had no heart to discuss it with Dismas before he'd gone out.

"I just talked to him again, you know. Your husband. He wanted to know if . . . he wanted to know some things about my parents. He didn't mention anything about last night."

"Was he here?"

Jennifer shook her head. "He called on the phone. It's a hassle getting up here anyway and he just had a couple of questions. No, you and he are . . . separate." She paused. "Men are separate. That's just the way it is. I tell them what they need to know. They ask me questions and I answer them."

"So what about your father? What do you think he's going to do?"

"I don't know. Against another man? I don't know. Or my brother either."

"Do you think they'd hurt our kids? If they touched . . ." Frannie stopped, unable to say it.

"You'd kill them?"

Frannie nodded, startled by the sudden realization that she would kill to protect her children. "Is that what happened?" she asked. "Larry started hitting Matt?"

For a moment, she thought Jennifer was just going to nod and say yes." But there was a withdrawal, something in her posture, her eyes. Her hand came away from the Plexiglas.

"I wouldn't worry," she said finally. "I think it's okay. My father won't do anything. Besides, men only hit when they think you won't hit back." Jennifer sat forward, legs crossed. "I'd kill for a cigarette," she said. And added, "One time Ned, my first husband, decided this dentist was coming on to me and he went over, pounded his chest a couple of times — or at least he said he did — then came back and beat me up." Her face broke into a sad, almost wistful smile. "Same as always."

"What did you do?" Frannie was leaning forward, her hand alone pressed to the glass. "How could you let that go on?"

Jennifer sighed again, crossing her arms and staring into the middle distance above them.

"I'm listening," Frannie said.

Jennifer's hand moved to the Plexiglas. Her face seemed to harden with the memory, whatever it was. She was whispering, intent, eyes on Frannie's. "You don't want to know."

Hardy had mentioned it more or less casually — an annoyance more than anything else — but Abe Glitsky did not like the fact that Phil and Tom DiStephano had gone proactive on his best friend. It wasn't so much the threat itself — after all, nothing had really happened, no serious crime had taken place. Glitsky's view that all but the most heinous acts went uninvestigated and unpunished in San Francisco did not mean, however, that uncivilized behavior was okay by him. His days as a beat cop were not so far behind him that he didn't remember the force a policeman could bring to bear on an individual who needed a lesson in etiquette or control.

Phil DiStephano was a plumber who worked out of a medium-sized shop near the Kezar Pavilion. The dispatcher told Glitsky that Phil and two of the other guys were out to lunch and ought to be back within fifteen minutes, so he decided to wait.

It wasn't that long. Glitsky stood up, the scar through his lips stretching into a white line as he found himself enduring the half-hostile stares of the three rednecks. Half-Caucasian, sometimes he found himself hating white people more than he ever hated all but the most repugnant of blacks. He thought it was probably a flaw in his character. He'd work on it someday, he really would.

The dispatcher said something and the biggest of the three men turned around. He spoke in mannered polite tones, ostensibly cooperative. "I'm Phil DiStephano, is there a problem?"

Glitsky had flashed his badge earlier and no doubt the dispatcher had passed along the information that this casually dressed strapping black man was the law. The other two plumbers flanked Phil but seemed to be waiting for an excuse now to go to the back room or their truck or wherever it was they went while they waited to fix drains and unplug sewer lines. He took out his badge again. "If you could spare a couple of minutes."

He motioned outside — a jog of his head. Opening the door, he didn't look back, but went halfway across the sidewalk and turned, arranging it so that the sun was behind him. When he turned, Phil had followed him and stood off a few steps, squinting, beginning to sweat.

Glitsky let him.

He took it for about ten seconds, which seemed like a very long time. "We got a problem here, Officer? I've got some calls I've got to —"

"Dismas Hardy." Glitsky wanted it so quiet that Phil would have to listen carefully.

"What's that?"

Glitsky repeated it. "Your daughter's attorney? Guy you visited last night?"

Phil put up a hand. "Hey, now you wait a minute. Hardy came by *my* house. I don't know what he's telling you but he's the one . . ."

Phil went on a while longer, the sweat now shining across his forehead. When he wound down, Glitsky asked him if he was all finished.

"I don't know if I am." Phil seemed heartened by Glitsky's tolerance, his quiet patience — arms folded, hearing him out. "I'm thinking maybe I should call in some report on him, you know. He's gonna keep up this kind of harassment —"

"I'm harassing you?"

"No! No, I didn't mean that. I meant him coming to my place, bothering my wife."

It had gone on long enough. Glitsky thought that another of his flaws was that he hadn't sufficiently enjoyed burning up ants under a magnifying glass when he was a kid. He nodded his head, as though he'd taken in all of Phil's information, considered it carefully. "Hardy didn't bother your wife."

"Sure he did. He was there and —"

"And if I hear that you've threatened him again, you're going to find life in this town very hard. You're going to get speeding tickets. You're going to get towed whenever you park."

Phil was moving into Righteous Indignation, Act I. "Are you threatening me?"

"It's entirely possible you could even lose your job. Bosses don't like employees who have the cops down on them. It's bad for business."

"I don't have to listen to this. What's your name again? You can't do this."

Glitsky's scar shone bright through a cold smile. "I'll bet I can." He lowered his voice. "The name is Inspector Sergeant Abraham Glitsky — you need me to spell it? I'll give you my badge number if you want."

Phil stood there, the sweat running down his face. Glitsky moved a step closer. "Hardy's a friend of mine. I'd make him a friend of yours, too. In fact, I'd say it's in your best interest to see that nothing bad happens to him — because if it does, I might be tempted to think you were part of it, and that would be unfortunate for you."

He turned and left Phil sweating in the sun. Getting into his car, he heard and ignored the explosion of obscenity. He had expected it and it rolled off. He had delivered his message, put out the word. It was what he'd come down for.

26

By Friday, in spite of her assurances to the contrary, Donna Bellows had not called back with news of any connection between Crane & Crane and Larry Witt. Freeman was chomping for any crumbs he might use at the trial, so Hardy, covering the bases, thought that he'd call down to LA again, though he entertained little hope that there was even a tangential link between Simpson Crane's murder in Los Angeles and Larry Witt's in San Francisco.

On reflection, the whole thing was so tenuous that he didn't want to pursue it at all. Which was why he had hoped Donna Bellows would have called him back — so he wouldn't have to chase this phantom himself. Nevertheless, he was doing his job, following leads that so far led nowhere. Freeman wanted them all to juggle, see how much he could keep in the air — as he'd often done in the past — sufficiently dazzle the jury with his legerdemain so they wouldn't notice it was being done with mirrors.

Look this way, now look at this. What about this? Whoa! There's a neat trick. Anything to distract, to draw attention away from the evidence they both thought had a good chance of damning their client.

Hardy's feet were on his desk. The door out to his hallway was open and so was the window over Sutter Street behind him. Faintly, he smelled the Bay. The cross-ventilation felt good in the room. The phone down in Los Angeles was ringing and he picked up a quick dart and tossed it across at his board — it landed on the "1," a quarter-inch from "20."

He spoke to a monotonic receptionist, who put him on hold. Waiting, he threw another dart, this time hit the "20," and was talking to an extremely formal secretary.

"Mr. Crane is in a meeting right now. May I help you?"

Hardy tended to respect secretaries — even formal ones like Phyllis — but he had a hard time with the Secretary-as-Keeper-of-the-Gate school. He thought that in the long run, for important issues, it wasted far more time than it saved. Principals ought to talk to principals.

He was polite. "If Mr. Crane is in, I'll be glad to hold. It's a matter of some urgency regarding a murder trial."

There was a sigh, another long hold, then a weary man's voice. "Todd Crane."

Hardy raised his victory fist in the air, introducing himself, expressing his condolences. But Crane kept it to the point. "Maxine said this was about a murder trial. How can I help you?"

Hardy explained about the Post-it he'd found under Larry Witt's blotter with Crane & Crane's number written on it, the word "No" underlined and circled several times.

"I'm afraid I don't . . . What was this victim's name again?"

"Larry Witt. Dr. Larry Witt."

"Sorry. I'm drawing a blank on that."

Hardy took a shot. "How about the Yerba Buena Medical Group? YBMG?"

"Okay. Was Witt with them? We handle their business development. That's Jody Bachman." He spelled it for Hardy. "You want me to connect you?"

The telephone — presumably in Jody Bachman's office — rang ten times before Bachman's voice mail picked it up. Thinking here we go again, Hardy left his name and number and a brief description of what he wanted.

He got up, threw the last dart on his desk and hit the "5" on the other side of "20," then turned around and looked down out the window onto Sutter Street. In spite of Bachman not being in, he found himself somewhat encouraged.

There was, finally, a link between Larry Witt and Crane & Crane. Sure, he knew that there would have had to be since the Post-it had had Crane's number on it, but the relationship had proved elusive to establish. And now he'd done that. Like the cross-ventilation, it felt good. Finding out facts felt good.

Of course, what those facts supported — what they even meant — was another issue altogether, and since it was Friday afternoon, Hardy didn't feel much in the mood to pursue that line. Facts related to the "other dudes" line of defense seemed to lead to a fork in the road to the truth that led to a dead end.

He had uncovered a fact. But did it lead anywhere?

The police in Los Angeles thought, although they couldn't prove it, that a hit man had murdered Simpson Crane and his wife. Simpson's firm — one of the partners anyway — handled the business development of the medical group that Larry Witt belonged to. Even a genius like David was going to have a difficult time establishing any provable causality between those two bits of data.

At least Hardy felt like he'd done his job. Bachman would call him back about details before they really got into the trial, which probably wouldn't be for another month or so. Glitsky had consented, reluctantly, to see what he could find out about the Romans on the day of Larry's murder. Over the next weeks he might see Nancy DiStephano again and try to get a line on where Phil and Tom had been on the Monday after Christmas.

So Hardy had "other dudes" by the carload. For the time being, his job would be to assist David Freeman, research legal issues that might come up, prepare for his own phase of the trial, the penalty phase, if Jennifer got convicted.

He was going to see what David Freeman could do with his brains, his showmanship, his fabled, much ballyhooed *je ne sais quoi.*

PART THREE

27

On Monday, July 19, Oscar Thomasino had slammed down his gavel and sent the case of *The People of the State of California v. Jennifer Lee Witt* to Department 25, the courtroom of Judge Joan Villars. That formality was quickly followed by a flurry of motions made and denied. Jury selection would begin as scheduled on August 23.

David Freeman had immediately filed his pro forma Penal Code 995 motion for dismissal, arguing that there was insufficient evidence to proceed and, as expected, Judge Villars had thrown that out. If a grand jury had found sufficient evidence to indict on three counts of murder, it was an unusually brave or foolish judge who would cast aside their decision.

Jennifer's hair had grown out, her bruises had disappeared. When she appeared in the courtroom for the first time flanked by two bailiffs, a buzz went up in the gallery. The defendant looked like a movie star.

Gone was the red "jail escapee" jumpsuit; gone were the leg irons and handcuffs. Judge Villars, prodded by Freeman, had agreed that they would be prejudicial to his client. Also, there would be no need to shackle her to her chair at the defense table. Although Jennifer had broken out of jail, even Powell admitted that there was little risk that she would bolt and escape the courtroom.

Jennifer wore low heels, nude hosiery, a stylish, muted coral dress with a hem an inch above her very attractive knees. Freeman had arranged to have someone come into the jail and do her hair, and now it shone clean, blonde, just long enough to be feminine and proper. Diamond stud earrings. A tasteful touch of make-up.

They led her in before the judge entered, while the members of the media as well as the eighty potential jurors were finding their seats behind the rail. Hardy, who had been talking with Freeman at the defense table on the left side of the courtroom, heard the noise in the gallery and looked up, stopping in mid-sentence. "My goodness," he said.

Freeman half-turned. A few flash bulbs went off — Villars would put a stop to that as soon as she came in, but for now Jennifer was fair game. She smiled in her ambiguous way — either shy or posing — and more bulbs went off.

The bailiffs delivered her to Freeman, who put an avuncular arm around her waist, guiding her to a chair between himself and Hardy. "You look good," Freeman told her. "Just right."

"I'm scared," Jennifer said.

Freeman rubbed a hand over her back. "It's all right, that's natural. You just sit here and relax."

Hardy noticed that her hands were shaking. She clasped them together on the table in front of her, her fingers tightly intertwined. Freeman came around on her right and covered them with one of his gnarled paws.

Over the past weeks Hardy had seen the earlier animosity between lawyer and client dissipate as they worked together fashioning a defense. Now, though Freeman still apparently believed that Jennifer was lying about her innocence, he had somehow convinced her that he was her best and most trusted friend — that he, personally, was her only salvation. Accordingly, she had come to cling to him, her life raft in a stormy sea. That was all right with Hardy, who might yet have his own role to play, and it would not be as liaison between Jennifer and David Freeman.

It was 9:23. Villars would enter in seven minutes. Dean Powell and his associate, a young Assistant DA named Justin Morehouse, were conferring, shuffling papers on their table a dozen feet to Hardy's right.

"Jennifer."

Dr. Ken Lightner had come up to the rail, and Jennifer turned in her chair, then stood and put her arms around him. One of the bailiffs came moving up fast, but Freeman held out a hand and somehow restrained him from breaking them up. It was over in seconds anyway, Jennifer pulling away, kissing Lightner's cheek.

Hardy made a mental note — probably Freeman did too — to caution Jennifer about these kinds of public embraces. They could too easily be misinterpreted. Both Hardy and Freeman knew about the bond between Jennifer and Lightner, but it would be difficult to explain to a jury. Woman accused of killing two of her husbands hugs another man as her trial begins. No, it wouldn't look good.

Jennifer, Freeman and Lightner were huddled, whispering together at the railing that separated the gallery from the courtroom proper. Walter Terrell had appeared and was having a few words with Powell and Morehouse.

Even though he would play no active role in this part of the trial, Hardy's mouth was dry, his stomach jumpy and sour. He turned in his chair to pour himself a glass of water in time to see the door open behind the judge's bench, the clerk intoning that all should rise, Department 25 of the Superior Court for the City and County of San Francisco was in session, Judge Joan Villars presiding.

The concept of *voir dire* — the questioning and selection of jurors — had undergone a sea change in California since the passage in June 1991 of Proposition 115. Before that time, attorneys on both sides of a case were given a wide latitude in questions they could ask prospective jurors. What did they do for a living? How many brothers and sisters did they have? What were their hobbies? Favorite books and/or movies? Feelings about puppies? Cats? Goldfish? Almost anything went if it might serve to bring out a prospective juror's character. Often the questions were thinly disguised speeches designed to sway prospective jurors. And because of this, jury selection in a capital case such as this one could easily take as long as two months and in some cases longer.

Since Proposition 115, however, *voir dire* was conducted by the judge and — as the proposition had contemplated — tended to go much more quickly. Attorneys could supply the judge with a list of questions they wanted to see asked, but often these were ignored. Likewise, in the case of Jennifer Witt, Freeman had asked Villars if he might ask direct questions of some of the jurors. The answer had been no.

Lawyers for the prosecution and the defense still had their twenty peremptory challenges — the right to dismiss a prospective juror for any reason whatsoever or no reason at all — but the empaneling of the jury was now much more outside the perceived control of either counsel. It was the judge's show.

Jurors were asked if they had read about the case in the newspapers, if they could sit through a three-month trial and, perhaps most importantly, if, in the appropriate case, they could vote for the death penalty. Out of the first eighty jurors, after perhaps three days of questioning, maybe four would be available for service and they would be told to come back at the end of September. They would be part of the pool from which the twelve jurors and six alternates would be chosen. Then Villars would send for eighty more.

Except for the half-moon reading glasses, Judge Villars was Hardy's notion of an elderly Joan of Arc. With her helmet of gray hair over a benign and handsome face, Villars might strike a casual passerby on the street as a grade-school principal, fair but firm, perhaps even with a rogue streak of humor.

But as Freeman had told Hardy when they had drawn her for this trial, looks could be deceiving. Villars was close to humorless, an authoritarian on the bench. Freeman did not think it was purely the luck of the draw — although it was supposed to be — that had brought this capital case to her courtroom. He fancied that he smelled the sulfurous machinations of Dean Powell behind the scenes.

Villars was also the least likely judge in Superior Court to be reversed on appeal. If Powell got a conviction in her courtroom, there was a likelihood that it would stick.

Hardy did not like something else — Judge Villars wasn't likely to overturn a jury's recommendation for the death penalty, if it came all the way to that. When they had drawn her, Hardy had tried to convince Freeman to challenge out of her department. Similar to their rights with jurors, attorneys for either side in California had one peremptory challenge of the judge assigned to any given case. The result in theory was to keep judges from getting too uppity, inserting too much of their personalities or beliefs into trials designed to be objective. If a judge made things too tough for the prosecution, for example, the DA's office could decide to challenge that person "out of the building," and a few judges over the years had found their careers ended when they had been too free with mandating from the bench some uniquely San Francisco notions of fair play.

Legally, in theory, judges had tremendous responsibility and leeway — even in a capital case, months of a prosecutor's hard work and a jury's long-contemplated decision could be overridden by any judge who decided — for almost any defensible reason — that justice was not being done. But it was also true that any judge who exercised that privilege too often might be off the bench.

Hardy had wanted to challenge Villars. In spite of her gender, she had acquired the reputation of being especially hard on women. Throughout her career she had, it seemed, leaned over backward to avoid giving the slightest appearance of favoritism to female attorneys, staff, defendants. A few years earlier she had been in the vanguard of a successful effort to dump the Chief Justice of the California Supreme Court — a woman — because of her "soft stand" on the death penalty.

Villars was nobody's pussycat, all right, but Freeman had been adamant. He *wanted* her. He'd been delighted with the choice. He could win with her.

Why? Because Freeman believed that Villars was, in fact, absolutely impartial, and very few other judges were. It wasn't that Villars was so tough on women — it was that she treated them exactly like she treated men. And in San Francisco, filled with vocal minority groups of every stripe, Judge Villars played it by the book. She thought men and women were equal before the law in every way. That was how she treated people and it was how she judged them — men, women, whites, blacks, Hispanics, gays, everybody.

So Freeman was confident that, with Villars on the bench, he stood the best chance of winning the guilty-or-innocent phase and wasn't inclined to challenge. The down side, of course, was that, if Freeman lost, Villars would be a very unsympathetic choice for judge in the penalty phase.

For the eighth time in five weeks, eighty people filed into the courtroom. The clerk read off twelve names and those people came out of the gallery and filed into the jury box. All eighty swore to answer truthfully any question pertaining to their qualifications to serve as jurors.

Judge Villars began: "Jennifer Lee Witt has been charged with three counts of murder in the first degree and special circumstances in an indictment returned by the grand jury for the State of California." She continued, asking the standard battery of initial questions: Did anyone on the panel know the defendant? The victim? How about the attorneys representing them? Had anyone been a victim of a violent crime? Did anyone have a policeman as a relative? A lawyer? A judge? Did anyone consider themselves familiar with the case from reports they'd seen on television or read in the newspapers? Had any of them been arrested? Hands went up in answer to each question, and the lawyers took notes.

And so it went. Jennifer leaning close to Freeman, occasionally turning to Hardy with a question or comment. They were making notes on their peremptory challenges, deciding who they would dismiss, although there wasn't much to go on.

Jury selection, even in the old days of *voir dire,* was, of course, no exact science. Now under the new rules it was close to a crap shoot. Did Juror Number 5 look like she was sympathetic to Jennifer? Would the young stud, Number 11, want to give Jennifer a break because she was so attractive, or would he identify with Larry Witt, a hard-working guy who got stuck with the wrong woman? How about the Plain Jane who was Number 9? Would she be jealous of Jennifer's looks, or would she perhaps see her as a misguided sister who had been maligned and unfairly accused?

None of the first twelve survived the initial questioning. Twelve more were called. By September 27 there were ninety-two people eligible to serve as jurors. All the others had been excused for "good cause," hardship or bias disclosed during the initial questioning. Only now did the lawyers use their peremptory challenges. Powell challenged eleven times. Freeman used all twenty of his. They picked six alternates.

28

The six weeks of jury selection had passed for Hardy in a kind of haze. San Francisco had its allotted two weeks of warmth in early September, and every workday Hardy, Freeman and Jennifer had sat at their table, Powell and his young assistant Morehouse over to their right, going over the same critical routine again and again.

It was grueling, detailed work that was emotionally and physically draining. Hardy was needed in court. Everything he might otherwise actively pursue — the "other dudes," for instance — had to get put on hold. Every night, after leaving the Hall of Justice, Hardy and Freeman would discuss prospective jurors and strategies until they began to babble, then they'd do it again the next day.

At home, Frannie held on. Her husband came home late, left early, was distracted when he was there. They went away on two of the weekends — once without the kids to a cabin in the pines around Lake Tahoe. They decided they would get through this and have a real life again someday.

Now it was Monday, October 4, the players were assembled, the gallery was full, and Dean Powell stood at last, ready to begin. Hardy thought that the contrast between him and David Freeman couldn't be greater. Powell radiated authority and personality. He wore a well-tailored dark suit with a blue tie — no need to emphasize the power with red or with pinstripes. His face, chiseled, strong and bronzed, wore an expression of amiable concern. Occasionally he would run his hand through the mane of white hair, the only combing it needed.

In the middle of the courtroom he turned to face the jury that had been empaneled over the past weeks. "Your Honor, Mr. Freeman, Mr. Hardy, ladies and gentlemen of the jury. I want to thank you all for giving up your valuable time for this most important of civic duties. All of us here" — Powell included the defense table with a sweeping gesture — "are grateful."

Freeman and Hardy exchanged glances. They both knew the defense would be within their rights to object to this little massaging of the jury by the prosecuting attorney. Such a welcome was really the judge's prerogative, but many attorneys on both sides often tried to show what nice people they really were underneath the lawyer costume. Freeman wasn't about to object — the jury would find it mean-spirited.

Most judges let the welcome party go on a bit. Villars did not. Her gavel came down with a crack. "Mr. Powell, I've already welcomed the jury and thanked them for their time. This is your opening statement. Let's hear it."

Hardy kept a straight face. Freeman brought a hand up, perhaps to cover a smile.

Powell bowed slightly toward the bench. "Of course. Sorry, Your Honor."

He turned back to the jury. There were four

men and eight women, five blacks, four whites, three female Hispanics. One retired doctor. Three housewives. Two unemployed. Four secretaries and an office manager. A parimutuel clerk. Perhaps two gay men. You could break it down any number of ways and it still came down to a guessing game. No one doubted that Villars had done a competent and quick job of it, and no one had much of a clue what any of these people were like except that they all professed to believe in the death penalty if warranted.

Powell smiled the low-wattage version. "Judge Villars has asked me to proceed with my opening statement, and that's what I'm going to do." He nodded, making a little eye contact here and there. "What is an opening statement? Well, it's really quite simple. I'm going to talk a little about the defendant in this case, Jennifer Lee Witt, and the three people she killed — two husbands and" . . . here Powell stopped for effect . . . "and her young son."

Another pause. "The roots of this case go back a long way, all the way to 1984. The People of the State of California believe and will prove to you, beyond any reasonable doubt, that Jennifer Witt, on or about the 17th of September of that year, injected her husband at the time, Edward Teller Hollis, with a lethal dose of atropine, which is a derivative of jimson weed, more commonly known as deadly nightshade."

Powell wasn't using theatrics, wasn't playing the personality game he did so well. Perhaps he had taken the early cue from Villars, but his version of events was beginning to come out free of gimmickry, straightforward and plausible.

"At the time of the death of Mr. Hollis, and while she was married to him, we will prove to you that Jennifer Witt was romantically involved with another man, a dentist, Dr. Harlan Poole. Atropine is a common medication, available in most dentists' offices and specifically available nine years ago in Dr. Poole's office. It is used to inhibit the flow of saliva."

As though stricken with dry mouth himself, Powell went to the prosecution table and drank from a glass of water. Hardy found himself getting thirsty. Freeman drank. Even Villars took a discreet sip on the bench.

Powell came back to the center of the room. "Why did Jennifer Witt kill her first husband? The prosecution will introduce to you exhibits that prove the existence of a life-insurance policy in the amount of seventy-five thousand dollars, payable to Jennifer Witt in the event of her husband's death. Within four months of the death of Mr. Hollis, Jennifer received that payment in full. Seventy-five thousand dollars was a lot of money in 1984."

"Objection, Your Honor." Freeman half-stood. He had to say something to break up Powell's rhythm, even though this was the most innocuous of his statements. But while it could be debated whether $75,000 was a lot of money in 1984, it couldn't be that the opinion was evidence. It wasn't.

Villars sustained Freeman but gave him a look. Opening statements could not argue the law and they could not editorialize, but a wide latitude was often given, and Villars was telling Freeman that if he was going to object to Powell's peccadilloes in these areas, she would sustain Powell if he tried to do the same to him. The interplay of the trial was beginning.

If Freeman's intent was to bump Powell's rhythm, he failed. The prosecutor was sailing and this objection was nothing to him. As soon as Villars said "sustained," he plunged ahead. "As all of you ladies and gentlemen of the jury are aware, this is a capital case, alleging special circumstances. And one of the special circumstances is that this killing of Edward Teller Hollis was a cold-blooded murder of a human being for monetary gain. It does not matter that this act occurred some years ago. There is no statute of limitations on murder."

Jennifer, sitting between Hardy and Freeman, sat ramrod stiff on the front half of her seat. Everything about her *seemed* in tight control, except her nostrils tended to flare with her breathing.

Powell looked directly at her and paused in his statement. Was it a challenge to him, her cold gaze of dismissal? He allowed himself a nod, almost friendly, and next to Hardy, Jennifer shifted.

"A year after her first husband's death, that is, in 1985, Jennifer married Larry Witt, who had left the woman who had put him through medical school . . ."

Freeman stood again, objecting. Again he was sustained, this time more forcefully. This was the beginning of what would possibly be many attempts at simple character assassination and Villars was giving Powell warning that she wasn't having it. It wasn't evidence. Don't try to introduce it.

It was a small good sign and Hardy made a note on his pad. Had the silent exchange between Jennifer and Powell lured him away from his game plan, or had it been an unintentional gaffe?

But the prosecutor had a lot more to get out and he had everybody listening. "In 1985 Jennifer married Larry Witt, who was just setting up a medical practice. They had a son, Matthew, the following year. As Dr. Witt's practice grew, they bought increasingly larger amounts of life insurance until, at the time of his death on December 28 of last year, Larry Witt was insured for two-and-a-half-million dollars."

This was the time for a pregnant pause, and Powell took it. A susurrous breath went through the courtroom.

"Two-and-a-half-million dollars, ladies and gentlemen. We will show you this policy as one of the People's exhibits, and you will see that it contains a clause providing for double indemnity should Larry Witt die a violent death. As he did. That brings the amount of the payment on his death to five-million dollars. And I needn't tell you that *that's* a lot of money in *any* year."

Powell glanced with a smile at Freeman, making nice-guy points with the jury. Freeman, who didn't do suave as a rule, gave his impression of a smile back. Villars picked up her gavel but reconsidered and put it back down.

"Of course, the presence of an insurance policy is no proof of murder. Let's be clear on this. We will show you — and prove to you beyond a reasonable doubt — that the actions of Jennifer Witt on the morning of Monday, December 28, will allow for no other explanation than that she shot her husband *and* son with her own handgun, then left her house in an effort to provide herself with an alibi for the time in question.

"Fortunately for the People of the State of California, we have two witnesses who will testify regarding this alibi. Between them, they will remove any doubt about Jennifer being in her home when the shots were fired. She was *there,* she had the *gun,* and she used it to kill her husband for his insurance.

"And finally, most tragically, we have young Matthew Witt."

Next to Hardy, Jennifer slumped slightly. The anger either had passed or given way to something more powerful. For the first time, she hung her head. Freeman looked over and put his hand over her lower arm. She looked back up.

"Frankly, we cannot tell you why Matthew Witt had to die on that Monday morning. But die he did, shot with the same gun as the one that had killed his father. We will even concede that it might have been a mistake — the boy could have accidentally come into the line of fire. He could have startled Jennifer —"

"Your Honor, please. These conjectures have no place in an opening statement."

Powell preempted the judge, apologizing. Freeman was right, he was sorry. He looked at the judge, slowly, up one row and back the next. He ticked the next points off with his fingers.

"Motive, means, opportunity. These *facts* remain, and we will prove them. And the *facts* will show that Jennifer Witt killed her husband for five-million dollars — *motive.* The murder weapon was her own gun, which she and her husband kept in the bedroom of her house — *means.* She was alone in the house with her husband and son when she turned the gun on them — *opportunity.* We will prove these beyond a reasonable doubt, and in so doing, will recommend that a person capable of these crimes has forfeited her right to live in our society. Such a person — male or female — should be given the ultimate penalty. Such a person should be condemned to death. Thank you."

In California, the defense has the option of delivering its own opening statement immediately after the prosecution's, somewhat as a rebuttal, or of waiting until the prosecution rests its case. Freeman had done it both ways in various trials in his career, and this time he was choosing the latter. He wasn't sure how things were going to break as the evidence accumulated, and he thought he would make more of an impression introducing things — if indicated — later on. He did not want to tip his hand.

The drawback to this way of proceeding was that it did seem, at the outset, to give the prosecution a lot of time in possession. Powell had barely sat down when Freeman announced he would be waiting — giving his opening statement at the beginning of the defense's case.

The prosecutor was quickly back up, calling Inspector Sergeant Walter Terrell as his first witness.

Freeman and Hardy had speculated on the order of witnesses, and neither of them had picked Terrell as leadoff. Looking younger than usual in slacks and an aviator jacket, Terrell aggressively pushed his way through the railing separating the gallery from the courtroom. Taking the oath, his eyes were everywhere.

"Why is he so nervous?" Jennifer asked.

"First murder trial." Freeman did not take his eyes off the inspector. "Mistake," he whispered half to himself.

"For us?" Jennifer turned to Hardy, who shook his head no. At least, he didn't think so. Freeman didn't answer, and Powell was moving forward, talking to the judge.

"Your Honor, for the record, we are going to be conducting this trial by first concentrating on the murder of Edward Teller Hollis. We will be calling witnesses again to testify when we get to the Larry and Matthew Witt phase of the trial, and Officer Terrell will be one such witness. I just wanted to make that clear."

Since this had been covered in pre-trial conferences with Villars, there was no objection from Freeman.

Powell turned to Terrell. "Officer Terrell, could you please tell the jury how you came to be involved in the investigation of the murder of Edward Hollis?"

Terrell nodded, swallowing, trying to smile. "That's Ned, is that right? The first husband?"

There was a brief chorus of nervous laughter, some even from the jury box. Terrell reacted to it, offended. He didn't mean to make anyone laugh. Powell remained calm. "If it please the court, we'll refer to Edward Teller Hollis as Ned

Hollis." Back to Terrell, he repeated his question.

"I am an inspector with the homicide department. Last December I was the investigating officer in the homicide of Larry and Matthew Witt. In the course of doing background on the suspect, the defendant, Mrs. Witt, I asked about her first husband. She told me he had died of a drug overdose and that she'd collected on an insurance policy. I thought that was a coincidence worth looking into."

All this was true, and Hardy realized that calling Terrell maybe wasn't such a mistake at all. Terrell's testimony would establish the similarities between the alleged motives behind the two homicides, and would do it before introducing any of the evidence that linked the murders to Jennifer. Actually it seemed a pretty slick opening and Hardy wondered what Freeman was going to do about it. Come right at it and try to knock it down, was the only answer.

"Your Honor."

In the courtroom, Freeman's voice took on a more sonorous tone, which couldn't be anything but purposeful. Everything Freeman did on this stage was, if possible, rehearsed, although nothing appeared to be. Freeman's voice in other situations tended to the gruff — with a coarse edge, low and guttural. Here, rising, the personification of gentle reason, there was authority, but the tone was that of a kindly grandfather.

Villars waited while Freeman got all the way up. It took longer than it had to, but the trial had just begun and the judge could be expected to incline toward patience.

"Your Honor," he repeated, "it's a little early for coincidences. No evidentiary link has been established."

As Hardy knew, motives were Terrell's weakness. The young inspector, red-faced now, veins visible on his neck, half-stood, leaning forward in the witness box. "The man was killed and she collected the insurance, what do you want?"

Bam bam bam.

Villars eyes were on fire, although she controlled her voice. "Inspector Terrell, that's enough. Mr. Freeman is addressing the court, not you. Is that clear?"

Terrell got himself back down. He straightened his jacket, still angry.

"I asked you a question, Inspector. Is that clear?"

"Yes, Your Honor. Sorry."

Villars nodded once, apparently holding no grudge, satisfied. Even the glaring eye was gone. Nothing personal but make no mistake — there was going to be order in her court.

For two seconds Villars looked at the ceiling, then back down to Freeman. "The objection is sustained. Mr. Powell, you'll have to be a little more specific." She turned to the jury box, from firebrand to functionary in a few seconds. "Ladies and gentlemen, please disregard the inspector's comments about coincidence. It's up to you to make the connections between facts, remember that." Back to the prosecutor. "Mr. Powell?"

Powell, who had had the control of the courtroom taken from him in less than the time it took to tie his shoes, was suddenly hyper-aware. His first witness was now a demonstrable hothead with a fraction of his original credibility and they had a long way to go. He smiled his unruffled smile. "Officer Terrell, let's take a new line, shall we?"

He walked Terrell — carefully, a step at a time — through the interview with Jennifer, leaving out reference to the reasons they had finally gone back and exhumed. The jury, as Villars had said, would have to make that leap. The fact was that they *had* exhumed, and that they had found a concentration of atropine in the left thigh. Powell did not go near any question of how it might have gotten there.

Ned did have an insurance policy for seventy-five-thousand dollars. Jennifer had provided a copy of the policy and the check from her tax records. Here it is, ladies and gentlemen of the jury, People's Exhibit 1. Jennifer was the beneficiary. Here's her canceled check, People's 2. That's all for the prosecution, Inspector Terrell, thanks very much. Here comes your cross-examination.

Hardy was sure he wasn't alone in the impression that Terrell had gone up there intending to say a lot more, stay a while longer, make more of a splash.

He was still, obviously, pumped up both from nerves and adrenalin. Freeman was playing that against him, shuffling some papers, fumbling up out of his chair, straightening his wrinkled tie. It wasn't quite slow enough to prompt Villars into moving him along, but it clearly was playing all hell with Terrell.

Finally, finally, Freeman got to the center of

the courtroom. "Good morning," he said genially, and waited some more. The gambit threw Terrell further off-stride, until at last he nodded and mumbled something like a greeting back.

"Now, Inspector Terrell, you have testified that Ned Hollis had a seventy-five-thousand-dollar insurance policy and that Jennifer Witt was the beneficiary. That's correct, isn't it?"

The witness looked up at the judge for an instant, then to Powell, finally back to Freeman. "That's right."

"What did Mrs. Witt tell you would happen if she died instead of Ned, then what?"

Another pause, thinking about it. "Then Ned would have gotten the money."

"In other words, it was a joint policy — a husband and wife, if-one-of-us-dies-the-house-is-paid-for kind of policy."

"Yes, that's right."

"And, in fact, did Jennifer tell you that she and Ned owned a house together at this time?"

"Yes, they did."

"And you checked it out, and that was the truth, wasn't it?"

"Yes, it was."

"In your investigation, did you come upon any records on the value of that house?"

Terrell cast a what's-all-this-about look at Powell. Freeman knew that if Powell objected to hearsay — what someone had told Terrell out of court — that the objection would be sustained. But Freeman could prove the value of the house anyway, with other records and witnesses if he had to. And the jury would remember that the prosecutor had tried to keep it from them.

Powell said nothing. Terrell answered that yes, Jennifer and Ned had bought a shoebox down near Daly City, putting down twenty-thousand dollars.

"So their loan was eighty thousand dollars?"

"I don't know. I'd assume so."

"You know they put down twenty thousand dollars, but you don't know what their loan was?"

Powell stood up, trying to save Terrell, at least for later. "Your Honor. Relevance?"

Villars was curt. "I think so. Go on, Mr. Freeman. Inspector?"

"Their loan was around eighty thousand dollars, yes."

Freeman did a little awkward half-turn, almost a pirouette toward the jury. "And, again in your investigations, did you discover whatever became of that loan?"

Terrell pulled at his suddenly tight collar. "I believe Mrs. Witt paid it off."

"With the insurance money?"

"Yes, I believe so."

"You believe so or you know so, Inspector?"

"I know so. She paid off the loan."

"Indeed she did." Freeman went back to his table and took out a fat photocopied document. He had it marked as Defense Exhibit 1 and passed it up to Terrell. "You've seen this before?" As Terrell was looking at it Freeman turned to the jury. "In other words, Inspector Terrell, from this document you knew that Jennifer Witt did not take a year-long vacation to Las Vegas, for example."

Powell was on his feet. "Objection."

"I'll withdraw the comment, Your Honor." Freeman had made his point — if Jennifer had killed Ned to take some money and live the high life, she might have been expected to have kept at least some of it to party with. "There's just one other thing I'd like to ask you about, Inspector. You said Jennifer — Mrs. Witt — told you that Ned Hollis used drugs."

"Yes."

"She said he *experimented* with drugs, isn't that right?"

"That's right."

"You interviewed people who corroborated that?"

Powell got up again. "Your Honor. Hearsay. Mr. Freeman is badgering the witness."

"Not quite, but I take your point."

Freeman waited, silent.

"Mr. Freeman?"

"I was waiting for your ruling, Your Honor."

Villars was not amused. She had the reporter read back the previous dialogue, then said that, *for the record,* the objection was sustained.

Freeman nodded, then continued with Terrell. "How many of Mr. Hollis' friends did you interview?"

"All that I could find."

"And every single one of them confirmed that Ned experimented with drugs, isn't that true?"

"Objection. Hearsay."

"Sustained."

Freeman: "Did any of them deny that Ned experimented with drugs?"

"*Objection.* Hearsay."

"Sustained."

The old defense attorney stood for a beat. Then: "During your exhaustive investigation into the death of Ned Hollis, did anyone ever describe Mr. Hollis' drug use as other than experimental?"

Like a weary jack-in-the-box, Powell again rose. "Objection. Hearsay."

Villars had had enough. "Mr. Freeman, no matter how many different ways you ask the question, I'm going to sustain this objection every time. Please move on."

Freeman was contrite. "I apologize, Your Honor." Back to Terrell with a kindly smile. "I have no further questions."

29

They're shooting themselves in the foot on Ned. You notice Powell said little about it in his opening, especially, didn't even put Jennifer in the county when he died, much less the room."

Freeman chewed on his sandwich — a thick fist-ful of dry Italian salami on a sourdough roll. "Villars should have bought my 995." This was the motion he had filed before the trial, asserting that there was not sufficient evidence in the Ned situation to convict, which Villars had denied. "Unless they've got some big surprise, this one can't fly."

It was the lunch recess. They had cabbed up to the office on Sutter and were sitting on benches in the small brick-and-glass enclosed garden just outside the conference room. Above them, in the aperture formed by the surrounding buildings, the sky burned a deep blue. Indian summer, San Francisco's finest season.

Hardy picked at the bread of his sandwich, threw it in the direction of some sparrows foraging in the low shrubbery.

"You with us?" Freeman asked.

"Sure." Hardy flicked another crumb. "Just thinking."

"About the case?"

Hardy shrugged.

"You don't have to tell me, but are things all right with you? You doing okay? Getting enough sleep? The first days of these trials can be tough."

Leaning forward, Hardy let out a long breath. "I don't know what's going on at home, David. It feels like I'm losing my wife."

"Literally?"

"I don't know. Maybe not."

"But maybe so?"

Hardy stood up, crossed the small opening, stared at blank brick. Without turning around he said, "Something's happened the last couple of months. I don't think it's the trial, all this preparation. I don't know what it is, but it scares me to death."

"You ask her?"

"Couple of hundred times, one way or the other."

"And nothing?"

Hardy shrugged, finally turned. "Not much. Not enough. We've got this tradition where we go out on Wednesday nights. Date night. Or we had it 'til a month ago."

The birds were chirping over the crumbs and Freeman broke off a bit of his bread and tossed it across the patio. "Something happen a month ago?"

"I wish it had. I came home one night, thinking we were going out, and she's in a nightgown reading. She tells me I ought to go out by myself, shoot some darts. She's just tired."

"Maybe she was tired?"

"Time was she'd be tired on a Wednesday night, we'd grab a blanket, go out to the beach, take a nap. This date night idea was something we'd decided to do, tired or not, kids or not. The marriage needed it. We need it for ourselves."

Freeman contemplated his sandwich. "How old are your kids?"

"Two and almost one, but it's not that." At the skeptical look, Hardy said, "I don't think it's that. You think it is?"

"I barely know Frannie, Diz. But she wouldn't be the first woman to decide her kids needed her more than her husband. Priorities change."

"Well, they haven't changed with me."

Freeman allowed himself a smile. "Life's unfair, like JFK said. If only we could find somebody to sue." He shifted on the bench, popped the last of his sandwich. "Does she think *you* need her?"

"Come on, David. Need? Who knows need? I love her and I think she knows that."

"I don't mean to sound presumptuous, but your kids know need. Frannie knows need."

"Well, hell, I need her, too. I mean, we're adults, though. We've both got things we've got to do. I've got this trial. She's got the kids. What are we supposed to do? That's what date night was supposed to be for — to keep us connected."

"It doesn't sound like you're too connected. You just said it — you've got this trial, she's got the kids."

Hands in his pockets, Hardy found himself pacing. Arguing with David Freeman, proving his point that Frannie — perhaps — shouldn't feel what she was feeling, whatever it was, didn't alter the fact that something pretty fundamental seemed to have changed between them, some balance had shifted.

Maybe what Freeman had implied was true — that she didn't feel as though he needed her much anymore. He had to admit he wasn't giving her much sign of it — leaving for work early, getting home late, drafting motions, doing research, following up his investigations, reviewing files on weekends.

As far as that went, he didn't feel like she was needing him much either. She was doing her jobs, caring for the children, taking care of the home. They were, he believed, committed to each other, and that had to be one of the main ingredients of what they both called adult love.

"I'd surprise her." Freeman had come up next to him and put a hand on his shoulder. "Break up the routine. Maybe she's just burned out. Maybe she sees you're not there for her and she's afraid you won't be and she's pulling away."

"But I *am* there. This trial's just starting. What does she expect?"

"Maybe the question is what does she need?" Freeman patted his shoulder, opening the glass door back into the conference room. "Let's get back to court. Her Honor frowns on tardiness."

John Strout, the coroner for the City and County of San Francisco, was already a familiar figure to Hardy and every other professional in the courtroom. An authority with a national reputation, the drawling, well-respected medical examiner had appeared at almost every trial, grand jury and preliminary hearing that involved a murder in San Francisco — perhaps once a week for the past thirteen years — and now he sat his lanky frame down in the witness box, comfortable and relaxed.

Powell, showing no sign of a post-lunch slump, combed his white mane with his fingers and greeted Strout genially, old friends, for the jury's benefit. Then he got right to it, preempting what Hardy thought would be Freeman's tack on cross.

"Dr. Strout, did you do the initial autopsy on Ned Hollis back in 1984?"

"Yes, I did."

"And what were your findings at that time?"

Strout backed his chair up in the witness box and crossed his legs, his broad and open face creased in a smile. "We ran an *A* scan and returned with a finding of accidental death due to an overdose of cocaine mixed with alcohol."

"An *A* scan? Would you explain to the jury what that is?"

Strout leaned forward and gave a two-minute explanation — most poisons and/or volatile compounds were found in the *A* scan, and it was cheapest and quickest. If a cause-of-death could be found at the *A* level — without a police report indicating a suspicion of foul play — the scanning tended to stop there.

"And the *A* scan did find traces of cocaine and alcohol in Mr. Hollis' system, is that it?"

Strout frowned. Making it simple for the jury wasn't his job. He was already on the record as having missed the true cause of death in this case, and he wanted to keep it precise. "There was a potentially lethal level of coca-ethylene, which gets a little technical, but basically it is the by-product when cocaine and alcohol mix in the blood."

"And when you determined the presence of this coca-ethylene, you stopped the autopsy?"

"Well, no. But we stopped looking so hard for a cause-of-death. A man's got a knife sticking out of his head, we don't necessarily go looking for a coincidental heart attack." A brush of low laughter. "But we didn't complete the autopsy with that finding. In fact, the lab tests and the physical examination are related but separate procedures."

Strout explained about blood samples being sent off to the lab while the autopsy proper concerned itself with the body and its organs. "When we get back the lab results, we check to see if anything we've discovered in the physical examination might throw some new light on the lab's finding or vice-versa."

"And in this case?"

"Well, we found the coca-ethylene. There weren't any appreciable amounts or physical indications of the presence of barbiturates or alkaloids. So we had a probable cause of death at the *A* level and stopped there."

Powell nodded to Strout, then turned first to the jury, then back to the defense table, making eye contact with Jennifer again. Hardy glanced at her out of the side of his eye. Was she *smiling* at her prosecutor? He touched her arm, and she stiffened, her face now a mask.

The direct examination continued without any surprises. Both prosecution and defense counsel might have stipulated to all of this forensic detail — the facts were largely undisputed — but neither

Powell or Freeman had shown any inclination to do so. They had their reasons. Powell wanted to make the long-ago death of Jennifer's first husband real to the jury. He might have been dead a long time now, but when he died he'd been a healthy twenty-six-year-old man. Powell wanted the jury to know that, to get a sense of a young life snuffed out, to watch his accused killer react to it all. When he'd finished outlining the *C* scan and discovery of the concentration of atropine in Ned's left thigh, Powell led Strout into an area that did not strictly concern his findings in the lab or at autopsy.

"Now, Dr. Strout, atropine is a prescription drug, is it not? It's not available over the counter?"

Strout agreed.

"And what is its principle use?"

"It's used in anesthesia and to inhibit the flow of saliva." Strout was good at including everybody. He smiled all around, smooth and comfortable.

"Were you surprised when you found it in the scan you've described?"

"Objection." Freeman was up like a shot, and almost as quickly, without discussion, Villars sustained him. Powell remained impassive.

"Dr. Strout, to your knowledge, does atropine get much use as a recreational drug?"

Hardy could see Freeman getting poised to object again, but he sat back, seemingly content to let Powell continue with this line of questioning.

"If it is, it's not a common one."

"It doesn't produce a so-called high, or anything like that?"

Again, Hardy glanced over at Freeman. Powell was leading the witness all over the place, and

Freeman was sitting back in his chair, lips pursed, listening.

"No."

"In combination with other drugs, does it have some hallucinatory or euphoric effects?"

"No."

"So if a person were an habitual drug user, and looking to get high, he or she would not —"

Here, finally, Freeman raised a hand, keeping his voice low. "Your Honor? Speculation."

Again he was sustained. Powell smiled, palms out, apologized in his gentlemanly way and nodded to both the judge and the doctor. "That's all, then. Thank you, Dr. Strout. Your witness, Mr. Freeman."

The rumpled defense attorney, no less genial than Powell had been, although — Hardy thought — more believable in this guise, walked to where Powell had been standing, then moved three steps closer to the witness box, lifting one hand in a casual unspoken greeting to Strout, telling the jury by gesture that he and Strout, too, were professional colleagues. Just because he was with the defense, it didn't mean he was with the bad guys, or was one of them.

"This exhumation business . . . I don't suppose it's much fun, is it, Doctor?"

Strout was still relaxed. There had been trials where he had testified for the better part of a week. He looked on his witness time as a break from his work in the morgue. He spread his hands. "It's part of the job. Sometimes it gets pretty interesting."

"Was this, the Ned Hollis exhumation, one of the particularly interesting ones?"

Strout thought for a moment, then added, "I'd have to say it was."

"And can you tell the jury why that was?"

Strout liked this, the opportunity to sit back and chat. "Well, in any autopsy the search for a cause of death is a bit of a puzzle. As I've explained earlier, we run laboratory scans for various substances and examine the body, hoping we can point at something when we're finished. In a case where someone has died a long time ago, the puzzle can get complicated. I guess that's what I mean by interesting."

Freeman, apparently fascinated, had now wandered closer to the jury box. "What kind of complications, Doctor?"

"Well, the body decays, for one. Certain substances break down — chemically, I mean — or turn into something else, or disappear entirely. Evaporate. Over time, of course, eventually you can lose almost everything."

"And had that happened with Mr. Hollis?"

"Well, to some degree, yes."

"And yet this was a particularly interesting . . . puzzle, I believe you called it."

The medical examiner nodded. "That's because we believed we had another poison and we had to find it — not just the substance itself, but how it had gotten into the body." Strout, the ideal witness, was forward in his chair again, addressing the jury directly. "During the first autopsy," he explained, "we had, of course, examined stomach contents and so on, but now we were looking to see if we missed anything the first time, so we tried again. But there wasn't much there. Although the scan found the initial trace of atropine, we couldn't get any concentration approaching a lethal dose."

"And your next step?"

Hardy glanced at the jury. This was gruesome stuff, no one was sleeping. Strout continued, showing enthusiasm for his work. "Now here's where the puzzle gets interesting. If there's been a recent death, you might find some needle marks, bruises and so on, but here we took samples from various locations, hoping to find a concentration, and we got lucky."

"How was that?"

Strout got technical on some muscle names and so on, but Freeman brought him back, making it clear that the injection had gone in two-thirds up the front of the left thigh.

"You're sure it was the front of the thigh? It could not have seeped through, so to speak, from the back?"

Stout was certain. "There's no chance of that. The muscles aren't connected." More medical detail, but gradually the picture came out — the lethal injection had been administered to the upper thigh.

To Hardy, it seemed like a long journey to get to something they already knew. Until Freeman asked, "This location on the thigh, could someone self-administer an injection there?"

Unflappable and friendly, Strout said of course.

"Was there anything about your examination

that indicated that the injection had *not* been self-administered?"

"Such as?"

"I don't know. Maybe a scratch where he might have tried to fight off the injection. Anything at all?"

Strout thought. "After all this time, no, nothing."

Freeman went back to the exhibit table and lifted People's Exhibit 5, the original autopsy report. "Did you notice anything nine years ago, Doctor, that would have argued against Mr. Hollis giving himself the shot?"

Perusing the page, Strout handed it back. "No. But, of course, there were tracks — needle marks."

"There were needle marks? And where were these, Doctor?"

"On his inner arms."

"Consistent with where a drug user might inject himself?"

"Yes."

"Did you notice any needle marks on his thighs?"

Again, Strout glanced down at People's Exhibit 5, his early autopsy diagram. "No, not that I noted here."

Across the room, Hardy saw Powell sitting, his hands folded in front of him, his head down. He was getting killed and he knew it. Freeman, with half a losing point — the needle marks on the thigh — wasn't even ready to concede that. He'd come back nearly to the edge of the witness box during the rapid-fire questions, and now he moved back to the center of the room. "But it's possible, is it not, Doctor, that you might have missed even a recent needle mark?"

Nodding amiably, the doctor, relentlessly honest, went him one better. "Not only could I, Mr. Freeman, it seems likely I did. The injection went in his thigh. It's the only way the atropine could have concentrated itself there. Needle marks are notoriously difficult to locate and catalog. Autopsies miss them." Strout spread his hands one last time. "It happens," he said.

30

Dropped off on the seventh floor by the bailiff, then escorted by her two female guards, Jennifer Witt undressed in the open room, hanging her good clothes carefully on the wooden hangers, watching as the guards made space for them in the changing locker. She turned and faced the wall as she removed the feminine underthings that Freeman had bought for her. She slipped a runner's bra over her head, turned back around, took the proferred plastic bag from Milner — a sweet-faced, overweight redhead with a gappy smile and freckles — and dropped the articles, one at a time, into the bag.

The other guard, Montanez, sullenly held out the red jumpsuit. From out in the pods, through the building, they heard the sound of bars clanging, strident voices rising and fading. It was near to dinnertime, getting darker a little earlier, a few weeks before the end of Daylight Savings Time.

"How's it going down there?" Milner asked.

Jennifer shrugged. "Bunch of men talking a lot."

"Ain't it, though?" Montanez started moving them together toward the door to the changing room.

"The judge is a woman, though. Her name is

Villars. There are a few on the jury, too."

But these considerations didn't much concern either Milner or Montanez. The two guards flanked her in the dim and ringing hallway, their belts and hardware creaking as they walked. From behind them, the lockup guard called out, "Is that Witt? She's got a visitor."

Dr. Ken Lightner had been in the courtroom for at least some period of time during each of the four days of the trial so far. Not being a lawyer, he had not been allowed into the tiny room next to the guard's station but, like Frannie, had to content himself with the more public arrangement — hard wooden chairs and telephone lines on either side of the Plexiglas.

He was already sitting there, waiting. His head was cradled wearily against the heel of his hand. When Jennifer sat down he stared at her for a long minute. Finally he reached for the telephone. "How are you holding up?"

"Nobody's hitting me anymore. Maybe they think I'm going to win." She allowed her face to crack into a brittle smile. "I'm starting to have a little faith in Mr. Freeman."

Lightner nodded. "What does he say?"

"He won't ever commit to anything. He says it's a long haul. But I hear him talking to Mr. Hardy, I see the response he's getting from the jury. He seems confident."

"And how about you?"

"I miss you, Ken. I miss talking to you. Everything. The people here . . ." There was nothing to say about them. They lived on a different plane.

She stopped herself, swallowed. "It's so different. I don't know . . ."

The phone nearly fell from her hand.

"What, Jen?"

She swallowed again, giving the impression of pulling back, even through the Plexiglas. "About going on."

"What about going on, Jen? You've *got* to go on."

Shaking her head, she became silent.

Lightner leaned forward, his face an inch from the glass. "Jennifer, *listen* to me. You've got to go on. You can't give up now. You're winning now, the worst may well be over."

"No, the worst isn't over. Mr. Freeman says the worst hasn't started yet . . ."

"He's a big help."

"He's trying. He is, Ken. I'm at least sure of that. It's not even the trial, you know, not mostly. It's everything else being so different. All these people here" — she gestured around her — "this whole place. I think sometimes I'll never get back to anything I recognize, anything I want." A tear broke from her eye and rolled down her cheek. This time she didn't wipe it away. It didn't matter if she looked weak, if she broke down in front of Ken, that's what he was for. And she was weak — they'd proved that. She didn't care about the old things anymore. "I'm so confused, Ken, I'm so confused . . ."

Lightner watched her, waiting for something, he couldn't say exactly what. Jennifer seemed inside herself, suffering, and he wanted to get her past this, but he didn't want to push. You let people find their own way out if they could.

"I'm still here," he said finally.

She allowed that brittle smile again. "I sometimes think you're the only reason I'm alive." A half-sob, half-laugh. "It's funny, you know. Remember when I thought if we could just get away from Larry, everything would work, everything would be better? It'd be a whole new world."

"I remember. It could still be there, Jen. We've talked about this over and over, working through the changes."

She shook herself, almost began rocking. Her head moved back and forth, a heavy weight held by a thread. "But that's just it, that's the problem. I don't believe it anymore. I don't know if I believe it anymore. The thing with Matt . . ." The flow of words stopped, her eyes suddenly dead, without any energy. "It would be better if it were just all over with. That'd be the end of it."

Maybe it was a test. Jennifer searched through the glass for something in his eyes, some answer. She scratched at the counter in front of her, reached her hand toward the Plexiglas, then withdrew it. "It's not going to get better, no matter what happens. I'm just the kind of person that everything beats up on . . . men, things, situations. I'm a loser, that's all."

Lightner was sitting forward now, his hand pushing against the glass. "You're not a loser, Jen. You've been victimized. We've talked about this. It's natural to feel the way you do, with what you've been through. But you're not a loser. I wouldn't stick with you if you were a loser, if I thought there wasn't some end to this, some time when things are going to be better."

"Tell me when."

"Come on, Jen. No one knows that exactly. But —"

"I think you'd stick with me anyway, Ken, even though I am a loser. And you know why. I've figured this out. Because I'm a challenge to you, some classic case study."

"Jesus, Jennifer, how can you say that after all —"

"Because it's true, isn't it? You don't really care, do you? I mean about *me*. Who could ever love somebody as messed up as *I* am? As soon as I do get turned around, the minute it happens, if it ever does, the challenge or puzzle or whatever I am would be over. You'd be gone, too, wouldn't you? And then where would I be? I'll tell you where — where I am now, which is nowhere. Nowhere, nothing, never coming back, oh, god*damn* it all . . ."

She threw the phone down, pushing the chair backward, knocking it over, standing, looking around, tears falling freely now. The guard was moving up, hand on her stick.

Lightner stood, his own hand on the Plexiglas, watching. Jennifer said something to the guard, slumping. She didn't turn back to look. They moved toward the door back to the cells, and Lightner sat again in the hard chair, trying to control his own feelings.

Suddenly she was back at the glass, hands splayed against it. Crying for real now, her body half-falling, half-leaning, her weight against the partition. Shaking her head, her face set, reaching for her stick as if she might really need it, the guard was coming up behind Jennifer — who was forcing words out between the sobs.

Even if he couldn't hear clearly he knew what she was saying. It was what she always said when she hit her own bedrock, when she felt it was all on her and she had to accept it.

"I'm sorry," she was crying, over and over, trying to reach him through the glass as though he were in another dimension. "I'm sorry, I didn't mean it, don't be mad at me . . ."

And then the guard's hand was on her shoulder, pulling her backward, turning her around and back to the door.

Lightner stood there breathing deeply and thinking that Jennifer might be right. She might be hopeless, an incurable loser.

And after all he'd done for her. It hit him like an electric shock, forcing him back down into the chair — the realization that she might never, ever get herself straight. He realized he was shaking, trying to get it under control, but what he *wanted* was to wake her up, knock some sense into that confused, lovely head of hers.

Frannie could not believe that Hardy had made all these arrangements — calling Erin, Rebecca's grandmother, to see if she would mind taking the kids overnight, sending a cab to pick everybody up and drop them where they should be, making reservations at this luxurious Bed & Breakfast.

Hardy was modest. "I'm a virtual treasure trove of surprises."

"What made you think of this? What about the trial?"

Hardy sat on a red crushed velvet settee drinking an old tawny port from a cut-crystal wine glass. "I figured we owed ourselves about four date nights, call it twelve hours minimum. The trial can live without me a day — this is primarily Freeman's phase, anyway, remember."

Frannie stood at the window, arms crossed, her hair up, taking in the view of the Golden Gate Bridge from the back window of the California House, an old Victorian on Upper Divisadero Street that had been refurbished and reincarnated as a Bed & Breakfast. They were in the Gold Rush suite, complete with stocked bookshelves, jacuzzi, fireplace, port and sherry with crystal service and, of course, The View, which added eighty dollars to the room charge.

He had made the reservation from the Hall of Justice as soon as they had recessed for the day. Erin had told him it would be no problem to come by, get the kids, feed them their dinner. Hardy had the feeling that if Erin simply showed up with a plan there'd be less chance that Frannie would demur. A cab came to their house and picked her up at 6:15. And now here they were.

Hardy still wasn't sure Frannie was altogether thrilled with the surprise. Her arms stayed crossed. Her face was set. He didn't think it was anger — in spite of the distance she hadn't been acting as though she were mad at him. Her jaw was tight, her eyes alert and thoughtful, inward looking — as though she were bearing up under some physical pain she didn't want to burden him with.

His fear was that the pain was the result of some change, that she'd realized that she didn't want him and their life together anymore. Her eyes came to him from across some chasm. A half-smile. "Hi."

He realized he'd been holding his breath, watching her, literally afraid to breathe. If he didn't breathe, maybe the moment would stop and he wouldn't have to find out what the next one held. He put his port on the end table and let out his breath in a rush. "So how's life, Frannie?"

"How do you think?"

"I think not good. I've had a stomach ache for a month. Since you stopped smiling. I thought maybe you'd like to talk about it."

She turned back to The View, her face in profile to him. He saw the muscle working in her jaw. He wanted to get up, go to her, but something — perhaps the knowledge that if she pushed him away now, didn't let him gather her in and hold her, then they might not get it back, not ever — something rooted him to the chair.

The words came out mumbled and he told her he hadn't heard what she'd said. They took a minute to come again.

She turned to face him directly and met his eyes. "Secrets."

He digested the word, and as the most obvious interpretation hit him, his stomach churned. He felt his head go light, as though he were going to faint. "What secrets?" It was the only thing he could think of to say.

She stood in the same posture, facing him

straight on, arms crossed. "Secrets are what you don't tell."

Hardy leaned forward in his chair. He lifted the glass of port next to him and took a drink, then put it back down. "Okay," he said.

"It's not just that," she said.

"I don't even know what *that* is."

"That's right. You don't."

Hardy brought his hand up to his forehead, squeezed at his temples. "Okay, Fran, but I've got to know." His palms found their way together. Praying. "Is it another man? Can you tell me that?"

He saw her shoulders settle, her eyes close. All her body language said that some crisis had just passed. Her arms uncrossed, untangled, came to her sides. She moved toward him, kneeled in front of him.

"What are you talking about, another man? There's no other man. There couldn't be another man." She had her hands on his face, her eyes into his, searching, outlining his features with her fingertips, her arms then around his neck, pulling him to her, against her. He felt himself shaking under her. It was all the emotion he so much tried to keep in check, to control.

That was why he'd married her. Because he trusted her enough to let her see him like this, see who he really was. She was part of him, the catalyst that let him be whole again.

She rocked him, his head in her hands, holding him, feeling the waves of emotion coming out of him, surfacing.

She held him as tightly as she could.

This was her man and he needed her. If he could

do this, trust her with what he'd call his weakest self, she didn't have to worry. She could lay herself out for him — her own doubts, her own failings, inadequacies. He wasn't going to leave her for them. He wasn't going to leave.

"I was afraid you wouldn't understand."

"I probably don't, but I try."

"You expect life to be perfect all the time and —"

"I don't."

She shushed him, a finger to his lips. It was full dark now, later, the bridge lit out the window, a candle by the bed.

"I didn't want to let you down," she said, "and I was just so damn sad. And it wasn't you, it was me. It was *my* sadness. It was Eddie, my so-called youth, everything. I guess it just caught up to me."

Hardy lay there, quiet.

"I didn't want you to know. I didn't want it to hurt you."

"I think I know life's not perfect, Frannie. God knows, I know that."

"But you want ours to be, our home life, don't you? Sometimes you even think it can be."

"Don't you? Don't you think that's something to shoot for?"

"I don't know. I thought I did. And then this, this whole thing, feeling trapped, all of it . . ." She shifted in the bed, moving her head from the pillow to the crook of Hardy's shoulder, her leg over his middle.

"I didn't try to trap you into this, Frannie. Into being married. I thought you were happy . . ."

"It wasn't you, Dismas. I can see now it wasn't you. It was my life. All of a sudden, I don't know what it was, it all just came back at me. And then I felt so much like I'd failed — I mean, I wasn't happy and I should have been and who's fault is that?"

"I generally blame a consortium of Arab investors."

"So do I, usually, but this time it didn't work, and I couldn't tell you. It wouldn't be fair with your trial coming up and all, and then I began to resent that . . . that I couldn't tell you, and then I convinced myself that you wouldn't care anyway, that this was just all stupid female stuff that isn't very linear anyway and can't be —"

"Whoa, whoa, whoa . . . what is that? Stupid female stuff? We didn't invite any stupid females to this party."

"You know what I mean."

"I don't know what you mean. And linear?" He turned up on his elbow, looking down at her. "I don't know what you mean," he repeated. "Really."

Frannie closed her eyes for a breath. "I saw Jennifer."

"I know you did."

"No." She shook her head. "More than once. I snuck out. I left the kids with Erin and went and saw her."

"How many times?"

"I don't know. Three or four."

"At the jail?" He answered himself. "Of course at the jail." Hardy sat all the way up, pulling the sheet around him. Frannie put a hand on his leg.

"The first time . . . I guess we connected. Then I didn't think you'd approve, or I didn't want to ask for your okay . . ."

"Frannie . . ."

"But then I talked myself into being mad that I felt like I *had* to clear it with you every time. That didn't seem right, that I had to ask permission."

"She's my client, Frannie." He was shaking his head, trying to fit this in somewhere.

"I know, I know. I should have talked to you, but it . . . it all seemed to fit in with the other stuff, being so depressed, feeling like I was trapped. Jennifer . . . well, she listened to me."

"Jennifer listened to *you?* Jesus." Hardy threw the sheet off and swung his legs off the bed. He walked to the window, not to see The View but because it was the only destination in the room. He stood stock still, then, without turning, whispered, "You talked to Jennifer about you and me? What's she got on us now?"

He heard her voice, small behind him. "It wasn't like that. Don't be mad at me now. Please."

He stood another minute, trying to piece it together. The images out the window — the lights on Union Street far below, the Golden Gate, the Presidio evergreens blurring the western horizon — they were piling up, falling over each other kaleidoscope fashion. Turning back, he sat again on the settee. "This was the secret?"

Frannie was at the edge of the bed. She paused, framing an answer. "All of it was a secret. It was all connected."

Hunched over, Hardy had his hands crossed in

front of him, his head down.

"Dismas?" She was off the bed now, on the floor, on her knees in front of him again. He felt her hands on his legs.

"I'm not mad," he said. "Let's get that straight. I'm not mad at you and I'm glad we're talking about this. But did it occur to you that she might be using you?"

"She wasn't. I just told you it wasn't like that. At least I didn't think it was like that —"

He jumped at the difference. "You didn't think it was like that then, but you do now? You think it might have been?"

Frannie got up, grabbed the blanket and drew it around her, then sat on the edge of the bed. "No, I didn't say that." She took a deep breath and reached out again, the space between the bed and the settee. "I wish you wouldn't interrogate me. I want to talk about this, Dismas, but when we get into it like this I feel intimidated. It doesn't work, it doesn't get us anywhere."

"Where do you want us to get to, Frannie?"

"I want us to be able to talk again. I'm trying to tell you how it was."

In the candlelight her face was an amber cameo. He found he couldn't take his eyes off her. He nodded. Her arm was across the space between them, touching his leg, reaching out. He put his hand over hers.

This was not the time to argue, to tell Frannie that Jennifer might have had an agenda far removed from the one she'd led Frannie to believe. He came over next to her, pulling the blanket around both of them. "You're right," he said, kissing her, holding her against him, "I'm sorry. Talk to me."

"She told you Larry beat her?"

"Everybody has beaten her. She couldn't believe you never hit me, or Eddie never hit me. She didn't believe me, I could tell. Like the idea is completely outside her experience."

"It probably is."

They were still huddled together at the edge of the bed. "Let's not ever hit our kids, okay?" Hardy said.

"We don't."

"I know. Let's not start."

Frannie leaned into him. Muffled night sounds came up through the closed window — a truck's brakes squealing as it inched down the north Divisadero escarpment, a girl's carefree laugh from outside one of the clubs on Union.

"I still feel a little like I've abandoned her. Jennifer, I mean. I just . . . it got feeling wrong somehow."

"Well, *I* haven't abandoned her, so I guess it's still in the family, right?"

"I know, but —"

"*Shh.* Look. Maybe just hearing your story — some woman who doesn't get hit — maybe that'll give her hope that it's possible."

"If she believes it."

"And if she doesn't, you seeing her more isn't going to make her, is it?" He held his wife against him, breathing in her scent. The candle sputtered briefly. Hardy looked over and saw a thin rope of wax snake its way down the crystal holder, pooling on the dresser's surface. "I'm not trying to talk you out of anything, you know. If you want to see her some more, just tell me, okay? Let me know."

"I won't." She sighed. "There's some things . . . it's just too wrong."

"You said that. But if you're not going behind me . . ."

"No, that's not what's wrong. It's her, really, Jennifer. First I thought we . . . you know, we were two women . . . we could talk. But then she cut it off. She was about to tell me something important and then closed up, said I didn't want to know. I began to wonder if maybe . . ."

"If maybe she's guilty?"

"Maybe. I couldn't handle that. Except I don't believe she killed Matt, even accidentally, or Larry. Maybe her first husband, I don't know. And if she did, I don't know whether I could handle it. *If,* I said. But she told me, why did I think she was fighting this thing so hard. The answer is she didn't kill them."

"Although Larry beat and abused her?"

"Please don't cross-examine me, Dismas. She told me Larry beat her. But she also said she didn't kill him, or Matt — not by accident or mistake or any other way or for any other reason."

Hardy looked at her, wondering if she was trying to convince herself. He certainly knew how that felt.

31

No one seemed to know where the storm came from, but rain slashed almost horizontally in gusts around Bryant Street, the temperature was in the low fifties and the gray paint on the Hall of Justice seemed a bruised and burnished blue as Hardy ran, raincoat flapping, from his parking space to the courthouse steps.

It was 12:42 when he entered the building. He knew they would be at recess, which was how he had planned it. He wasn't going directly to Villars' department anyway.

Freeman and Jennifer were having lunch in an abandoned office back behind the courtrooms.

Hardy nodded at the bailiff standing watch outside the door, then waited, getting his breathing under control from the run through the rain. He watched them through the wire-lined glass window in the door, talking, chatting really, at opposite sides of a pocked old green metal desk. He pushed open the door.

Freeman, his mouth full, raised a hand. "Greetings. We're killing 'em, Diz. Their feet are up, I swear to God."

Jennifer was pushing some three-bean salad around her white Styrofoam tray with a white plastic fork. He was struck again by the figure she cut — demure yet sophisticated, innocent and unattainable. It was as if she were Freeman's creation now — clay-molded by an artist.

Hardy had unbuttoned his dripping trenchcoat and now pulled a chair around backward and dropped himself over it. A gust delivered a fresh torrent of rain, slapping at the window in front of them hard enough to make everybody stop and look.

"More good news. The drought's over again." Freeman shoveled some tubular pasta in a glutinous red sauce. He mopped his mouth with an already spotted napkin. "Hey, Diz, listen up. I'm kicking some serious tail in there. I'm thinking about what I'm going to say in there." He pointed back behind him to the courtroom. "That's where I live, you hear me? You want some advice? No? I don't care, I'll give it to you anyway. You want to give good trial, that's where you'll live, too." More milk, another swipe of napkin. "It doesn't get in there, Diz, it doesn't count. And that's the truth. The truth is also we're winning right now."

A long moment went by while everyone looked at one another. More rain got flung against the window. Over downtown, lightning arced into a rod on a hotel rooftop, and seconds later the crash of thunder rolled through the room.

Jennifer, kitty-corner to him, put her manicured hand over his. One part of him registered that it was cool and dry, so he thought it was odd that it seemed to burn where she touched him.

"Jennifer never admitted to Harlan Poole that Ned was beating her. In fact, she always denied it. His opinion that she was being battered is totally speculative," Freeman said. "He can say he and Jennifer were having an affair. He can say he had atropine in his office. Period. I filed an early 1118 yesterday after we crucified Strout. And Poole is turning into a bigger disaster than Strout."

The 1118 is a motion for a directed verdict of acquittal, by which the judge is asked to rule that no reasonable jury could convict the defendant, that as a matter of law there isn't sufficient evidence to prove guilt. If the motion was granted, the charge would be dismissed and could never be retried.

"I'd bet Villars grants it after the recess." Freeman's eyes seemed to glow. He put a hand on Hardy's other sleeve. "He maybe can chew gum and walk, but I don't think Powell can run a campaign and a trial at the same time. This thing's going south for him."

The bailiff knocked and entered. Judge Villars was coming out of her chambers. Trial was going back into session.

Hardy sat listening as Powell tried to find some wedge to introduce Harlan Poole's testimony.

The dentist was a wreck. It was hard to imagine that this portly, balding, bespeckled, sweating man had ever been Jennifer's lover. Also, the "low profile" that Terrell had promised him had turned out to be impossible to maintain. Like it or not, and he obviously hated it, Poole was a central figure here, one of the prosecution's star witnesses in a capital murder trial. From his eyes, the role was playing havoc with his life.

"Dr. Poole." Powell was recovering from another sustained objection. Freeman had jumped up as he liked to do, and Villars criticized Powell for again referring to the fact that Ned had beaten Jennifer, which they hadn't been able to establish because it was hearsay.

In his frustration, Powell was walking in circles, facing the bench, then the jury, back to the defense table, then his own table, all the way back around to Poole. "Dr. Poole," he said, "you have testified that you were intimate with the defendant?"

Poole studied the ceiling, avoiding his wife in the gallery. He wiped a handkerchief across his eyebrows. "Yes."

"During your intimate moments did you have occasion to see the defendant naked?"

"Your Honor! Objection!"

But Powell had given this some thought. "Your Honor, at your insistence, we have to take this testimony out of the realm of hearsay. This is not a direction I would have chosen to go, but it is relevant and it is not hearsay."

Villars had her mask on. Eyes straight ahead, unmoving, she could have been a mannequin. "Let's have counsel up here."

Hardy rose along with Freeman. No one seemed to object, or even notice. They were before Villars, looking up.

Villars spoke quietly. "I'm not sure I'm going along with the relevance, Mr. Powell. What does Mrs. Witt's nakedness have to do with the alleged killing of her husband?"

Freeman, still feeling he was on a roll, incautiously spoke right up. "It doesn't."

A mistake. Villars glared. "When I want your answer or argument, Mr. Freeman, I'll address you, is that clear?" Without waiting for his response, she went back to the prosecutor. "Mr. Powell?"

"Your Honor, it speaks to motivation. We know that her husband was beating her and that —"

"Wait a minute. Up to now all I've heard about is the insurance and an affair . . ."

Hardy suddenly noticed that the court reporter wasn't there. He surprised himself by speaking up. "Excuse me, Your Honor, is this conference to go on the record?" The court reporter was supposed to take everything. Nothing in a capital case was off the record.

The judge seemed to realize for the first time that Hardy was even there. The look of surprise gave way to her usual intimidating glare, but Hardy didn't back down. "Perhaps we could go to chambers?"

"We just got out here." Extremely displeased, she frowned down at the three men who were waiting on her. "What's your point, Mr. Hardy?"

"We don't have to go to chambers, Your Honor." Powell was Mr. Conciliatory. "I'm sure we can settle this right here."

Villars straightened her back, drew in a quick breath. "I'm getting pretty damn tired of asking one person a question and getting an answer from another one. I ask Mr. Powell a question, Mr. Freeman answers me. I ask Mr. Hardy a question, Mr. Powell answers me. Now everybody listen up.

I'm asking Mr. Hardy. You want this conference in chambers?"

"Yes, mam."

She leveled a finger at him. "Yes, *Your Honor,*" she corrected him, "not 'yes, mam.' "

"Yes, Your Honor. I'm sorry."

Villars was moving papers around in front of her on the bench. She lowered her head, shaking it back and forth. "This really pisses me off," she whispered to no one.

She stood up. "The court reporter will accompany us to chambers. We're taking a short recess. Dr. Poole, you can stand down 'til we get back. It shouldn't be too long. Or you can stay where you are."

She led the parade out.

Her chambers were not much more impressive than the cubicles used by the Assistant DAs. The room itself was bigger and had its private bathroom and a sitting area away from the oak flat-topped desk, but even with two nice throw rugs and some framed prints the place had that public-building feel.

Hardy was now facing the wrath of Villars. "All right, Mr. Hardy, we're on the record in chambers. What are we in chambers for, if you don't mind?"

"Mr. Powell was discussing the relevance of—"

"I know what he was doing."

Hardy stepped back. "Okay, then, Your Honor, if he'd like to continue his argument. It might come up in the penalty phase, if there is one."

Villars reminded him of an angry bird, head tilted to one side, ready to peck his eyes out. She shifted her gaze to the prosecutor, who was sitting in one of the leather chairs. "All right, Mr. Powell, let's hear why Mrs. Witt's nakedness is relevant."

"Your Honor, Dr. Poole's testimony will give direct evidence that Ned Hollis used to beat Jennifer regularly, which of course would have given her another reason to have killed him. Surely that's relevant."

But also a point in mitigation, Hardy thought.

"You're saying this is a burning-bed case?"

"It may have those elements. It's a question of fact and we ought to let the jury decide."

Villars shook her head. "You realize you are introducing BWS here?" Referring to the battered-woman syndrome. "Do you have any evidence that what's-his-name, the second husband . . . ?"

"Larry?"

". . . that Larry was beating her, too? Is that your argument?"

"Excuse me, Your Honor." Freeman wanted to get onto the boards. "*We're* not claiming BWS. She is not saying she had a reason — we're not saying she killed them because they beat her and they deserved it. We're saying she did not kill them at all."

Villars pushed herself up until she was sitting on the edge of her desk.

Hardy glanced at his partner. Freeman was leaning against one of the bookshelves, seemingly at ease arguing the position that Jennifer had not killed anybody for any reason.

Villars, her arms straight down on either side, palms flat on the desk, stared through the one window at the driving rain outside. "So I assume, Mr.

Powell, that we're going to hear that Mrs. Witt had bruises, black and blue marks and so on, all over her body?"

"That's right, Your Honor."

"And the fact that Dr. Poole personally saw them takes this out of the realm of hearsay?"

Powell, seeing where she was going with this, began to squirm. The leather chair squeaked as he shifted. Still, he persisted. "The bruises themselves, Your Honor, are admissible. Dr. Poole saw them himself."

"And you would then ask the jury to somehow connect these marks on Mrs. Witt's body to her husband?"

"Your Honor, the truth is that her first husband, Ned, beat her. The implication can be drawn —"

Freeman stepped away from the bookcase. "That's just not true, Dean." He turned to the judge. "Pardon me, Your Honor, but my client has consistently denied that she has been a battered wife, or that this will be any part of her defense. The jury cannot draw any implication at all from bruises that may have been caused by anything."

"Oh, get serious, David." Powell was halfway out of his chair. "You know as well as I do that —"

"Gentlemen! Let me remind you that we are on the record here, and that any remarks are to be made to the court." She wasn't waiting for a response but moved off the edge of the desk, facing both men. "Mr. Powell, from what I've seen here so far, you've got an evidence problem of substantial proportions. Are you planning to call somebody who's going to give us any testimony about the day Mr. Hollis died, where Mrs. Witt was on that day, anyone who saw her take the alleged atropine out of Dr. Poole's alleged drawer, or the alleged syringe, or who saw her dump it afterward?"

Powell was standing, hands in his pockets, trying to affect a casual posture. Hardy wasn't convinced and doubted anyone else was. "Your Honor, with the insurance, the pattern here —"

Villars held up her hand. "I asked you a simple yes or no question. Are you calling anybody to address any of the issues I just raised?"

"Your Honor, I —"

"Yes or no, damn it." She looked over to the court reporter. "Adrienne, strike that profanity." Then, back to Powell: "Yes or no, Mr. Powell."

A faraway rumble or thunder rolled through the room.

"Not to those specific issues. No, Your Honor."

"Are there *any* specific issues you'd like to preview for us that you can think of that would fall more or less into the category of evidence and not hearsay? Take your time."

Powell sat back down, leaning forward, his forearms on his thighs. "Lieutenant Batiste, who was the investigating officer for Ned Hollis' death, is scheduled to testify."

"Is this the same Lieutenant Batiste who did not see fit to arrest Mrs. Witt for murder nine years ago, presumably because there wasn't sufficient evidence to bring charges?"

Powell was combing his hair straight back with his hands. "We have several other witnesses, Your Honor."

"I'm sure you do, but are any of them going to say anything that might be remotely admissible? You know the law as well as I do, you tell me."

In the middle of his worst nightmare, Powell came up for the third time. "Your Honor, after much deliberation and at some expense, the District Attorney's office decided to exhume Ned Hollis and run scans for poisons. We found the atropine, which is not a recreational drug, in a lethal dose."

"Your honor," Freeman broke in, "their own witness says Hollis experimented with drugs. He wanted to see if atropine could get him high, that's all."

Villars ignored Freeman's interruption, her eyes on the prosecutor. "As you know, Mr. Powell, the point is not whether you think it, which I believe you do, but whether you can prove it — beyond a reasonable doubt — that Ned Hollis was murdered. Now, what I see is an insurance policy that was used for its original purpose, to pay off the house. I see a recreational-drug user experimenting with a dangerous drug. And here you are waffling on your motive — if Mrs. Witt didn't kill her husband for the money, then she killed him because he was allegedly beating her. Do you have any reports from doctors documenting these beatings? Did she ever report them to the police?"

There was, finally, nothing Powell could say.

Nodding, Villars crossed her arms and walked around behind her desk and stood there a moment. Everyone waited. The rain beat against the window and the clicking of the court reporter's keys stopped. Villars leaned over her chair and picked up, then dropped, four or five stapled pages of legal brief.

She shook her head, taking in the assemblage. "I'm going to be taking a moment to consider this situation. I'd like you all to return here to chambers in fifteen minutes."

Back in her chambers, Villars told Freeman and Hardy that she was prepared to declare a mistrial on Ned Hollis if they wanted it. Of course, in that case, Jennifer could — and would — be retried for the Witt murders only.

Obviously, the jury had been prejudiced — they had heard that the DA, at least, thought that Jennifer had killed her first husband. Also obviously, the jury must have a poor impression of Powell, who was bringing charges that "no reasonable juror" could believe.

Freeman and Hardy wrestled about who got hurt more — the prosecution or the defense. In the end, though, it was Jennifer who made the decision — she did not want to sit in jail while they set a new trial date and started all over again.

They put it all on the record with Villars.

"Your Honor," Freeman said, "I believe the grounds for a mistrial were caused by prosecutorial misconduct that has violated my client's due-process rights. I believe the case must be dismissed in its entirety and that all further prosecution is barred because Mrs. Witt has been placed once in jeopardy."

Villars hated this. "Nice try, Mr. Freeman. Are

you asking for a mistrial or not? If you ask for it, the defendant can be retried. If you don't request it I am not granting it on my own motion."

Freeman, not really expecting to have it both ways, was satisfied nonetheless. But he kept a straight face. "In that case, Your Honor, although I believe the trial has been fatally tainted, we elect to proceed. I have explained the situation to Mrs. Witt, and she elects to go forward. Isn't that true, Jennifer?"

Jennifer looked up. "Yes."

They all trooped back into the courtroom, where Villars announced to the jury that she had decided to grant defense counsel's 1118 motion regarding the murder of Ned Hollis — there wasn't enough evidence as a matter of law to convict Jennifer Witt of killing her first husband. They would be moving on to the next phase of the trial on Monday, but until then, Villars added, why didn't the jury go home early and get a weekend of rest?

Hardy shucked himself out of his wet raincoat, tossed it to the other end of the seat and at the edge of the banquette at Lou's. Freeman slid in opposite him.

It was not yet four o'clock, a dark early afternoon. At the bar Lou was playing a quiet game of liar's dice with one of the regulars; his wife watched a soap opera on the television up in the corner. They were the only other people in the place.

Coffee arrived and Hardy curled his fingers around the mug to warm them. Freeman took his time, adding two spoonfuls of sugar, pouring some cream. He stirred, sipped, added more cream, stirred again.

"Diz, I've got something to tell you and you're not going to like it."

Hardy was trying to keep his hands from shaking. "How long have you known this?"

Freeman studied his own nails. "Longer than you'd like to know, Diz."

Hardy nodded. What could he do? Freeman had just told him that Jennifer had, in fact, killed her first husband, Ned. She'd shot him up with atropine. Just as the prosecution had contended. And Freeman had known all along.

"You know, you are a true son of a bitch," he said.

The older man nodded. "I can understand why you'd think so, but I didn't really think —"

"*Fuck* that, David. You didn't really think? Give me a break."

"Diz —"

"No. No, Diz anything. She told you?"

Freeman nodded.

"And you could go on with this? This incredible charade?"

"Of course."

The blood was pumping. "Of course, even. I really love that. Not just 'sure, Diz,' but 'of course.' "

"She's a client. Of course she's guilty. We're supposed to get her off. And, I might add, we just did."

"We just did. Jesus. Give us a medal, would you."

"It bothers you, does it?"

Hardy lifted his tired eyes. "Bothers me? I think that's fair, David. More than fair, even just, if the word has any meaning for you." He took a long pull at his beer. "But as a matter of interest, since I'm punting out of this case, did she kill Larry, too? And Matt even? What else have you known all along?"

"No."

"No, what?"

"No, I don't think she killed Larry. Or Matt."

"You don't think so?"

"Diz, I said no."

"No, David, you said you didn't *think* so, which, I need hardly tell you, is fairly open to interpretation, as if you didn't know."

Freeman was picking at the frayed wrist seams on his shirt. "You can't punt out. What do you mean? Quit? Now?"

Hardy gave him a long look. "I know you're not much into popular culture, David, but yes, punt means quit. I'm out of here. I'm off the case, okay? Dropping it. You think I could stick around and be part of this? I get a woman off when she murdered her husband? She *admits* it. Is that supposed to make me feel good? Why do you tell me now? You think the irony appeals to me, is that it?"

"No, I don't think that."

Hardy waited, his breathing labored.

Freeman picked some more at his shirt ends. "It was so complicated, Diz. And . . ." he seemed, uncharacteristically, at a loss for words, "and I valued you. I didn't want to lose you, and I know I would have."

Flattery. Bullshit. Hardy's nose was getting refined.

He sucked the rest of his beer. "Well, David, the hell with you. And the hell with her."

Rising, he slammed the bottle down on the table and headed for the door.

Freeman, forgetting his own drink, was up after him, out into the rain.

"I want you to just listen to her, I want you to hear it for yourself." Freeman had followed Hardy out to his car, had gotten himself into the passenger seat and now they sat, the rain pelting on the roof, the windows steamed, in the public lot across from the Hall.

Hardy shook his head in disbelief. "What's she going to say? What can she possibly say?"

32

I had no choice. He would have killed me, would have hunted me down and killed me. How long do you have to take that before you can do something?

That's what they all say, right? That's what you're thinking? Well, if that's what they all say, maybe there's something to it.

The first year or so we both had jobs, we bought a house, we were going to be like our folks. He wasn't doing much coke yet. If he hit me one time in a fight, he'd be all sweet afterward and we'd make up.

I went home to my mom after the first bad time. You know what she told me? She told me she hoped he stopped but she'd better not tell Dad because he'd get all upset and what could he really do anyway? Except maybe go on over to Ned's and get himself in trouble. Either him or Ned, and either way it would be trouble so I'd be better off in the long run if I could just work it out with Ned and not involve my dad.

That's what wives did, Mom said. They worked it out and tried not to complain, and maybe if I was just a little nicer, maybe Ned wouldn't get so mad. If I wouldn't get so bitchy, you know.

So I did try but the thing was, I couldn't get any control over Ned when he was drinking and doing coke and all that other. He was just plain mean, and even worse after he lost the job with Bill Graham — he was like one of the chief roadies for a couple of years — and then they let him go —guess why? — and he had to go back to little clubs and just got meaner all the time. And of course in those music scenes there was all that coke.

Anyway, I had this girlfriend, Tara, down in LA, and I kind of ran away to stay with her. I made the mistake of calling Ned and telling him I was gone, I wasn't coming back but he shouldn't worry about me. Isn't that great? I didn't want him to worry about me. I just wanted it to be over.

But he didn't want it over. It was a mistake to have called. I never dreamed he'd come after me. Stupid, I know now. He came down and was so weirdly calm. He wasn't stoned or drunk. I think that's what scared me the most.

We let him in. I never thought he'd . . . well, he just walked up to Tara and didn't say a word and punched her in the stomach as hard as he could. Ned was a big man, you know, six feet, two hundred pounds. Then he stood over her and said he'd kill her if she ever hid me again or helped me or called the police.

And me, too. He'd kill me, too, if I called the police. I believed he would, too. I had no doubt at all. He grabbed me by the hair and the arm and we got to the car and drove back all night and he wouldn't let me go to the bathroom. Then when we got home, he hit me because the car was dirty and he made me wash it.

It sounds strange, but during all this time we were trying to live normal lives. I mean, I was working with Harlan, I was his receptionist, thinking someday to be a hygienist — oh, you didn't know that? Yes, that's how that started. I didn't plan it, to be unfaithful. That wasn't who I thought I was. But everything with Ned was falling apart and Harlan was very nice to me. Gentle. So it was easy to keep the relationship hidden. It wasn't like I had to sneak out at night. I mean, we'd just close the doors at lunch.

And then, after we were together, he saw the . . . he saw what Ned had done and said I should report it, call the cops, do something. I kept telling him Ned hadn't done it. They were accidents, that's all.

Well, you saw Harlan. He thinks you do everything you're supposed to do and things somehow will work out. So finally, I think I'm in love with him — Harlan. I know he's fat now, but in those days he was just big. I've always had this weakness for big men.

Now I decide to wait until Ned isn't drunk or stoned and try to talk to him, tell him I'm unhappy and can't take him beating me anymore and I'm going to leave. I don't mention Harlan, of course. Thank God. I tell him there's no other man, nobody else. It's not that. It's just between him and me that we're not working out.

I kept thinking that if I don't run away, if I'm reasonable, his reaction is going to be different.

Which it was. He sits there in his chair for about an hour and then — real calm again, which should have been a warning — he says he's going to go out for a while and think about things.

By midnight he's not home and I finally fall asleep.

I wake up screaming, but there's a sock or something in my mouth and I can't breathe or make any noise and there's this awful awful pain down . . . down in me . . . and Ned's on top of me, holding me down.

The next day I can't move. My insides feel broken, ripped up, I still can't breathe, there's blood on the sheets and my hands are tied to the bed. I see that my closet is open and half the clothes are pulled out, cut into shreds, thrown around the room. On the floor I see the knife — it's a butter knife — he's used the dull end, poking it in me.

I wake up again and he's there, untying me, he's straight again. Helps me get in the bath. I'm scared every second now. He's being calm and says he can make things disappear without a trace. I'll find out it's true, he says.

So I take a sick day — I couldn't have gone in anyway — and then it's the weekend and one of the nights Ned has scored some coke and he wants me to get high with him. We'll have fun, he says. It'll be like old times. What old times? I never used drugs.

Well, I can't do it. I'm so scared, I'm still hurting bad. Ned starts to get upset with me again — I've got to stop that. I can't take any more, not right then, so I try to be nice, do what he wants, and he wants to have sex.

Can you believe this? I'm pleading with him, saying I hurt real bad, but he says so what, I'm his wife, get on your back. And I do. And I'm not sure at the moment I'm going to die.

But I don't. That was the worst, not dying. You know how many times I wished I had just died then? How many other times? I mean, truly die, not wake up, just be gone from all this? And believe me, once you feel that — like you really want to die — it's not too far to want someone else to be dead. Why does it have to be me?

I wake up sometime early and Ned is lying next to me, not moving. For a long time I watch him, thinking, hoping, he might be dead. I pinch him in the leg and there's no reaction, then he snores or snorts or something. But the idea stays, the germ of it.

A couple of days go by and I'm starting to heal and things look different, the way they do. No one really wants to believe there's no hope, do they? Even though, really, there isn't.

I'm back at work, I'm putting Harlan off with some excuse and suddenly I realize I haven't seen Boots — Boots was my cat — I haven't seen her in days. Sitting at the front desk at Harlan's, then, all of a sudden, I know. And then I know, I just know, the only way out, what I have to do.

Don't kid yourself, there wasn't any escape. Ned can make things disappear without a trace. He was proving it. I was next.

I arrange it so he thinks we're going to get high. I'm sorry I've been so difficult, I'll be a fun person the way I used to be . . .

This time it's easy. I give him the shot, take a long hot shower, drive out to the beach and bury the stuff, go to my parents' house for breakfast — just visiting, which I still did back then. When I get back home I call the police, tell them my husband's had an accident.

The tiny airless interview room smelled of sweat and wet wool.

Freeman sat, legs crossed, in the chair that he had pushed back against the wall in the corner away from the door.

Hardy's mouth was dry, his back stiff. He had not moved a muscle in fifteen minutes. He found that he believed every word she had said, and was struggling to keep his perspective. "You could probably have pled that as a Murder Two," he said, "which would take it out of capital."

Freeman said, "We got a dismissal. That takes it out of capital, too."

"I don't care what the law says." Jennifer brushed her hair away from her face. "I knew him. There was no other way."

"You should have tried calling the police. They could have done something." Hardy, arguing against himself now, realized how lame it sounded.

Jennifer allowed a one-note laugh. "No they couldn't. Don't you understand? This had been going on for two years and they couldn't have done a damn thing even if they wanted to, even if they believed me."

"Why wouldn't they believe you?"

"Because that's not how it really works. You should know better. You think the law's here to protect *potential* victims? Wrong. What the law does is punish people who've already broken the law. Until somebody's already hurt or killed, they've got no business —"

"But you were hurt. And Ned did break the law, he would have been punished —"

"Jesus, in your dreams." Jennifer looked to Freeman. "Is this guy for real? Does he live in the real world?"

"I live in the real world, Jennifer, and you can't —"

"Oh? Well listen, here's the real world. If I'm

lucky, Ned gets no bail — impossible right there — and then gets a year, if that, for a first offense. Meanwhile I've got maybe a year to move, change my name and my life. Then, guess what? — Ned gets out of jail and comes and gets me, wherever I am, and I disappear just like Boots. My cat. Do I have to explain this? Do I have to draw you a picture? I'm the one whose life is ruined, if I stay alive."

Hardy leaned back in the chair and tried to stretch the crick from his neck. In the guards' room through the glass a woman had just come in for the night shift and was shaking out her raincoat, hanging it on a peg by the door, saying something to somebody outside of Hardy's vision.

"I don't know, from my perspective, I'd say Matt's life is pretty ruined. Even if Larry was beating you —"

"I've told you, Larry wasn't beating me," she said, glaring at him.

Hardy slammed the table with the flat of his palm. "Oh, cut the shit, Jennifer!" He was standing now. The chair tipped, crashed to the floor behind him. "I know for certain that Larry was beating you. I know the doctors you went to see and I know the lies you told them."

He picked up his briefcase and grabbed for the chair to set it upright. Freeman still hadn't said a word.

"I did not kill my son —"

"Good for you."

"I didn't kill Larry, either."

"Or if you did, I'm sure you had a good reason."

"I *didn't,* goddamn it, *I didn't kill them. I have no idea who did.*"

Suddenly she was in his face, coming at him, arms flailing. He tried to back away but in the constrained space there was nowhere to go. The back of his knees hit the chair behind him and he lost his balance, falling over.

Somehow Freeman had gotten between them and maneuvered Jennifer back down into her seat, giving the high sign that everything was all right to the guards through the window. Hardy was pulling himself up, and Freeman, who was aware that he stood blocking the exit, said that in his experience every trial worth its salt produced at least one good display of honest emotion. "I think we can all get through this," he said. "It's to all our advantage."

It had been a tense five minutes, but they were all seated again, clustered around the table. Hardy had agreed to talk, to listen. Now he stared at his partner. "You don't care what, in fact, happened, David. You've made that point a hundred times."

"No, that's not strictly true. What I said was that, *legally,* it doesn't matter what the facts are if they can't be proven. Personally, though, I care. I care a great deal. It's why I'm a lawyer. Which is telling you more than you deserve to know. I could ruin my reputation."

Hardy turned to Jennifer. "Here's a quick-quiz question: Did Larry beat you or not?"

"Yes." Finally.

"A lot?"

She nodded. "But if I admitted that, especially with what happened with Ned, no jury would believe I didn't kill Larry, too."

This was the issue. Jennifer had killed Ned because he beat her. Larry, too, had beaten her, and she was contending, insisting, that she had not killed him.

"I had to lie," she said. "Once it came out that they both hit me . . . ."

"What's to make me think you're not lying now?"

"I'm not lying now. I'm telling you."

"All you're doing is telling me another version. Whatever flies this week."

"Diz." Freeman put a hand on his sleeve. "Please. Look at it strategically. She's free on Ned. We're halfway there. She certainly didn't kill her own boy. Accident or not. She wasn't any part of that. I think you and I both believe that."

"I don't know what I believe anymore, David."

Jennifer put her hand on his other arm. "I did what I did with Ned almost ten years ago." She was talking quietly, almost whispering, not trying to look at him to persuade with her eyes, which he took as a good sign. "If I had a choice, as you say I did, well then at least you should believe that I didn't *think* I had a choice. I was scared for my life and I didn't know what to do — I thought there was no other way out.

"With Larry, it hadn't gotten to that yet. Maybe it would have, I don't know. I wanted to think not. It's why I started seeing Ken Lightner, trying to make the family work. I'm screwed up, I admit, I bring things on myself. Even Ken tells me I'm too much a victim. I was trying to change. . . And then somebody . . . somebody kills Larry, and my son, and out of the blue I'm arrested for it. And suddenly I'm supposed to trust my whole life to two men I didn't even know six months ago? No way. Men haven't been so good to me, you might have noticed, so I made my own plan and stuck with it."

Hardy crossed his arms. "I did notice one other thing, though. You managed to tell David here the truth."

Freeman cut in. "I sandbagged her, Diz. That's how I work. It came out."

"And you didn't tell me."

"That was my decision, not hers. Okay, it was a mistake on my part, bad judgment. I should have included you, but I didn't think you'd need to know until the penalty phase, if then."

"Need to know, huh?" It had become dark outside through the guardroom window. Friday night. The weekend lay ahead, with time to decide what he was going to do. Hardy let out a long breath. He turned to Jennifer. "If you have any other secrets, Jennifer, now would be a good time to talk about them."

But the veil had come down again, her passion spent. "Just find out who killed my baby, would you? Can you do that?"

33

He didn't know what he was doing, driving in the morning rain out California to Miz Carter's, then changing his mind, turning down through Golden Gate Park, avoiding the tree limbs that littered Kennedy Drive, knocked down by the force of the storm. He didn't really know where he was going. Maybe his brain had shut down from lack of sleep.

It all had come down to whether he believed her. This time. Even though he knew she had lied to him — about damn near everything — from the beginning. Could he still believe her?

He thought he did. That was what had kept him awake, tossing next to Frannie until the cloud's gray became visible out their bedroom window.

He had told Freeman that Jennifer's story was flawed, but the truth was that he found it credible. He'd been around and around on it, and every time it came up more logically sound.

Jennifer had to kill Ned. From her perspective, it was pure self-defense. She truly believed he was going to kill her, and why wouldn't she?

She'd tried to run away and he'd tracked her down. Then she'd told him she was going to leave and he'd beaten her almost to death, violated her with the blunt end of a kitchen knife, killed her cat as an obvious, classic threat, and threatened her with her own death if she did anything to stop the rampage.

He had read everything Lightner had given him, plus twenty or thirty other articles and briefs on the subject. Battered women did not feel like they could get away. They were forever trapped in a situation from which they could literally neither run nor hide, and which would someday, in all probability, kill them.

Hardy believed Freeman could prove that Jennifer taking Ned's life had been justifiable, a sometimes valid form of self-defense that the courts had begun to recognize. Even with Judge Villars, even with the legislature failing to pass a law codifying BWS as a defense, Hardy was fairly confident they could get Jennifer off. Certainly, as he had pointed out, no jury in the State of California would call for the death penalty.

Jennifer was not stupid. She knew that if she agreed to assert the battered-woman syndrome, then her life, at least, would be removed from the equation — it would no longer be a capital case.

So the recurring question was: Why wouldn't she plead to it? *Her* reason was that it implied a defense against guilt, and she said she had no reason for a defense against something she hadn't done.

And she could not very well plead to one murder and not the other. No one would believe her. Powell would laugh at it. A jury would be insulted. No judge would be sympathetic. Yet Hardy found himself believing it. Jennifer Witt did *not* kill her son, she had not been there when he had been killed, she had known nothing about it. Matt rang true, and if he bought that — which was not at all the same as believing a jury would buy it — then, working backward, all the other apparent duplicity made a perverse kind of sense.

She could not admit to any similarities, especially in so far as battery, between her lives with Ned and with Larry, especially once they'd gotten as far as trial.

There was no evidence that she had been beaten, and if they admitted at trial that she had been, in the jury's mind that would only make it more likely that she had killed both of her husbands. So her position had to be that no one had ever abused her. It was the only story that worked . . . And of course, truthful or not, David Freeman the lawyer gobbled it up and made it his own.

There was a pause in the downpour. Hardy was wearing tennis shoes, jeans and a green waterproof jacket. He got out of his car, and from where he stood, near the top of Olympia up the block from Jennifer's house, he could see a band of blue widening at the horizon. Even this early in the morning, and it was before seven, the air was strangely humid and heavy, laden with the smell of eucalyptus.

He didn't know why he had driven out here, or what, if anything, he expected to find or accomplish. Light-headed, he walked from his car up past the Witt house to the edge of the grove surrounding Twin Peaks, leading up to Sutro

Tower, the source of the eucalyptus scent. A mother deer and her two fawns were rooting through the foliage there, fifty or sixty feet back into the trees.

The deer bolted, startled, disappearing into the woods. In the deep shade, Hardy blinked his stinging eyes, trying to clear his vision, stunned to see Jennifer Witt in a bright blue jogging outfit break from the cover of the trees and run toward him on the trail, then past him — no, close up it wasn't, of course, her — out to the street, where whoever it was turned down Olympia.

As he stood there, drizzle began to fall again and he ran, following her footsteps, around the corner and down the long block to his car. The woman, jogging faster than Hardy could sprint, had turned downhill on Clarendon.

The car spun on the wet pavement, then straightened. Hardy took the corner at Olympia and hydroplaned again, his wheels this time bouncing off the concrete before he got the car under control again.

He was alongside the woman, slowing down and honking his horn, motioning for her to pull over. She flipped him off, stole a glance at her watch and kept going.

Hardy slowed, rolled down his passenger window and gunned it up to her again, honking. "I need help," he called out to her. Driving ahead another hundred yards, he pulled to the curb, throwing open his door and getting out. He held his hands wide, spread out at shoulder height, offering no threat. The woman slowed abruptly, stopping fifty feet up the street. The rain started coming in sheets.

"What?" she gasped. "Can't you see I'm trying to run?" Hardy took a step toward her and she put her hand to her hip. "I've got mace here on my belt and I'll use it."

"I need to ask you a question."

A car passed going the other direction, slowed to look, then sped up the street.

"A *question?*" She shook her head in disbelief. "Christ, this city."

"It might save a woman's life."

"Sure it will." She checked her wristwatch again. "Who the hell are you? Leave me alone."

Hardy wished he could try the old badge trick but he didn't carry it as a matter of course. It was at home, there if he decided he might need to use it.

"I'm going by," the woman said. "You'd better leave me some room." She was, in fact, holding what looked like a spray can in her hand and Hardy had no doubt she'd use it.

He had to talk fast, find some lever. She was coming toward him cautiously. "You ever hear of Jennifer Witt? I'm her lawyer."

"Good for you. I'm a runner."

She turned it on, going by the other side of his car. There wasn't so much as a glance back as she flew down the street, around a curve and out of his sight.

Back in his car, Hardy consoled himself that it was probably nothing anyway. But then, three blocks later, he realized the truth of what he'd just done — he thought he might have stumbled on a nugget of truth in one of Jennifer's explanations — so he hadn't given up on her.

Jennifer had said she always started out walking for a couple of blocks when she left her house to go jogging. She had insisted that was her routine, and she followed it on the morning of December 28. And somebody else, with a resemblance to her, came running by her house just as some shots were fired. That person stopped, saw nothing, and continued running, right from Jennifer's gate. And was identified as Jennifer by the State's star eyewitness, Anthony Alvarez.

It almost gave him real hope.

Glitsky called after dinner and told them they should turn on the news because David Freeman was on.

Moses and his new wife Susan were over, and everyone was at the front of the house. While Hardy turned on the set, Moses plopped himself on the sofa. "That guy gets more air than a hot-air balloon," he said. Turning around, Hardy said that David Freeman *was* a hot-air balloon. When it suited him.

The man himself appeared on the screen. Unshaven, hang-dog, his tie askew over his wrinkled shirt, with sleeves partially rolled up — here was a man who'd been working all night and all day on behalf of his client. He was sitting on the edge of the desk in his office, his lawbooks visible behind him — and the sound came up. ". . . victory but, to be quite candid, I expected it. I have fought from the original arraignment to have this case dismissed for lack of evidence, and, of course, the judge's ruling here corroborates what I've maintained all along — Jennifer Witt is innocent. She did not do these things."

Hardy and Frannie, now sharing their own secret about Ned, exchanged a glance. "He is some piece of work," Hardy whispered.

The young female reporter spoke earnestly into the camera. "And, obviously buoyed by yesterday's victory, Mr. Freeman had some even stronger charges to make."

This was edited tape, and again the sound bite picked up in midsentence. Freeman was answering another question. ". . . there's the political motive. I hate to bring this up, but it's true — Dean Powell is running for Attorney General on a pro-death-penalty ticket. At the same time, you can't have a death penalty just for black men. He needs a case like this, and he needs it right now. If Jennifer Witt hadn't come along he would have had to invent her." Freeman hung his head, genuinely saddened by the flawed nature of humankind. "Unfortunately," he said, "that's essentially what he did."

Suddenly they were back in the newsroom and the anchorman was saying to his partner, "Those are some pretty strong accusations, Shel, and we'll be following that trial every day here on Channel 5."

"That's right, Jack." Shel beamed at the camera, filling the screen. "Want to know what happens when three sisters fight over the family dog?"

"Slick segue, Shel," Frannie intoned.

Moses, leaning forward on the couch, shushed his sister, speaking to the TV, "Yeah, three sisters and the family dog. I want to know what happens, I do."

Shel was continuing. "Sounds like a case for Solomon, doesn't it, and it's developing right now down in Daly City. That's up next. Don't go away."

Hardy was up, also talking to the tube, turning it off. "Sorry, Shel, got to go."

Moses jumped up. "Come on, Diz. I'm dying to know about the sisters and their dog."

Susan hit him on the leg. "Pervert."

"How can you do that? Turn off Shel?"

Hardy was moving back to his chair. "Years of training and therapy have helped me here. Why do I get the feeling that Jennifer's trial is going to be getting nasty?"

"It's that amazing sixth sense you have." Frannie rubbed a hand over his arm. "It must have been an awful slow news day."

Susan was smiling and relaxed, leaning against Moses on the couch. "He's your partner, Dismas?"

"Cute, isn't he?"

Moses, cut adrift, moaned that he wanted to know more about the girls and their dog.

"They ate it," Frannie said.

Susan nodded. "Cut it up into little pieces. Fried the ears and served them with roquefort dressing."

Hardy stood up. "I'd like to go on the record here by saying how nice it is to be among people who are so in tune with the big issues. I'm going to get dessert."

Because of the afternoon nap he'd taken, he wasn't tired. Moses and Susan went home at a little after ten, and Frannie, who would have Vincent's first feeding at one, said she thought she would turn in.

Hardy added a log to the fire in the front room and sat in his chair with a copy of John McPhee's *Oranges*. He'd barely begun when the telephone rang. He grabbed it halfway through the first ring.

It was Glitsky saying his man Freeman was a star. "Trial by television. It's what makes this country great."

"That and concentrated orange juice." Hardy explained the McPhee connection, knowing that Glitsky, like himself, had a weakness for the obscure fact. "But I sense you didn't call to talk about citrus."

"Normally I would," Abe said, "except I thought you'd want to be the first to know about something else."

Hardy silently counted to five. A log popped on the fire. "I love this game," he said.

"I called the Detail on an unrelated matter about ten minutes ago. They were interviewing a guy down there named Marko something. Ring a bell?"

"No. Should it?"

"I don't know. I thought you might have run across it in your travels. He's saying he killed Larry Witt."

Marko Mellon had not begun watching the news report on Jennifer Witt during the Freeman section, as Hardy and company had. He had watched from the start, when they showed her picture — the one the stations and newspapers had used before she had been charged with the murders — smiling, vivacious.

Marko, a twenty-five-year-old Syrian exchange student at San Francisco State who had been following the trial in a fairly dedicated fashion up to this point, was familiar with, Hardy thought, a surprising amount of facts about the case, so much so that it took police inspectors — one of whom was Walter Terrell — nearly five hours to determine he could not possibly have killed Larry Witt.

His motive for killing Larry, he said, was that he loved Jennifer. As it turned out, his motive for the confession was that he had decided he loved Jennifer from her picture. It was a spiritual connection he was sure they had, and if he confessed she would of course want to meet him, after which they would fall in love, get married, have more babies to make up for Matt. It was a no-lose plan, because eventually they would find out he, Marko, hadn't really done it, and then he'd be free and they could live happily ever after together.

"I don't think he thought the whole thing through." Hardy was talking to Freeman. The storm had passed and there were pink clouds in an early morning gray sky over the Oakland Hills across the Bay. They were by the door to Hardy's car, standing in a deserted Bryant Street outside the Hall of Justice after the decision had been reached that they weren't going to be charging Marko with Larry Witt's murder.

"It staggers me that it took them five hours to come to it," Freeman said. "The boy's got the IQ of a turnip. Of course, then again, some of the inspectors . . ."

"He did know a lot of details, David. They had to let him cross himself up."

"Rats in mazes know details. That doesn't make them smart. They should have just asked him when his visa runs out."

"Why would they ask him that?"

"You check. Dollars to donuts his visa runs out in the next month or so. He figured he'd get arrested, get to stay longer over here."

"In jail? On a murder charge?"

Freeman shrugged. "You ever been to Syria, Diz?"

Hardy let it go. Freeman might be right. "I saw you tonight on the tube, by the way. I don't think Dean's going to be too pleased."

Freeman waved it off. "It's good press. I'm doing him a favor." There was a silence between them, a residual tension that banter wasn't going to camouflage.

Hardy pulled open the door to his car and, in the predawn light, asked if he could drop Freeman at his apartment. He'd taken a cab down. The old attorney said no, he'd walk.

"This time of the day through this neighborhood? Come on, David, get in."

Freeman slammed his hand on the roof of the car. "Take off, Diz, I'll see you tomorrow."

"David . . ."

Freeman spread his hands theatrically. "We've been working together long enough, you ought to know by now. I'm bullet-proof."

At sunrise Hardy was still in his car, waiting

on Olympia Way as though he were at a stakeout. If the jogger came by again he was going to get a few words with her if he had to sprint alongside her for six blocks breathing Mace.

She did not appear.

34

Freeman was wrong. Powell did not take it as a favor.

They were in Judge Villars' chambers again. It was 9:40 on Monday morning and the jury was in the courtroom, waiting. Adrienne, the court reporter, was perched with her portable equipment next to one of the easy chairs, but she was the only one sitting. Her presence was necessary, as no meeting was ever off the record.

Freeman, Hardy, Powell, his young assistant, Justin Morehouse, and Villars were taking up most of the rest of the space in the room. Or maybe it just felt that way. Everyone stood in a knot, too close, an invisible bubble surrounding them, the pressure building within it.

"I've never been more serious, Your Honor." Freeman looked especially wan in a ten-year-old brown suit. "I've given this a lot of thought over the weekend, since your generous granting of my 1118 —"

"There was nothing generous about that. Don't put a personal spin on this . . ."

"The fact remains. I'm convinced this would not be a capital trial if Dean here weren't running for AG."

"Your Honor." Powell wore his substantial self-control on his sleeve, but it was wearing thin. "Mr. Freeman knows full well that we've still got two sets of specials on both remaining counts. This is a death-penalty case."

"It's politically tainted and you know it, Dean."

"There's nothing political about it."

Freeman turned to Villars. "Let him prove that, Your Honor, if he can. Continue this trial until after the election. See how hot our dedicated prosecutor is to fry Jennifer Witt then."

"Your Honor, I resent defense counsel's implication —"

"I'm not *implying* anything, Your Honor. We've got grounds to appeal right now, and I think we're skating mighty close to another due process violation. I might have to ask for a mistrial after all."

Freeman, though he said the magic word, did not win a hundred dollars. Instead, Villars raised herself up and pointed a finger at him. "On Friday you said you didn't want a mistrial, Mr. Freeman. I am not going to let you take opposite sides of the same issue."

Powell, his temper beginning to show, cracked his knuckles and ran his fingers through his hair. "If he wanted to calendar the case after the election, he could have requested it anytime. Now we have a jury impaneled, we have witnesses who've rearranged their schedules to be here. To continue the trial at this point —"

Villars moved a step toward them both, the color high on her normally gray cheeks. She spoke quietly but her voice had the crack of authority. "All right, now, both of you, listen up. Unless Mr. Freeman requests it *right now* we're not having a mistrial, we're not having a continuance. I'm going to give some instructions to the jury this morning and then we're going to proceed in an orderly fashion until we get to a verdict." She reached to button her robe, then stopped. "And one more thing — I don't want to see this case on television, or read about it in the newspapers over the next few weeks. Consider this a gag order. My clerk will have a written order by the recess. I trust we're clear on this."

"Ladies and gentlemen."

The judge was still angry — furious at Powell for what she considered the sloppiness of the first half of the case, and at Freeman for at least a half dozen reasons — blurring the mistrial issue, threatening to appeal, attacking Powell personally, going public with his accusations, dressing like a bag man in her courtroom. Hardy wondered if her anger was as obvious to the jury and to the standing-room crowd in the gallery, who had no doubt showed up in response to Freeman's appearance on television followed by the front-page story in yesterday's *Chronicle*.

Jennifer Witt had become big news again.

Though Villars had more reasons to want to flay Freeman, she appeared to be equally hostile to both sides, and this — Freeman felt — would ultimately help him. Of course, Freeman was of the opinion, Hardy reflected, that a mass murder in the courtroom would ultimately help the defense. His credo was that any disturbance in the steady accretion of incriminating evidence helped the defense. It was why he acted so disruptively.

But in spite of the huge crowd, Villars might as well have been alone with the twelve jurors in a small room. She did not so much as glance in the direction of the gallery, of the attorneys' tables. In a conversational, almost intimate tone, she was giving instructions intended to keep her trial from becoming a reversal — the nightmare of every judge and doubtless the root of her most immediate anger.

"I won't try to deny that this trial has taken an irregular turn. It is highly unusual to dismiss one charge in the middle of the People's case and I won't insult you by pretending it is not. Some of you may feel a little strange that we are going on at all, and I want to address that issue now.

"Mrs. Witt had been charged with three separate counts of murder. On Friday, you will recall, I ruled that there was not sufficient evidence introduced, as a matter of law, to prove beyond a reasonable doubt that Jennifer Witt killed her first husband, Ned Hollis.

"However, I want you to understand that this should not in any way prejudice your feelings about the People's case on the remaining two charges on the one hand, or Mrs. Witt's defense on the other."

She took a sip of water and cast another withering gaze at counsel — on both sides of the courtroom.

"That said, let us now put Ned Hollis behind us. He has no integral connection to the remaining charges filed against Mrs. Witt. If any of you feel that you cannot in good conscience accept this instruction, please raise your hand now and I will excuse you from the jury."

No hands went up. Hardy would have preferred to see one or two because he knew, in fact, that this was an instruction that would be difficult if not impossible to internalize. Now all twelve jurors were sitting with the personal knowledge that Jennifer's first husband had died, and afterward she had collected a lot of money. No hands meant that it was not going to be acknowledged in deliberation over the verdict — but it was going to be there, a snake in the weeds.

Villars nodded. "Now, the remaining two counts still include multiple murder and murder for profit, and these are among the special circumstances defined in California for which the State can ask the death penalty. The deaths of Larry Witt and Matthew Witt should be your *only* concerns during the remainder of this trial. The court appreciates your patience in sitting through this exercise and assures you that we will not have a repetition of it during the coming days or weeks."

Villars took a final drink from her glass, then abruptly turned to face the courtroom. "I trust, Mr. Powell, that you are ready with your next witness."

"I am, Your Honor."

"All right, then, let's get this show on the road."

Not only was Dean Powell unhappy and angry, the confrontation with Freeman in Villars' chambers seemed to have galvanized him. Now he didn't just want to win for another notch in his belt or a leg up on his campaign. Freeman, always angling for an edge, had raised the stakes and now — for Powell — it had become personal. He was not just going to win by getting the jury to convict Jennifer Witt. He was also going to whip David Freeman.

Hardy flipped open his binder and found the tab for the Federal Express driver. He pushed it over in front of Jennifer so that Freeman could review it, too, but Freeman either did not need it — could it be he had the whole file memorized? — or was reluctant to show that he did.

Mr. Fred Rivera, the Lou Christie fan — Hardy had had "The Gypsy Cried" going through the brainpan for weeks, it was driving him crazy — took the stand, slightly ill-at-ease to be the first witness but clearly pleased to be part of all this excitement, plus getting paid to take a day off. He wore his Federal Express uniform and sat forward in the witness chair, wanting to take it all in.

"Mr. Rivera." Powell stood on the balls of his feet, rocking forward and back, fifteen feet or so in front of the witness, in the center of the courtroom. "On the morning of December 28 of last year, the Monday after Christmas, did you deliver a Federal Express package to 128 Olympia Way?"

"Yes, sir, I did."

So it began, Powell walking Rivera through the delivery at precisely 9:30 A.M., when Larry Witt and Matt were still alive. Fred identified a picture of Larry. It was stamped as an exhibit, as was the Federal Express invoice containing Larry's signature for the package. Nailing the time down,

Powell introduced the computer printout showing that Fred had punched in his verified delivery at 9:31.

Powell started his next line of questioning: Rivera had seen no one walking up or down Olympia Way that morning. Then, without changing his rhythm, the prosecutor departed from what Freeman and Hardy had predicted would be the script. "Mr. Rivera, you had a talk with Inspector Terrell about the events of that morning and you described Dr. Witt's behavior, did you not?"

"You mean I said he was pretty uptight, like that?"

Freeman raised his index finger and objected that this was speculation and called for a conclusion. Villars sustained him. Powell rephrased it. "Mr. Rivera, what did Dr. Witt do when he opened the door?"

"Well, he only opened it a third, maybe a half way. I gave him the package and then tried to give him the clipboard so he could sign for it, but he was holding the package, no place to put it down. It seemed to make him mad."

Freeman, wondering where all this was going, raised a finger again. "Your Honor? Same objection."

Villars leaned over to the witness. "Mr. Rivera," she said gently, "just say what you saw him do, not how you think he felt about it."

Rivera's composure was slipping. Throughout all of his earlier conversations with lawyers and policemen, nobody had made him respond in this way before. Welcome to jury trials, Hardy thought.

"What did Dr. Witt do then?" Powell was suddenly his good buddy, helping him, drawing him out.

"Well, he turned half-around to give the package to the boy."

"Did you see the boy?"

"No, I didn't see him, not then. He was behind the door."

"Then how do you know it was the boy?"

"I saw him go running off to show the package to his mother."

At the defense table, Freeman was flipping pages on Rivera's interviews. "You ever hear this before?" he whispered to Hardy and then, without waiting for an answer, stood. "Your Honor, I object. The witness can't possibly know the boy's intentions going off with the package."

Freeman appeared agitated and he had reason to be. If the prosecution could show that Jennifer had been *home* at 9:30, and until now nothing in the record had indicated that they could, it would be a significant loss.

Villars all but rolled her eyes. "I'm sure Mr. Powell will rephrase."

Powell, still not skipping a beat, smiled at Rivera and said, "Dr. Witt handed the package to the boy behind the door. Did the boy then say anything?"

"He said, 'I'm going to show this to Mom.' "

Powell turned to Freeman, stopping to make sure the jury understood what Rivera had said. "Your witness."

It was a classic example, Hardy thought, of

why trials were both so addictive and so nerve-wracking. Freeman had interviewed Rivera twice and the man had never wavered in his story — he hadn't seen Jennifer. He had wanted to get back and hear the Golden Oldie, win a trip to Hawaii. He'd been at the door with Dr. Witt for a minute at the most.

So the entire thrust of Freeman's interview had been to establish the time of delivery — not whether Matt had gone running upstairs calling for his mother.

The old bear got up slowly, but by the time he had reached his spot in front of the bench there was no further sign that he had taken a blow. He smiled at the witness, nodded to the jury. "Mr. Rivera, we've had a few conversations over the past couple of months, have we not?"

"Yes, sir."

"And during those conversations, did I ever ask you if you saw Jennifer Witt while you were delivering this package on December 28?"

"Yes, sir."

"And how did you respond?"

"I said I didn't see her."

"Did you hear her? Was she, for example, singing in the shower or something like that? Moving furniture around?"

Freeman was taking advantage of the rules that allowed defense in cross-examination to lead witnesses, and Freeman was also using this bantering tone to get back into a more relaxed mode with Fred, showing him what a regular Joe he could be.

He got his small reward. Rivera grinned, loosening. "No, I didn't hear nobody singing or moving things around."

"When the boy ran off, did he yell for his mother? Did he run up the stairs yelling 'Mom!' or anything like that?"

A risky question — if the answer was yes it would hurt. But given the repressed nature of what they knew to be the tone in the Witt household, Hardy thought it would pay off.

It took a moment of reflection. Hardy glanced over at the jury. They were following every nuance. Faces were on Rivera. "No, I don't remember that."

Some of the damage perhaps repaired, Freeman allowed himself a breath. "Let's go back, if we may, to what Matt said to his father. Can you tell us again what it was?"

Seeing this new trap, Powell was on his feet. "It's in the record, Your Honor. The reporter can read back what Mr. Rivera said."

Villars considered Powell's point a little too long for Freeman's comfort. Knowing that a trap could sometimes spring on the person who set it, Freeman withdrew the question. He did not want the jury to hear again how Matt had said "I'm going to show this to Mom." He had been fishing, hoping that Fred would come up with another paraphrase of the same idea, something like "I'll see if Mom will like this when she gets home." But no such luck.

Smiling, Freeman turned back to the witness. "So, to summarize, you did not see Jennifer Witt in the house at 9:30?"

"That's right."

"You did not hear her either?"

"No, I didn't."

Freeman paused and realized this was about as good as he was going to get, and it wasn't all that good. Giving the jury a confident grin, he said to Rivera, "Thank you, sir. No further questions."

Powell, smelling blood, stood quickly and said he had a short question or two on redirect. "Mr. Rivera, when Matt went running off with this package, what was Dr. Witt doing?"

"What was he doing? I guess he took the clipboard, looked at his watch, signed it and gave it to me."

"Did he speak to his son?"

"No, I told you, the boy went running behind him."

"Yes, you did say that. He didn't remind the boy, though, for example, that his mother wasn't home?"

"Objection!" Freeman was up, shot from a cannon.

Villars pointed at Powell. "Sustained. Mr. Powell, you know better. Strike the last." And she directed the jury to disregard the question, which they would try to do. But Powell had done more damage, and he knew it as he graciously dismissed the witness.

Freeman was fuming. Over Jennifer's objections he had insisted that he and Hardy return to the Sutter Street offices. He needed to vent and didn't want to do it in front of his client. "He never, never mentioned Matt going to show anything to anybody!"

Hardy was drinking cranberry soda out of a bottle, picking pretzels out of the bag on the center of the conference table. "Well, he did today, David. Did you ask him?"

"Shit."

"Does that mean you didn't?"

Nothing, it seemed, dimmed Freeman's appetite. He was having liverwurst and onions on a rye roll, drinking one of the popular non-alcoholic beers that were so politically correct in San Francisco but which Hardy thought were a blight on the earth. "I asked him ten times if he'd seen Jennifer. Was Jennifer there? You're sure you didn't see her?"

"You think she was there?"

Freeman swallowed what he was chewing. "The *jury* thinks she was there, Diz. We've got to convince them she wasn't 'cause if she was, guess what?"

Hardy knew too well the answer to that one. He sat a moment, part of him savoring the experience of Freeman choking on his arrogance, a victim of his own oversight.

After lunch they breezed through the coroner, Dr. Strout again, and this time he delivered his testimony without incident. It was no surprise that both Larry and Matt had been shot at close range with Larry's gun and had died almost instantly from the wounds. Freeman could have stipulated to most of what Strout had to say, but he held onto a small hope that once again the doctor would put some spin on his testimony that might cast doubt on the essential and undisputed facts. He did not.

There was no point in boring the jury. Freeman had been willing to stipulate to the validity of the forensics report identifying Larry's gun as the murder weapon. But on the matter of fingerprints, he had a few thoughts.

The witness was the police department's expert, Aja Farek, an attractive Pakistani woman of perhaps thirty-five. Powell had elicited from her the testimony that Jennifer's fingerprints had been on both the brass bullet casings and clip that held them.

Freeman shuffled to center stage. "Ms. Farek, did you find any fingerprints at all on the outside of the gun — the barrel, the grip, anyplace like that?"

"No. Except the person's who found the gun, of course."

"The person who found the gun? Who was that?"

Ms. Farek consulted some notes. "His name is Sid Parmentier. He's the man who found the gun in the dumpster, I believe."

"The dumpster? What dumpster?" Freeman knew all about the dumpster. Still, he raised his eyebrows, including the jury in his shock at this surprising new development.

Powell stood up. "Your Honor, the People will be calling Mr. Parmentier about his discovery of the murder weapon. Ms. Farek is a fingerprint expert."

Villars nodded, her face a blank. "Stick to the point, Mr. Freeman."

"All right. Fingerprints." Freeman again included the jury, this time in his disappointment. He guessed that they, too, would have to wait to find out what they all wanted to know about the dumpster. Well, it wasn't his fault. He was trying to help them but the judge and prosecutor weren't cooperating. Back at the witness, he was gentleness itself. "How long do fingerprints last, Ms. Farek?"

The witness frowned. "They can last a long time."

"A long time? A month? A year?"

"Yes. Easily."

"And how old were the fingerprints of Jennifer Witt that you found on the casings and the clip?"

"I don't know. There's no way to tell that."

"You can't test them for residual dryness, anything like that?"

"No. Fingerprints are oil-based. They don't get dry in that sense."

"So she could have handled those bullets and the clip at almost any time?"

"Yes."

"Not necessarily on the day of the shooting or anywhere near it?"

Powell raised himself from his chair again. "She's already answered that, Your Honor."

Freeman piped right up. "So she has." Beaming all around, as if he'd made a point he'd been laboring over for weeks. "No further questions."

Despite the lead-in, Sid Parmentier, the man who had found the gun, had nothing either new or startling to say about the gun or the dumpster. Nevertheless, it was not in Freeman's nature to pass on even neutral testimony. He must have felt he had already used up his quota for the day by not cross-examining Strout, because he jumped up ready to go when Powell had finished.

Mr. Parmentier was heavy-set, with a Neanderthal-like hairline. His black sports coat was shiny. His over-starched white shirt was too tight, and, evidently, so was the black tie he constantly tugged at.

Freeman, loving a man who shared his sartorial tastes, stood close to the witness box, hands in pockets, relaxed. "At any time, sir, did you see the defendant, Jennifer Witt" — he pointed for effect — "at or near this dumpster?"

"No."

"Did you see her throw anything into it?"

Powell raised a hand. "Asked and answered, Your Honor."

Villars sustained him, but Freeman hadn't had his say yet, or he had another card to play. Hardy suspected the latter. "Your Honor, it bears repeating."

"I'm sure the jury heard it the first time, Mr. Freeman. If Mr. Parmentier didn't see Mrs. Witt at or near this dumpster, then it follows, doesn't it, that he didn't see her throw anything into it?"

Silently, apparently deep in thought, Freeman nodded. He half-turned around to the defense table, thought some more, then gave the jury a look.

Villars wasn't having it. "Mr. Freeman, do you want to excuse the witness? Let's stop these histrionics."

Contrite, sincere, Freeman apologized — lost

in thought, as though he'd forgotten where he was for the moment. "It just occurred to me, Your Honor, that this testimony here falls into the same category as that you ruled on during the earlier part of this trial."

No one in the courtroom — not Hardy, not Powell, not the jury or Villars — knew where he was going, and he took the opportunity he had created to push forward uninterrupted. "We've got a gun in a dumpster, just like we had a hypodermic needle in a leg years earlier." Freeman turned directly to the jury, suddenly raising his voice, suddenly furious. "You see what he's doing, don't you? Mr. Powell keeps leaving out any *agent* who delivers these *objects* to their destinations. He wants you to assume that it's Jennifer Witt and he *can't do that.*"

Bam bam bam.

Powell was on his feet. "Objection! Your Honor . . ."

Villars sounded angry: "Mr. Freeman, get hold of yourself. You don't address the jury like that. The reporter will strike those last remarks."

But Freeman kept his voice up, indignant, outraged. "Your Honor, my client's life is at stake here, and there's no evidence whatsoever that Jennifer Witt even *held* this gun that somehow got into the dumpster."

"Your Honor!" Powell had come around his table into the forum of the courtroom, "her *fingerprints* were on the weapon."

Villars used her gavel again. "Sit down, Mr. Powell, we're not arguing this right now." She pointed a finger. "You, Mr. Freeman, are out of order. Are you finished with this witness or not?"

"I am outraged —"

Now Villars slammed the gavel, the sound echoing in the wide, high room. Next to Hardy, Jennifer jumped.

"Anything but yes or no and you'll go to jail, Mr. Freeman."

Suddenly Freeman got himself back under control. He nodded, swallowed hard. "Yes, Your Honor."

"Yes, what?"

"Yes, I'm through with this witness."

The judge was still holding her gavel, ready to crack it down again. But the moment had passed, Powell was back in his seat, Freeman was returning to his.

Villars perused the room from her bench. With no one else to talk to, she looked down on Mr. Parmentier. "The witness may be excused," she said. "We're going to take a short recess."

"They're hating you," Jennifer said.

Freeman was walking around by the window, looking out, then back, pleased with himself. He, Hardy and Jennifer had retired for the recess to their semi-private conference room behind the bailiffs' area.

"I don't think the jury is hating him," Hardy said.

"They love me," Freeman declared.

"But Mr. Powell was right." Jennifer was sitting on the desk, hands and feet crossed. "There was something connecting me and that gun — it was mine and Larry's — even if I didn't put it in that dumpster. It wasn't the same as the needle."

"It doesn't matter," Freeman said. "After what the judge did with Ned, every person on that jury is going to have it in their minds. They're going to think it's another Powell railroad because that's what they're going to be looking for. I think we just put 'em away —"

Hardy was standing by the door, hands in his pockets, taking it in. "It's a different set of facts, David. I think the jury's going to go with the facts."

Freeman stalked back to the window, looking out and down. "Bunch of spoilsports."

There was a knock and the door opened. One of the courtroom bailiffs stuck his head in, gave Hardy a look and told Freeman that the judge would like a word with him in her chambers.

35

Hardy decided that he should probably swing by Olympia Way and spend an early morning hour going over notes and hoping his phantom jogger would reappear. If she ran by that way even semi-regularly there was some chance that she might be useful. The defense would open its case in the next week and he wanted as many "other dudes" as he could for David to pull out of his hat.

Not that, strictly speaking, Hardy's jogger was another dude. Or even a dudette. He had different plans for her — Freeman wouldn't attempt to implicate her in the killings as a possible suspect. But he might be able to use her to discredit the damaging testimony of Anthony Alvarez, the neighbor from across the street. What if he had seen this phantom jogger that morning — and not Jennifer — at the gate? And therefore not in the house. If a question about Alvarez's identification of Jennifer could get planted in the jury's mind, the jogger would be worth putting on the stand.

Sipping some coffee out of a traveling mug, cramped behind the wheel of his Honda just after sunrise, he realized that during the past week, while the focus of the trial had been on the Ned Hollis murder, he should have been preparing overviews on Tom DiStephano and the Romans if Freeman was going to use them as defense witnesses.

But in fact he hadn't spoken to Tom DiStephano since he'd gotten threatened by him and his father a couple of months ago, and Glitsky hadn't seemed particularly inclined to move on finding an alibi for the Romans on December 28. Glitsky might be his friend, but he was first a cop, and a busy cop with other priorities. When the directed verdict of acquittal came in so early on Ned, he realized that time was getting short and he had to have significantly more if Freeman was going to be able to use any of the information he'd gathered on these people.

He'd have to put the needle in Abe — see if he could get him to move on the Romans, and he knew the answer might well be that he couldn't. He also came across the name Jody Bachman and realized that the Los Angeles attorney had never gotten back to him on Crane & Crane and YBMG. These were all areas that would have to be shored up before the defense began its case in earnest.

Yesterday, Monday, they had never gone back in to trial. Villars had evidently gotten herself good and fed up with David Freeman's grandstanding and after repeated warnings on the record had fined him five hundred dollars — privately — for contempt of court. He knew the rules as well as anyone and if he wasn't going to play by them, it was going to get expensive for him in a hurry.

By then it had been late in the afternoon and Villars had sent word out via the bailiff to excuse the jury for the day. On his way to do that he had stopped by the room where Hardy and Jennifer had been talking, told them what had happened, and Hardy had taken the cue and cut out.

He was parked at the corner so that he could see where the jogger had appeared out of the woods the last time. Looking down, going over one of Florence Barbieto's interviews with Walter Terrell, he almost missed her when she emerged again.

Throwing his notes onto the passenger seat, he started the engine in time. Sure enough, she ran down the same route, turning the corner onto Jennifer's street, just flying. Hardy pulled across the street, into the driveway just as she arrived at it, cutting her off.

He opened the door and got out, facing her across the roof, smiling. "Hi again."

Today she was wearing maroon shorts and a Boston Marathon T-shirt, a maroon headband, and the can of Mace. Panting, seeing Hardy, she closed her eyes briefly, then opened them. "What's your problem?" she asked, sucking air. "Why don't you leave me alone?"

He really wasn't into ruining this woman's day but he also didn't want to let her get away again. He had a card out, ready, and held it up over the hood of the car. "Just grab this as you run by — would you? — and call me. It might be important. It might even save a woman's life."

She stood there a minute, staring, as though she hadn't heard him. "You're a lawyer? Really?"

"That's right."

"Last time you didn't look much like a lawyer."

He grinned. Clothes make the man. Now he was in one of his suits, on his way to court, a real-life lawyer. "I was in disguise."

She was still breathing hard but more controlled than when she first stopped. Hardy figured that even if he could run as fast as she was going, which he couldn't, if he had come from the Sutro Woods down to here it would take him ten minutes to get his breath back. She was already back to being able to talk without gasping. It was impressive.

She reached over and took the card, glanced at it, then at her watch.

"I don't want to keep you, but if you've got time for one question, we might clear up something right now."

She looked again at her watch, took a deep breath. "What is it?"

"Do you run down this street often?"

"Almost every day. I've got a regular route when I'm working out."

"Not the same time, though?"

She shook her head. "Depends on when I wake up, how the morning's going. Why? You been waiting around here?"

"A couple of days, early. So sometimes it's later?"

"Sometimes." She was getting leery again. "This is more than one question."

"Yes, it is. Sorry. How about this one: Do you ever remember running by this house here" — Hardy pointed — "and hearing something like shots, something that might have made you stop for a minute? That's the special one question."

She gave it her attention, breathing normally now. She ran the wristband over her forehead, frowning in concentration. "When would this have been?"

"Last winter, right after Christmas."

She gave it another second, then slowly nodded. "Yes . . . I do remember that. It was like bang, then bang, right together. They were shots? I think I convinced myself that they were just backfires."

"But you did stop?"

"Just for a minute. I'm on a schedule. I like to keep running. I didn't see anything else, or hear anything. I decided it must have been a backfire so I just kept on."

Hardy stayed where he was, just outside his door on the driver's side. He wasn't about to spook her now. "You mind telling me your name?"

There was a last bit of hesitancy but it gave way. She even half-smiled at him. "Lisa Jennings. This is for real, isn't it?"

"As real as it gets, Ms. Jennings."

Hardy came up the gallery aisle — out of the corner of his eye he saw Terrell in the front row on one side and Lightner on the other — and let himself through the swinging gate at the rail. It was almost eleven and Dean Powell had a diminutive Filipino woman on the stand — Florence Barbieto, Jennifer's next-door neighbor.

Hardy sat down next to Jennifer, touched her arm and whispered, "Jackpot. The woman who started running away in front of your house . . . I found her."

"Where?"

Hardy didn't get a chance to answer. Villars interrupted Powell's questioning with a tap of her gavel, a glare at Hardy. The message got across. He sat back with a gesture of apology. He didn't feel like incurring a five-hundred-dollar fine, and his information, though useful, could wait.

Powell turned back to his witness. Apparently she hadn't been on the stand very long, they were going over the events of last December 28 and hadn't gotten very far.

"To repeat, Mrs. Barbieto, you heard them fighting?"

"Oh yes. The houses aren't far apart. They were yelling at each other and the boy was crying."

"Could you make out any words?"

Mrs. Barbieto brought her finger to her lips. "No," she said at last, "not that morning." Leaving the implication that on other mornings she had. But Powell knew better than to prod there. Freeman would be up if he did and he'd be right. This was the morning they cared about.

"All right. Now, could you tell us about the events leading up to the shots themselves?"

"Well, I was in my kitchen cutting up chicken for *adobo*. The kitchen is against the wall by the Witts' house, by the window."

"You were standing right by the window?"

"I was cutting at the counter. The window is over the sink. There's another window back a ways, which I had open a crack because of the vinegar."

"The vinegar?"

"For the *adobo*."

Powell nodded as if he knew what she was talking about. "I see. And so you could hear what was happening next door?"

"But not anymore. They had stopped."

"They had stopped yelling, you mean?"

"Yes."

"And for how long was it relatively quiet over there, next door at the Witts?"

"Not too long. A minute maybe. I put away my coffee, I cleaned the cup and put it in the washing machine" . . . Hardy had a vision of a washing machine full of porcelain chips, no wonder the damn thing wouldn't work — "then took out the chicken and I was cutting it, and suddenly I heard somebody yell out *'No,'* and then this awful noise. It had to be a shot. Still, I was thinking about all the fighting this morning and all the weekend and then there is this noise so I go to the window."

"The one that was open a crack?"

"Yes, that one more in the back. When I get to it I hear another shot. It is so loud, I almost feel it hits me."

Powell nodded some more, then turned around, his eyes taking in the defense table. Jennifer sat forward, hands clenched on the table in front of her. She met his gaze.

"And then what did you do?"

"Well, there's a chair there, by the window. I sat down, trying to think. I didn't know what to think."

"What could you see from this chair?"

"Some of the hedge, then the side of their house to the back?"

"I'm sorry. Do you mean the side of the house or the back?"

"The side, but you know, in the back. Except

nothing happens. I don't see anything for a minute or two, I just sit there, trying to think what to do. Then I think maybe I'd better go out, but maybe I should call my husband, I don't know." Mrs. Barbieto was reliving the moment, twisting the fabric of her dress in her hands, squirming in the witness chair. "Then I decided I have to go see. If something is wrong, maybe I can help. It is so quiet now, more quiet than before even when they weren't fighting."

Powell was up close to her, soothing but persistent. "And what did you do then?"

Mrs. Barbieto took a breath. "I went next door and rang the bell. Then I wait and then again I ring. But no one is answering, and I know the noise came from inside the house, just a minute before, so somebody must have been in there. But no one answered."

She was shaking her head, stealing glances at Jennifer, clearly afraid to look at her. Perhaps, to the jury's eyes, afraid of her.

Powell brought her back, repeating the safest question there is in a courtroom. "And what did you do then?"

"I waited another minute, and then nobody came, so I tried the door to unlock it but it wouldn't move, and then I became afraid and ran back to my house and called the 911."

"And what did you do then?"

"I sat down by the front window until the police car came, maybe a couple of minutes. I was afraid to stay outside."

Powell continued to walk her through the next hour or two, after the police car had pulled up,

Jennifer's return from her run, the arrival of the homicide team, Mrs. Barbieto's actions and impressions. It was a straightforward narrative that Hardy didn't think was very damaging to Jennifer. After all, someone had been in the house and done the killing — but none of Mrs. Barbieto's testimony necessarily convicted Jennifer. It could still be argued that she hadn't been there.

When Powell turned the witness over to the defense, Freeman didn't get up from his chair. Instead he looked up at the judge and then the witness. "I need one minute, Your Honor, if it please the court."

He sat there, unmoving. He didn't look at his notes. His arms were crossed on the table in front of him. After about ten seconds of silence, a ripple began in the courtroom, people moving in their seats, throats being cleared. Freeman seemed oblivious. Hardy looked over to him; so did Jennifer. The seconds went by.

Powell got up after about half a minute. "Your Honor . . ."

Villars agreed. She pointed her gavel. "Mr. Freeman, are you going to cross-examine Mrs. Barbieto or not? If you are, please get to it."

That exchange took about ten seconds, and Freeman, at last, began to move. Slowly, he got his body straightened up, out of the chair, grabbing up his yellow pad as a prop. He still hadn't spoken. Sighing, he moved forward, glancing at his watch. "Now!" he exclaimed. Half the jury jumped, as did the witness.

Freeman circled quickly in front of the bench, taking in the whole room. "That was one minute."

He walked directly up to the witness box and smiled. "Now, Mrs. Barbieto, I'm sorry for that little display and if it startled you, I apologize. But we've got some substantial problems with time in your testimony, and I thought it would be helpful to think about what a minute is."

He was out of line. He wasn't questioning the witness. Villars was about to reprimand him but he went right to work. "You've testified that the yelling stopped at the Witt house quote about a minute unquote before you heard the voice shout '*No,*' and then the shot, is that correct?"

Mrs. Barbieto was looking at Freeman as if he were possessed, and she could have been at least half-right. She nodded, yes.

The judge looked over and down at her. "Please use words in your responses. A nod doesn't work."

"I'm sorry," Mrs. Barbieto said. "What was the question again?"

Freeman repeated it, and this time she said that yes, it had been about a minute.

"Just to be very clear on this, during the time that you were sitting there drinking your coffee, you heard them yelling across the way at their house?"

"Yes?"

"Right up until you finished your coffee and got up?"

"Maybe not."

"Maybe not?"

"But during. While I was there, yes."

"About a minute before?"

"Yes, about."

"Okay, and during that minute you got up from

drinking your coffee — where were you drinking it, by the way?"

"Just by the window, there, by the back."

"All right, by the back window. You took your cup up front to the sink, is that right?"

"Yes."

"And then what?"

"And then I washed it."

"With soap?"

Powell stood up with an objection, Villars overruled him. She might think Freeman was an ass but he was following a visible trail here, and it might even lead somewhere.

"No, I just rinse and put it in the washing machine."

Freeman smiled, but clearly *with* her, not *at* her. "I don't mean this as a criticism, Mrs. Barbieto, but do you mean you put the cup in the automatic dishwasher?"

There, see, he wasn't so bad. Mrs. Barbieto smiled, embarrassed. "Yes, I meant the dishwasher."

"All right." Freeman went on to recap what she'd done so far, walking around pantomiming her actions in the area in front of the witness box. "And what did you do next?"

Powell tried again, saying she'd already answered these questions. Villars overruled him.

"You mean cutting the chicken?"

"If that's what you did next, yes."

She stalled now, her face clouded. "The things I did in the kitchen, that's what I did."

"Did you leave the kitchen during this time?"

She was silent.

"Mrs. Barbieto, did you leave the kitchen during this time?"

The witness looked up at the judge. "I have to go to the bathroom."

"Mr. Freeman," Villars said, "are you close to wrapping this up? The witness has to go to the bathroom."

"No, no, no!" Mrs. Barbieto's embarrassment was acute. "That's what I say . . . said. I've got to . . . I had to go to the bathroom then."

Freeman stood stock still for a bit. "You went to the bathroom before you cut up the chicken? Do you recall how long you were in there?"

The witness was squirming, clearly uncomfortable with such talk. "Not long, maybe a minute, I don't know."

In the courtroom there was a low rumble. Freeman, his point made, ignored and tried to bring Mrs. Barbieto back to his side. "All right, let's move along now. You've testified that you began to cut up a chicken. Where was the chicken before this?"

Freeman maddeningly led her through each step — the chicken had been wrapped in the refrigerator, she'd come over across the kitchen from the refrigerator to the sink, unwrapped it, threw away the wet wrapper, washed the chicken in cold water, dried it with a towel. First she'd cut off the wings, then both leg and thigh quarters. Next she'd separated one leg and thigh portion — and just before she was about to cut the other one she heard the yell and then the shot.

"Now, Mrs. Barbieto," Freeman concluded, still friendly and helpful, "this is why we began with my little demonstration of what a minute is. It's not, as you know, just a short amount of time. It's an exact amount of time — sixty seconds. And you've testified that you heard Jennifer fighting with her husband a minute — sixty seconds — before you heard the first shot."

"No, it was more than that."

"It could have been a lot more, couldn't it? Perhaps as much as, say, ten minutes?"

"I don't know. I didn't look. It just seemed like, you know, not too long."

But easily, Hardy thought, long enough for Jennifer to have left the house and "another dude" to come in and commit the murders.

Freeman let the jury take it in, consulting the notes he held in his hand. Reaching his decision, he looked to the bench. "Your Honor, it's almost twelve-thirty. I have a lot more questions for this witness but this is a good breaking point if the People have no objection."

The People did not.

36

Time-out.

Hardy had a black, cast-iron frying pan that his parents had given him before he went away to college. It was his only artifact from those long-ago days, a relic from his own lost youth. It weighed about five pounds, and its cooking surface was as smooth and black as hematite. After using it he cleaned it with salt and a wipe with a towel, although every couple of years he spent an hour rubbing it down with oil and extra-fine-grade steel wool. So far as he knew, soap had never touched it.

Frannie was reading to Rebecca before putting her down for the night. Hardy had discovered shallots and had cut up four of them and tossed them in the pan with butter and olive oil and some parsley. He took a drink of his Chardonnay and dribbled a few drops of wine into the pan. A small pot of rice was on another burner and he lifted the lid, checking it. Timing was all. He turned the heat off under the cast-iron pan. The prawns would only take two minutes and he wanted to wait until Frannie was finished with the Beck. Leaving his wine, he walked through the bedroom and into what had been his office for ten years.

Now, the walls painted light blue and surrounded with a menagerie of stenciled animals, it was a child's room. Rebecca was wearing her new turquoise silk pajamas. They were Daddy's favorites and so she wore them every night — soon he'd have to get her another pair. She sat surrounded by half a dozen of her "buddies" — a teddy bear and a rabbit and a cabbage-patch doll and some others, all with names — half on Frannie's lap on the rainbow children's loveseat, draped, enthralled by Good Dog Carl. Hardy stood in the doorway, taking it in. He came over and sat with them, and the Beck rearranged herself so as to be lying over both of her parents. Hardy put his arm over Frannie's shoulders and she leaned into him, smelling good.

He didn't particularly like it that Frannie continued talking to Jennifer, but Frannie just didn't feel right about abandoning her and she didn't want to go down to the jail, so she'd talk to her on the phone from time to time.

"She seems confident David's going to pull it out after all."

"I hope so." Hardy picked up a prawn by the tail and took a bite. "I'm getting good," he said. "These are good."

Frannie disagreed. "They aren't good, they're perfect. Anytime you feel like throwing a little something together for dinner like this, you go right ahead." Frannie had finished breast-feeding Vincent. She was having some of the wine now. "You don't sound too sure."

"Well, David does put on a good show. He was

something else today. You leave that courtroom feeling you've got your money's worth."

"But . . . ?"

"But I don't know."

Frannie put her fork down and looked across the table at him in the candlelight. "Are you really worried?"

"I'm really worried." He moved some rice around. "He had Florence Barbieto up there today for maybe six hours and proved that every time she'd said the words 'a minute' — and she said them a lot — it really didn't mean a literal minute. But if this guy Alvarez, the neighbor across the street, comes on and says he saw Jennifer leaving the house within — pardon the phrase — a minute after the shots, then she was there."

"But this other woman you found. The jogger . . ."

"Well, sure. David will trot her out — and I *am* glad that I found her — and she'll say she heard the shots, or noise like shots, and stopped and started running right from the gate, but all Powell will have to do is ask her how she even knows it was the same day. She doesn't. If Alvarez sticks to his identification, that still puts Jennifer in the house, and very probably we lose." He pointed at her plate, his face softening. "Eat your shrimp, woman, it'll make you strong."

Frannie dutifully took a bite but her heart wasn't in it. "I can't believe somebody — this man, Powell — who's talked to her and seen her is so determined to put her to death. God. I mean, she's a nice person, maybe a little confused but . . ."

Hardy shook his head. "I don't mean to argue

with you, but I don't think she's such a nice person. She's lied and she did kill at least one person" — he held up a hand — "*okay,* maybe she had reasons, but I don't want to go overboard on what a sweetheart Jennifer Witt is."

"Well, she sure didn't kill Larry and Matt."

"I don't *think* she did."

"Dismas, you *know* she didn't."

"I don't know that. I hope it and it's true I can't imagine that she killed Matt, but I don't know for sure. Nothing I've found, and I've been looking, proves she didn't do any of it."

"But nothing proves she did, and that's what it comes down to, doesn't it? That's what Powell's got to prove."

Hardy nodded. "In theory."

"Well?"

"Well, in fact quite a bit seems to indicate that she did it. That's the problem. She's got five-million dollars if she's cleared, and she's out of her abusive marriage and —"

"And Matt?"

"Sure, except that . . ." Except Hardy knew that there were a host of so-called human beings on the planet who were capable of killing their offspring without remorse. He really didn't believe Jennifer was one of them, but. . . .

"I don't think that's her."

"I don't *either,* Fran, but it's not impossible. That's all I'm saying."

"Well, I hate it. And I hate to hear you even suggest it."

"I'm not all that fond of it myself."

They sat, across the table from one another,

the food forgotten. Hardy reached out a hand and Frannie took it. "I've got a really startling idea," he said. "How about if we don't talk about Jennifer Witt or the law at all for oh, I don't know, let's try five minutes? And if we make it, let's go for the whole night."

It wasn't easy, but later on it was sweetly worth it.

37

As Hardy had feared, Anthony Alvarez was trouble.

It didn't help that he looked like Ricardo Montalban, the cosmopolitan spokesman for whatever quality car it was — little clipped white mustache, ruddy yet handsome chiseled face — except that his snow-white hair didn't flow, it was Marine-cut. His business suit was neat — neither showy nor run-down. His posture was relaxed yet commanding and his vocabulary impressive. He had worked for the City for thirty years as a fireman before retiring seven years ago, rising to the rank of Assistant Chief. He was at home most of the time now, tending to his wife who was bedridden with a lung condition. In short, had he been a defense witness he would have been a godsend. But he was the prosecution's witness — in fact, he was their star.

At Powell's careful prodding he was telling the story again from his own perspective, talking about the shots. "It was very unusual. It's a quiet street most of the time, and one noise like that, it was surprising but I didn't think too much of it. But then with the second one, right away like it was, I thought I ought to go and look, see if there might be some serious disturbance."

"And what did you do then?"

"Well, Mary's room . . . Mary is my wife . . . is up the stairs, the second room back. I had been in with her, reading to her, and after the second shot I walked up the hall to the window at the head of the stairs, which looks down over the street — Olympia Way."

"And did you see anything then on the street?"

"Yes. I saw a woman dressed in some kind of a running outfit standing by the gate to Dr. Witt's house across the street."

Powell had clearly coached Mr. Alvarez on how to answer his questions, and now he had him at the crux. "Is that woman in this courtroom, Mr. Alvarez?"

The witness did not hesitate. "Yes, she is, sir. She's right there" — he pointed — "at the defense table."

Powell nodded, the nail driven. "Let the record show that the witness has identified the defendant, Jennifer Witt."

There was the expected buzz in the courtroom, and next to Hardy, Jennifer hung her head, shaking it. Villars tapped her gavel a couple of times, calling for order, and Hardy took the moment to whisper to Jennifer. "Look at him. Look right at him."

Her head came up but she apparently couldn't sustain her defiance. Alvarez was staring directly back at her, conveying that he was committed to his accusation — it was you and there's no mistaking my certainty on it. Jennifer slowly crumbled, crossing her arms on the table in front of her, lowering her face until it rested on them.

Powell took it all in. There was a moment when he looked at Freeman, declaring himself the victor. Then it was gone. He turned back to the witness.

"What did she do then?"

Hardy was constantly surprised by the many guises of David Freeman. He never rose to cross-examine the same way twice. Sometimes, as he had demonstrated with Mrs. Barbieto, he didn't rise at all, waiting for an invitation — more an ultimatum — from the bench. With Anthony Alvarez, when Powell had finished with him, Freeman figuratively leapt at his throat.

"Mr. Alvarez, you have just stated that you saw Mrs. Witt, standing by the gate, looking back to the front door, within a minute or so after the shots, is that correct?"

"Yes."

"Did you see her leave the house?"

"No, she was by the gate when I saw her."

"And your inference was that she had come from the house?"

"Yes."

"That she was in the house when the shots were fired."

"Yes."

"And came out directly afterward, within a minute or so, which is when you saw her?"

"Yes, that's right. I did infer that."

"She could, though, have been *anywhere* when the shots were fired, isn't that correct? Up the street, down the street, halfway across the city for that matter."

Alvarez frowned and Powell objected.

"Are you going somewhere with this, Mr. Freeman?" Villars said.

Freeman nodded. "I am clarifying, Your Honor, that the witness could not possibly have known *where Jennifer Witt was when the shots were fired.* He assumed that she was in the house because of his purported identification of her at her gate immediately after the shots. Because he thought he saw *her* at the gate, he assumed she was inside at the time. But if it was *not* Jennifer at the gate . . ."

Villars nodded. "All right. I'll overrule the objection. You may continue, Mr. Freeman."

It was a good exchange, Hardy thought. Of course, it didn't preclude that Jennifer had been inside at the time of the shooting, but for the first time the jury was listening to a prosecution witness testify that he could not say for certain that she was. And after Freeman brought up Lisa Jennings, the doubt that she had been there at all would be even greater.

The question was read back to Alvarez and he reluctantly conceded that yes, in theory, Jennifer could have been anywhere when the shots were fired. "Except that she couldn't have gotten to her front gate in one minute from across the city," he added.

Freeman smiled warmly. "Indeed she could not," he said. "This is why I want you to be absolutely certain of your testimony, Mr. Alvarez, that you saw *Jennifer Witt* standing at her front gate. You are certain of that?"

Alvarez was not flustered but he surely was getting impatient. "Yes, I'm certain."

"But you've testified that she was looking back at the front door?"

"Yes."

"And after that she began running down the street?"

"That's right."

"And her house is where, in relation to yours?"

"It's just across the street."

"And Olympia Way is a flat street, is it?"

"No. It's fairly steep. Maybe a three-percent grade."

"And the Witt home — is it exactly across Olympia from you, or a little uphill or downhill?"

Alvarez, with no clue what Freeman wanted, remained relaxed. He took a beat, though, to make sure that there wasn't a trap here. Not seeing it, he answered: "I consider it just across the street, but you're right, it is slightly down the hill."

Freeman remained crisp. "I didn't say anything I could be right about, Mr. Alvarez. You're saying it."

"Yes. I'm saying it. It's slightly down the hill."

"So you were standing in your upstairs window, looking across and down the hill at Mrs. Witt, who was standing by her gate, and then, immediately, she began running down the street — that is, away from you. Is this your testimony?"

"Yes." Alvarez sat back, crossing his legs. His patrician face had gradually tightened and now he was frowning.

Freeman pounced. "All right, then, when did you see her face?"

Alvarez leaned forward. "When did I see her face?"

"That's right, Mr. Alvarez. If she was facing away from you the whole time, looking at her house, and then she started running downhill, *when* did you get a chance to see her *face?*"

Alvarez went with the only story he could salvage. "Well, I must have seen it from the side."

"You *must have?* You *must have?* Did you or didn't you?"

"Yes I did. I did. I saw her profile. I knew it was Jennifer Witt. It never occurred to me it wasn't."

"You mean it could have been so it must have been?"

"Your Honor!" Powell was on his feet. "Counsel is badgering the witness."

Freeman raised his hands theatrically. "Your Honor, this is a crucial eyewitness for the prosecution, and the jury needs to know that his positive identification of Jennifer Witt is, in fact, highly questionable."

Villars pursed her lips, disliking Freeman's histrionics but knowing he had a point. "Nevertheless," she said firmly, "Mr. Powell is right. You're badgering the witness. We'll strike the last question. You may proceed."

Freeman walked back to the defense table, took a sip of water, then turned back to the witness. "Mr. Alvarez, let's talk about the gun, shall we? Did you see the gun?"

"The gun?"

"Yes. The murder weapon which somehow made its way to a dumpster down the street by the park. That gun. Did you notice if the person you identified as Jennifer Witt was holding that gun as she stood by the gate?"

"There was something bulging at her side."

Freeman shook his head. "Mr. Alvarez, please, just answer the question. *Did you see a gun?*"

Alvarez didn't like it and neither did Powell, but there was nothing he could do about it. "No, but she was holding —"

Freeman held up a palm. "Please, Mr. Alvarez, that's all. Let's move along, shall we?" Freeman turned again to glance at Jennifer and Hardy. This, of course, conveyed his expression to the jury as well — they would know that at least from his perspective he was eating Alvarez's lunch. He turned back to the witness box. "The final point I'd like to ask about is along the same line I pursued with Mrs. Barbieto — how long is a minute?"

Villars pursed her lips, ready to squelch any histrionics before they got out of hand, but for all of his penchant for showboating, Freeman was playing this cross-examination very straight, and Hardy doubted that he'd let his flamboyance sideswipe him when he was on such a roll.

"You've told us that you were at your wife's bedside, reading to her, when you heard the shots?"

"That's right."

"And then, after the second shot, you got up to look across the street, is that right?"

Alvarez nodded wearily and Villars instructed him to answer questions with words. Nodding again, he said, "Yes, I got up after the second shot."

"Immediately? Within a minute, say? Or less?"

"Perhaps slightly less. Somewhere between immediately and a minute."

"And then you walked to your front window?"

"That's correct."

"And how far is that from your wife's bedroom?"

"I don't know exactly, maybe twenty feet, I'd guess. Something like that."

"And you walked directly to the window? You didn't stop, for example, to go to the bathroom on the way?"

There was a nervous titter in the courtroom — Freeman was pushing the limits of Villars' endurance and knew it, but it played beautifully for the jury.

Alvarez didn't see the humor and answered soberly, "Yes, I walked directly to the window."

"And the person you saw at the gate was already there when you arrived, looking back at the house?"

"Yes."

The picture was clear to Hardy, but he wondered how many of the jury saw it. All of them would, he believed, after Freeman got through with his opening statement for the defense: Could Jennifer have killed Larry and Matt upstairs in her house, then run down the stairs, through the house, out the front door and up the walkway, and then shut the gate in the time it took Anthony Alvarez to walk twenty feet, give or take less than a minute? He doubted it, he thought the jury would doubt it, too, especially once Freeman tied in his jogger, Lisa Jennings, for the misidentification by Alvarez, mistaking Lisa for Jennifer.

But Powell was not about to let Alvarez stand down on this, for him, low note. Trial rules permitted direct examination by the side giving its case-in-chief, then cross-examination by the opposition, then another round of questions should they be required by the side that had called the witness in the first place. This last round was the redirect, and Powell was up and rolling before Freeman got back at the defense table.

"Mr. Alvarez, just a couple more questions — how long have you known Mrs. Witt?"

"We've been acquainted for about four years. We went over and introduced ourselves when they moved in."

"Four years. And during that time, I take it you've seen her walking away from you?"

"Yes."

"And, obviously, in profile, haven't you?"

Alvarez finally started to loosen up with the friendly tone. He broke a smile. "Of course. Many times."

"And you have no doubt, personally, that the woman you saw at the gate across the street after the shots was Jennifer Witt."

To his credit, realizing what it meant, Alvarez took some time, staring at Jennifer. "I have nothing against the woman, but it was her."

"Your Honor!"

"All right, Mr. Freeman. The jury will disregard that last answer. Mr. Alvarez, please just answer the question."

The court recorder, Adrienne, read back Powell's question, and this time Alvarez answered simply: "No. No doubt at all."

To which Freeman could not object.

Officer Gary Gage took the stand in his uniform. He was about forty, a veteran patrolman, the officer who had responded to 911 and who had discovered the bodies.

"And the front door was locked when you arrived?" Powell said.

"Yes. The neighbor" — he consulted his notes — "Mrs. Barbieto, came out when I got there. We talked for a few minutes and then I went over and knocked on the door, and then I tried to open it, but it was locked."

"And what time was this?"

Gage reluctantly replied. "I got there at 10:10, so this must have been maybe 10:15."

Powell frowned. "But you received a dispatch from 911 much earlier than that, didn't you?"

Officer Gage nodded. "Yes, sir. We received a DD call — that's Domestic Disturbance — at 9:40."

"Exactly 9:40?"

Gage again looked down at his notes. "That's what I've got here, sir, 9:40. They radioed it through to me." Gage shrugged. "It was after Christmas. A lot of people were having family fights. Sometimes it takes a while."

Powell nodded, walked back to his table and took a yellow sheet from his assistant, read it, put it back down. "What did you do then?"

"Well, I was going to go check around the back,

but just then Mrs. Witt came back from running. She asked what I was doing there, and I explained about Mrs. Barbieto's call, hearing some yelling between her and her husband, maybe some shots."

"How did she respond to that?"

Gage fidgeted slightly, raising his eyes to take in Jennifer. He wanted to get it out straight: "She, uh, she told me there wasn't a problem anymore. She had just been out running. Obviously, if there had been a fight, it was over."

"Did you get the feeling she was dismissing you?"

Freeman objected to that and was sustained, but Powell didn't break stride. "What did you do then?"

"I told her I'd rung the doorbell and no one had answered. She said her husband had probably gone out to cool off, just like she had. And taken her son."

Next to Hardy, Jennifer was whispering to Freeman that she hadn't wanted the cop to have to confront Larry because she knew he would beat her up for getting the police involved.

Gage was going on. "I said I'd like to see the house, make sure, in view of the suspected shots, that everything was okay. She again told me she was sure that everything was in order but I insisted, so finally she opened the door."

"And then what happened?"

Gage swallowed. "Well, I smelled the gunpowder immediately, so I told her to sit on the couch. I drew my weapon and began to walk through the rooms of the house, first downstairs then up, until I found the bodies."

The courtroom was still. Gage was sweating, apparently reliving the moment — Jennifer seated on the couch in the living room, waiting while he looked . . .

"And what did you do then?"

Gage took a breath. "I came out onto the railing and looked over and down at the defendant, at Mrs. Witt there. I said, 'Stay here, please. There has been a shooting.' "

"And what did she do?"

"She looked up at me and said, 'I know.' "

After the lunch recess Inspector Sergeant Walter Terrell took the stand for the second time.

The Walter Terrell who was sworn in this afternoon was not the eager young man of only a few days before. Gone was the flight jacket and casual slacks, the hair half-uncombed, the designer shirt buttoned to the neck. For his testimony this time he wore a three-piece charcoal pinstriped suit that had to have set him back plenty — a lawyer's suit — complete with red tie and white shirt. He had cut his hair and it lay where he had put it.

Even the aggressive demeanor had been tempered. Hardy knew that if you wanted to succeed in this theater you sometimes had to grow up in a hurry, and obviously two things had happened since Terrell's last appearance as a witness in the hardball of a capital murder trial — someone had spent time coaching him, and he had wanted to learn.

At first glance it looked as though Powell had made Terrell understand something that had been foreign to him before — that a witness didn't need a macho personality out on his sleeve to be effective. If Terrell wanted to help put Jennifer Witt away, his effort was best placed in a careful arrangement of the facts.

Powell, for whatever his flaws in preparing this case, continued to exude confidence — that he was winning.

It was unsettling.

"Inspector Terrell," Powell began, "since your credentials have already been established, let's begin with your arrival at the murder scene, the Witt house on Olympia Way. This was when?"

This time up Terrell didn't break out his winsome smile — all business, not trying to please anybody, just here doing his job. "I arrived at the scene at 10:43. There were already officers there and the room had been secured."

"Did you see the defendant, Jennifer Witt?"

"Yes. When I came in she was sitting on a couch in a large room off to the right of the entrance. One of the officers there pointed her out to me and I went over to speak with her."

"What was her demeanor at that time?"

"She was sitting with her feet tucked under her, her hands crossed in her lap. She was quiet."

"She was not crying?"

"No, sir."

"And she could speak coherently?"

"Yes, sir."

"Did you, Inspector Terrell, have any reason to suspect that Mrs. Witt had committed the murders at that time?"

Terrell thought for a beat. "Not really, other than that, statistically, spouses often kill each other." Terrell sat back, for the first time comfortable in the hard witness chair.

Powell probably looked genuinely puzzled to the jury. "But didn't Officer Gage tell you about Mrs. Witt's saying 'I know' when he told her about the bodies upstairs?"

"Yes, but I guess I chalked that up to shock. Plus she might have come to that conclusion while waiting for him to check the house."

This was good, but not for Jennifer. Terrell was repairing his hothead image of the other day. He hadn't jumped all over Jennifer like a rabid dog. He had waited for the evidence to pile up. And Powell was leading him toward it, toward his certainty that Jennifer had done it. "During later interviews, did you ask Mrs. Witt who she thought might have done this?"

Now Terrell sat forward. "Well, in law enforcement we always ask the question *'cui bono?,'* which means who benefits? And, of course, when I learned that Mrs. Witt would inherit something like five-million dollars, well, it got my attention. I asked if anyone else would inherit. She said no."

"Go on."

"The next thing was that she had told me her husband had no enemies, and if that were so, the motive for the murders had to be impersonal. Robbery, for example. I asked her to search the house and list anything — however small — that was missing."

Hardy had heard all this before, but it was now coming out in a believable and damning fashion. The gun never mentioned as missing by Jennifer, her belated memory of the strange swarthy man in a trenchcoat walking up the street as she walked down it.

When Powell was finished and turned the questioning over to Freeman, the defense attorney started with the same line Hardy would have taken — the only pinhole in an otherwise seamless fabric.

"Mrs. Witt told you her husband had no enemies, is that so?"

"Yes, sir."

"And in the course of your investigations, you looked into this assertion?"

"Yes, I did." Terrell was volunteering nothing, playing Freeman's game, pausing before he spoke, never giving a word without thought. He met Freeman's stare with his own.

Hardy knew a little of what made Terrell tick — the inspector was daring Freeman to try and come get him. And somehow he was pulling it off without appearing belligerent. Powell had trained him well.

But something was up. Suddenly Hardy put together Powell's confidence and Terrell's attitude — the defense was walking into a trap. He raised a hand. "Excuse me, Your Honor."

Freeman, interrupted as he was trying to find his rhythm, turned around, glaring. "I'd like to request a short recess."

Villars frowned — the afternoon had been long enough without these constant interruptions. "If there are no objections." There were none. She called a fifteen-minute recess.

"There's something going on," Hardy said.

"We're going to get sandbagged."

He and Freeman were standing nose-to-nose just inside the door to what they had taken to calling their suite. The windows were sealed shut and the heat either was working too hard or the air conditioner wasn't working hard enough. In any case, the temperature was at least ninety degrees.

"On what? I'll bring up a couple of other dudes with Terrell and sit my weary ass back down."

"I know that's what you want to do. What I'm saying is, don't do it. Terrell's got something he's dying to leak out. You hurt Powell on Alvarez and he knows it and still he's a Cheshire cat out there, and I don't think it's faked."

"Everything Powell does is faked."

"Unlike your own sincere self, right?"

Freeman let it go. "Goddamn, it's hot as hell in here. What do you want me to do, just dismiss Terrell? Stop right here?"

"How could it hurt?"

The look Hardy got in response wasn't flattering, but he didn't care. He was convinced that they had closed to within a length of a good chance of acquittal after the testimony of Barbieto and Alvarez. After all, they were talking reasonable doubt here, not certainty, and Hardy thought they had it.

Further, even though Gage and Terrell hadn't gotten them any points, neither had they put too many on the boards for Powell. That, though, could change in an instant. One false move now could turn the momentum of the entire trial. It was a time to be conservative in the literal sense — conserve what you've already got. Don't let the other side score.

This, however, had never been David Freeman's style. "You ask me how it could hurt? It isn't presenting the best defense for our client, that's how. Terrell's on the record as implying nobody else in the world had a reason to kill Larry Witt. He's built it on our client's saying Witt had no enemies. You want to let that go by? You don't think that's important?"

"Sure it's important, but we can get to it next week —"

"We can introduce it now. Get the jury primed to accept the details later."

Hardy saw that he wasn't going to convince his partner, which was no surprise. Well, perhaps he was wrong; it was, after all, just a feeling. Maybe Terrell's presence put hunches into his gut. Anyway, he'd tried to warn David, satisfy his conscience, put his two cents in. And, as in the rest of the world, two cents were essentially worthless.

Freeman pulled open the door and went out into the blessedly cool corridor.

"Inspector Terrell, we were talking about Larry Witt's lack of enemies, I believe. You looked into Mrs. Witt's assertion that he had no enemies, is that right?"

"That's part of any homicide investigation, finding out who had a motive to kill the deceased."

Freeman, still flushed from the heat of the suite, glanced down at the yellow pad he was holding. "And were your efforts to uncover enemies for Dr. Witt successful?"

Terrell's opinion about who might be Larry

Witt's enemies — in fact, this whole line of inquiry — as speculative, argumentative and irrelevant, but Powell didn't appear to want to object.

Terrell was in no hurry. He pushed his back against the chair, stretching, lifted his shoulders, let them fall. "In what sense?"

Freeman looked to the jury. Surely a cooperative witness could understand this question. But he bravely pressed on. "In the *sense* that you found people who might have had a motive to kill Dr. Witt?"

"Might have, perhaps."

"And in your thorough investigation, did any of these people become suspects?"

"No."

"No? Why not?"

Terrell explained patiently: "Because at the time there wasn't any evidence linking anyone else to the crime."

A good answer. But Freeman had at least gotten the concession that "perhaps" there had been other people with motives. Hardy thought he should take that and sit down. But again it wasn't to be. His heart sinking, Hardy recalled Malraux's dictum that character is fate. Was Freeman pressing on to his fate — to Jennifer's?

"At the time, you say. You mean that since the defendant has been in custody you've come upon such evidence?"

Freeman turned to the jury, including them in his reaction. "Linking another person to the crime?"

"Yes." Terrell making Freeman pull it out. Hardy was silently begging his partner to stop, sit down, call it off. But it was already too late. Now it would have to play out.

"And still you've kept Mrs. Witt in jail? Even though there was another suspect?" Again that inclusion of the jury.

"I didn't say there was *another* suspect. In fact, this individual only strengthened Mrs. Witt's motive. There was nothing that tied him to the crime scene."

Jennifer gripped Hardy's arm.

Terrell could hold it no longer. Without being asked, he declared: "Mrs. Witt was having an affair. She was sleeping with her psychiatrist."

It was speculation, it was obviously based on hearsay. It was totally inadmissible, but David had asked for it and he got it. He didn't bother to object. The damage was done.

38

It was the battle of the anchors, each channel outdoing the other trying to bring out dirt on Dr. Ken Lightner, alleged lover of Jennifer Witt. They weren't having a lot of luck.

Even though it was date night, Hardy called and told Frannie he was sorry but he wasn't coming home. She could find out why by watching the television. He had a lot of catching up to do.

After he left the Hall of Justice he went back to the office and watched some television himself. A few of Freeman's associate red-hots hung around in the conference room trying to figure out how to salvage something from this disaster. Nobody had any good ideas, although all agreed it was a bitch when your client lied to you, or seriously withheld information from you.

Freeman himself, after an hour-long argument with Jennifer during which she had continued to deny any affair with Lightner, in spite of the fact that they had stayed in the same room in Costa Rica for a week, had said he was going out to dinner alone at the French restaurant below his apartment. He was going to drink a good bottle of wine and then he was going to drink another one.

Once Terrell's testimony opened the dike, the flood swept over Freeman. On redirect, Powell revealed the details of Jennifer's extradition — how they had found her. Then he had called Lightner and gotten it confirmed. Everything, that is, but the affair itself, which Lightner strongly denied.

The jury, however, would draw its own conclusions about that from the facts. They would probably be the same as those drawn by Hardy, Freeman and every other soul in the courtroom — which was that your heterosexual male was not likely to go and stay in a hotel room on a beach in Costa Rica with a world class beauty like Jennifer Witt for a week and not have the physical creep in from time to time. Or to assume that this relationship might not be a preexisting condition from who knew how far back.

After she had broken out of jail, Terrell had played one of his famous hunches. He had figured Jennifer would have to contact someone, and from his earlier investigations he tagged Lightner as the most likely, indeed the only possible, person. Jennifer had no close friends and was estranged from her natural family — there really had been no other choice.

And because it was a capital murder case, because Powell, the candidate, was so strongly in his camp, because Jennifer's escape had infuriated the judiciary, Terrell had somehow squeezed enough juice to get a warrant on the phone company's list of Lightner's outgoing calls.

The outgoing calls to Costa Rica were good

enough. Terrell was going in to question Lightner in person when — lo and behold — the doctor had gone off to Costa Rica for a week, a much-needed vacation. Terrell had followed him down, lying low, getting enough to come back and start the extradition proceedings.

Hardy would have bet a lot that the money for all this had come from Dean Powell's campaign fund. There was no way that the San Francisco Police Department could pay the freight to fly an officer down to Costa Rica to investigate some alleged hanky-panky.

Hardy realized that he had for too long let himself be diverted by Freeman's theatrics and boundless confidence. This case was far from won — in fact, it might now be lost. It was one thing that Lightner had gone down to Costa Rica, although that was bad enough. But Terrell's testimony that she and Lightner had shared a *room!* The fact that there had been another man in the picture all along — and who knew for how long? — would work against Jennifer with the jury. Now in their eyes she also had a *personal* motive for killing Larry — it had not just been the money. She was cheating, too!

Hardy understood what the jury would feel — Jennifer was a woman who did what she wanted, took what she wanted and the world be damned. She would seem exactly the kind of person one would expect to do what she had been accused of.

He knew now that whether or not Freeman chose to address this Costa Rica business in the defense's case-in-chief, they were going to need to distract the jury by presenting their other dudes — someone else who might have had a plausible motive and an opportunity to have killed Larry Witt and the means to have done it. Hardy had his briefcase open, the files on his desk. Forcing himself — he had to start somewhere — he looked up the number of Jody Bachman, the Los Angeles–based attorney for the Yerba Buena Medical Group.

Since it was eight-thirty, after hours, he wasn't surprised to get one of those automated answering devices that asked if you knew your quarry's last name or extension. Dutifully, he punched in the first four letters — B. A. C. H.

The phone rang once.

"Jody Bachman." A youngish voice, not exactly squeaky but enthusiastic peppy.

"Mr. Bachman, my name is Dismas Hardy. I'm an attorney in San Francisco and left a message for you several weeks ago. I'm following up." Tardily, he added to himself.

There was a longish pause. "I didn't call you back?"

Hardy had to smile. They ground down these guys so far in the corporate mills they had to look up to see down. "You might have," Hardy admitted. "I didn't get any message, that's all."

"I'm sorry. It's been crazy here. Maybe you know."

They schmoozed a moment, non-billable lawyer talk about the rat race and working until all hours, then Hardy got to it, saying that Todd Crane recommended talking to Bachman about YBMG. "Sure, I represent them. If I can help you — but you said this was a murder trial."

Hardy explained.

"Witt? Witt? I can't say it rings any kind of bell, but I've been awake for four days running now and sometimes I don't recognize my own name." He laughed weakly. "The glamour of the LBO."

"What's that?" said Hardy, the innocent.

"What? LBO? Leveraged buyout. Where have you been, Mr. Hardy? The wave of the past, or future, depending on your politics. Or your money."

"Same thing, aren't they?"

"Not exactly but that's often a good guess. So listen, about this Dr. Witt . . ."

"I'm pretty sure he called your offices last December. I don't know who he would have talked to."

"Probably me," Bachman admitted, "but I really don't remember. I'll have my secretary look it up and get back to you, how's that?"

"That'd be good. Thanks."

"Sure. No problem."

"It's the real you at last," Hardy said to his friend Abe Glitsky, who stood in the doorway to his apartment wearing a clown costume — big floppy feet, white pancake make-up, a cute little red nose. "Let me guess . . ."

Glitsky cut him off. "It's Jacob's birthday party." He turned back into the apartment, Hardy tagging behind. Flo came up, bussed him on the cheek and asked if he wanted some cake or ice cream. There were about fifteen ten-year-olds in the cramped kitchen, none of them meditating.

"Abe looks good."

Flo gave him a look. "You wait. You'll do it too."

Hardy thought that she was probably right. He couldn't, at this moment, though, imagine himself as a future reincarnation of Bozo the Clown, but he had to admit it was possible. "Is he going to be done soon?"

"Ten minutes," Flo said, "maybe a little more. He just does a little act."

"I'd love to see it."

She moved closer to him, a hand on his arm. "I think you'd cramp his style. You can wait in the boys' room."

All three of the Glitsky boys had the same bedroom, and it wasn't a big one. Jacob and Isaac shared the bunk bed, and OJ, now almost five, used a little daybed against the opposite wall. Hardy sat on it listening to the laughter from the kitchen as his friend the homicide inspector did his clown tricks. He took the opportunity to rest his head for just a second on the pillow.

"I hate to wake you but my kid needs to go to sleep."

Hardy looked at his watch. He had crashed for nearly an hour. Glitsky was back in normal clothes, holding out a cup of hot coffee. Hardy took it, sitting up, rubbing a crick in his neck with his free hand. "I had a dream about you in a clown suit," he said. "It was horrible."

Glitsky shook his head and turned around. Hardy followed him into the kitchen, sat down at the table with his coffee cup. Glitsky poured some boiling water into a cup and started fiddling with the chain at the end of his silver tea strainer. In the back rooms they could hear Flo finishing up with the boys, supervising the washing up, getting them into their pajamas, ready for the sack.

"But enough small talk," Hardy began. "What did you ever find out about the Romans?"

Over by the stove Glitsky dipped the strainer up and down in his cup and watched the steam rise. "I know they were after the Greeks but beyond that it gets a little fuzzy." He picked up his cup, holding the tea chain in his other hand, crossed to the table and sat. "Latin wasn't my thing or I'd probably know more."

Hardy drank coffee. "Cecil Roman, father of Melissa Roman, deceased patient of Larry Witt. Mr. Roman accused Witt of performing an abortion and killing his daughter."

The tea was by now as dark as Hardy's coffee and still Glitsky kept dipping the strainer. "Oh, *those* Romans. No, I haven't found out anything. I probably would have told you if I had." He finally took the strainer out and took a cautious sip. "You really going to need it?"

"I'd like to know if Roman, or his wife for that matter, has an alibi."

Glitsky nodded. "The case falling apart?"

Hardy told him about the events of the afternoon, the allegation about Lightner, how it would be helpful if they had at least *one* other person who might have had some good motive and opportunity to kill Dr. Witt.

"It sounds like this guy Lightner kind of sticks up. He was sleeping with the lady and he could have —"

"They both deny they were lovers."

Glitsky gave him the eye. "I'm sure."

Hardy shrugged. "It doesn't really matter. The jury's going to believe it."

"So there's a motive for him."

"Except he was working that morning. At his office. With secretary in attendance. Terrell already checked it out."

Glitsky slurped some tea, his eyes out of focus somewhere behind Hardy. "I'm not sure I understand why I want to help you point the finger away from a murder suspect who looks to me like she's guilty. You want to explain that part to me again? I'm a cop, remember? I'm on the other side."

"I could say to serve the ends of justice but I sense you'd gag or something."

"Or something."

"Okay, I won't say that. How about we're such good friends and I'd do the same thing for you?"

"Nope. No good."

Hardy got up for more coffee. At the counter he turned back around. "I've got it — you might get the collar on the real killer."

"Except we think she's already on trial."

"Well, what about if it isn't her? Look, Abe, the Romans hated Larry Witt. All I'm asking you to do is find out if they were in Tahiti or some place on December 28 so I can cross them off."

"That's all, huh? Find out what somebody was doing on a certain day ten months ago? You saw them, didn't you? Why didn't you ask them?"

"I think it was that the opportunity never came up."

"So I go find out, right? Piece of cake. Speaking of which, cut me a little of that, would you?"

The remains of Jacob's birthday cake, pretty well destroyed, were on the drain, and Hardy scooped some of it onto a paper plate and brought it back to the table. "See what a friend I am?"

Glitsky rubbed a finger through the frosting, popped it into his mouth. "Absurd," he said.

Hardy shrugged. "But so much of life is."

Freeman did not have two bottles of wine at his French restaurant. Instead, after the first one, he decided he had to take another crack at Jennifer, get to the bottom of this affair issue.

But he didn't make it upstairs to the jail. Ken Lightner was coming down the wide steps at the front of the Hall of Justice when Freeman arrived. Not given to hesitation in any event, Freeman jumped out of the cab, bumping his head on the door and calling, "Dr. Lightner, wait a minute, would you?"

Fumbling for some money, Freeman threw a mixed handful of coins and bills through the cab's front window. Lightner had come down the steps. "Mr. Freeman, I'm sorry, but it's late and I'm very tired. Whatever this is, it's going to have to wait."

"It's not going to have to do anything of the kind, sir. I need the truth from you and I need it now."

Lightner gestured back toward the building. "I

told the truth in there this afternoon."

"And tomorrow, if I choose, I get to cross-examine you about that, about what you said. Would you rather we get to it then? What have you been doing in there? Visiting my client?"

"Visiting my *patient*, Mr. Freeman. My patient."

"And your lover?"

This time Lightner's response was measured. "I've denied that under oath. You're going to have to accept that."

"I don't accept it," Freeman said. "I don't believe it, and that makes *you* my best suspect."

"*Me?* Are you joking?"

Freeman jabbed a finger. "Yeah, you. No, I'm not joking. If you were having an affair with Jennifer, you've got at least as good a motive as she does to have killed her husband." Of course he didn't really believe that, but he had to try. "So I'll look forward to talking to you tomorrow on the stand, and if you think you're tired now . . ." Freeman headed for the wide doorway.

"Now just a minute . . ."

Freeman turned. "It's going to take a sight more than a minute, Doctor. You got the time or not? If not, I've got better things to do."

They were ten feet apart, Freeman flat on his feet like a fighter. Lightner scratched at his beard. "All right," he said. "But not here."

"I know a place," Freeman said, already moving, leading the way across Bryant, through the doors and down the steps to the underground labyrinth leading to Lou the Greek's. This time of night the place was nearly empty. Lou was wiping up, the TV was dark. Two regulars quietly nursed beers and shots at the bar and a couple were wrapped around each other in a side booth. Freeman took Lightner to the back, to another booth. When Lou started toward them, Freeman waved him away.

"My only concern, Mr. Freeman, is Jennifer." It hadn't been warm outside and Lou's wasn't any better, but Lightner had a sheen of sweat on his brow that he seemed unaware of.

"Well, good, Doctor, that gets us off on the right foot." Freeman knocked on the table, loud, calling out. "On second thought, Lou, bring us two cold ones, would you?" Back to Dr. Lightner, he crossed his hands in front of him. "I'm listening, Doctor."

Again the beard got scratched. "It's complicated. She thinks she's in love. With me. It's a common phenomenon, transference, reinforced by the situation she had at home."

"Transference? Where you sleep with her?"

Lightner shook his head. "Look, Mr. Freeman, I am not a therapist who sleeps with his patient. I don't really care if you believe that or not. That would really damage her. She doesn't need that, she didn't need that, even if she thinks she did . . ."

"And she thought she did?"

Lou came back with the beers, put them on the table, disappeared. Freeman put a hand around one and drew it to him, drinking, listening. Lightner sat there, reflecting, ignoring his bottle. "It was not an easy week," he said. "Down there, I mean. In Costa Rica . . ."

Freeman took another swig of beer. "So you didn't sleep with her. But why didn't you tell us about how she felt?"

Lightner was shaking his head side to side, as though lecturing a child. "That would have been rather stupid."

"Why?"

"Because it would announce to the jury that Jennifer wasn't in love with her husband, that she wanted out of the marriage. You think that would help her, help your case?"

Freeman shrugged. "It's out now, Doctor. How about that?"

"It *came* out. Nobody volunteered it. There's a difference." Lightner's voice was down to a near-whisper. "Listen, please, do you think if I thought it would help Jennifer that I wouldn't have lied? I'm human, I'm even at least a little in love with her." He shook his head. "It happens both ways in therapy. A professional recognizes it and controls it." He seemed to notice the beer for the first time and pulled it toward him. "Don't you see, she realizes that, it gives her the freedom to feel as she does and not be afraid I will take advantage of it. It's in part why she trusts me."

"But she stayed with you."

"She was scared, Mr. Freeman. She wanted to stay with me. I decided to allow it. It may have been bad judgment. As I said, I'm human too. Even though I am a shrink." He half-smiled.

Now Lightner took a drink. "That's all of it, Mr. Freeman, and you can believe me or not. I could not turn her out. We draw our own lines. I let her stay in the room with me. Platonically."

Freeman crossed his hands in front of him again. He sighed. It was not impossible. "I still say you could have told me this earlier."

"I didn't want it to come out *at all,* don't you understand that? *Nothing* about it. I was afraid it would hurt Jennifer at this trial. It would *seem* to say that she had a strong motive — in addition to the money, or whatever else they're saying, to get rid of her husband. Wouldn't it? It would cast her in the role of a cheating wife."

"And now it has."

Finally, Lightner seemed to lose his patience. He slapped at the table. "Well, that was not *me.* I did not make that happen. And if you want to bring it up again tomorrow and hammer at me, if you think you'll be doing Jennifer any good, then so be it. I'll repeat what I've told you here and you can watch while the jury takes in the fact that Jennifer had a strong emotional reason to kill her husband, maybe even her child, maybe even on purpose . . . so that she could run away and start a new life with her shrink." He grimaced. "If you really think that's going to help her . . . well, you can't possibly. The best thing you can do for Jennifer, Mr. Freeman, is forget about her and me."

Sipping his beer, Freeman nodded. "It also lets you off."

Lightner shook his head again, as though regretting what he was about to say. "Mr. Freeman," he said, "I was in my office that morning and I can establish that. I'm afraid the jury is going to focus on Jennifer, on her supposed motive, or motives, on the fact that she didn't love her husband anymore, that she wanted out of a terrible marriage." Lightner drank off half his beer. "My God," he said, "*you're* the lawyer. Do you think I wanted this to happen? Do I have to draw you a picture?"

His eyes sad, dispirited, Freeman spun his empty bottle between his hands. "You just did," he said.

39

Good morning. I'm not going to take up too much time with my defense statement this morning. You probably feel you've been here long enough. I don't want to bore you on the one hand or insult your intelligence on the other.

"But I do think it will be useful to recap what's happened here in this trial, so far as the evidence is concerned, because evidence is what trials are really all about. Does the evidence prove beyond a reasonable doubt that Jennifer Witt killed her husband and son? Well, looking at the evidence, which we've now seen every bit of, the answer, ladies and gentlemen, is *no*.

"Let me repeat that: The evidence we've seen so far does not prove that Jennifer Witt killed her husband and her son, and that's what it has to do."

Freeman, voice low, in his least aggressive tone, spoke in place, gesturing occasionally with his hands, but seemingly content to let his words do their work. He stood before the jury box, directly in front of the table shared by Hardy and Jennifer. He did not so much as glance at Judge Villars, or turn to Powell and Morehouse at the prosecution table. This was his statement to the jury and he was going to play to them.

"The evidence has to *prove* that Jennifer Witt has done these terrible deeds. It must allow for no other reasonable explanation. It is not enough to say, 'Well, maybe she could have been there and done this.' You must be absolutely convinced. There must be no doubt."

"Your Honor." Dean Powell appeared saddened by the need to interrupt. He conveyed how much he just hated to break Mr. Freeman's rhythm, but alas, he really had no choice. He spoke with considerable control. "This is argument, not an opening statement."

Surprisingly, Villars overruled Powell. Hardy thought it was the first time in the trial that he'd seen Villars blow a call on the law. Freeman was out of bounds — this was clearly argument. Evidently it was an argument that appealed to the judge.

But Freeman had no cause to gloat. He knew it, and picked right up. "And what do we, the defense, have to prove? Do we have to prove that Jennifer Witt was not at her house? That she did not use the gun? That she did not have a lover? That, perhaps, she did not know about her husband's insurance policy and the double-indemnity claim? The answer is that we do not have to prove a thing. The burden of proof is on the prosecution and it never goes away from the prosecution. Mr. Powell here" — and Freeman turned slightly — "his job is to prove Jennifer Witt did these things, and you know what? He just has not done it."

Hardy had to admire Freeman. The man was

a fighter. Freeman held up a finger. "One — no one — ever — has positively put Jennifer inside the house when the shots were fired. This is a fundamental flaw that, by itself, creates reasonable doubt.

"Two." Another finger. "And this is also crucial. The prosecution has offered no motive, no theory, no reasonable hypothesis at all for the shooting of young Matthew Witt. It is simply asking you to believe that Jennifer Witt, for some unknown reason, shot and killed her only child. There has been no effort to prove that she did, or why."

Jennifer still took any mention of Matt heavily. Her head went down for an instant and she sucked in a breath, swallowing hard. She reached for her water and drank.

"Three. The first witness to even put Mrs. Witt near the scene at the time of the shooting — that was Mrs. Barbieto, you'll remember — was not even close to being clear on the amount of time that had elapsed between hearing Jennifer next door and the shots. It might have been fifteen minutes. In fact, it quite possibly was.

"Four, Mr. Alvarez says he saw Mrs. Witt running down the street away from him within a minute of the shots. One minute. Let's recall the testimony of Mr. Alvarez on this famous one minute. He said that he walked directly from his wife's bedside to the window at the front of the hallway overlooking Olympia Way, a distance of perhaps twenty feet. And there was Jennifer Witt, already — in that short minute or less — outside the gate to her house, looking back at it."

This, Hardy thought, was clear by now. And it was a crucial point. Even if she had run, Jennifer could not have made it from her bedroom — where the killings had occurred — down the stairs, across the living room, out the door, down the walkway and out the gate, closing it and turning around in the amount of time it took Alvarez to walk twenty feet.

Freeman paused briefly to let it sink in. More quietly now, confident in his facts. "Let's go to Mr. Alvarez's identification of Jennifer Witt. Now, I'm not saying he didn't positively identify Mrs. Witt — he did that. I'll ask you, though, to consider how he could be so positive when he admits that he never saw her face. That's a hell of a trick."

Villars frowned at the mild profanity but — again surprisingly — let Freeman continue uninterrupted.

"Next, since it made such an impression on the prosecution when this came up, let's take a minute to talk about Mrs. Witt's alleged intimate relationship with her psychiatrist. Dr. Lightner, under oath, has denied it. Now you may be skeptical, but remember that Inspector Terrell's opinion that they were having an affair was stricken as speculation. Which means that, as a matter of law, this alleged relationship has not at all been proved. Has anything proved that Mrs. Witt and her psychiatrist were intimate at any time? The answer, again, is no." He paused, lowering his voice. "No. Nothing." And after the interview with Lightner, Freeman could assert this with conviction.

Freeman walked to the defense table and took

a sip of water. Raising his eyes for a moment, he briefly took in the gallery, seeing if he still held them, as well. Satisfied, or nodding as if he was, he turned back to the jury box, raising a finger again.

"Nevertheless, although we do not have to prove anything, we will demonstrate to you how easily Mr. Alvarez could have been — within the meaning of reasonable doubt — how he could have been, and indeed was, mistaken in his identification of Mrs. Witt as the woman who went running off after the shots. Further, and finally, we will show you evidence — powerful, compelling, incontrovertible evidence — that Jennifer Witt could *not* have killed Larry and Matthew — because in fact she was not in her house when the shots were fired. *She could not have been there.* Just as this court found that there was insufficient evidence to prove that Jennifer Witt had killed her first husband, Ned Hollis, there is none to prove that she killed her second, or, for God's sake, her child." He pointed a finger for the last time at Jennifer. "There sits a woman who truly has been wrongly accused. A victim, not a criminal. Mrs. Witt is more than legally just not guilty — she is in truth, and in fact, an innocent woman."

In his bleaker moments, Hardy wondered if it was something in the San Francisco air. He had often heard that there was supposed to be something — some mold or spoor or other magical substance — in the local salt-tinged windy ether that was responsible for some of the wonderful gastronomic delights of the city — sourdough bread and Italian dry salami, for example. But he found himself wondering if there was a less benign side to it, some as a yet undefined parasite or chemical or meteorological phenomenon that produced hope at the outset of an endeavor only to dash it before it could be realized.

Witness the 1993 Giants. Had a team ever come so far only to crash and burn just enough to fall short by one game? You could talk all you wanted about their sore pitching arms and lack of basic team character, but it was damn tempting to blame the air. Here it was October, and Hardy wasn't watching San Francisco in the playoffs. And back when the Giants had been ten games ahead at the All-Star break, he'd also entertained the belief that Jennifer would be acquitted — now he worried that that was another dashed hope, like the pennant. For in spite of David Freeman's antics and experience, in spite of his "other dudes," in spite of the victory in the Ned Hollis portion of the trial, even in spite of Freeman's really brilliant cross-examinations of the prosecution's major eyewitnesses, Florence Barbieto and Anthony Alvarez, he believed now that they were probably losing.

With the Lightner business being introduced, despite David's efforts to neutralize it, the wind had seemed to go out of the defense's sails. Of course, Freeman would never admit defeat, or the likelihood of it, and he was doing his best to keep the ship sailing, but the ballast — the weight of all of Jennifer's apparent lies — now seemed to be just too much. There was a scrambling feel to the defense now, a sense that all the arguments and pyrotechnics weren't leading to the truth, weren't in the service of justice, despite Freeman's arguments.

The jury wasn't going to vote your way if you didn't convince them there was an alternative truth that perhaps they just weren't seeing. For a while, even he had believed in the possibility of an alternate truth that might be convincing. He thought the jury would, too, and what was reasonable doubt if it wasn't that?

Now — maybe it was, after all, something in the air — but like the Giants and their sore arms, Freeman had started well but with the failure to come up with at least one convincing other dude, and the bombshell about Lightner and Jennifer, well, he feared the season could be over.

On Monday Jennifer was escorted into the courtroom by David Freeman on one side and the bailiff on the other. As opposed to the fashionable clothes she had been wearing throughout, she wore a maroon runner's outfit and some high-tech tennis shoes. Her hair was tied back in a ponytail, and Hardy thought she looked about seventeen years old.

When Villars ascended to the bench she immediately noticed the change and frowned. "Mr. Freeman, would you approach?"

Hardy watched his partner chatting with the judge, nodding, gesturing. Voices didn't get raised, and in a minute Freeman was back at the defense table, smiling. "What could she do?" he said.

Freeman called Lisa Jennings, the other jogger, who was dressed identically to Jennifer. The gallery caught it, and Villars rapped her gavel a couple of times, calling for order.

Lisa did not look exactly like the defendant, but in their matching outfits, with their hair cut the same — Freeman had paid Lisa to cut hers — there was no denying the similarity. Lisa was a little thinner and an inch or two taller, but they were both medium-boned, attractive blonde women in their twenties.

Hardy thought Freeman shouldn't have Lisa say a word. He should just call Alvarez and see what happened. But Freeman could no more do that than he could whistle with a mouth full of thumb tacks.

Though Hardy had warned Freeman — often and vigorously — that Lisa's testimony could be chopped up and masticated by Powell, still the old dog wanted to introduce it to the jury. "It'll ring true," he had told Hardy. "You wait."

And, in fact, he was right. Lisa's testimony itself — stopping at the house, hearing the shots, running off after a minute or so — all of it did ring true.

The problem, as Hardy had argued again and again, was that even if it had happened, they had no way to prove it had happened on December 28.

And Powell — no surprise — did not seem inclined to let that omission slide.

"Ms. Jennings, how often do you run down Olympia Way in the course of, say, a month?"

"Several days a week, I'd say." She may have been nasty to Hardy when he had first tried to corral her, but Lisa came across as a cooperative, even friendly person. Now that she was here, committed, she wanted to please. "Maybe . . . fifteen, twenty times a month."

"And you've been doing that for how long?"

"A couple of years, I'd say. Almost three."

"So you've run by Mrs. Witt's house what . . . about two hundred times? Something like that?"

"Yes."

"And do you keep a log of where you've gone on which days, which route you've run?"

Lisa looked at Freeman, then back at Powell. "No, I just run."

"So, you don't know for a fact when you heard these noises on Olympia Way that you've just testified about, do you?"

"Well, I only heard them once."

"Two noises, like gunshots?"

"Yes."

Powell nodded, taking his time. He looked over at the jury, his face showing a question mark. "I see. And hearing these gunshots, did you report them to the police?"

"No." Lisa rolled her shoulders, moving in the seat.

"Why not?"

"I don't know. I guess I didn't think they were gunshots."

Wide-eyed wonder broke over Powell. "Oh? Why didn't you think they were?"

"I'm not sure. I guess at the time I thought they were backfires or something."

"Could they have been backfires?"

Freeman, trying to save her, stood up and objected, but before he could even give grounds,

Powell withdrew the question. But came right back. "You've mentioned the phrase, 'at the time.' This was on December 28, last year, is that right?"

Again, Lisa looked at Freeman. "I didn't say that."

"No, you didn't. That's why I ask." Powell smiled, a gentleman, only trying to get to the truth of the matter. "Take your time."

"I don't really know what day it was."

The wonder appeared again. "But surely it was last winter."

"I think it was, I know it was several months ago."

"Might it have been longer?"

"Your Honor! Counsel is badgering this witness." Freeman was standing, but he was going to lose and he knew it. He did.

"I don't think so," Villars said. "Overruled."

"Might it have been longer ago?" Powell asked again, mildly.

Suddenly Lisa's voice rose to a near-shout. "I don't know *when* it was!" Shocked by what she'd done, she stared at Powell, then at the jury. Finally she apologized to the judge and repeated, in a near-whisper, "I don't know when it was."

"Thank you, Ms. Jennings. I have no further questions."

It was getting to the end.

Freeman had been intending to call Alvarez and get him to point at the two women — Lisa and Jennifer — in the back of the courtroom, at least demonstrate to the jury that a mistake in identifying one or the other would have been possible.

In a sense, having Lisa simply appear accomplished the same result, although in Hardy's opinion it was nowhere near the victory he had been hoping for when he waited those mornings out in his car on the off-chance that Lisa would go jogging by.

Now, with Powell's undoing of the mistaken-identity argument, Alvarez would not be called. They were down to the ATM, their last best hope.

No one was exactly asleep, but it was a Monday afternoon, and even Hardy, who had memorized the numbers and carefully honed the theory to its present form, had to admit that this was the kind of testimony that reminded him of his after-lunch high school physics class, the one he had largely slept through.

Freeman was up with Isabel Reed, the young black woman who had been so taken with Abe Glitsky when he and Hardy had gone to visit her at the Bank of America half a year or more ago. In the course of a couple of interviews, the matter of the three-minute difference in times had come up and Freeman had brought it home strongly to Ms. Reed so that, on her own, without a direct question from him, she should not bring up the discrepancy. He wasn't sure, but it was possible it could get her in trouble.

This made Hardy uncomfortable — but again he got overridden. Freeman contended that if the prosecution knew about it and wanted to talk about it, they'd deal with it then, but they wouldn't feed them the extra three minutes. They might need them.

When he had Ms. Reed on the stand, Freeman had introduced Jennifer's own ATM receipt and a copy of the Bank of America's confirming report. Solid physical evidence that at 9:43, Bank of America time, Jennifer Witt had been standing at the automated teller machine, getting some spending money.

They were looking at a blown-up poster that had been set up next to the witness chair. It was a portion of a map of San Francisco showing the route from Olympia Way down Clarendon into the Haight-Ashbury district — the route Jennifer told Hardy she had taken that morning. On Friday, one of Freeman's witnesses had been Officer Gage again — he had been induced to talk about the distance from the Witt home to the bank — the shortest route along the streets — a long semicircle around the UCSF Medical Center, now outlined in red for the jury's benefit.

It really had nothing to do with Ms. Reed's direct testimony, but Freeman thought he saw a way to get in what he wanted, and he wasn't going to let a little thing like that bother him. His face assumed its most perplexed expression. "Ms. Reed, let's look at this map for a moment. You may have heard Officer Gage the other day testify that your branch office is 1.7 miles from Mrs. Witt's home."

"Yes."

Freeman kept frowning, trying to figure this out. "He said 1.7 miles. Does that seem right to you?"

"Your Honor . . ." Powell rose. "We'll stipulate that the red line represents 1.7 miles."

"Stick to it, Mr. Freeman," Villars said somewhat ambiguously. "What's your point?"

Now, the door open, Freeman smiled. "I'm glad to explain, Your Honor." He turned back to Ms. Reed. "You've said that Mrs. Witt accessed her account at precisely 9:43?"

"That's right."

"Well, we've heard a witness — Mrs. Barbieto — say that Mrs. Witt was home, that she heard her, a couple of minutes before she called the police at 9:40. I'm just wondering if you are sure about your time."

"It was 9:43," Ms. Reed said. She was well-dressed, self-assured, confident. A good, believable witness with a document — the computer printout showing the exact time that Jennifer had accessed her account — to back her up. It was 9:43.

"In other words, Ms. Reed, just to touch all the bases, and, Your Honor" — Freeman smiled up at the bench — "this is the point I've been laboring to make. We've got a picture of Jennifer Witt at her house at 9:38, which is, in Mrs. Barbieto's words, a couple of minutes before she called 911 at 9:40, and we are expected to believe that five minutes later, she was at her ATM machine, having covered a distance of 1.7 miles?"

This played very well. The jurors were struck by it as Hardy had hoped they would be. Behind him, he heard a satisfying, low buzz in the courtroom. Even Villars, doing the math in her head, seemed to him to be impressed. All might not be lost, after all.

The prosecution could not have it both ways

— either Jennifer left before the shots, in which case she obviously could not have done the killings, or she had left later, in which case she couldn't have made it to the bank. But she *had* made it to the bank. So she hadn't killed anybody.

"In fact," Freeman continued, "even if it had taken Mrs. Barbieto ten minutes to call 911 after the shots, that moves Jennifer's time back to 9:30. But the shots weren't at 9:30, either, because the Federal Express driver, Fred Rivera, was there until 9:31, at least."

Freeman was rolling, in his enthusiasm making a closing argument, and for some reason Dean Powell was letting him do it. Hardy looked over at the DA's table and his stomach tightened. The man was smiling.

The judge wasn't stopping Freeman either. He just rolled on and on, paying no attention now to the witness, speaking directly to the jury. "Let's even, for the sake of argument, say that Jennifer *was* home, upstairs, when Fred Rivera was there. Let's say Larry and Matt were shot within a minute of that, at 9:32. If she left immediately, or within a minute as Anthony Alvarez has said she did, then Jennifer would have had to cover 1.7 miles in ten minutes. This is a pace of better than a six-minute mile, which is almost a dead sprint for a real athlete. Jennifer Witt just could not have done it."

Villars, caught for a moment in the rhetoric, came back to herself. She sent a hard look at Powell, no doubt, Hardy thought, wondering why Powell was letting the defense get away with that without objecting. But the prosecutor didn't react to her gaze. Freeman was walking to his seat, and Powell was casually rising, straightening his jacket, combing his hair with his fingers, a man on his way to a party.

"Ms. Reed," Powell began. "Do you know if the clock on your ATM, your automatic teller, is accurate?"

Hardy leaned across Jennifer. "He knows," he whispered to Freeman. "How could he know?"

Freeman shook his head, tightening his mouth. Jennifer said "what?" and he patted her hand.

Ms. Reed gave it a valiant try. "I'm not sure I understand the question. Accurate? You mean does it keep time accurately? I'd say yes."

"That's not exactly what I meant." Powell smiled at her, then turned to the jury. "We've just heard so much about time in this trial — the Federal Express computer, the 911 dispatcher, your own ATM machine — that I wonder if you know if these are all connected by some big computer, or somesuch."

Ms. Reed, no fool, knew where this was going, but there wasn't anything she could do about it. If she was going to get in trouble, then she was. She definitely wasn't going to lie under oath.

It came out.

Powell, of course, feigned shock. "Do you mean to tell me that the defense knew about this three-minute gap and we listened to all this hoopla from Mr. Freeman and he never saw fit to mention it?"

Villars, Hardy thought, was almost smiling, and that was chilling. In her eyes, it seemed, Powell had just vindicated himself.

"Yes."

"Why didn't you bring it up? Didn't it seem important?"

"Well, it did, but Mr. Freeman had said I might get in trouble."

"Mr. Freeman said you might get in trouble?"

"Yes."

"How would you get in trouble?"

"I don't know. With the police maybe. That's what Mr. Freeman said, anyway."

Hardy covered his eyes with his hands for a minute. It occurred to him that it didn't look good to do that, but in lieu of a hole to crawl in, it seemed a reasonable second choice.

Powell pushed on. "So with the three-minute difference, we've got a *thirteen*-minute run, don't we? Or a pace that makes a seven-and-a-half-minute mile, which is fast but nowhere near requiring a trained athlete."

"I don't know . . ." Ms. Reed was near tears, either from fear or from anger at being placed in this position.

"Objection." But Villars just pointed her gavel. "Don't you dare, Mr. Freeman," she said.

Powell waited, naturally pleased with the ruling, then continued: "Since the defense has brought this poster up here, let's use it for a minute, shall we? You've testified about this famous 1.7 miles, is that right?"

"Yes."

"But look here, this red line skirts the property of the UCSF Medical Center. Are you familiar with these grounds?"

"Yes, they're just up the street. I eat lunch there sometimes."

"You mean, they're not closed off to the public? Anybody can walk through them?"

"I do all the time."

"Ms. Reed, would you mind taking the red marker we've been using and draw a line through the grounds of the medical center so that the jury can see it."

Everyone in the courtroom was watching. It was almost a straight line from the Midtown Terrace Playground at the end of Olympia down to Parnassus Street.

"And is this a level area, Ms Reed?"

"Objection."

"I don't think so," Villars said again.

"No, sir, it's all uphill."

"Or *downhill* from Olympia Way?"

"Yes."

"So," Powell concluded, "if you ran through the medical center, you had only to cover a *half-mile* of ground as the crow flies, and all of it downhill. Even if the defendant had left her house at 9:40, she could almost have walked it . . ."

By Friday, Hardy was going crazy sitting in his office, or strolling down to Freeman's, or going by the jail to talk to Jennifer, or looking into store windows. Waiting for the verdict was its own special hell.

And if they lost, the case would become his and his alone. It had begun really to sink in that Freeman wouldn't even be there in the courtroom with him anymore — there was no reason for him to be. Freeman had been the guilt-phase attorney and — win or lose — his job was now over. He would write his appeal, if necessary, try for a new trial or a reversal, but as far as the courtroom was concerned, Freeman would play no more active role.

When Freeman had first asked him to be Keenan counsel — the attorney for the penalty phase of the trial — Hardy had not fully realized its implications. He should have, he told himself.

Now he alone would have the responsibility of convincing the same jury that convicted her, if it did, that Jennifer should not go to the gas chamber, that there were factors in mitigation. It would be his job to tell the jury what those factors might be.

But of course all this led back to his belief, now, that the jury might find her guilty. It wasn't, he felt, that the prosecution had done such a bang-up job proving that she'd killed her husband, and accidentally, in some undocumented fashion, her son. Nor, he was convinced, had Freeman been inept, in spite of what Hardy considered to be his occasional lapses of judgment.

No, if the jury convicted Jennifer it would be because they had become convinced that she was selfish, cold, a liar who stole from and cheated on her husband, a woman who mostly had shown anger rather than contrition — exactly the sort of human being who would do what Jennifer had been accused of.

And — the source of much of Hardy's angst now — if the jury believed Jennifer was such a cold-blooded person, they could also not implausibly believe that she deserved the ultimate penalty . . .

Hardy had asked Frannie if she could leave the kids with Erin for a couple of hours and have lunch with him, and now they were standing at Phyllis' station outside Freeman's office, making small talk, waiting on Freeman, who had invited himself along, when the telephone rang at Phyllis' desk.

"David Freeman," she said formally — her standard response to incoming calls — then listened, lips pursed, nodding once or twice. "Thank you." Hanging up, apparently forgetting the presence of Hardy and Frannie, she pushed the button on her intercom. "Mr. Freeman, the jury's coming in."

The gallery had filled up with media representatives in a remarkably short time. Hardy finagled a space for Frannie next to a reporter he knew on the aisle in the second row.

Jennifer was escorted in and brought to the defense table. She was wearing a white blouse and tan wraparound skirt with low heels. Freeman patted her hand, though she seemed not to notice, sitting without expression, showing no emotion.

When Villars directed her to, she stood at attention, staring straight ahead, flanked by Freeman on her right and Hardy on her left. The judge took the paper from the clerk, read it carefully, handed it to the clerk.

"As to the first count, we the members of the jury find the defendant, Jennifer Lee Witt, guilty of the murder of Larry Witt, in the first degree, with special circumstances."

Hardy felt his stomach churn. Half-turning, he noticed that Jennifer's reaction was the one he would have predicted — none. No, not quite. A muscle on the side of her jaw was moving, but otherwise she might have been waiting for a streetlight to change. He glanced at the jury box — they were seeing it, too. A cold woman, they must be thinking.

Behind them, in the gallery, there was an insistent buzz, but Villars, after a perfunctory tap with her gavel, was bent on the job at hand. "As to the second count," the clerk read, "we the members of the jury find the defendant guilty of the murder of Matthew Witt, in the first degree, with special circumstances."

Freeman was holding her elbow. She did not appear to need the assistance.

I'm not going to break. I'm not going to let them break me.

They beat on you every way, every day, and their satisfaction is watching you fall apart. Then you break down. You beg them to give you another chance, promise you'll do better, anything you want. You'll change and be different and you won't even be yourself anymore if they would only stop making you hurt.

Which is all the time, now. Especially since Matt.

But I'm not going to let them anymore. Crying doesn't help. It never helped with Larry, with Ned, with Ken, even with these lawyers. They think it's an act, anyway, if I show how I feel. They don't know and even if they did, they wouldn't care.

Why do I want to convince everybody? Of what?

That I'm not a monster? *Why should I bother? Of course they found me guilty. They always have . . .*

I am guilty in a way. I am *to blame for getting myself to here, for becoming who I am — empty, used up. You let them beat on you long enough, eventually who you really are, that person goes away. Hides.*

Well, I won't give them that satisfaction anymore. That's something. Maybe a start . . .

"I honestly didn't think they'd convict." Freeman's hair was all over the place in the late-afternoon wind. The sky was a thick gray blanket over the steps in front of the Hall.

Hardy had his arm around his wife, who was feeling sick, her hand clutched to her stomach. She had waited in the courtroom until it had cleared, until Hardy had come out after going into the private suite with Freeman and Jennifer. Where Jennifer hadn't wanted to talk about anything.

At least not with Freeman.

She told Freeman, a smile of fury on her face, that he was lucky he had made her pay up front. If she had known he was going to lose . . . wasn't he supposed to be the best?

He told her it wasn't over yet, of course that was her understandable reaction. But he'd be working on the appeal. There were grounds . . .

Hardy had listened to part of it, then excused himself — he would talk to Jennifer later, without Freeman — and came out to Frannie. She wanted to go home.

But Freeman caught them on the steps, wanting

more post mortem. He was still fighting the case. He *was* going to appeal. "It came down to the three minutes . . ."

Hardy felt he had to say something. "That was my fault. I thought it was a big deal."

Freeman hit him on the arm. "That's bullshit," he said. "The whole thing was my show, don't kid yourself. I mean, I should have walked the route myself. If there was any way in the world she could have got to that bank in five minutes instead of eleven it was my responsibility to have found out how. Too many eggs in that basket." He pulled his jacket more tightly around him. "Anyway, I can probably get a new trial. Villars should have stopped this one after she granted my 1118."

Whistling in the dark? Hardy had a hard time imagining that Freeman wanted to go through this exercise again. He also doubted whether as a matter of law Freeman was right. But he really preferred not to get into that. Instead he said, "Maybe you should have crossed Lightner. That's when it went south. If they were having an affair we could have made the case that he had as good a motive as she did."

Freeman shook his head. "*If,*" he said. "And *if* we could prove it, and *if* he hadn't had an alibi, which he did. Not to mention he pretty much convinced me he just wouldn't do that. No, I'm afraid Lightner just gave *Jennifer* a better motive, Diz. The less the jury saw of him the better."

Frannie finally spoke up. "Guys, please. I'm really not feeling good, Dismas." She looked at Freeman. "Sorry, David, I can't handle this very well.

Jennifer did not do this. How could they have found her guilty?"

A gust whipped between them, stopping what Freeman was starting to say. Reconsidering, forced to really see her expression at last, he moved closer and put an arm out, encircling them both. "Go on home, Frannie. Get some rest. Diz, go on, you two go on home."

In the car, Frannie was crying quietly. Hardy had the windshield wipers going in the drizzle. She held his hand in both of hers on her lap.

"You're more upset than she was."

Frannie shook her head. "No. She was just holding up, trying to hold herself together."

Hardy glanced across. "Well, she's some kind of superhuman holder-upper then."

Nodding, Frannie said that she had to be. "She did *not* kill Matt, Dismas. She didn't kill Larry, either. I still believe that."

Hardy looked over at his wife. He squeezed her hands, not knowing what to say.

PART FOUR

40

Before she had known that the jury would be coming in that day, Frannie had made plans for the weekend. She knew that her husband would probably want to stick around, hang out with Freeman, discuss and analyze and worry. She didn't think that would be wise.

So when they got home from picking up Rebecca and Vincent at Grandma's, although she still felt sick to her stomach, she helped Dismas pack the car and then got him in the passenger seat and drove north for ninety minutes, up to the small town of Occidental, near the Russian River.

She had rented adjoining rooms in the old Union Hotel where there was nothing to do except eat huge plates of home-style Italian food and drink in the bar and dance to country music and, in the soggy daytime, drive around some more looking at redwoods and water and playing with your children.

In spite of her own feelings, she gave Dismas until they got to San Rafael — about thirty-five minutes — to get out all of his frustrations and impressions about the trial and verdict and plans for the upcoming penalty phase.

Right now they were having a family weekend.

The penalty phase would take over their lives soon enough. This was an opportunity for some quality in their lives. She had gone to some lengths to arrange it. And she was going to demand it for herself, for her children, for her man.

The rest of the world could wait until Monday.

Hardy knew it was one of the reasons he loved her. She did things like that.

His own inclination was to keep pushing and pushing until something gave, but she had taught him on a couple of occasions that sometimes it didn't hurt to back up a step and look at the direction you were pushing. A different angle of perspective might get more accomplished.

He had originally planned to go right on up and talk with Jennifer, but on Monday morning, marginally refreshed from the food and simple beauty of the north coast — although he hadn't slept much — he found that sometime over the weekend he had decided to call on Ken Lightner.

Lightner had been not exactly a thorn but a presence since the beginning — in any event his involvement was greater than Hardy had originally suspected and he wanted to get to the bottom of it if he could. Not only that, he was considering the battered wife issue again — he felt he had to. The jury had decided that Jennifer had killed Larry and Matt, but he thought they might be persuaded that she wasn't a cold-blooded killer deserving execution if they knew how often and/or how badly she had been beaten.

It was worth a try. He didn't have much else.

Lightner had sounded pleased, perhaps relieved,

to hear from him. Maybe he'd felt ostracized since the allegation of the affair had come out and they hadn't wanted to bring him to the fore because his relationship with Jennifer could appear to give her one more reason to get rid of her husband.

The office was across from Stern Grove in a large mixed-use apartment complex called — cleverly — The Grove. It was a glass and brown-shingle contemporary building surrounded by trees, the parking lot on this morning half-filled with a disproportionate sprinkling of high-end German automobiles. Rent here wouldn't be cheap.

In spite of a morning sun, autumn was in the air. After he had parked, Hardy stood a minute by his car, arrested by the scents of eucalyptus and wood smoke, although where the smoke came from was a mystery. No one was supposed to burn anything outdoors anymore — it was illegal.

Lightner's office seemed to take up most of one of the back-corner modules. Hardy rang, waited, was buzzed in. He walked down a long hallway of muted color. There were six or eight non-representational framed things — works of art? — on the walls.

Lightner's bulky frame appeared in the light at the end of the hall. "Mr. Hardy," he said. "Welcome."

Hardy shook hands and was introduced to Helga, Lightner's secretary. The reception area was bigger than it had to be but still, somehow, cozy. The two couches were overstuffed. There was an easy-chair and ottoman in hot orange, yellow, blue and black, the only brightness in the office. Helga herself — she preferred, she said, Helga to Ms. or Miss Brun — was about forty and wore no rings. She had a low black desk, the surface of which was clean except for a green felt blotter. A low shelf held a typewriter — no computer here — with what Hardy took to be a six-line business phone and intercom set up next to it. Helga asked if they would like coffee and both said they would.

Lightner led the way to his consulting office, a room that was small but warmer than the reception area. It wasn't pastel, for one thing. Done in greens, leathers, carved woods and glass, it was restful, its windows looking out onto one of the older groves, sunlight coming through the trees. Hardy avoided the couch and took one of the two leather armchairs. Lightner left the door to Helga's area open and sat in a chair by the door.

"I'll come right to it," Hardy began. "You went to Costa Rica for a week and stayed with Jennifer." He figured he didn't have to say anymore.

Lightner frowned. "Are we going through this again? I thought I'd covered this with Mr. Freeman."

"Freeman?" Somewhere in the back of his mind, Hardy figured he must have known this, though he'd never made the overt connection. Yes, Freeman must have talked to Lightner. He had said right after the trial that Lightner had convinced him he hadn't done anything wrong with Jennifer, been intimate with her. At the time, right after the trial and the verdict, it had gone right by him. And, just like Freeman not telling him about Jennifer being guilty of killing Ned, he hadn't reported to him about this interview with Lightner either. Typical David.

The psychiatrist nodded. "So now what, Mr. Hardy? Now you too want some assurance I was not violating every code in the book and having sex with my patient?"

The burden of saving Jennifer had been building steadily on Hardy, or probably he wouldn't have resorted to the extreme ploy he was now about to try. "Dr. Lightner, your patient and, I gather, friend, Jennifer, told me otherwise." Of course, she hadn't, but if it would smoke out some mitigation for her, some alternative . . .

Lightner looked shocked, then saddened. "Mr. Hardy, I find it hard to believe that, I really do, I'm sorry. But if, indeed, Jennifer did say this, well, there are psychological reasons, but you would only say they were self-serving. I tell you that I did not have intimate relations with my patient. I testified to that. I believe, I thought, Mr. Freeman believed me."

Hardy shrugged, feeling increasingly uneasy about what he was doing. "So where does that leave us, Dr. Lightner? You've wanted to help Jennifer, and, believe me, I'd love it if you could. So . . . ?"

Lightner stood and crossed the room. He opened a door that led out to a patio, motioning to Hardy, who got up and followed. Outside, Lightner walked a few steps into the grove, then turned. "I'll take a polygraph if you'd like. You know how much I care about Jennifer, but I can't have it said I've been intimate with a patient, taking advantage of the relationship. I'm sorry, but Jennifer is just not telling the truth."

Finally, Hardy relented. "Sorry. It's me who isn't telling the truth. It was a bad try."

"Okay, here's what happened, just as I told Mr. Freeman . . ."

He and Jennifer had stayed in the same hotel room in Costa Rica because when Lightner had arrived she had become scared all over again, realizing that she hadn't run that far if he could be there on such short notice. She had felt vulnerable, alone, checking out of her own room, thinking she would be leaving no paper trail.

It stretched Hardy's belief to the breaking point, but the explanation was plausible, if foolish, from Lightner's point of view. Still, people did foolish things — it could have happened the way Lightner told it. And now Hardy felt he needed Lightner if he was going to have any real chance to save his client's life. And he had to think of it that way . . . Freeman's appeal working out was not to be counted on.

Between answering the phone Helga had managed to bring the coffee. They were back in their chairs, more relaxed now, though not totally allies. Lightner had not been impressed or pleased with Hardy lying to him, he said. Still, they were on middle ground, working for the same result. They didn't, after all, have to be pals.

Hardy sat with his coffee perched on his knee. "What do you personally think is the situation here, Doctor?"

"What do you mean?"

"I mean, what in your gut do you believe?"

"I believe her, Mr. Hardy. But as I've said, *if* she did it, she was driven to it. It's not a frivolous defense, you know." Placing his cup and saucer on the low table next to him, Lightner turned toward Hardy and leaned forward in the chair, hands folded. "I've said this all along — I've never understood Mr. Freeman's concepts —"

"He was obeying his client's wishes about the abuse, the same thing you'd do." Hardy wasn't about to listen to Lightner criticize anybody. His own judgment, after all, was a long way from exemplary.

"But the fact remains, he lost. And Jennifer loses." He held up a hand. "My point is that he could have called several witnesses — myself included — who might at least have planted the seed. Did you visit any of Jennifer's past physicians?" At Hardy's nod, he continued. "Okay, then you *know* there was abuse. And there were more people, people I've talked to — her own mother, for example. An abused person as well, as you may know. Even Helga has seen Jennifer come in here, staggering with the pain, limping. It was a classic situation — Larry Witt was literally beating her to death."

"But Jennifer told Freeman — she ordered him — not to get into that."

"He should have overridden her. He was her lawyer. His job was to clear her, not allow her to be convicted. She is a *victim*, Mr. Hardy."

Hardy raised his voice. "She would have fired him, don't you understand that?"

Lightner sat back, his face working. "And why is that?"

"If she admits she was beaten, to her it's the same as admitting she killed Larry. And if she killed Larry, that's admitting she killed Matt."

"She doesn't have to admit anything, does she?" Lightner said. "You can call all these people as witnesses, can't you? Get them to talk about what they've seen with Jennifer. Maybe nothing overtly even about Larry. I could come on as an expert witness — I've done it before. This kind of denial is common. I wouldn't have to talk specifically about things Jennifer told me. I'd just discuss the syndrome, and then let the jury make the connection."

"That she killed Larry because he beat her?"

"They've already convicted her — it can't hurt her any worse and it might help. Show the jury what she's been through. It might, if nothing else, move them to some sympathy. This woman has done nothing but suffer her whole life. Maybe you can end the cycle."

Lightner shook his head. "God, this is a travesty."

"Yes it is," Hardy said.

Lightner walked him out to his car. As Hardy opened the door, Lightner reached into his wallet and took out a card. "I expect to talk to her today, as I've been doing, but I want you to feel free to call me anytime if you feel I can help you, if I can come in with you and perhaps try to convince her to agree with a defense, anything at all. I'm always here."

"You don't go home?"

Lightner's face lit in a brittle smile. "My ex-wife

and children have the home. I've a space behind the office" — he motioned back to the building — "bedroom, kitchen and whatever I was able to keep. But it's all right, I'm getting along. Shrinks have a notoriously high divorce rate. We're often better with other people's lives than our own."

"Mr. Hardy?" It was Phyllis on the intercom. "There's an Emmett Kelly down here to see you."

Hardy pushed his files away, smiling. "Send him up."

A minute later Abe Glitsky's form filled the doorway. "I couldn't resist," he said. He walked across the room and looked down onto Sutter Street, then turned back and plumped himself halfway over the couch, laying his head against the armrest. "I think I'll take the afternoon off, get in a nap. Naps are rare among the ranks of homicide inspectors. I should do a study."

"You should," Hardy agreed. "But in the meanwhile . . ."

Glitsky sat up. "In the meanwhile I have made an ass of myself yet again in your behalf, although I realized on Friday the horse got out of the barn. I thought I'd make sure it all got covered, so I went out to see the Romans, told them we were finishing up some paperwork."

"And you found out?"

Glitsky grinned his horrible grin, the scar through his lips stretched white, the eyes with no mirth in them. "I found out that they have no idea what either or both of them were doing on the Monday after Christmas last year, which is the worst possible news for you."

"Why is that?"

"Because," Glitsky held up a finger, lecturing, "if they had spent any time being guilty and thinking up an alibi, I believe they would have remembered it and trotted it out. That's what guilty folks do. As it was, they just looked at each other." Glitsky stood. "They had no clue, Diz. There's nothing there."

By this time it was getting to be no surprise. "Well, at least I feel like I've covered the bases." Then, remembering the other thing he'd been meaning to put to his friend. "You filed a report on that visit to the bank we made, didn't you? The three-minute thing."

Glitsky had gone over to the dart board and was coming back to Hardy's desk, having pulled out Hardy's near-perfect round. "Sure. I was on duty. I thought Terrell could use it. Why?"

Hardy shrugged. "Just following up."

Glitsky threw and the first dart hit the wall a foot below the board. "These are heavy," he said. "My kids' darts don't throw like these."

"Twenty grams." Hardy grimaced at the hollow sound, at the hole in the wall. Another dart flew, smacking the wallboard high and wide of the target. "They're made out of tungsten. They're pretty good darts."

Glitsky fired the last one. It grazed the bottom of the board before sticking, again, in the wall. The inspector headed for the door, stopping when he got there. "I don't know," he said. "I think they might be broke." Then he was gone.

He was almost through the first, and had another four working days — Villars had given everyone a week off before the penalty phase was to begin. Hardy was grateful for the prep time, but the probable reason for it galled him — Powell was in the stretch run for his election and it seemed Villars was cutting him some slack.

He couldn't, of course, prove it, but that didn't make him any less suspicious.

Freeman hadn't been to the office either, which was just as well. He was sick to death of Freeman and his histrionics. He was also sick of himself, of his waffling — every chance he'd got, he'd backed off in the face of the older man's resolve and personality. Half a dozen times he should have just stood his ground. Said this was what was what and take it or leave it. But partly he'd *wanted* to believe that Freeman was right and would prevail. Partly because if Freeman won he wouldn't have the burden of trying to save Jennifer's life. He had wanted so badly to get out from under the responsibility that he'd convinced himself that Freeman's strategies would likely work.

He had been whipping himself over his own deficiencies. Time and again he had driven from Olympia Way down to Haight Street, trying to find a shortcut that would undermine his argument about Jennifer getting to the bank.

But through it all ran a common thread. He had believed — he had never questioned — that Jennifer had run where she said she had. At least she had run on paved streets. He had dutifully consulted his map. No, he'd convinced himself there was no flaw. Even if Jennifer had taken a slightly shorter route, as long as she stayed on the streets she could not have made it to the bank and also killed Larry.

Now he realized he had ignored the UCSF medical center, about ten square blocks of campus and buildings at the base of Mount Sutro between Jennifer's home and her bank. He had seen it, of course — he knew it was *there*. But he had never gotten out of his car and walked through it. On the map, it looked impenetrable, a dense maze of impassable structures. The huge medical buildings gave the impression of a fortress, not a park anyone could simply stroll through. It did have a wall — why did he think it was solid, without gates? Why didn't he get out and stroll through and look?

Because he was too clever for his own good, and Freeman's and, most important, Jennifer's. All his careful calculations about time and distance and how Jennifer couldn't possibly have made it to the bank and accessed her account when she did and still get back home in time to commit the crimes didn't really signify what he had been convinced they did. He had set Freeman up for Powell's devastating rebuttal. And that, in his opinion, even more than Freeman's ego and tactical blunders, had cost them the verdict.

Hardy had always, in theory at least, considered himself more or less in the death-penalty camp. He didn't pretend it was a deterrent. What it did do, though, was eliminate the possibility that the person who was executed was going to kill another innocent citizen — either when they got out on parole or, if they were doing life without parole, during their life behind bars.

He had favored what he called the mosquito argument — if you killed a mosquito that bit you, you at least guaranteed that *that particular mosquito* wasn't going to bite you again. Other mosquitoes didn't have to know about it and tell each other and get deterred — if another one bit you, you killed that one too. That way, at least you had less mosquitoes in the population.

But he *knew* Jennifer. She was not a mosquito. He understood why she had done what she had done *if* she had done it. And he didn't think she should get the death penalty for that.

Here, he knew, at least generally speaking, he was getting on shaky ground. Every murderer had somebody who knew him — or her. Somebody who understood that they'd had a lousy childhood or whatever it was that had made them believe it was somehow okay to kill as an expression of rage or frustration. The flip side to that, of course, was that the victims also had people who had loved them, whose lives were ruined and hearts broken. What about them?

To say nothing of the victims themselves. They didn't ask to be victims, did they? They had done nothing wrong and now they were dead, and generally that's where Hardy drew the line — the people who made innocent people dead deserved to die.

Hardy believed that at some point, adults in society had to take responsibility for what they were, for who they'd become. If as grown-ups, they'd turned into killers, they didn't deserve any breaks. *Adios,* you had your chance and you blew it.

It was a tragedy all around, there was no denying that. It was a tragedy that children got atrociously bad starts in life, that people turned out bad. But it was the world. It was a worse wrong, a worse tragedy, to keep giving bad people the opportunity to do truly bad things again and again.

But what about someone like Jennifer, who had two husbands who beat her? Whose life had been a living hell? Where did she fit in?

41

The next morning, as he was gathering his things, getting ready to go to the jail to see Jennifer, the telephone rang.

"Mr. Hardy? This is Donna Bellows with Goldberg Mullen & Roake." As soon as she said the name Hardy recognized the sultry voice. Ms. Bellows, the lawyer who had referred Jennifer to Freeman, was another lead he probably hadn't followed up enough, another unreturned call that he hadn't pursued. He said hello somewhat warily.

"I found out about the verdict over the weekend and I was out of town yesterday, but I realized I never called you back. I'm sorry. I suppose it's too late now anyway."

"It's never too late if you've got something," Hardy said. "I'm sure David Freeman's working on the appeal right now."

"Well, I don't think I have anything."

Hardy waited. Finally he said, "Whatever you do have, I'll take. I did find out that Crane & Crane was YBMG's law firm, although what that means about Larry Witt . . ."

Bellows sighed over the telephone. "That's what I found, too, where I had heard the name." Again Hardy waited. "I've had a busy few months, and

I've had two secretaries quit on me, and my files are a mess, so I came in a couple of weeks ago and tried to get some of this cleaned up. It should have been filed with Larry's stuff but it wasn't. In any event, I can't imagine it's of any importance —"

"What is it?"

"It's an offering circular. Larry had sent it around to me with some questions but I'd been on vacation over Christmas."

"Maybe that's why he called Crane — to answer the questions."

"He did call them? Directly?"

"Once. From his home, anyway."

"Well, okay, but by the time I saw it, Larry was dead. I'm afraid that between my reaction to that and my other pressing business, I just laid the circular aside. Larry's questions were moot by then anyway. But it sounds like you got your answer."

Remembering how foolish he had felt asking Jody Bachman what an LBO was, Hardy hesitated a moment but then went ahead. The way to stay ignorant was not ask questions. He admitted that he didn't really know what an offering circular was.

"It's pretty much what it says — it's a brochure outlining a stock offering. In this case, YBMG was reorganizing to change their not-for-profit status. I guess Larry had some questions, so he came to me, then when I wasn't here he went to the horse's mouth."

"He wrote the word *'no'* under their phone number."

"He probably decided he wasn't going to invest. It doesn't look like it was much of a deal, anyway."

So that was that.

Hardy, being thorough now, asked if Ms. Bellows would send him a copy of the circular so that he could look it over. She said she would messenger it over that afternoon.

She was dressed in her reds. Her hair was all over the place. The guards let her in and she stood, arms crossed, leaning back against the closed door. She had asked Hardy to bring her a pack of cigarettes, and he shook out one and gave it to her. San Francisco County Jail was officially a smoke-free environment. This created a cottage industry among the prisoners who smuggled in cigarettes and sold them the way they sold cocaine, marijuana, and heroin. Hardy just couldn't believe they'd bust Jennifer, convicted of murder and up for the death penalty, for having a smoke in the attorneys' conference room.

Her eyes squinted against the smoke, drilled into him. "Now what?" she said.

"Now I think we talk about how Larry beat you."

She squinted some more, seemed to shrink into herself. "And that's why I killed him?"

Hardy nodded. "That's our best shot. It always was." He took a step toward her but she stared him back. "How are you holding up?" he asked gently.

She laughed briefly, more like a bark, then coughed, choking on the smoke from her cigarette.

The small room was filling with smoke. "I'm real good," she said. "Real good. I love being here." Tears filled her eyes, overflowed onto her face. She left them there.

Hardy again tried to move forward, but she held out her hand. "You stay *away*." She turned a shoulder into the door and stood there, shaking, her body heaving, trying to control the sobs. The cigarette fell to the ground at her feet. "This isn't me . . . ." After all the other scenes, *this* was not an act. She was talking to herself. "I can't have got to here."

Hardy didn't know what to say. Or do. He had some of the same reaction — that this wasn't real, they couldn't have gotten to here. Yet here they were.

One of the women guards looked in through the window, leaning over slightly with no expression at all. The two people in the room, one crying and one standing, might as well have been part of the furniture. The guard ignored the cigarette smoke.

There was no point in pushing. Hardy took one of the chairs, pulled it around backward and straddled it. He crossed his arms over the back of the chair and waited.

Eventually she had to sit down. She turned her chair to the side, resting an arm across the table. "I don't know why he needed to do that."

"Who?"

"Larry." She nodded. "I always tried to be a good wife, a good mother. But I know who I am. I guess Larry knew it too, maybe better than I did. He was trying to protect me from myself,

I think, keep me from making mistakes . . . And he wasn't mean like Ned was. Even when he was mad he wasn't mean about it — it was more like it was his job to do."

"To keep you in line?"

"It wasn't every day, you know. Most days, sometimes for a couple of weeks, nothing would happen. But then it would just get to me — this, this feeling that if I didn't do *something*, something for myself, I'd go crazy. A couple of times I think I did go crazy. Threw things, tore up the house. The anger just took over. Do you know what I'm talking about at all? I realize it sounds pretty strange."

"But you couldn't leave him?"

She hit her fist on the table. "I didn't even want to leave him. I loved Larry and . . . oh, God, I loved Matt. It wasn't the way it was with Ned. Not at all. I really hoped we would work it out, someday."

This was, Hardy thought, the straightest — and saddest — talk he'd ever gotten out of her, but if it was going to do them any good he had to get more. "I'm sorry to ask this, Jennifer, but what about Ken Lightner?"

It was as though she expected it, nodding to herself. "I talked to him. He told me about your lying to him about me saying we'd slept together. But I'm not going to pretend I don't feel something strong for Ken. I do." She stared straight ahead for a long moment. "But no," she said at last, "I wasn't going to leave Larry and Matt for him. We talked about it. It was okay. I wanted to, at first especially. But that was just more of the same behavior — Ken made me see that. Doing something I knew was wrong so I'd get punished. Ken said I should break the cycle, don't do the wrong thing to begin with. That way I wouldn't feel like I deserved to be punished."

"What about him? How do you think he feels about you?"

She shrugged. "He thinks I'm attractive. He told me that, so I wouldn't think he was rejecting me." Her hands were crossed in her lap, her head down, her voice almost inaudible. "Men find me attractive, but once they get to know me, they don't like me so much."

"He's sticking with you all through this," Hardy said. "That counts."

"I guess."

Hardy took a breath — this was the moment. "If we can talk about this, talk about Ken, lay to rest the talk about your having an affair, say exactly what you've just said to me, how you just snapped and did some crazy things — I think we might have a chance."

She just looked at him.

He spoke quietly. "We can get another shrink — or even Ken if you want — to argue for leniency based on the stress you were under."

Now shaking her head.

"What?"

"No," she said. "I told Ken. No."

Hardy stopped. What did she mean, no?

"That's again saying I killed them, isn't it? I'd be saying I just snapped one morning and killed them." Her body had straightened, her head was up now, eyes getting life back into them. "As soon as I say that, then there really is no hope."

Was this *déjà vu?* Or *déjà, déjà déjà vu?* Hardy had been through this a million times. If she didn't have something new to say, the jury was going to vote the death sentence. Didn't she see that?

"I'm *not* going to tell anybody, ever, that I killed Larry!"

Hardy met her eyes, defiant and hard. He noticed she didn't include Matt, and before hadn't named him. *"Them,"* she said. She could say Larry, but not Matt. She might let people — Ned or Larry — control her up to a point, but when she moved out from that control it was on her own.

It occurred to him too that she had changed over the past year — maybe she'd decided not only that she wasn't going to take it anymore with Larry but with any other men as well. She'd just gotten assertive, cured of the submissive streak that had allowed her to accept being beaten.

If she were getting better Hardy was glad for her. Still, he thought, strategically it couldn't have come at a worse time.

What was he going to argue in front of the jury? What could he say that might induce them at least to spare her life?

Since he was in the building anyway he thought he would drop by Dean Powell's office on the third floor, see if he was putting in his time at his desk while he campaigned.

He was. Sitting alone, reading what looked to be a police report, Powell started at Hardy's knock. After the surprise, the genial candidate appeared. "Hardy! Come on in, take a load off."

Half out of his chair, hand extended, he could afford to be gracious. After all, he had won. "How's Freeman? Not taking it too hard, I trust. I ought to give him a call, congratulate him on a good fight."

Hardy closed the door behind him. He leaned back against it, not moving toward the seat in front of the desk. "Dean," he began, "I want to be straight with you a minute. Off the record, is that all right?"

The smile remained, but Powell's expression went a little sideways. He sat back down. "Sure, Mr. Hardy."

"Dismas is okay if Dean is."

The smile flickered back. Hardy hadn't had much luck reading Powell. He couldn't really blame himself. Powell was in an unusual predicament — on the one hand he wanted votes so badly that it was almost painful to watch. On the other, the two men's relationship was adversarial. It must be awkward, Hardy thought, to feel like your adversary might wind up voting for you, to *want* your adversary to vote for you, even to like you.

"Dean's fine," Powell said. "I assume you're here about Jennifer Witt."

Hardy nodded. "This is off the record," he repeated. "I don't want this to be construed as a pre-sentencing conference or anything formal, and I'd prefer if what we say here doesn't leave this office."

"You have my word."

Hardy would rather have heard "sure" or "okay" or anything but "you have my word," which he thought clanged with insincerity if not downright duplicity. Still, he was here and determined to press ahead.

"I wanted to talk about the death penalty."

Powell folded his hands in front of him on the desk. "All right," he said mildly. "Talk."

"I don't think it's just."

Powell waited.

"You and I both know that there are people out in the system with sheets a mile long that make Jennifer look like a den mother, and these guys are getting ten years for armed robbery with priors and serving six."

"That's true. It's one of the reasons I'm running for AG. That's got to stop. We need more jail space. We need tougher sentencing."

Hardy didn't need the campaign speech. "Dean, my point is that going capital on Jennifer Witt is going overboard."

Powell looked up at him. "A woman who's killed not one, but *two* husbands" — he raised a palm to stop Hardy's argument — "we don't have to be legalistic, Dismas. David Freeman won that one in court, sure, but since we're off the record, we know the truth about that. Let's not kid ourselves. This woman has twice plotted and killed in cold blood for money, and in this second case, also managed to kill her own son. If that isn't a death penalty case I don't know what is."

Hardy braced his foot back against the door. "Have you talked to her? One on one?"

"Why would I want to do that?"

"Maybe to get a handle on the fact that she's a human being."

Powell sat back. "Let me ask you one — have

you tried to visualize the crime? Can you imagine the kind of person who takes out a gun and shoots her husband at point-blank range and then turns and" — Powell exploded in righteous anger — "and blows away her own *child?* Can you *imagine* that?"

"She didn't do that, it wasn't like that —"

Powell slammed his desk, coming halfway up onto his feet. "Bullshit! That's just what it was like. The jury says that's what she did. I *proved* it. Beyond a damned reasonable doubt." Gathering his control, he sat himself down, lowered his voice. "If you want to call such a person a human being, you're welcome to, but don't expect any tears from me. Or any mercy, either."

There was a knock at the door and Hardy stepped aside, pulling it open. It was Art Drysdale, Hardy's old mentor, the ex-officio administrative boss of the office. "Everything all right in here? How you doin', Dismas?"

"We're fine, Art," Powell said evenly. "Everything's fine. Just a little disagreement among professionals."

Drysdale looked from one man to the other, raised a hand and closed the door again.

"You really think she did it, don't you? You know her husband — Larry — was beating her?"

"So what? Nobody's talking battered wife here. Freeman never did."

"We should have. I should have. Jennifer wouldn't allow it but she was wrong." He almost said dead wrong. "She thought it would prejudice the jury, make them think she was using it as an excuse." Sitting down, he gave Powell as much as he could of the short version. "I'd just like you to consider if it was self-defense."

"Bring it up in the penalty phase, I'll consider it. I'm not a monster, Hardy."

"I *can't* bring it up. I've just told you why."

"You can't bring it up?" Powell went all the way back in his chair, looking up at the ceiling, running his fingers through his mane the way he did. He took a long moment, running it around different ways. Finally, he came down. "This is pretty goddamn sleazy."

"I'm not —"

"Don't try to lay this human-being guilt trip on me now, Hardy. To tell the truth, it was heavy enough deciding to go capital on this, but I've played by the rules from the get-go. I don't give a shit what spin you put on it, we're sitting here talking about circumventing the system, and as far as I'm concerned this is an unethical conversation and it's over right *now*."

Powell was up out of his desk, around it, to the door. He pulled it open. "I'll see you in court," he said. "Not until."

Hardy's first reaction was that he needed a drink. His stomach was in knots, his breathing coming shallow. He stayed thirsty until he got inside the door of Lou's, then abruptly decided not. It was still early in the afternoon, and a drink or two now would end his day. And he needed all the time he could get.

He was at his desk, going over his options.

Lightner's motion to introduce de facto witnesses to Jennifer's pain and suffering at the hands of her husband wasn't bad — might well garner some sympathy for her. But as soon as Jennifer saw the way the wind was blowing there — and it wouldn't take long — she would either go berserk in the courtroom or insist on testifying that no beatings took place.

So given that, what was he going to do next Monday? If Powell's reaction was any indication, Jennifer hadn't won many hearts in the courtroom. Dressed in a way that separated her from the commoners, for the most part sitting without expression at the defense table, she hadn't testified on her own behalf. Another of Freeman's questionable decisions.

The package arrived, messengered over from Donna Bellows. Grateful for the distraction, Hardy opened it, little more than an envelope, depressingly thin.

There was the letter from Larry Witt to Donna Bellows. There was a covering letter to go with the offering circular. Finally, there was the circular itself.

Dear Donna:

I wonder if you could take a look at the enclosed. As you will see, the YBMG Board is offering all doctors (we are called "providers" in the brochure) an option to buy into the new for-profit plan. The shares are a nickel each, and the tone of both the covering letter and the brochure is very negative — there's slim to no chance that this is a worthwhile investment.

So why did they bother sending the thing out?

My concern is that the Board has only given us three weeks to exercise the option, and that they sent this circular now, over Christmas, when so many providers are either on vacation or swamped with personal business at home.

I realize that the most shares any individual can buy is 368, so potentially the greatest personal exposure to any provider in the group is only $18.40, but —

Hardy abruptly stopped reading.

Larry Witt, control freak extraordinaire, was asking his two-hundred-dollar-an-hour lawyer to look into a maximum exposure issue of less than twenty dollars?

He must have read it wrong, got the decimal misplaced. He looked at the last line again. ". . . the greatest personal exposure to any provider in the group is only $18.40 . . ."

Shaking his head, thinking what an absolute pain in the ass Larry Witt must have been, Hardy stood, stretched, and gave up for the day. He went downstairs to watch the World Series in the conference room. Maybe his side would *win.*

Frannie had her feet up on the couch, a book face down on her chest. Her eyes were on her husband and she was trying not to nod off.

"No, listen, this is really interesting."

His wife shook her head. "Anytime you've got

to say that, it isn't."

Hardy put his paper down. "You used to be more fun."

She raised her eyebrows. "Let me get this straight — you're sitting in our living room on a balmy October night, you didn't taste the fantastic dinner I made, you didn't even want wine with it, and for the last ten minutes you are reading to me aloud from some stock proposal that isn't worth anything anyway, and *I'm* the one who used to be more fun?"

He nodded. "A lot more. I remember. I know it can't be me."

Frannie swung her feet to the ground, patting her lap. "Okay, come here."

Hardy crossed the room. "What am I going to do, Fran? She still won't let me use the only thing that might save her."

"I don't think you're right, about it being the only thing that can save her. It's not just the beatings . . . Jennifer's life with her husband was terrible, but she didn't kill him, Dismas. She never lied to me, not even about Ned. She never *denied* to me, about him. She just didn't say she did it. But she absolutely denied killing Larry. She had no reason to lie to me, she *avoided* it in the case of Ned."

Hardy could think of at least one reason why Jennifer might want to lie to Frannie. Frannie was his wife, he was Jennifer's lawyer. It would be better if he believed she didn't kill Larry and Matt.

Frannie went on. "This is *not* just an instinct, you know. Or woman's intuition, although I wouldn't put that down if I were you. You're forgetting what you proved. Never mind if she could have done it or not, Jennifer in fact did *not* run through the Medical Center. It did take her probably fifteen minutes to get to her bank, not five. And *that* means she didn't kill anybody. She had left her house. She ran to the bank the way she told you she did. Talking about that morning, telling me about it, she *volunteered* the way she'd come — down Clarendon, through the Victorians, the old Haight, she talked about that, how the neighborhood calmed her down. You don't make that stuff up." Sometimes you do, Hardy thought. But it wasn't a bad point. "So what you — Dismas Hardy the person — forget the lawyer, what you've got to do if you really want to save her is to stop doubting her, stop even considering that she might be guilty."

"Frannie, they found her guilty. That part's over."

Her fingers felt good against his scalp now. "*I* say she did not kill Larry and her boy."

"I can't prove she didn't. She did kill Ned —"

"That was different."

"Not so different," he said. "Ned's dead. Larry's dead —"

Frannie stood up and walked over to the fireplace. She spent a minute rearranging the small herd of brass elephants that liked to graze there. "I still say you're thinking too much like a lawyer. You're thinking what arguments you can make."

"That's kind of my job, Fran."

She faced him. "I'm not attacking you, Dismas. I'm telling you she did not do it. That's reality, not law, not what the jury found."

"It's *one* reality, Fran. Yours."

"Damn it! *Listen* to me. You want to argue and fight about words, you go ahead. But there's a major thing you're forgetting."

"Oh? What's that?"

"Sure, go ahead, get mad. That's a real help."

Hardy was mad. He had gotten up, found himself standing by the couch with his fists clenched. He closed his eyes and took a breath. "Okay, I'm sorry. What am I forgetting?"

"If Jennifer didn't do it, *somebody else* killed them, and did it for a reason."

Hardy was shaking his head. "I've been all through the possibilities there — by myself, with Terrell and Glitsky and Freeman and the whole known universe."

"Then you missed something."

"Except if Jennifer did do it. How about that?"

Frannie didn't budge. "She didn't. I think you know it and I know I know it. Powell got it wrong both ways."

"I don't know that."

Frannie was heading back through the dining room. "I feel like a glass of wine. Several. You can join me or not, I don't care."

"The hit man?"

The mood had mellowed some. It was ten-thirty and they'd finished most of a bottle of Chardonnay. Hardy had run all the people with motives by Frannie, and finally they had arrived at Frannie's suggestion that one of these people, although armed with an alibi for his or her personal time, had hired someone to kill the family.

Hardy shook his head. "Don't you suspect a professional hit man would bring his own weapon? You ever hear of a hit man shooting somebody with their own gun?"

Frannie had her legs over his on the couch. She sipped her wine. "I don't know. It's not exactly my area of expertise."

"Plus, how did he get in or out?"

"Maybe he just walked. Is there a back door? A window? All I'm saying is it had to be someone. Someone besides Jennifer."

"The problem is, Fran, even if I agree, this takes us back to police work. And they didn't find anybody else. No hit man, no nobody."

"Maybe Abe . . ."

Hardy shook his head. "Abe is a good guy but he's done on this one. Everybody's done. It's down to me."

Frannie finished her wine. "And you don't have a lawyer argument that's going to save Jennifer, do you?"

"No. She won't —"

Frannie shushed him. She knew all that, she reminded him. "Okay, then. There's only one option left."

"I'm listening."

"You've got to find out who killed them."

42

Hardy sensed that he and Walter Terrell weren't friends anymore. He had reached him by telephone at the homicide detail before nine the next morning, and they had had a brief discussion. After Hardy had introduced himself, saying he just had a couple of quick questions, Terrell had replied, "Why don't you take your questions to somebody who gives a shit?" And then the inspector had hung up.

Hardy held the receiver for a long minute, until it started to beep at him. Okay, he thought, I can take a hint.

He had a problem — nobody was going to talk to him. Terrell was the first indication, but as he sat flipping through the interview folders and copies of police reports on his desk, he realized that he had about run out of folks who might be willing to give him the time of day, much less a substantive interview.

Tom and Phil DiStephano — forget it. Nancy — too scared, and rightly so. The Romans — he could go get in Cecil's face, but there was no leverage even if he had a grounded suspicion, which he didn't. There was Sam, the gay receptionist at the Mission Hills Clinic, but that could get awkward and was still once removed from any even remotely potential suspect.

Hardy went downstairs again, watched more World Series action, drank a cup of coffee and schmoozed with Phyllis. David Freeman was in his office this morning but had a client with him and Phyllis wouldn't interrupt, not that Hardy wanted her to. It looked like another murder case. By the way, he'd been working while he'd been at home — she had typed the first papers on the Witt appeal this morning.

The ever-spinning wheels of the law depressing him, Hardy went back upstairs. He threw darts — 20, 19, 18. The numbers falling, the clock ticking.

The only human being left was Ali Singh, the office manager at YBMG. Hardy thought he'd take him out to lunch, see if there was any other avenue he hadn't explored regarding Larry Witt's work. Maybe he had stolen another doctor's patients? Singh's avowal that Larry had been popular with his fellow workers — on reflection — just didn't seem to be possible. The man had been difficult with everyone, and all work environments created frictions. At least it was worth a shot. Not to mention that it was the only shot Hardy had.

Except that Singh no longer worked there.

"Do you have a forwarding number?"

The efficient voice said they weren't allowed to give out that information, which Hardy had somehow known was coming.

"It's very important."

The voice was sorry. There was nothing it could

do. Hardy's karma on a negative course.

"Okay, then, how about this? How about I give you my name and number and you call Mr. Singh and ask him if he'd like to call me back?"

"I may be able to do that," the voice said. "I'll check."

Assistant District Attorney (and candidate for Attorney General) Dean Powell and his boss Chris Locke were having lunch together at a corner table fifty-two floors above San Francisco in the Carnelian Room at the top of the Bank of America Building. Powell had asked for the lunch.

The special was Santa Barbara rock shrimp risotto, and both the attorney and his boss the DA had ordered it. Powell had decided he wanted a half bottle of Meursault to go with it. Locke wasn't having any until it was poured, and then he allowed himself to be talked into a glass. They did not click their glasses together.

The upcoming election was now less than two weeks away, and Powell was leading the pack of contenders in the latest poll by four percentage points. After a few minutes of chatter about that, Powell came to the point, filling Locke in on Hardy's visit to his office, the one he had promised not to talk about.

When he had finished, Locke said, "He's only been with Freeman how long and he's pulling this? 'Course, he's capable of doing it all on his own."

Powell nodded. "It's pretty transparent." He stabbed a shrimp. "He tells me his client won't let him bring it up but nevertheless it's the truth and I'm a cretin if I don't believe him."

"Still, though, Dean, this issue has been floating around since the beginning."

"Or course. There's little doubt the woman was hit a few times. But it's nowhere in the record."

"Yes it is, Dean. At least once."

"Not with Larry. Not with the second husband."

A bit annoyed, perhaps only impatient, Locke snapped, "I know who Larry is." Then, "What's he doing with it? Hardy, I mean."

"Well, that's just it — he says Jennifer has forbidden him to bring it up in open court."

"He say why?"

Powell shrugged. "She says it gives her a reason to have killed Larry and she didn't do it."

"She's feathering her bed for the appeal." Locke finished his short glass of wine and Powell poured him a little more, to which he did not object.

"That's how I read it, too. She's just stonewalling, and she's smart, figuring if she admits to being beaten she's admitting to the murders."

"I don't think she killed anybody because she was being beaten," Locke said.

"Right. She did it for the money. Twice." Powell looked out over the sparkling city, the view clear to Napa. He sipped at his own wine. "I just wanted to alert you. I think you can expect a personal call from Mr. Hardy, calling on you to tap those reserves of sympathy for which you are so justly famous."

Locke, never able to stand Hardy, allowed himself a small smile. He brushed his lips with his napkin. "If it's not in the record it doesn't exist, Dean. That's how I run my office. Always have."

Powell was satisfied. "Yes, sir, I know." He nodded. Locke held out his glass for the last drops of the Meursault, and Powell poured.

At least Hardy had found a couple of questions he hadn't yet asked. It gave him a glimmer of hope.

Not that this particular question — what was in the Federal Express package and/or who sent it? — appeared to have much to do with the matter. But it *might*. At this point, he was considering a "might" of resounding relevance.

The files were piled in a half-circle around the periphery of his desk, in places a foot high.

The other consideration that had occurred was Phil DiStephano's co-workers. Glitsky had told him about the redneck feel of the plumbers' workplace. Hardy thought it was at least possible that here, from a pool of blue-collar workers, might surface a moonlighter who augmented his hourly wage by a sub-speciality in taking people out.

Again, this was the long shot to end them all . . . who said blue-collar workers were disposed to professional killings — and besides, plumbers were not exactly economically depressed. But what else did he have? If he was going on the assumption that Frannie's feelings, convictions, were accurate — which he now was — then he had to have missed *something*.

When the telephone rang now it startled him. He had been trying to figure out a way to contact one of Phil's friends: Hi, I think one of your co-workers might be killing people on the side. Anybody talk about anything like that? Unlikely.

"Hello."

"Mr. Hardy, is it?" The welcome voice of Ali Singh, not that he was likely to know anything either.

"It's a little late," Hardy said, "but if you haven't eaten yet, I'd like to take you to lunch."

It was a different setting than the Carnelian Room.

The Independent Unicorn was one of those San Francisco coffee houses in the avenues that always seemed to be empty and yet had been operating in the same location for thirty-some years. A poster next to the front door announced poetry readings on Wednesday nights, open-mike music on a few others, randomly. The place had picture windows, but they were covered with paisley cotton sheets, keeping the room suitably dim. There was sitar music and faint smells of patchouli and curry. A shirtless bearded man and a long-haired thin young woman dressed in black were playing chess at the counter.

Singh waved tentatively from his table at the back. Hardy's eyes, not yet adjusted to the light, made out the form, and he moved toward it, knocking into one of the tables on his way. A cat meowed at Hardy's feet and jumped up to the window ledge.

Hardy studied the table, moving on. Singh shook his hand, weakly. The little efficiency expert seemed somehow diminished, beaten down, though he put on a brave smile. When Hardy thanked him for the meeting, Singh said, "It is my pleasure for you to come down. There is not, you see, much . . ." His voice stopped. He gestured around the room.

"Is this your place?" Hardy asked. "You own it?"

A polite laugh. "Oh no, no." He leaned forward, confiding. "It is not expensive. They let me sit in here all day sometimes. It is better than being home. It is a place to come to, like work."

The shirtless man had put on an apron for his waiter's duties, and was at their table offering the menu. Espresso, teas, whole grain bread products, lentil soup, brown rice, tabouli. Hardy ordered hummous and a salad. Singh asked if Hardy minded if he had the vegetable curry, at $4.95 the most expensive thing on the menu. Hardy said sure, anything, lunch was on him. Hardy, the sport.

When the waiter had gone, Hardy asked Singh what had happened to his job. Singh smiled sadly. "Well, the business climate, you see . . ." he began, then trailed off again. He was still wearing his thin tie and his white shirt. The sportscoat was draped over the chair behind him. "No, it is not that. I think it is just greed."

"Greed?"

"No, that is not fair, not right. I suppose it is just business, but I am . . . I was with the Group for seven years and I thought . . ." He shrugged.

"What happened?"

"Well, the restructure, yes? The bottom line." Singh drank from his water glass, no ice. "I did not see this coming. It is my fault. I should have known. This is how profit is made — you trim the fat." He laughed. "I never saw myself as the fat, though. You see? I thought I was valuable, providing a service. Now, of course, I see."

Hardy, having read the offering circular three times, was by now familiar with the facts: The Yerba Buena Medical Group had been in the process of changing its status from non-profit to for-profit, for well over a year — the HMO needed to attract capital if it expected to compete for patients, and it couldn't attract capital if it didn't make a profit.

"So they just let you go?"

Singh shrugged. "Somebody else could do it more cheaply. Maybe not so well, I don't know. But I was staff, not a doctor, so . . ." Another shrug, the conclusion obvious. "In any case, how do I help you? You did not come to talk about me."

Hardy sat back on his chair. "That's all right, Mr. Singh. I don't mind hearing about you. You might have heard that Dr. Witt's wife was found guilty of killing him . . ."

"No, I did not. I do not follow the news since . . . his wife . . . ?"

"She's my client. I'm trying to keep her from being getting sentenced to death."

"I do not believe in that. I think execution by the State is just another form of murder."

"Then you might want to help me?"

"If I can. But as I told you, Dr. Witt was respected."

The food arrived, slightly more appetizing than its description. Hardy broke off some pita and dipped it in his hummous. Singh ate hungrily, beginning almost before the food was on the table.

"You also said that you and Dr. Witt had some problems over how money got spent."

"But that was the Board, their decisions. It never came to anything. Dr. Witt did what he did in his office, what he wanted. I think he wanted more say, more control, in how the plan worked, in the decision-making." Singh stopped eating for a second, a smile on his face. "What he would do now, I don't know."

"What do you mean, now?"

"Now there is no Ali Singh to discuss it with. Now, with the takeover."

"You mean the change to for-profit?"

Singh shook his head. "No, Mr. Hardy. That was last March. I mean the takeover, the buy-out." He forked in some more curry. "If he had not bought in . . . almost no one did, but I think Dr. Witt, he would have arguments over this."

Hardy stopped the pretense of eating. He felt a tingling at the back of his neck. "I'm afraid you've lost me. I thought we were talking about the company going for profit."

"Yes, it did that."

Hardy waited.

"And then — this is separate, you see? Later, this summer, the Group was bought."

"Who bought it?"

Singh had finished his curry. He pushed his plate aside. "These are the people who let me go. The insurance people — PacRim. They paid $40 million in cash."

Hardy pushed his own plate away. "$40 million."

Singh was going on. "When it filed with the State for the status change — the fee is to pay the State for your worth — it came to $535,000 dollars. That was the Group's net worth. The offer of $40 million was a great surprise, you see? No one thought the Group had that kind of value."

Somebody did, Hardy thought. No business suddenly discovered its value had increased from $500,000 to $40 million in less than six months.

Yet the offering circular had described YBMG's financial future in the most conservative terms. No sale was contemplated — publicly — last Christmas. There had been no potential buyers and the market had been scoured at the time. The circular had been clear on that. The members shouldn't expect any windfall profit; it probably wasn't even worth the members' time to buy the nickel shares. They'd never be worth any more than that.

The tingling sensation was spreading.

"If I had been a member, I would have bought," Singh said. "Not many members bought but I would have. And everything now would be different."

"The members did all right?" Hardy asked. "The ones who bought in?"

Singh, the accountant, knew the figures. He couldn't help smiling bleakly in admiration. "They offered forty-nine percent to the members, the doctors. That's 140,000 shares at five cents a share. How much you could buy depended on how long you had been with the Group. The most — for any one individual, you see — was 368 shares, which would be a total investment of $18.40."

Hardy remembered that figure — "less than twenty bucks."

"I have been over these numbers so many times," Singh said, "and it is still very difficult to believe. Do you know what a nickel share is now worth?"

"I could do the math."

Singh smiled his sad gentle smile again. "No need. I have done it. One hundred forty-two dollars and eighty-six cents. Per share."

Hardy whistled.

"Fifty-two thousand, five hundred seventy-two dollars and forty-eight cents," Singh said.

"What's that?"

"That's what you have now if you bought your three hundred and sixty-eight shares for eighteen dollars and forty cents."

"Interesting, if true. But so what?"

Freeman was on his own turf. Unlike his austere apartment, the surroundings in his office were sumptuous. A twelve-by-eighteen-foot Persian rug covered the center of the dark hardwood floors; fine leaded crystal was on display on the mirrored shelves behind the fully stocked bar; two original Bufanos and a Bateman hung on the sponge-painted walls. The corner room was large — three times the size of Hardy's — with full bookshelves, two full-size couches, several armchairs. There were drapes — not the ubiquitous louvered blinds — on the three sets of windows. Freeman's desk was a five-by-seven-foot expanse of spotless, shining rosewood.

It was six o'clock and Hardy was sitting in one

of the armchairs. After his discussion with Ali Singh, he had tried unsuccessfully to reach Donna Bellows again. He had also left a message with Jody Bachman at Crane & Crane. Then he had spent an hour or so going over the YBMG offering circular in some detail. In light of what he had discovered with Singh, it didn't read the same way it had.

"So what?" Hardy replied. "So something, at least."

Freeman grunted, handed Hardy a cold beer and went back to the bar, rummaging around down behind it.

"It's a lot of money," Hardy persisted. "It's a hell of a lot of money."

Freeman came up with a bottle of red wine. "I agree." He was taking the foil off. "But again, so what? So a bunch of doctors made a lot of money. Happens every day."

"Not a bunch. Only a few. This accountant, Singh, said he didn't think more than fifteen, twenty guys bought in."

Freeman pulled the cork, sniffed it and laid it on the bar's surface. He lifted one of the large-bowled crystal wine glasses from behind him and poured himself a quarter of the bottle, holding it up to the window to check its color, its clarity, its legs.

Hardy crossed a leg. "Let me know if I'm bothering you, David."

He sipped at the wine. "Not at all," he said, taking another mouthful, flushing it around his mouth, gargling, finally swallowing. He came around the bar. "The '82 Bordeaux are not overrated. You really ought to try a glass."

Choosing an armchair, placing the glass on a marble-topped end table, he sat down. Hardy defiantly pulled at his beer.

Freeman sat forward. "I would love to put something together here, Dismas, believe me. I'm not seeing it."

Hardy sat back, trying to formulate his position. It would be good practice if he had to present it to Villars, or a jury. Maybe it wasn't as clear as it seemed to him. "Let's be generous. Say a maximum of fifty doctors bought the stock. There are about four hundred doctors in the Group."

Freeman waited, hearing him out, sipping his wine. "Okay?"

"Okay, so from my perspective, and I admit it's almost a year later, the cover letter looks like an outright deception."

"A year ago you hadn't started your first trial," Freeman reminded him. "You didn't work here. You didn't have two children. You'd never met Jennifer Witt, and Larry and Matt Witt were alive." He swirled more wine. "A lot can happen in a year. Perspectives change."

"I think the reason Larry got in touch with his lawyer, and then this guy down in LA, was because he thought something was fishy — back then, and he was calling them on it."

"Calling who?"

"The Board, the attorneys, I don't know. Whoever drew up this thing, whoever concocted the scam."

The bushy eyebrows went up. "Now it's a scam?"

"A scam is the only way it helps Jennifer."

Now Freeman sat all the way back into his chair. "Don't hang your hopes on the way you *want* something to be, Dismas."

"I don't think I'm doing that."

Freeman shook his head. "You want it to be a scam because if it is a scam — and you can prove it — then, maybe, you can help Jennifer with it. Although how you plan to do even that eludes me." He leaned forward again. "All you can do this round is get the death penalty mitigated. She's already guilty. You can't get her retried."

"If I can get Villars —"

"You're talking about Joan Villars, the Superior Court judge, I presume? Get serious. The woman's about as flexible as concrete. You're not going to convince Villars to do anything."

"So let me try to convince you."

Freeman sat back again. "I've been listening. I think you said fifty doctors bought stock. Continue."

"The *reason* the other three hundred and fifty did not was because of the wording of this cover-letter and the offering circular. Together, they made this dumb nickel investment sound like a waste of time. Then they sent it out to their doctors during the holidays, when only a few of the guys would be likely to take the time to read it, and limited the option period to about three weeks."

"I'm with you so far. Did Larry buy or not buy?"

"Larry smelled a rat."

"And then?"

"And then he threatened to blow the whistle on this multi-million-dollar scam. That was the call to LA."

Fingers pressed to his eyes, Freeman sighed. "I was afraid that's where you were going."

Hardy had been talked out of enough good ideas by David Freeman over the past weeks. He was not in his most receptive mode. "David, the managing partner in the LA firm handling this was shot to death within a month of Larry Witt."

Freeman tipped his glass. "You said that. I fail to see, though, how any of this is going to mitigate Jennifer's sentence, even if you could get Villars to listen to it, which you can't. You're saying now, I take it, that there was in fact some mysterious hit man, the existence of whom, by the way, the defense — that's us — never hinted at during the trial, and of whom there is no physical evidence."

"That doesn't mean he doesn't exist."

"Do you think he does? You think Jennifer is telling the truth?"

Hardy said he still didn't entirely think that, but the jury might. "I'll let them decide."

"Villars won't let you introduce the theory. And if she'd be inclined to, which she won't, Powell will object and win unless you've got some shred of evidence, which doesn't exist, no doubt because this didn't happen this way."

"Which leaves Jennifer hanging," Hardy said.

Freeman noisily sipped the rest of his wine. "It always has," he muttered.

But he wasn't going to take any more of Freeman's advice, even if it was right. He still had four days, and he thought if he did succeed in finding that shred of evidence Freeman had talked about, he could get Villars at least to listen.

After all, this was a capital case. This was life and death, not some moot-court discussion, not petty politics. If he got something real, he had to believe she would listen to it.

Of course, this did beg the question of whether or not anything real in fact existed, but Hardy had nothing else — he had to assume it did. Somewhere.

43

The next day he interviewed three doctors at YBMG, two of whom had not invested and one who had. The first two felt understandably snake-bit, but neither one saw a grand conspiracy at work in his bad fortune. The Group had done well and they both wished they had been more a part of it, but it was like the lottery. Who would have predicted the windfall? It was a fluke, and they'd been given their chance.

The lucky one, Dr. Seidl, was a younger member of the Group, only entitled to ninety-two shares. Paying his monthly bills in December, he had sent in his $4.60 and promptly forgot about it. Last month, when he received his payout of $13,143.12, he thought it was very nice, but after taxes it was a little under ten grand, and after all his credit cards he was back to square one. It sure beat a swan dive into a dry swimming pool, but it wasn't really going to change his life.

Hardy was starting to think it was going to be hard to sustain his conspiracy theory, even to himself, if he didn't find somebody who had made a bundle, and theoretically, at least, would have had reason to shut up a whistle blower if that's what Larry Witt had been.

In the afternoon he went to the library and looked up the members of the YBMG Board in the business reference section, but the names were all unfamiliar. He did learn that the corporation as an entity was scheduled to hold fifty-one percent of the stock, and the doctors forty-nine percent, if all of them bought in. He wondered if there was a provision for outstanding, unbought doctor stock, some kind of secondary buy-in, but he saw no mention of it in the published prospectus.

He did some figuring, realizing that if only ten percent of the doctors bought their stock, then there appeared to be a little over 125,000 shares out there somewhere — unclaimed — with a value of something like $17 million.

On Friday morning, he was in his office, talking on the phone to the Los Angeles Police Department. He still had discovered no evidentiary connection between YBMG's business dealings and Dr. Larry Witt. He had talked to Jennifer again last night, pressing her, but she could recall nothing Larry said or might have said regarding the proposed buy-out. Hardy was tempted to tell her to make something up just so he could get it in front of somebody, but he restrained himself.

Then it struck him — there had been two homicides in Los Angeles, and there must have been an investigation. He knew that policemen got sensitive about their unsolved backlogs — their skull cases, they called them — but he might be able to drum up a little enthusiasm — tie the old crime to another one?

"Restoffer. Homicide."

It was an older voice but not a tired one. And Hardy had gotten through the huge bureaucracy faster than he'd have thought possible. Maybe it meant something.

Hardy introduced himself, trying to talk fast and still be as clear as he could be — he was a defense attorney in San Francisco and maybe had discovered a possible link between his client and the murder of Simpson Crane.

There was a longish pause. "What'd you say your name was?"

Hardy told him. Another pause. "Just a minute. Hang on, would you?"

When Restoffer came back on, there was less background noise. "You said you were in *San Francisco?*"

"That's right."

"I'm listening."

Hardy went through it, more slowly this time, filling in the blanks. When he'd finished, Restoffer said, "That's pretty tenuous, Mr. Hardy."

The inspector was right, of course, and Hardy admitted it. Simpson Crane ran the law firm that represented the medical group of which Larry Witt had been a member. Crane himself hadn't been YBMG's lawyer, or Witt's. For that matter, even Jody Bachman hadn't been Witt's lawyer.

Hardy knew better than to push. It was the quickest way to turn a cop off — a citizen, especially a defense lawyer, lobbying for an unsupported theory. The facts were either going to intrigue Restoffer or not. "Well," Hardy said, "I just thought I should report it to somebody, get it off my chest."

It was Restoffer's cue to hang up if he was going to, but he stayed on. "We're pretty sure it was union muscle but we couldn't find any kind of trail. They did it right . . ."

"Same up here. Except they've convicted my client — Witt's wife — of killing him for the insurance."

"They've convicted her already?"

"Last week. My problem is she's got no defense, other than saying she didn't do it. She says she saw somebody walking up the street. Maybe it was some kind of hit man, so I've been trying to find a reason for a hit man to want to kill Witt. This might be it."

There was a long silence. "I've got four months before I retire," Restoffer said. "I'd love to close out these two. Crane was a prominent guy. So was his wife. But I've got five live cases right now. When am I supposed to fit this in?"

That was his problem, and Hardy let him wrestle with it.

"You got a paper trail, anything at all?"

All Hardy had was the offering circular and the prospectus from the library, which he'd fax down if Restoffer needed it.

"How much money we talking about?"

"I figure about seventeen million dollars."

"Seventeen *million.*"

"You think that could motivate somebody to do something serious?"

Restoffer grunted. "Seventeen dollars does it down here, sometimes seventeen cents." The line hummed, empty and open. “Okay,” he said, “why don’t you send your stuff down? I’ll take a look at it.”

Now it was Hardy’s turn to hang up, but much as he wanted Restoffer’s help, he didn’t want to mislead him. It was full-disclosure time. “Inspector . . .” he began.

“Floyd,” Restoffer said.

“Okay, Floyd, there is one other thing you ought to know that argues against this hit man theory. It might make the whole exercise not worth your time.”

“I’m listening.”

“I don’t know what the practice is with professional killers — if they do this. But Witt was shot with his own gun.”

The silence hung. Hardy thought he heard Restoffer let out a deep breath. “So was Crane,” he said. “Send down your stuff.”

At least some things seemed to be falling together, even the details that did not appear to have particular relevance. For example, the FedEx package.

While Hardy was filling out his subpoena form to call Ali Singh as a witness for the defense, it had come back to him that the FedEx invoice had been entered as an exhibit, and all he had to do was look up who had sent the package.

He had done that, and seeing that it had come from Nancy DiStephano, he had remembered — putting things together — that Tom had gone over to Jennifer’s house the week before the killings to deliver his own present, but that Nancy was going to wait to deliver hers in person when the Witts came to visit on Christmas. So what had happened was that after the Witts had blown off the family visit, Nancy had sent her present to her grandson Matt by Federal Express. What the gift had been didn't matter — it had obviously vanished into the gaping and insatiable mouth of Christmas presents, into the mountain of Matt's new toys.

But, like Restoffer's cooperation, and though it was not what he'd call hot evidence, the information gave Hardy some small consolation. The unanswered questions had been distracting, and there weren't many left now.

There seemed something fishy in the YBMG takeover. Hardy's theory was a long way from completely developed and even further from proven, but what he was beginning to suspect drew him like a moth to a candle. Hell, any possibility did. Suppose that both Larry Witt and Simpson Crane had, for different reasons and by differing paths, somehow threatened to expose and undermine an extremely lucrative and shady business transaction. So whoever was behind it had these two obstacles to eliminate — Simpson and Larry — before the deal could proceed. Someone was hired to do the dirty work, and the murder of Simpson Crane (and his wife, who just happened to be there) looked like some kind of radical union hit, while the murder of Larry Witt (and his son, who also just happened to be there) got laid off on his wife. It was at least a tantalizing parallel.

Sunday morning, frying eggs and bacon in his

metal pan. Frannie in her bathrobe reading the paper in the sunny kitchen. Rebecca and Vincent enjoying the special treat of sitting next to each other, Rebecca the big girl helping her mommy, feeding the baby, getting fully twenty percent of the squashed banana into Vincent's mouth.

Hardy taking it all in out of the corner of his eye, one of the life moments that he'd committed himself to recognizing, savoring. From the front of the house came the strains of the *Grand Canyon Suite* — more Freeman influence. He walked a couple of steps across the kitchen and planted a kiss on Frannie's forehead.

"Um," she said, kissing the air distractedly near his face.

And the telephone rang. It always did.

"Don't get it," Hardy said. He was standing right next to it and was fighting the temptation pretty well.

But Frannie was already up. "I know it's Susan. She said she'd call me. She might be pregnant." She picked it up, listened, then frowned. "Just a minute, he's right here."

He gave her a look, but what could he do?

It was Floyd Restoffer. "I've got good news and bad news," he said, getting right to it. "The bad news is I'm off the case."

"You're off the case?" Hardy had gone around the corner to the workroom off the kitchen. "What happened?"

"My guess would be politics. After I got your stuff on Friday I talked to the younger Crane, Simpson's kid, Todd. Asked him if he didn't mind, which he didn't, if I interviewed some of his partners, although he had no idea what I wanted from him. Anyway, I didn't tell him much — just following up a new lead on his parents' deaths. I asked if his dad did any work with Yerba Buena."

"And?"

"No. It was this guy Bachman and a couple of associates."

"Okay."

"So Bachman and I have a chat. He seems like a nice guy, cooperative." Hardy remembered that had been his take on Bachman, too. "I ask him if he knows Witt. He says he's heard the name. Then he remembers — you'd called him, Bachman, I mean. He says he forgot to call you back, the message got lost. He writes himself a note this time — I'd expect a call from him if I were you. So we talk for a while about the deal, if Simpson had been involved somehow. Bachman can't think how, and I don't have any more questions, so that's that. I get the impression he doesn't know Witt from Whinola."

"Did you mention the seventeen million?"

"Yeah, he said he thought that figure might be pretty exaggerated but he'd look into it. There might have been some slush, as he called it, given as bonuses and so on, and he was pretty sure the members of the Board had a buy-back option, but none of this was a secret."

"So why are you off the case? Somebody took you off?"

"Somebody asked, that's all. Yesterday, called me at home."

"Who?"

"My deputy chief. But there wasn't any pressure, more like a suggestion — what am I doing messing with a ten-month-old murder when I'm counting four months to pension city? Clear my plate and get out, that's what I ought to do."

Hardy was staring out at the city's famous skyline across the rooftops in the Avenues. The thought occurred to him: "How did he know you were on it to begin with? Did you tell him?"

"I asked him the same thing. Evidently it came down from the chief himself, who in turn got an earful from Mr. Kelso."

"Who's Mr. Kelso?"

"Oh, that's right, you're not a local. Frank Kelso is one of our illustrious supervisors. Called the chief and wanted to know why we were hassling — that was the word — why we were hassling the pillars of our legal community, and grief-stricken ones at that. I took it he meant the son, Todd."

A Los Angeles supervisor! My, Hardy thought, but this is heating up. Whatever else he might be doing, he had touched a nerve here. It pumped him up. "So where do we go from here?"

"Me? I'm afraid I don't go anywhere. I'm in don't-rock-the-boat mode, Hardy. The brass wants me to leave it, I leave it."

"They just tell you to forget about a murder?"

"Every few years, yeah." After a beat, he said seriously, "I asked the same question. You know what the answer was? Did I have anything solid to go on or was I just fishing? So I told him a little about your client, what you'd told me — just the high spots but enough — and he said it sounded like I was fishing. I told him sometimes it pays to fish and he said it wasn't one of those times." Restoffer sighed. "It's all a numbers game here, and I do have five live ones they want cleared by the time I'm gone."

Hardy took a moment, then tried again. "You're okay going out with unfinished business like this?" It was a lame attempt at a guilt trip, but Hardy didn't want to let it go.

Restoffer laughed. "You know how many open cases I'm leaving? You don't want to know, but one more isn't going to make any difference, I can tell you that. There's just no percentage in it for me. You might have some luck with a private eye. I could recommend a couple of guys down here."

"Floyd, I need a pro. Someone inside." Maybe sugar would work. Restoffer had access and a history no private detective could approach.

"Can't do it, Hardy. Sorry."

"Okay, Floyd. Thanks for your help anyway."

He was about to hang up, waiting for Restoffer to say good-bye. Instead, the inspector said, "Aren't you going to ask me about the good news?"

"Okay." Hardy played along, although even the bad news was good in a sense — the involvement of supervisors and police chiefs was corroboration that it wasn't *all* a chimera. *Something* was getting covered up. "What's the good news?"

"The good news is that last night I think this whole thing stinks, so I did some research of my own this morning. Downtown we've got lists some guys in White Collars use for whatever they do, you know? It's all public record, although sometimes it's a little hard to get access to. Contributors to various causes, that type of thing. I thought I'd check the list of Supervisor Kelso's contributors against the Yerba Buena Board, see if I found anybody who might feel comfortable leaning on our good supervisor for a favor or two. Guess what?"

"You found one."

Hardy could almost see him nod. "Margaret Morency. San Marino old money and lots of it."

"She called Kelso?"

"I can't prove it, but it's a safe bet."

"Can you go to your deputy chief and tell him about it? Seems like this takes it out of the fishing department."

"Not enough, Hardy." Restoffer was off the case and he was clear about that — he wasn't going to jeopardize his retirement with his last months on the job. Hardy was grateful, taking what he could get — at least the man was helping. "This only looks like something if you're already disposed to see it," Restoffer was saying. "I've got nothing hard at all, nothing to connect the dots."

"Do you know anything about this Morency woman?"

"Nothing. She's probably on ten boards — that's what these people do, isn't it? Sit on boards, keep the money in the family, take a small stipend — say, my salary — for their efforts. And the rich stay rich. Hey, listen to me. I'm four months from life by a lake in Montana in a cabin that's paid for. Get out of this zoo for good, so what am I bitching about?"

"Sounds great."

"It will be, believe me. The first year I don't

think I'll do anything but paint. I haven't painted since I was a kid. I used to love it, then I ran out of time to do it."

"I used to make things out of wood," Hardy said. "No nails."

There was a silence, then: "Life, huh?" Restoffer said. "Anyway, I thought I'd give you what I found, see if you get lucky."

"Well, I appreciate it, Floyd, I really do."

"Listen, if you get so you're closing in on this, I'm here."

"Got you."

"Later."

44

Hardy climbed the Hall of Justice steps. It had turned cold overnight and the morning sun shone bleakly, as though through a gauze, just enough to cast its long shadows.

He had never believed he would miss David Freeman, but the schlumpy, gruff, arrogant presence would have been welcome now. He entered the building, passed the metal detector and went downstairs to the cafeteria, not yet mobbed as it would be later. He ordered a cup of coffee, went to a table and opened his briefcase, taking out a fresh yellow legal pad and a black pen.

It was 7:40 and the penalty phase was to begin at 9:30.

He had wrestled with his options for an hour before talking to Floyd Restoffer, and in the end had decided that time had simply run out to pursue things on his own down in Los Angeles. If it absolutely came to that, he would, but meanwhile he had a defense to conduct — Jennifer Witt would be sentenced to death unless he had some reasonably effective argument that she should not be.

And, of course, he couldn't use his best one.

But the penalty phase of the trial gave him more leeway than Freeman had had. The guilt phase was interested in the weight of evidence, in proof, in determination of the facts. By contrast, the penalty phase explicitly contemplated — indeed mandated — the introduction of factors that might persuade a jury of the defendant's mitigating human qualities. So Hardy could bring up those things about Jennifer — her life as a wife with her husband, what a good mother she had been. He could talk about her childhood, her friends, even her pets. His problem was that over the past week, at the rate of a couple of hours with Jennifer every day, he hadn't discovered much more about her life than he'd already known, and he suspected that not much of Jennifer's life story — the part he could tell — was going to move the jury to empathy.

Larry Witt had not allowed her to make or keep any friends, and she had acquiesced. She wasn't even allowed to be involved in Matt's school life. She didn't visit her parents or her brother. There were no pets. Those few times they went out to dinner, or to one of Larry's social engagements, she played the role of an aloof beauty, the wife as a trophy.

She insisted on denying the terrible reality that she had been found guilty. Hardy hammered over and over the fact that from the jury's perspective she was a multiple murderer. This was a hard truth but it was the truth. She avoided it, as she had so many other hard truths in her life.

Finally, they did reach a compromise of sorts. Hardy could bring up what he saw as humanizing issues, in effect pleading for her life as though she were in fact guilty, so long as he left out any reference to Larry beating her. In return, Hardy must continue to bring up alternative theories for the killings; she was not letting go of her idea that this possibility — that someone else had done it — would at least plant enough doubt to keep the jury from voting the death sentence. And no matter her situation and Hardy's dose of reality, she still seemed to cling to the hope that somehow the real killer would be found and she would be entirely cleared.

So, based on the YBMG material, and in the face of David Freeman's warnings, Hardy spent half the night arranging and, he hoped, buttressing the argument that a hit man had killed Larry, and the reasons he had for doing so. To that end he had subpoenaed Ali Singh.

Trying to portray Jennifer as a model of sweetness and light proved to be somewhat more difficult. She just wasn't the girl next door and had never pretended to be. A difficult, moody child, she had grown up, as everyone in the courtroom had seen, or thought they had seen, into a difficult, moody adult — haughty, cool, secretive, self-destructive. That was too often her persona, showing rarely what was beneath it. The jury could not properly consider many of the things she had done since the arrest, but Hardy believed that one way or another they knew as much as he did, and would be unlikely to be able to forget it.

Here was what the jury was working with, Hardy noted down: After killing her husband and son, Jennifer had gone out for a jog, setting up an alibi — her stop at the ATM — that almost had sold them. Then by a clever ruse she had broken out of jail, remained at large for three months, during which she continued an affair with her psychiatrist (so much for the loving wife).

Though the judge had instructed the jury that there was insufficient evidence to convict Jennifer of murdering her first husband, Hardy doubted that any member of the jury didn't think she had. They'd no doubt remember that, too, when the time came.

Yes, she was pretty. To some of the men she might even be beautiful, but even that, Hardy suspected, played against her — she seemed by her appearance of aloofness to think she was above it all, including the law. More tears would have helped, but Jennifer fought tears.

It had taken Hardy almost a whole day to hammer out the jury instructions that Villars would give after argument, just before the jury got the case.

"Ladies and gentlemen. Good morning."

Powell stood in the at-ease position about twelve feet in front of the judge's bench, eight feet from the jury box, facing them. His voice was low, his tone relaxed — though it carried well enough. It looked as though he was going to be keeping out the theatrics, reasoning that the jury might well have had enough of them.

Another problem was that Powell's lead in the polls had jumped over the weekend — he was now leading his nearest opponent by seven points and seemed to be heading for election on the first ballot. Hardy had a feeling some members of the jury were aware of this, and if that were the case, it was more bad luck for Jennifer. Powell's authority and stature would tend to increase if the jury saw him as the Attorney General of the State of California rather than as just another working stiff prosecutor. But this, again, was something Hardy could do nothing about.

Powell continued: "Around these United States of ours, a murder is committed about once every two hours, every hour of the day, every day of the week, every week of the year. Until only a few years ago the death penalty was a relatively common punishment for a person convicted of murder, as well as for so-called lesser crimes such as rape, and even some types of armed robbery.

"That has changed now in our so-called enlightened age and we live in a society and a state that sanctions the death penalty for only the most heinous of crimes — murders involving special circumstances, which include, as Judge Villars has told you, multiple murders, lying in wait, murder for financial gain, murder of a police officer.

"You have found Jennifer Witt guilty of murder, and guilty of two of the special circumstances I have just referred to — murder for financial gain and multiple murder. *That* is no longer in dispute. In this phase of the trial, I am going to be showing you why the State of California is asking for the death penalty.

"First, in the strictly legal sense, the laws of this state have decreed that the nature of these crimes compels the ultimate punishment. But, of course, there is an even larger issue here, and that is the nature of the murderer, a nature so devoid of mercy and feeling that she could — and *did*

— cold-bloodedly plan and execute the murder not only of her husband, but of *her own flesh and blood, her only son.*"

Hardy as well as Powell knew that this was the baldest of opening-statement rhetoric, but it was powerful and *legally* accurate. While no one had ever before in these proceedings claimed that the murder of Matthew Witt had been anything but accidental, his death by gunshot had occurred *in direct consequence* of and *during the commission* of another "cold-blooded" crime. Any person planning the first crime would have to see, inherent in it, the possibility of the second. That, at least, was the prosecution's point. In that sense, legally, the two crimes were of the same magnitude, or sufficiently close so that Hardy decided he couldn't object and be sustained.

Powell stopped and turned his whole body toward Hardy and the defense table. Jennifer, now on Hardy's left — she had been on his right throughout the guilt phase — seemed to jut out her chin and stare straight back at Powell. Hardy had his hand over her wrist — she was shaking. He squeezed to signal her — it wouldn't help her to get involved in this visual exchange of defiance, a game of chicken.

But the references to her son Matt earlier in the trial had been few and glancing — this was an escalation, and Jennifer was taking it hard. She pulled her hand from under Hardy's.

"You're such an asshole," she said out loud, unable to restrain herself.

The courtroom exploded.

Powell stood open-mouthed, but no doubt

pleased. Let her hang herself. Villars was calling for order, pounding her gavel. Behind Hardy, the gallery was humming. He put his arm around his client, pulling her to him and telling her to shut up right now.

Over the din Villars was trying to be heard but to little avail. Jennifer was starting to stand up, about to say something else. Hardy squeezed her arm again, trying to keep her down, to save her. *"Ow."* Turning on him. "You're hurting me. Let me go." She wriggled her arm free, now facing the judge, now the jury. A fury, cornered and suddenly mute. The two bailiffs were closing in on the defense table.

Hardy leaped up, reaching for her and at the same time trying to motion to the bailiffs that they didn't need to interfere. His voice quiet, hands outstretched, he kept repeating, "It's okay, it's all right . . ." Except, of course, it wasn't. She was killing herself.

Villars stood at the bench, her gavel forgotten. Behind Hardy someone said Jennifer's name and she turned. Ken Lightner had gotten to the front of the gallery and Jennifer went into his arms across the railing separating them. Protectively, his big hands caressing the top of her head, as a parent might do to comfort a child, he held her.

The bailiffs, rooted where they had stopped, waited. The crisis had lasted less than a few moments and appeared to be over. Villars sat down. Powell appeared bemused. The judge tapped her gavel and called for a recess, then ordered Hardy to see her in her chambers.

Villars' usually gray visage was almost crimson. Powell did not say a word.

"She won't do it again, Your Honor —"

"Damn right she won't do it again!" The judge spoke quietly, standing behind her desk, hands down on it, leaning on them. "If I don't gag her and she *does* do it again, Mr. Hardy, I'll hold you responsible. You won't sleep at home for a week."

Hardy, expecting a rebuke, was brought up short by Villars' tone — more personal than he'd expected. He decided it would be a good time to bring it out into the open if something was there.

"Do you have a problem with me personally, Your Honor?"

"I have a problem with your client disrupting my courtroom. *That's* my problem. You got a problem with *that?*"

"I don't think that's it," Hardy said.

Villars straightened up. "What?" She squinted at him. "What did you say?"

"I said I don't think that's it."

The judge's eyes narrowed. Her voice came out raspy, choked with anger. "My courtroom is a goddamn model of fairness, Mr. Hardy. Justice is hard enough to come by, so I bend over backwards to go by the rules and try to be evenhanded, and I resent the hell out of anybody suggesting that I don't."

"I haven't said it got into your courtroom, Your Honor. But I noticed you fined David Freeman for contempt and now you're threatening me with the same thing or time in jail."

"I'd do the same to Mr. Powell, don't flatter

yourself." She glanced at the prosecutor, who was doing his wallpaper imitation. "Nobody gets to yell obscenities in my courtroom. Nobody. Freeman got out of line, as he does often. It's not a personal thing with me, as you seem to think. The main reason I'm not going to gag your client is that it would further prejudice the jury against her. Beyond what she's done all on her own. Nevertheless, you have guaranteed her behavior and if she goes over the edge again I'll take appropriate steps. Against her and against you. Clear?"

"Perfectly."

She continued to glare at him.

"Your Honor," he added.

Powell's statement took another hour, taking them to lunch. As he went on, Jennifer kept a grip on Hardy's arm, sometimes squeezing hard enough so it felt like she was cutting into his skin through his coat sleeve and shirt.

The thrust of Powell's new argument "in aggravation" was that implicit in Jennifer's planning to kill her husband for the insurance was the realization that it might be necessary to kill her son too! That it *wasn't* a "mistake." The boy hadn't just gotten in the way. She knew he would have to be there and she knew she might kill him, might have to.

Hardy thought Jennifer might leap out of her chair and attack Powell, and he almost felt the same. Powell was really going all out.

"Who will speak for the victim?" Powell had concluded. "If a person who has planned to kill a child has not forfeited her right to live, then what, as a society, have we become? What greater violation of trust can there be? And what punishment, other than the ultimate, can begin to balance the scales?"

Miraculously, Jennifer had somehow borne it quietly. Tears, quickly and angrily wiped away, had begun on several occasions, but by the time he had finished she seemed composed.

"Cut that bastard's balls off," she said to Hardy as Powell was walking back to his table. He prayed that none of the jury had heard her.

"You've heard Mr. Powell characterize Jennifer Witt as a person who, by the very nature of her crimes, has forfeited her right to live. And if, in fact, she has committed these crimes, I might agree with him."

Without standing, Powell raised a hand. "Objection, Your Honor. The defendant's guilt has been established."

"I've acknowledged that, Your Honor." Hardy hoped he had, enough. He thought his only chance — and it was slim — of getting any other theory of the murders admitted was to be crystal clear on what the jury had already determined. He wasn't trying to undermine them — merely give them alternatives to consider.

Villars gave it a moment's thought. "Just so that's clear. Go on," she said to Hardy. It was enigmatic enough — Powell took it as though he'd been overruled and Hardy would take anything he could get.

He inclined his head to the judge, then went back to the jury. "The evidence in the first part of this trial persuaded you that Jennifer was guilty beyond a reasonable doubt. But now you are being asked to pass judgment on this woman's *life,* and there is a different standard — a mistake here that leads to her execution cannot be rectified. If new, exonerating or at least mitigating evidence appears sometime in the future it would be too late.

"The law recognizes a concept, and the judge will give you instructions regarding it, called lingering doubt. Lingering doubt does not undo what you have found beyond a reasonable doubt, but it *does* contemplate a situation such as we have right here before us. Though you have found Jennifer guilty" — Hardy thought he'd best keep repeating this to make a following distinction — "let's see what even the prosecution acknowledges that we *don't* have, and why each of you, if you should vote the death penalty, might find yourself, over the coming years, with some very haunting and serious lingering doubt."

Like Powell, Hardy had begun in the center of the courtroom, but as he began to loosen up, he moved closer to the jury box. He had all of their attention — this was, after all, his first appearance in a speaking role before them and there was a curiosity factor. But he thought it was more than that — up to this point, his statement seemed to be hitting a mark.

Slowing himself down, he went to the table, pretended to consult some notes, and took a drink of water. He returned to where he had begun. "Number one, ladies and gentlemen, we don't have anyone who saw Jennifer Witt shoot anybody. *Nobody. Not one witness.* We have heard a witness,

Mr. Alvarez, say that he saw Jennifer outside her house right after the shots. Mrs. Barbieto said that she heard Jennifer yelling inside the house before the shots, but neither of these are eyewitnesses to the shooting itself. And, let me remind you, Mrs. Barbieto was unclear as to how long exactly it was between Jennifer's yelling and the shots, and there is the possibility" — even though they'd apparently chosen to disregard it in their deliberations — "that Mr. Alvarez saw someone else outside the house on that morning and *thought* it was Jennifer."

"Objection, Your Honor. Counsel is arguing evidence."

"I'm reminding the jury of previous testimony. That's all, Your Honor."

"This is not a round-table discussion, Mr. Hardy. But the objection is overruled."

So he won one and got slapped on the wrist at the same time. Villars might, as she claimed, be fair to a fault, but that didn't make her any easier to deal with. "Thank you, Your Honor." He turned back to the jury. "What else does the evidence leave unexplained? True, Jennifer stood to collect five million dollars, presumably the motive attributed to her for these murders. But if that is the case — if this were a meticulously *planned* murder for money — where is the evidence of the planning? What was the fight about, the one overheard by Mrs. Barbieto? If Jennifer killed her husband, might it have been because they were fighting? Was it in the heat of argument, without any premeditation at all? Did Matt somehow, tragically, simply get in the way? These are questions that are not answered by the evidence. They cannot be answered."

He paused again, letting his words sink in. "There are two final points I'd like to make to you. The first is this: that Jennifer Witt said and says she did not commit these crimes. You may dismiss this as self-serving, but her stance, her position, has never wavered throughout this trial. She has pleaded not guilty, and she has stuck with that throughout. She is *not* claiming she was temporarily insane, or pressured by issues beyond her control or" — Hardy took a breath — "or trying to escape an abusive situation at home." He hurried on. "She could have said any of these things and hoped you would find her guilty, if at all, only of some lesser offense than first-degree murder, death-penalty murder. *But she did not do that.* She has *never* done it. No bells or whistles, no fancy defense moves to save her life, and believe me, my colleague David Freeman has a few he can pull out if he's asked to."

Hardy went back to the defense table and took another sip of water, gathering his thoughts. "The last point, ladies and gentlemen, concerns a crucial factor that has thus far been missing in the record of this trial — and that is the fact that because no one *actually saw* Jennifer kill Larry and Matt Witt, the *possibility* must remain that someone else could have done these deeds."

Powell stood quickly. "Your Honor, the verdict is in."

But again he was overruled. Hardy was not arguing a logical inconsistency nor, strictly, was he arguing hypothetically. He could continue, but "walk carefully, Mr. Hardy. There's a thin line here."

Acknowledging Villars' warning, Hardy turned to the jury. "I am not here to prove to you that your verdict was wrong. You worked long and hard coming to your decision and I respect your work. But the fact does remain — someone other than Jennifer *conceivably could* have had a *reason* to kill Larry Witt, and someone other than Jennifer *conceivably could* have done it. So as this portion of the trial proceeds, you are going to be hearing some about Larry Witt — the kind of man he was, his business dealings, some of the other matters he was involved in. I believe that a number of these considerations are persuasive and might bring you to that lingering doubt I mentioned earlier."

He paused, took a breath. "Ladies and gentlemen, there is one last, painful thing. Mr. Powell has gone to great lengths in his opening statement —"

Powell wasn't having it. "Objection. This is not the time for rebuttal."

Villars didn't hesitate. "Sustained." She waited. Hardy almost felt she was daring him.

"All right," he said, turning to the jury, including them in his frustration out of Villars' line-of-sight. "Now I must, *I must,* say a word about the death of Matthew Witt." Again he paused, and it was not just for dramatic effect. He could not tolerate having the tragedy of the boy's death, however it had transpired, misrepresented to the jury. "*No evidence has been introduced, nor will any be, that Jennifer Witt was an abusive mother*. If there were doctors out there who could testify that Matthew Witt was the victim of any kind of abuse, believe me, they would be here as witnesses for the prosecution. There are none.

"And why is that?" Hardy turned and pointed now at his client. "Because Jennifer Witt was a remarkably *good* mother. No one contends or even suggests that she was not. She loved her son. She has been devastated by his death. She did not concoct any plan that — however remotely — might have put her son in danger. And *that,* ladies and gentlemen, is the plain truth."

Hardy glanced at Villars, waiting for Powell to object again and this time be sustained. But it did not come. He had kept it vague enough and, after all, this was just an introduction. Letting out a breath, he decided this was about as good as he was going to get at this stage. He thanked the jury and sat down.

It was six-thirty and Hardy was sitting at the bar of the Little Shamrock, working on a Black & Tan, a mixture of ale and stout. Moses and Hardy (back in his full-time bartender days) took pride in how they made the drink, separating the two brews cleanly, stout on top. But the new kid, Alan, had not gotten the knack, so that the fresh drink tasted old, flat. Maybe it was just the way the day had gone, how Hardy felt.

After the full day at the trial, the emotional drain of finally getting up and beginning to work, Hardy didn't think going home with his edge on would be wise. The shift in personal mode from near-adversary to ally was not a toggle switch, and he had called Frannie explaining he needed some unwind time — if she could handle it, if she wasn't too burned on the kids.

That early on a Monday, there were only five other people at the bar, two couples at tables near the dart board and a really lovely young woman up by the window talking to Alan. Hardy spun his pint slowly on the smooth wood before him. Willie Nelson was singing Paul Simon on the jukebox, about the many times he'd been mistaken, the many times confused. Hardy understood that.

The young man behind the bar brought a new attitude to the Shamrock. Moses called it the "look of the nineties" — short hair, shaved face, dress shirt and slacks. Moses said they were getting a lot more single female customers than they had had with Hardy behind the rail, to which Hardy had replied that maybe that was true, but probably they were shallower people, into the good-looks thing. He — Hardy — was into substance, character, depth, real stuff. Moses said the real stuff was all right, but it didn't sell as much booze. Besides, Moses said, since Susan, he'd been into the good-looks thing himself. Times changed.

The woman by the window said something and Alan laughed. Swirling, checking on Hardy's progress with his drink, he was smiling as though no one had ever lied to him. Maybe that was it, Hardy thought — I'm in a business where most everybody lies. It's expected.

He took a last sip for politeness sake, pushed a few bills into the gutter, raised a hand saying good-bye. A stranger in his own bar.

It was just getting to dusk, and there was one light on in the DiStephano house, in the front left window. No cars in the drive.

Hardy parked down a half-block. He put the folded-up subpoena form in his shirt pocket.

Going up the walkway, heart pounding, he wondered how Frannie would feel about this segment of his unwind time.

He walked a few steps onto the lawn. Through the lighted window he saw Nancy moving about in the kitchen. On the porch, he stopped to listen. There was no conversation. If Phil was home he would bull his way through, or try.

He rang the doorbell.

The overhead light flicked on. She stood inside the screen. "Hello," she said. She looked around behind him, up and down the street.

"Phil isn't home?"

Shaking her head no, she opened the screen door. "He's on a call." Again, Hardy was struck by how young she looked — Jennifer had gotten her good bones from her mother. He thought those bones had played a big role in getting their men — perhaps it wasn't the blessing it was cracked up to be.

"I wanted to come and ask you if you'd like to talk about your daughter. On the witness stand."

"Talk about Jennifer? What do you want me to say?"

"I want you to talk about how much you love her."

Nancy swallowed, her eyes wide. "I *do* love her," she said.

"I know you do. I want you to tell that to the jury."

"Why?"

"Because it might help save her life. Because it's something they can see, something human."

Her eyes became hooded, haunted. Jennifer got that way often enough, too; Hardy thought it was whenever either of them thought they were about to do something that would get them hit.

He pressed the point. "I need you, Nancy. *Jennifer* needs you. The DA is pulling people out of the woodwork and they're painting a very bad picture of Jennifer."

"I know, I watch TV." She scanned the street again, then stood silent, volunteering nothing.

"What is it?"

"It's him." Hardy had met women before who referred to the current man in their lives, always, without preamble, as "him." And it always chilled him.

"Phil would want you to save his daughter's life, Nancy. Don't tell me he wouldn't want that."

"This whole thing . . ." she began, then stopped again. "He hates it. He hates that everybody knows it's his daughter on trial."

"He's worried about how that affects *him?*"

"He's not just worried, he's furious. He said he wishes we never had her. He won't even let me talk about it, about her."

"Nancy, how's he going to feel if they execute her? How are you going to feel?"

The plea in her eyes was clear — don't ask me such a question. She loved her daughter and was scared to death of her husband. If he had to bet on it, she hoped more than anything at this moment that he would just go away.

But he didn't drive out there just to go away. He took the paper from his breast pocket. "This is a subpoena for you to appear, Nancy. I need you to be there. I need somebody to say that Jennifer loved her son, that she herself has something to offer, that she is at least worth saving. Show the jury that *somebody* cares."

Nancy held the paper close to her.

"Nancy, how old are you?" Hardy asked suddenly.

She tried to smile but it came out broken. "Forty-eight," she said.

"It's not too late," he said.

She clutched the subpoena form against her, in a fist held tight against her stomach. She sighed, almost shuddering. Any trace of even a broken-down smile was gone. "Yes, I'm afraid it is," she said.

In the middle of the night, the telephone rang. It was Freeman. "You heard yet? Anybody call you?"

Hardy blinked trying to focus the clock. Four-thirty.

"No, David, nobody's called me."

"Well, they called me. Jennifer's mother just tried to kill her old man."

45

They were both at Shriners' Hospital — Phil under the knife in emergency surgery, Nancy in a guarded private room. Hardy was down there before six, before the sun was up, before any other lawyers or the media.

"She's going to be all right. Him I don't know."

The inspector, Sean Manion, had had a long night, but he worked out of Park Station; he had known Hardy from the Shamrock and they got along. They were standing in the hallway outside Nancy's room now. She had been sedated and was not going to be giving interviews to anybody for a while.

"What happened?"

Manion was strung tight. He was shorter than Hardy by half a head, with a pock-marked face, a reconstructed cleft pallet, a monk's tonsured hairline. Perpetually hunched, hands in his pockets, chewing gum, he talked in a rapid staccato. "Guy beat her once too often, I guess. She grabbed a knife and stuck him. Four times, I think. No, five."

"How bad?"

"Three on the arms. Standard slash, but a couple of belly whacks. Could have nicked his heart; they weren't sure last I checked. Guy lost a ton of blood. She called us, you know. After."

"You gonna charge her?"

Manion chomped his gum. "I don't know. Ask the DA. I doubt it. With what?"

"Attempted murder?"

Manion snorted. "Nah, shit, this was self-defense. You ought to see *her*. Son of a bitch ought to die. If he lives, anybody gets charged with anything, ought to be him."

"Sean, did you call David Freeman on this?"

"Who?"

"Never mind. Maybe she did before you got there." Hardy motioned back toward the room. "She's out, though, huh?"

Manion nodded. "Dreamland. Check her around noon."

"Can't," Hardy said, "I'm in trial."

"Lucky you." The inspector spread his hands. "Well, there you go. She'll still be here tonight. She's not going anywhere, I'll tell you that. Not today."

"That bad?"

Manion bobbed his head. "Pretty bad. But hey, she's alive. It could be worse."

Hardy knew he had caused it. If he hadn't gotten the idea in the first place, if he hadn't gone down with the subpoena, if he hadn't tried to talk Nancy into testifying . . . Then she and Phil had gotten into it and now they were both in the hospital.

From his lack of a night's sleep, he should have been exhausted, but when he entered the small interrogation room on the seventh floor at a little after eight, the adrenalin rush hadn't let up. He felt like he'd had a half-gallon of espresso.

Jennifer had not yet dressed for court. She was escorted in wearing her red jumpsuit. "So what's today's advice?" she began. She acted like she was losing hope in him.

He told her.

She had been standing in what had become her usual posture in that room, arms crossed leaning back against the door. Before Hardy was half done, she sat down, shell-shocked.

"Jennifer?"

"I'm here." Then: "What does this mean?"

"I think it means your mother was going to testify for you and she and your dad had a fight about it."

"But why would she risk that? She *knows* him . . ."

"How about because she loves you?"

Jennifer just stared at him, her mouth working in silence. She put her head down on her arms and began to sob.

A very unhappy Harlan Poole was back on the witness stand. The dentist appeared to have lost some fifteen pounds in the two weeks since he had been up before. This time he was not going to be relating hearsay.

Dean Powell was zeroing in. The election was around the corner and the candidate's whole rhythm was picking up. "Dr. Poole, you have said that after Jennifer's first husband died, you decided to call things off with her. Is that correct?"

Poole, sweating almost before he had begun, agreed.

"Can you tell us what happened then between you and Jennifer?"

"We . . . I just kind of tried to distance myself."

"Although she worked with you every day, did she not?"

Poole nodded. "She was my receptionist."

"And yet you needed to distance yourself."

"I . . . we stopped being intimate."

Poole seemed to be looking in all directions at once, pulling at his collar. He mumbled it out, just into the range of audible. "I couldn't perform . . . it may sound strange, but I was afraid of her —"

Hardy jumped up, objecting, but was overruled. He began to argue with Villars, saying that Poole didn't answer the question of whether or not he had stopped being intimate. Villars, pointing a finger, asked Hardy if he were hard-of-hearing — she had ruled on it. He had to stop. He risked a contempt citation but worse, he risked losing the jury's respect. The former he could handle, but the latter could doom Jennifer. He sat down.

Powell, for his part, was not about to risk a mistrial repeating why Dr. Poole had been afraid, but then, of course, he didn't have to — the jury would remember about Ned. He didn't need it anyway, as it turned out — the direction he did take was damaging enough. "So then what happened?"

"I tried to tell Jennifer it was no good, that it just wasn't working anymore, but she, uh, she . . ." He looked at Jennifer again.

"Take your time," Powell said.

Poole thought about how to put it. "I finally decided I'd have to break it off with her and fire her at the same time."

There was a little rush in the courtroom. Several members of the jury sat forward. So did Hardy. Once again, he hadn't heard about this one.

"And what happened then?"

"Well, she got pretty crazy . . ."

"How do you mean crazy? Threatening? Violent?"

"Both." He stopped and swallowed a few times. "I don't know what to say, sir. I'm sorry."

Powell was prepared. "Did she physically attack you?"

"Yes."

"With a weapon?"

"Well, some things at the office, yes."

"Sharp things? Medical instruments?"

"Yes."

"Were you hurt?"

"She scratched me pretty badly on my arms and face." He shook his head. "She was pretty crazy."

Hardy stood up again. "Your Honor, this is the second time this witness has characterized the defendant as crazy."

Villars, deadpan, addressed the jury: "Disregard the characterization," she said. "You're sustained, Mr. Hardy." She gave him a cold smile.

Powell picked it right up. "She scratched you on your arms and face?"

Hardy instinctively rose again. "Asked and answered, Your Honor."

Powell turned back to him, to the jury, arms

outstretched. Villars wasted no time.

"Let the prosecutor question this witness, Mr. Hardy. You'll get your chance. Overruled."

For the third time, the jury heard that Jennifer had scratched Poole's arms and face. Powell now asked: "You've also said that the defendant threatened you. What was the nature of that threat?"

Poole swallowed and croaked it out. "She said if I didn't take her back she'd kill me."

"She'd kill you," Powell repeated.

"Yes, sir."

"Did you think she would?"

Hardy, hating to but having to — Powell was baiting him — stood to object again, but Powell graciously smiled. "I'll withdraw the question. Your witness."

Now was when the fatigue was hurting him. If Powell had found his own rhythm, Hardy felt that he had lost his, but there was nothing to do but press on.

"Dr. Poole," he began, "this attack you suffered at the hands of Jennifer Witt — was it after you broke up with her or after you fired her?"

"Well, they were . . . it was pretty much the same thing."

"Okay. How long had you been intimate with Mrs. Witt before that time?"

"I think about six months."

"You don't remember exactly?"

"Not exactly, no."

This was Hardy's favorite answer from a hostile witness. He thought he'd try for it again. "All right. Would you please tell us what weapons she used against you — the sharp ones you mentioned earlier?"

"Well, they were office instruments."

"Yes, you said that, but which ones?"

Poole frowned. "I don't remember exactly. She was throwing a lot of them."

"Oh, she was throwing things at you? You broke up with someone you had been intimate with for six months, taking advantage of your position as her employer —"

"Objection," Powell said.

"It wasn't like that . . ."

Hardy's voice was rising indignantly and it wasn't an act. ". . . *and* fired her at the same time, and she threw some things at you in anger. Is that the attack you're telling us about?"

Villars rapped her gavel.

"Badgering the witness, Your Honor," Powell said.

"Sustained. Mr. Hardy. Is there a question somewhere in there?"

Hardy took a breath, turned to the jury and gave them a half-smile. "Doctor, can you tell us *any* instrument that Jennifer threw at you?"

"Well, yes. I mean no. But it wasn't just that. She trashed the office. She *cut* me."

"Let's take those one at a time. She trashed your office?"

"Completely."

"She did a lot of damage?"

"Eight thousand dollars. I had to close for a week."

"Eight thousand dollars. You must have reported that kind of loss to the police."

Poole was silent.

"Dr. Poole, did you report this incident to the police?"

"I didn't want to —"

"I'm sorry, Doctor, but it's a yes or no question. Did you report this to the police?"

Poole swallowed again, and again. "No."

"So there's no record that it happened as you say? Yes or no?"

"No, there's probably no record."

"All right, let's go back to her cutting you. Did she cut you with one of your instruments, perhaps?"

"No. It was scratches."

"Oh" — Hardy brought in the jury again — "now it wasn't cuts, it was scratches."

"She tore at my arms and face with her nails. That's the scratches I'm talking about."

"All right, that clarifies that. And you've testified that they were pretty bad? Did you see a doctor for them?"

"No, I didn't want —"

"Thank you. Do you have any scars from this alleged attack?"

His hands went to his face, as though there was a memory there. "It's been almost ten years," he said.

"That would be a no?"

"Yes, that's a no."

"Thank you. One last question, Doctor. Let's go on to this alleged threat. Do you remember the actual words Jennifer used?"

"No, I don't, not exactly." He was breathing hard, and suddenly rose in the chair and actually pointed to Jennifer. "But she *did* say she was going to kill me."

Villars told him to control himself, to calm down. "Did she actually try to kill you? Did she follow you around, call you on the telephone, hound you after that?"

"No. No, nothing like that. I never saw her again, at least not until I got here."

"You never saw her again. In other words, regardless of what she might have said in the heat and pain of the moment after being simultaneously jilted and fired by you, she disappeared from your life. Isn't that true?"

"Yes, that's true."

"Thank you. No further questions."

Hardy might have won that round on points, but he was afraid the victory would turn out to be Pyrrhic. The jury had been reminded forcefully of Ned, and regardless of what they were legally instructed to do, he doubted that many people, if convinced of Jennifer's guilt with Larry and Matt, would not come to the conclusion that she had also killed her first husband.

Additionally, Hardy worried that he had probably alienated Villars once and for all, and no good could come of that. And though he had supplied a reasonable motive for Jennifer's outburst, he had not been able to overcome the bare fact that she had gotten physically violent with Poole. Poole might have come across as a user, a wimp and a whiner, but Jennifer's character kept slipping, too — a highly unstable person that you crossed at your serious peril. Wouldn't such a person be likely to repeat her violence on others?

Powell had not relied much on photographs during the guilt phase, but as a courtesy he assigned his young assistant, Justin Morehouse, to inform Hardy as they broke for lunch that the prosecution was going to bring out the pictures in the afternoon — a member of the forensics unit for the color shots from the Witt home, the coroner Dr. Strout with the morgue shots.

It was gruesome but it made sense from the prosecutor's point of view. Powell was out to prove that the killing must have been cold and deliberate. His thrust in this phase was to emphasize the horror of Matt's death and Hardy, having seen the photos, knew that they would be tremendously effective to that end.

Justin was a strapping athletic young man in a well-tailored suit. He had been in Powell's shadow throughout the trial, taking notes, saying nothing, doing the grunt work as most young lawyers did. He had a fresh open face. Giving his message to Hardy, he seemed to be leaning over backward to avoid the appearance of the prosecutorial posturing that some start-up Assistant DA's adopted as their shield.

"This is going to be very rough on Jennifer," Hardy said. "Maybe you could pass that along to Dean."

"What will?"

"Looking at pictures of her dead son."

Justin shifted uncomfortably from foot to foot as though he had to go to the bathroom. "Maybe she shouldn't have killed him, then," he said. It seemed to come out reluctantly, as though he didn't want to sound heartless but it happened to be his honest belief, no shadow of doubt in it. It was a good reminder for Hardy.

To many people in the courtroom — perhaps most Hardy believed — Jennifer was an unredeemed multiple murderer who would likely do it again with the right provocation. Even Justin Morehouse — a seemingly nice guy — wasn't losing any sleep about getting her a death sentence. In fact, though he probably wouldn't admit it, he didn't feel too badly about having her suffer a little, too, by the display of pictures.

Hardy was afraid that Justin might be a pretty good litmus for how the jury was feeling, and if that were so, Jennifer was in serious trouble. Because for all the impression that his cross-examinations were having on Morehouse, Hardy figured he might as well not have come to court.

As soon as court was called to order after lunch, Hardy rose and asked if the judge would allow counsel to approach the bench.

"Your Honor," he began, and told Villars about Powell's plans for show-and-tell. "In view of the highly emotional response these photographs are likely to produce, I would like to request that you excuse Jennifer Witt from the courtroom during this testimony."

Villars pulled her half-moon reading glasses further down her nose, looking over them at Hardy. "We don't try murder cases *in absentia* in this country, Mr. Hardy. Your client stays."

This was the law, but strict adherence to it under

these conditions smacked of gratuitous cruelty. However, he couldn't very well argue that. "She may faint, Your Honor. This will be extremely difficult for her."

Villars rearranged her glasses, then took them off altogether. "If she faints, Mr. Hardy, we'll adjourn until she's feeling better."

As it turned out — and this seemed to be the trial's trademark — it was worse than he had feared. An emotional outburst — even a negative one — might at least humanize Jennifer. But she had no reaction at all. Instead, she seemed to Hardy to go into shock, sitting through it all dry-eyed, unmoving, clutching Hardy's arm with her right hand as the succession of photographs — blown up to fit on the easel next to the witness box — showed her and the jury how her boy had looked after he had been shot.

Half the jury reacted with tears or apparent nausea. But Jennifer sat still, her hand on her attorney's arm, looking straight ahead.

Unfeeling.

Dragging from fatigue, Hardy nevertheless forced himself back to Shriners' Hospital after court adjourned. There was still that bleak sunshine at the Hall, but he hit the fog just across Van Ness as he was heading west and had to slow to twenty miles per hour. In San Francisco, the fog didn't creep in on little cat's feet. It was a blitzkrieg that rolled in off the ocean at about a block every three minutes in a wide front that engulfed everything before it. The temperature dropped twenty degrees in half a mile. The wind whipped and wipers went on. People suddenly decided to jump off the Golden Gate Bridge.

Hardy's car crept out on Lincoln, the park on his right. He briefly considered stopping at the Shamrock again for a quick one, but last night he had done that and it hadn't improved his life that he'd noticed.

There was no guard outside the door to Nancy's room. These were visiting hours, and Hardy was able to get right in.

Jennifer's mother was half-upright in her bed, her eyes closed. There was a wide bandage over the bridge of her nose and, above that, her eyes were swollen orbs of black and blue.

Hardy cleared his throat and she stirred.

"It's the troublemaker," she said.

"Yeah," he agreed.

She pulled herself higher on her pillow and with some difficulty — grimacing — turned her head to face Hardy. "I told Phil I'd testify, that you'd been by."

Hardy nodded. "I figured that."

"How is he?"

Hardy had asked and been told at the nurse's station. "He's critical."

Nancy exhaled — relief? disappointment? — but then quickly sucked in a breath. Some of her ribs might be broken. "I don't know," she said. "What did I do?"

"It sounds to me like you defended yourself against someone who was hurting you very badly."

"I don't know . . . I'm scared."

"Of him?"

"Of what I did. Of what's going to happen now?"

"Have you talked to the police?"

She nodded, though every slight move seemed to cost her. "They've been by. I told them what happened." She sighed again. "But after that, what?"

"What do you mean?"

Half a dry laugh turned to a sharp cry of pain. "It does hurt when you laugh," she said. "I mean stabbing your husband. I think it means it's over, your marriage. Now I don't know what I'm going to do. What will happen."

Hardy didn't have an answer for her and beyond that, he thought her best bet was to figure it out on her own. In his opinion, she hadn't done badly so far. "What do the police say?" he asked. "Are they charging you?"

"They say not. Not yet, anyway." She looked down at her body, covered now. "They say Phil might have killed me. I think he just didn't realize . . ." She stopped herself. "No. I'm not going to do that. Not anymore. He knew what he was doing, he just kept coming. I asked him to stop, I begged him . . ."

"And that's what you told the police?"

"That's what happened," she said. She met his eyes. "So when do you want me to testify?"

"When do you get out of here?"

She shook her head defiantly. Echoes of Jennifer. "After this . . ." Beginning again. "You tell me when Jennifer needs me, I'll be there if I've got to crawl."

46

The prosecution rested on Wednesday afternoon. For the better part of four days Powell had called solid witnesses, remarkable for their lack of stridency, given that his goal in calling them was to persuade a jury to vote for the death penalty.

The jury had seemed to listen raptly as the psychiatrist that Powell had retained related his professional opinion, after three interviews during which Jennifer had, he said, remained uncooperative, that Jennifer was irredeemably sociopathic, unresponsive, hostile, dangerous.

Such a psychiatric opinion would not have been admissible until after Hardy had raised the subject by calling a psychiatrist of his own, but Jennifer had obliged the prosecution by assaulting their psychiatrist, thereby making his testimony admissible whether Hardy called a psychiatrist to testify or not. In their last interview she had burned him, stubbing out her cigarette on the back of his hand. ("I barely touched him. Besides, he asked me if maybe I'd killed Matt to shut him up about my sexually abusing him! Was that a possibility I was repressing? Was I afraid to consider that?")

Then there was Rhea Thompson, the woman from the jail who had exchanged identities with

Jennifer back in the spring so that she could escape. Hardy suspected that Rhea was a career snitch who had volunteered her information to cut a better deal for herself, but when she told the jury that Jennifer had said she'd "just have to kill" anyone who tried to frustrate her escape, it came across as credible.

"That was just a joke. Anybody could see that," Jennifer had said.

If Jennifer's life at home with her husbands paralleled the way she was with Hardy — equal parts bad attitude and bad judgment — he thought he was getting some notion of how she might have provoked the men. *Not,* of course, that he forgave them, not that it was for a minute acceptable, but so much of what Jennifer did seemed to involve some sort of self-destruction. She seemed to *need* to lose, to put herself in a position where she could say, See, I *told* you I was no good. And proving that was what she seemed to do best.

Hardy decided it was time for a heavy dose of reality talk.

They were in the suite for a fifteen-minute recess after which Hardy was going to call Ali Singh and let the chips fall.

"Jennifer, don't you realize people out there are trying to get a handle on who you are? That's really what this is about. So you call Powell an asshole in front of the whole world, you use the State's shrink for an ashtray, you talk about killing other people if you have to. You're killing yourself here, Jennifer, you know that?"

"What am I supposed to do, put on an act?"

There was a time when he thought that was what she was doing. Not now. "Yes! That would be a beautiful thing. I would love a little act right now. Let them see another Jennifer, some gentleness behind the front. Or rather, maybe drop the tough guy act."

"Why? Why show it to them?"

Hardy put his face down in front of hers. "Please. We've only got a couple more days, Jennifer. Could you try . . . ?" He turned around, away from her. "Goddamn," he said.

"You're mad at me."

Pacing across to the windows, he looked across the short expanse to the freeway, the faded buildings beyond, the gray sky.

"You are."

"Okay, so I'm mad at you. So what?"

He was aware of her moving, coming up behind him. She pressed herself against his back. He felt her hand come around to his stomach, low, and start to descend.

He whirled around, backing against the window. "What the hell are you doing?"

She looked up at him, her eyes surprised. "Don't be mad at me," she said, whispering.

Hardy tried to back away again but there was no place to go. She took a half step into him, against him.

This wasn't going to happen. For a second there was no room, no light. He gripped her shoulders, pushing her back as hard as he could, away from him. As quickly as it happened, somewhere in the middle of it, a vestige of control kicked in, made him hang on, kept him from throwing her backward across the room.

He held her at arm's length. As he came back to himself he realized how tightly he was holding her shoulders. She had her whipped look now. He let her go. "Don't you ever, *ever* do that again."

She backed away.

He had to turn again, to see something outside the room. The fog, the same freeway, the city beyond. He gulped air, trying to get a breath, to slow his blood down.

Behind him, she whispered, "It's just . . ." she began. "I'm sorry. Forget it."

He stared for a long minute at the nothing out the window. He knew now she wouldn't move. She was waiting. He sucked in another breath, then turned around. "Don't be sorry," he said. His legs still unsteady, weak under him, he walked across the room to the door. He was leaving her alone. The bailiff could watch her until they reconvened.

"Don't be sorry," he repeated. "Change."

Villars had them back in her chambers. Powell had let Hardy question Singh for about ten minutes before he had requested this private conference. Villars had — as usual reluctantly — agreed.

"Your Honor" — Powell was standing next to Hardy in front of Villars' desk — "the People have been patiently listening to Mr. Singh's fascinating story, but I fail to see any relevance at all to these proceedings. We've argued this before and Mr. Hardy keeps saying he's going to tie this into the Witt killings. I don't think he can."

Villars ruminated, then spoke: "Mr. Hardy, I have to agree. Can you tell us where this is going?"

Hardy took a minute, giving them the short version as well as he could — that the victims in both scenarios were killed with their own guns, the amount of money involved, the suspicion in Los Angeles that there had been a paid assassin in the death of Simpson Crane and his wife. When he finished, Villars was still puzzled.

"You're saying this Simpson Crane was killed with Jennifer Witt's gun?"

Hardy said no, Witt was killed by his own gun and Crane had been killed by his.

The judge turned to Powell. "Am I missing it?"

Powell jumped in. "Even if there is —"

Villars motioned him quiet. "*Is* there an evidentiary connection, Mr. Hardy?"

"This is a plausible alternative theory to these murders that the jury at least ought to hear."

"Perhaps you didn't hear *me?* I asked you if there was any evidentiary connection?"

"Yes, of course."

After a beat Villars asked if Hardy would favor them by telling them what it was.

"Witt was with the Yerba Buena Medical Group, Your Honor. He got wind of this stock scam and was going to go public with it. He was killed for that knowledge."

"By whom?"

"By whoever killed Simpson Crane."

Villars drummed on her desk. "How do you know that?"

"I think I can make a persuasive argument."

Powell stepped into the breach. "Your Honor, this is ridiculous. This is neither the time nor place for alternative theories. The jury has already found

Jennifer Witt guilty. If Mr. Hardy had any evidence, he should have had Freeman bring it up during the guilt phase."

"I didn't find out any of this until last weekend."

Powell threw up his hands. "Well, that's either too damn bad or damn convenient, isn't it?"

Villars held up a finger. "Gentlemen, please. This is a woman's life, and if justice is served, we ought to be able to find a place for it. *If* there is evidence, I want to hear about it anytime. Mr. Hardy, this Mr. Crane then was killed . . ."

"The investigating officer was a Floyd Restoffer. He's with the LAPD. I could subpoena him to come up."

"And they have a suspect?"

"No, but they're certain it was a professional hit."

Villars paused, not liking that very much. "All right, so this Restoffer, what has he found about this Group?"

"The Group was represented by Crane's firm, as I've told you."

"By Crane himself?"

Hardy hesitated, but there was no escaping it. "No, by another of the partners."

"Now *wait* a minute," Powell exploded. "Your Honor, does Mr. Hardy mean to tell us Crane didn't even represent this Group?"

"I hope not," Villars said. "That's not your evidence, is it, Mr. Hardy?"

This was not turning out pretty. "Well, no one's been charged, if that's what you mean, but —"

Villars' face had clouded, her volume increasing. "That's *exactly* what I mean. Does Restoffer have a case that relates here, or what?"

"It's an open case down there."

"*Ten months* and it's still open? What's this man Restoffer doing with a ten-month-old case?"

"Nothing, now, Your Honor. He's been taken off it."

Hardy well knew that alleged linkage here came across as pretty farfetched. Perhaps — no, certainly — he was damaging his professional credibility even bringing it up, but what else could he do? Jennifer was going to get sentenced to death if he couldn't pull something out of his hat. Was there really a rabbit in there? He didn't have any idea, but in his desperation he sure as hell would argue it. If the judge would let him.

All Hardy felt he needed was another ten minutes at least to try to explain the latest news he'd received from Restoffer: how he'd been told to drop the case after questioning Bachman; the wealthy woman in San Marino who was both a contributor to Frank Kelso, the LA supervisor, and a member of the YBMG Board. There had to be something there. He needed ten minutes alone with Villars — he had to get her ear.

"Your Honor, I wonder if we might speak *in camera.*"

Villars sat back in her chair. "No," she said. "There is nothing off the record in a capital case. Nobody's going to cut any private deals."

Her irritation with Hardy was palpable.

"Your Honor, I must say something." Powell stepped into the pause, polite but firm. Villars turned to him. "I'd like you to consider another possibility — as Mr. Hardy is having you do. And that is this: Regardless of what you ruled or what the jury might have found had matters progressed differently, let's consider the possibility that Jennifer's first husband, Ned, was in fact killed by this same assassin ten years ago. If we grant that, could it then become, in Mr. Hardy's words, a plausible defense?" Powell squared around, right at Hardy. "It's absurd. It's insulting."

Villars had given every indication she'd reached her limit before, but Powell's *reductio ad absurdum* hit its mark. The judge nodded, leaning forward. "I agree," she said. "You know, I've been listening hard, Mr. Hardy. I've been paying attention. I've been leaning over backward because, as you point out, this is a capital case. But for the life of me I can't see any reason this should be admitted."

"Your Honor, there's *got* to be a connection." Did he really *believe* that? Or was it his own desperation talking? "Give me a continuance for a couple of days, I'll fly down to LA —"

"Your Honor, please!"

She held up a hand, not needing Powell's input. "That's not going to happen. We've already taken more than two months of this jury's lives." She sat, still in her robes, her face set. She lowered her voice, which gave it even more authority, not that she needed it; there was no mistaking who was the boss in Villars' chambers. "You know, Mr. Hardy, I've been trying to figure you out. I hear you were a pretty good lawyer when you worked for the City. You seem like a sincere man. You appear to work hard. But time and again in this trial I've come up against your refusal to deal with the way we do things here in this state, or in any other state that I know of. In the last couple of weeks I've had to listen to how I was personally hostile to you and how that was affecting my decisions. Then we get this specter of the battered-woman syndrome, which you raise once, don't present any evidence of, and then drop. Today, your first real opportunity to bring up something to help your client, some witnesses that might want to argue for her character or her background or *something* . . ."

"Your Honor . . ."

Villars slammed her hand on her desk, but her voice remained low. "Mr. Powell is correct here. The guilt phase of this trial is over. We have played strictly by the rules. Your side lost. That's how we do it. That's why it's fair."

Hardy waited a moment to make sure he wasn't interrupting, that she was finished. "It may be fair, Your Honor, but they got it wrong. Jennifer did not kill her husband and son —"

"Then prove it, when this is over. I guarantee you, if you find another murderer, Mrs. Witt will go free. But in the meantime, your job is to argue mitigation. I want to know if you are prepared to do that or not?"

Hardy let out a breath. "One of the main thrusts of my argument was that somebody else killed them."

"With the evidence you've got, I'd say that was probably ill-advised strategy." Adjusting her robes, Villars checked the clock on the wall and shifted gears. "All right, gentlemen, it's four-fifteen. We'll go outside and adjourn for today."

She pointed a finger. "Mr. Hardy, tomorrow I expect witnesses who have something to say to the jury. Evidence talks here, Mr. Hardy. It's all that talks."

She rose and came around the desk, leading the way to the door, five steps ahead of the men. Powell hung back, letting Hardy come up abreast of him, then whispered, "Bullshit walks."

Hardy left the courtroom, head bowed, shoulders hunched, seeing nothing. It had fallen apart. Not only had he let down his client, he had sullied his reputation, such as it was, by misreading the fairest judge he was likely to appear before.

Out of the corner of his eye he was aware of Powell in front of the television cameras. He'd get a few seconds of air time looking good, but he wasn't about to defy the gag order, not at this late date and with things going his way. Instead he was carrying on about how crime was a huge problem, all right, he had a lot of thoughts on the subject.

Hardy had had his fill of Dean Powell. He wanted to slink back to his office, but Inspector Walter Terrell suddenly was standing in his way. Mr. Theoretical. But Hardy couldn't very well condemn him for that — he himself had fallen into the same trap. Because something *could* have happened didn't necessarily mean that it did. Or, in any case, that it could be proved. His job, the trust he'd taken on, was to prove, not speculate. He'd lost track of the obvious.

"They sent me down to get you," Terrell said

enigmatically. "There's somebody upstairs asking for you."

He stopped. It never ended. What did Jennifer want now? How did she get upstairs so soon? Then another question popped up: Why was Terrell giving him the message?

"On seven?" he asked, meaning the jail.

"No, four." The fourth floor was homicide. "We're talking to Mrs. Witt's mother. Her dad died a couple of hours ago. She wants her lawyer. Abe Glitsky told her he thought he knew where you might be."

Nancy had volunteered to come down. Homicide lieutenant Frank Batiste as well as Glitsky and Sean Manion were on hand. Nancy was not being charged with anything yet in the death of her husband. No one argued that she had killed him, but they needed her statement, even if it was self-defense.

Nancy was sitting in a yellow leatherette chair at the table in one of the interrogation rooms. Dressed up, with black eyes and a bandage across her nose, she could have passed for thirty-five, much as her daughter on a good day could pass for twenty.

Barely nodding to the assemblage, telling everyone that, first thing, he needed five minutes alone with her, Hardy entered the room and closed the door behind him.

She smiled weakly, greeting him. He saw immediately that her breathing was shallow, her color bad, too pale. "Are you all right? Should you be walking around?"

She nodded. "They let me out this morning. I'm just a little weak. I thought this would help," she said. "Anyway, if I came down here, maybe I could see Jennifer."

"We can probably arrange that. But what do these guys want?"

She shook her head. "I don't know. The inspector I saw in the hospital — Manion? — said they weren't going to charge me with anything, and then when . . . when Phil . . ." She forced a breath. "Anyway, after Phil died the younger man came out and asked if I'd cooperate."

"If you'd cooperate? He said that?"

This wasn't adding up. Either they were going to charge her or they weren't, and either way there was no point in getting her downtown in her condition to sit in an interrogation room at the homicide detail. He also wondered about the party outside — Batiste, Glitsky, Manion, Terrell. Everybody hanging around waiting on an interview with a woman they weren't going to charge with anything?

"Have you talked to them yet?" he asked.

But before she could answer, there was a loud buzz outside, clearly audible even inside their room. They stood and Hardy opened the door. The District Attorney himself, Christopher Locke, had come in, trailed by Dean Powell and half the television cameras in America.

It was all getting clearer.

Hardy didn't look at Locke. Their feelings about each other had been aired the year before. He walked out into the main room, around Locke and up to Powell. "You know, Dean, this is pretty outrageous. Not to mention insulting."

Terrell stepped forward, out of the pack, explaining to Powell: "She asked for her attorney." *Why should Terrell be explaining to Powell?*

"I don't know what you're talking about," Powell said to Hardy.

"I'll tell you what I'm talking about." The room continued to backfill with camera-wielding humanity. "I'm talking about this media circus. I'm talking about using this woman's" — there was Nancy, standing by the door — "about using this woman's personal tragedy so that the jury in her daughter's trial can read about it with their coffee tomorrow morning, and not incidentally so you can be on television again just before election day."

"That's ridiculous."

"I don't think so, I think it's on the money. I think you had Terrell sitting in the wings at Shriners' in case Jennifer's father died so you could drag his wife down here in front of the cameras . . . Like mother, like daughter. Right?" Hardy wished California sequestered its juries.

Frank Batiste was a no-nonsense professional cop who was out-gunned by the brass here, but he was in charge in this room, his domain. He moved forward toward the press of media. "Would all of you please step outside the door now?" He was herding them, prodding. "Just back up there. Thank you." When the last camera had gone, he closed the door and turned back to the room, suppressing a smile. "I'm sure they'll wait."

Locke thought he'd try to take charge. "It's the District Attorney's decision whether or not to charge a person with a crime, not the police department's."

"Hey, I already wrote it up." Manion, DA or no DA, had done his report and he wasn't about to stand by while his professionalism was questioned. "If this wasn't self-defense, you can have my badge."

"I'm not saying it wasn't." Locke as usual, in Hardy's view, was temporizing until he saw which way the wind was blowing. "But it is my decision."

Hardy didn't dispute that, but it wasn't the issue. "Why is Dean here then, Chris? You want to explain that one?"

This drew blood, but Locke recovered quickly. "Mr. Powell is a Senior Assistant District Attorney. He's got every right to be here."

Batiste took another step forward. "No question, sir. So you've decided to charge this woman? You want us to take her upstairs and book her?" Hardy didn't know Batiste well, but suddenly he decided he admired him. There was no irony in his tone; in fact, it was punctiliously correct. He was telling the District Attorney that if he had his facts right they should proceed with the next administrative step.

He was also calling Locke's bluff.

The District Attorney stood there flat-footed. The room, even without the media, felt jammed and overheated — Locke, Batiste, Powell, Terrell, Manion, Nancy, Hardy, three other homicide guys who happened to be there when it began. Locke for the first time looked at Nancy DiStephano, who was leaning wearily against the doorjamb to the interrogation room, her arms crossed, protecting her broken ribs.

"I haven't read the arresting officer's report," Locke said. "I was under the impression . . ." He stopped. "After I read it, I'll make my decision."

Powell followed him out, "no commenting" all the way down the hall. In the homicide room there was a long silence. Finally Batiste spoke to Terrell. "The District Attorney's office hires its own investigators, Walt. You want to be one, go apply. I'll expedite the paperwork." He walked into his office.

Hardy walked back over to Nancy, who by now looked to be on the verge of fainting. Hardy got her to the chair, helped her down. She was panting from the exertion. Glitsky joined them. "She could have called Freeman or you. I told her you were probably closer."

Hardy put a hand on Glitsky's shoulder, squeezing it, a thank you. "How about I take you home, Nancy?"

She was obviously in pain but she looked up at him, shaking her head. "Would you mind? I'd like to see Jennifer if that's okay."

After a short rest she felt she could handle the walk to the elevators, the short ride to the seventh floor.

When she got out of the elevator into the barred bullpen outside the heavy doors of the jail, Nancy put her hand to her mouth, a caricature of shock, except Hardy was certain it was genuine. There was the liniment and sweat smell — familiar to him. The way the sounds rang if they were close by — the elevator, the lock in the bullpen door, keys jangling. Far off, half-heard, haunting, voices were muffled yet the low hum was constant. They heard somebody scream, the crash of something being thrown. It was dinnertime.

Nancy clutched at his arm. "I didn't know it was . . ." She didn't finish. She didn't have to. Nobody knew what it was like until they'd been there. "I should have come down, but Phil . . ." Hardy knew that one too — Phil wouldn't let her.

He'd gotten permission for Nancy to enter the tiny attorneys' room at the women's jail. He was by the door as it opened when they led Jennifer in.

Nancy was sitting across the small room. She bit her lip, her face tilted up. The door closed. "Did they tell you about your father?"

Jennifer nodded, her hands flat against her sides. Nancy stood up, took a tentative step forward toward her daughter.

"Jenn . . ."

She barely whispered it. "Oh, Mom . . ."

They stood there, unmoving. Nancy held her hands out and Jennifer moved to her uncertainly. They came together, embracing, Nancy's arms around her daughter's neck, her face twisted with the agony of her broken ribs but not letting go, squeezing, from Hardy's perspective, as tight as she could.

"I have to find it."

"No," Freeman said, "you've got to drop it."

"I don't have anything else. The woman doesn't have any friends. She's got a mother, but that's the only trace of her past. She's legally as sane as you or me. This is the only chance. I've got to pursue it."

They were in Hardy's office. It was closing on eleven. He had remained in the interview room, a fly on the wall, for the hour that mother and daughter had talked or, more precisely, tried to reestablish some connection. It had been strained a lot of the time, with long silences and frequent tears, but they had held hands throughout and everything was personal — they never mentioned Jennifer's case.

After leaving the jail and making sure Nancy was okay to get herself home in a cab, he had come directly here. Freeman, of course, was working late, already on a new murder as well as preparing Jennifer's appeal.

Now Freeman was listening to his tenant and sometime partner, who had swept half his files off his desk and was raving out of frustration and fatigue. "You know how many people I've talked to these six months? And what do I have to show for it? I've got Jennifer's mother and Jennifer's shrink, and the jury won't believe her shrink. That's it. That's my case to save the woman's life."

"You've got Jennifer herself." Leave it to Freeman — he had eye for detail.

"Oh, there's a good idea." Hardy, pacing, stepped over a stack of folders. "Call Jennifer so she can look the jury in the eye and say, If you vote to execute me, then you can go fuck yourselves. That'll soften 'em right up."

Freeman had gone around to sit behind Hardy's desk, in his chair. "That's really all you've got."

Hardy stopped. "That's what I've been trying to tell you, David. She's totally separated from the world. As if you didn't know. She's too pretty to have other women trust her, and she's not the platonic type with men. Except for her son she didn't seem to give kids the time of day. After Ned killed her cat, she never even had another pet. Juries love cat lovers. Why didn't she get another one? The fact is I haven't found a soul who's got anything good to say about Jennifer Witt." Hardy leaned over and started picking up the files he'd thrown. "I really think I'm right, David. I know Simpson Crane found someone there screwing up."

"Do you also really think they killed Larry, or had him killed?"

"At least it's a reason."

"So is the abortion. Remember. We've been all through this, Dismas. Didn't Jennifer's brother hate Larry, too? And isn't the union squabble with Simpson Crane just as good as your scam idea? Might he in fact have been killed over that?"

"I don't know, I have no idea what Restoffer found there."

"It doesn't really matter, but obviously it was enough to keep him interested all throughout the primary investigation, wasn't it?"

Freeman's point was clear enough, though Hardy wasn't in the mood to hear it. He knew that any event in life could support an almost infinite number of possibilities, even plausible scenarios to explain them if imagination were the only criterion. Trials would never end so long as attorneys were allowed to introduce another way something *might* have happened without regard to evidence. Which was why, overworked as they were, courts were intolerant of hearsay, fabrication, unsupported theories.

At a trial, somebody had to see it, smell it, touch it or taste it, then swear to it. Because, in real life, it had only happened *one* way. And the court's job, perhaps more than justice, was making sure the story was righteous, in sync with the evidence.

Hardy sat on the floor picking up folders. "What am I going to do, David?"

"I wasn't entirely kidding before," Freeman told him. "First I'd let her mother get up, but then I'd call Jennifer . . ."

"But *you* didn't even do that!"

"That was a different situation. I had the luxury or thought I did. You *don't*. This is the last card. The jury has got to get a chance to know her, see who she is beyond —"

"Powell will eat her."

"He well may. She may condemn herself. It's a risk." He brightened. "But then, life's a risk, my boy. Besides, what's your option?"

47

The kids weren't awake yet — a miracle. It was just past six and Frannie was reading the morning paper, in the middle of the story. Even though charges weren't being filed, the mother of the convicted killer had killed her husband and that was hot news. So Powell, in spite of Hardy's efforts, had achieved his goals — not only was his name and picture again on the front page, the jury would get a glimpse of how the DiStephano/Witt women solved their problems — they killed their husbands.

"They make it sound almost Biblical," Frannie said, "like some curse through the generations."

Hardy nodded wearily. In his life he had probably been more tired but he couldn't remember when. He hadn't gotten home last night until after midnight, hadn't been able to get to sleep for at least an hour after that. "I just hope the jury doesn't see it that way."

Frannie put the paper down. Something in her husband's voice . . . "Are you going to lose?"

"It's a possibility." The prince of understatement.

Frannie wrestled with the awful thought. "Can I do anything?"

"Like what?"

"I don't know, help you in some way, any way . . ." She reached across the table and took his hand. "I feel real bad about this, you know. Like I've deserted Jennifer. They convicted her. What am I supposed to think? What am I supposed to do? I just couldn't keep on denying —"

"You don't have to explain anything to me, Frannie. She's one difficult woman. She drives people away."

Frannie bit her lip, squeezed her hand. "What will happen? I mean, if you lose?"

"If Powell gets elected and stays on the case, her odds on appeal go way down. He'll be the Attorney General and she's his baby. I mean, even if he wanted to, which he doesn't, it would be hard for him, politically, to do anything but keep pushing."

"This is just so wrong."

Hardy covered Frannie's hand. "It's not over yet."

He was going to have Nancy take the stand, then Jennifer.

A society reporter named Lucy Pratt was in the newsroom at the Los Angeles *Times* when Hardy called from Sutter Street an hour later. That early in the morning, the place was deserted and she was happy to talk to somebody about her work. A lot of people wanted to move on to hard news, but she loved being a society reporter. She loved people. She didn't like violence, world problems, all that stuff. She told Hardy that sure, she knew who Margaret Morency was. In fact, just the last weekend they had run her picture. She and her fiancé had hosted a wine-and-cheese auction to benefit the San Marino library.

"For some reason," Hardy said, "I thought she was this old woman. San Marino old money, you know?"

Ms. Pratt laughed over the line. "Old money doesn't mean you're old, at least not with Margaret. I don't think she's thirty yet. I could fax you her picture. She was one of the Rose Court in 1986, you know."

Hardy thought a picture wouldn't be necessary.

"The wedding's going to be at the Huntington in December," Lucy said. "The whole town's talking about it."

Hardy doubted whether the folks, say, in South Central, were as excited about the upcoming nuptials as Lucy was, but she seemed to be a nice kid so he listened. It seemed the polite question before he said good-bye so he asked it. "Who's the fiancé?"

"It's really a Cinderella story," she said. "Jody's from the west side, but down in the flats, not exactly Brentwood. But now . . ."

"Is that Jody *Bachman,* the lawyer?"

"That's the lucky man. Do you know him?"

"Sure," Hardy said. "All lawyers know each other It's like a big fraternity."

Lucy laughed again. She sure had good manners, though he doubted she got the joke.

He left a message with Restoffer. Even with the

cold he wanted time to think, so he walked across Market, a block out of his way down 5th (you took your life in your hands on 6th), to the Hall. He rounded up Powell and they caught Villars alone in her chambers.

In that, he was fortunate, although she was less than delighted to see them.

"I hope you've got something prepared for today, Mr. Hardy," she began. "I'm not entertaining any continuance motions. You still want to see me?"

Hardy said he did, and she turned her back to him, going back to the slingback chair where she had been reading the paper, having her morning coffee. But she didn't settle. Instead, she lowered herself onto the outside of the chair and pointed a finger. "The time for a personal appeal is after the jury's decision."

Villars was referring to the orchestrated ballet that surrounded death-penalty cases in California. Even after the jury returned with a verdict of death, that was not the end of it. The defense filed an automatic motion to set aside the verdict while, at the same time, there was a motion for a new trial, on almost any grounds and without any prejudice — in other words, without a mistrial. In the jargon, the judge became the thirteenth juror.

In practice, such motions were seldom granted. If a judge, sitting as the thirteenth juror, did in fact overturn a verdict and a sentence after the time and expense of a jury trial, the DA — by exercising his right to challenge out of any courtroom — would make it hard for that person to find work. Still, Villars was tough, and Superior

Court judges, it was true, could amass a great deal of power.

Hardy remained standing. Powell sat down, silent, listening. "I wanted to get a ruling on something," he said, and told her what he had discovered that morning about Jody Bachman and Margaret Morency. She didn't interrupt him. "So, Your Honor, I have a member of the YBMG Board who called off Restoffer's investigation in Los Angeles, who is also engaged to the attorney for the Group. I think the jury should hear about this."

Villars finally sat back. "How did this woman call off the police investigation?"

"She called Kelso, the supervisor. He passed it along to the chief."

"Do you have proof of that?"

Hardy knew this was the tough sell. "Ms. Morency both contributed to Kelso's campaign and is on the YBMG Board. I know it was Kelso who called the chief after Restoffer interrogated Bachman."

Villars spoke slowly now. "That's not proof."

"The standard is less in this phase, Your Honor. I'm trying to get the jury to lingering doubt."

Villars waited for more.

Hardy gave it to her. "Your Honor, these at least are facts, *not* conjecture. Simpson Crane was killed with his own gun. Larry Witt was killed with his own gun. There *is* a connection, the Group — okay, it's tenuous, but it's there — between these men, and a line running through Jody Bachman, and a lot of money unaccounted for. Crane's murder investigation is closed down. The fiancée of the Group's attorney has access and leverage over Kelso. Let the jury see all this and maybe they'll start to wonder about it. It's not just my theory. It springs from the facts."

Villars considered another moment. "But it's a house of cards."

"Your Honor . . ." Hardy started.

"May *I*, Your Honor?" Villars nodded and Powell stood up. "I took a hard line with you here, yesterday, Mr. Hardy, but in spite of what you may believe, I am not anxious to see anyone condemned to death. So after we adjourned last night, do you know what I did? I called down to Los Angeles and spoke to the head of homicide, who referred me to the chief of police. The homicide department is *positive,* unquote, that Simpson Crane was assassinated by someone paid by Machinists' Local 47 down here. It's not a closed case, although this Inspector Restoffer isn't on it anymore — it's gone federal with RICO. There is — again I quote — no suspicion that he was killed by someone with the Yerba Buena Medical Group."

"Still, they called Restoffer off." Villars was following it all closely, even taking some notes.

Powell sighed. "Evidently the inspector was a little miffed at the federal intervention. When he thought he saw a way back in — it's a high-profile case — he stepped on a few toes. He was called off because he was hassling people, because he wasn't being a good cop."

Standing up, not in her robes, the judge might have been a friendly grandmother. And her voice had no edge now. "Mr. Hardy, I've listened carefully to you, one last time. Now I'm talking to you and I hope you listen to me. All of what you say may be true as far as it goes. There may be all kinds of financial shenanigans going on down in Los Angeles, but it doesn't concern this case. And where it might appear to intersect, it still falls under coincidence. Larry Witt just wasn't involved in any of this, or if he was there's no evidence of it."

"He called Crane & Crane."

"About this? Did he talk to Crane himself, or Bachman? And if so, about what? Is there any telling?" She shook her head. "I'm sorry, Mr. Hardy, I really am. I can see you are trying your damndest, as you should, but I'm not going to admit unsubstantiated theories, and that's what this is."

She was moving him with her toward the door. "And now, please excuse me. I've got two hours of briefs I've got to wade through in" — she looked at her watch — "in forty-five minutes."

48

Evidently, a lot of people in the courtroom had read the morning paper, or seen the news on television. When Hardy called Nancy to the stand, the reaction was audible.

She was sitting in the first gallery row, next to Dr. Lightner, directly behind Hardy and Jennifer, and she stood stiffly, the way a person would be expected to stand with taped and broken ribs. She still had the bandage over her nose, her eyes black and swollen.

Reporters were snapping photos as she inched painfully toward the center aisle. Villars was not having this — she had allowed cameras inside the courtroom up to this time, so long as their use was unobtrusive, but this action crossed her line.

She rapped her gavel. "That's enough pictures. All of you sit down. As of this moment I'm forbidding cameras in this courtroom. Anybody who's got one can leave now. Bailiffs, make sure that they do."

The bailiffs moved up to the rail. In the ensuing hubbub, as reporters either left with their own cameras or gave them to assistants to remove, Nancy DiStephano made it through the rail, stopping at the defense table. Jennifer reached over and the two women held hands briefly, wordlessly. Her mother straightened up and forced herself to the front of the courtroom, to be sworn in.

Hardy assumed his position about ten feet in front of the witness box. "Mrs. DiStephano, what is your relationship to the defendant?"

"I'm her mother."

Apparently not everyone had known what the earlier commotion surrounding this witness was about because this admission caused another ripple of sound across the back of the courtroom. Villars didn't act so Hardy had to wait for it to subside.

"Mrs. DiStephano, may I call you Nancy?"

"Sure."

Hardy reasoned that his best odds were to face it head-on. "For the jury's benefit, Nancy, I wonder if you could tell us about your injuries?"

Powell jumped up. "Objection, Your Honor. Irrelevant."

Amazingly, Villars asked for an argument before her ruling. "Mr. Hardy?"

"Your Honor, Mrs. Witt grew up in her mother's home. The person she has become was formed there. The jury should be aware of this environment."

Villars said she would allow the line of questioning. Hardy thanked her.

It seemed to him that he and the judge had — perhaps by osmosis — reached some accord. It might be the more relaxed rules governing admissibility in this phase of the trial, but he sensed it was something more.

Hardy approached the witness stand. "Nancy,

you've recently been released from the hospital, is that right?"

"Yes."

"Would you tell us the extent of your injuries?"

Nancy described the broken ribs, broken nose, the kidney damage that caused her to urinate blood, the bruises on her breasts, torso, thighs.

"And how did you sustain these injuries?"

"My husband beat me up."

The courtroom was rapt, silent.

"Your husband, Phil DiStephano, the natural father of the defendant?"

"Yes."

"And was this the first time he'd beaten you?"

Talking about it, Nancy was starting to withdraw, to hunch her shoulders, the way her daughter did. Or was it more the other way around? She shook her head and Villars leaned over, speaking quietly. "You'll have to answer with words, please."

"No," Nancy said, "it wasn't the first time."

To give her a moment, Hardy stepped toward the jury box, turned to look at his client — Jennifer was frowning, not liking this. Hardy came back to Nancy. "Did your husband beat you often?"

The witness shook her head, then, remembering, said "yes."

"How long has it been since your daughter, the defendant, moved out of the house?"

"About ten years."

"And before she moved out, did you suffer these beatings at the hands of her father?"

"Yes . . . it's always been there. Phil would

drink too much and get mad about something and hit me."

"And did this ever happen in Jennifer's sight?"

"Yes."

"Did he ever hit your daughter?"

She shook her head. "No. He threatened a couple of times but I wouldn't let him. I got between them. He loved her." Tears had begun to show on her cheeks. "He just lost control."

"He just lost control," Hardy repeated. Taking a few steps again toward the jury, he continued: "In your opinion, Nancy, did this pattern of your husband beating you have any obvious effect on Jennifer's behavior?"

Nancy was toughing it out, letting the tears come. But, as Jennifer did, she spoke clearly through them. "We didn't talk about it afterward."

This wasn't the answer to the question, but it moved toward it. "You didn't talk about what?"

"They just happened and then they went away and everything went back to being the same."

"You denied that this was happening? The family denied it?"

"Yes. We just pretended."

"And Jennifer?"

"She got more and more quiet. And then she moved out."

"You'd say she became withdrawn, moody, mistrustful?" This was leading her all over the meadow, but he was allowed to do it in this phase and it would, he hoped, go a long way to explain to the jury Jennifer's apparent callousness in the face of the authority of the court.

"Yes." Nancy looked over at her daughter. "She was such a sweet little girl. She was my baby girl . . ."

Although she was maintaining her composure, Nancy's emotion lay over her like a blanket — her face was blotching with tears. Villars leaned over again. "Mrs. DiStephano? Would you like to take a break?"

They were moving on.

"Nancy, did your daughter ever talk about how she felt about Matt?"

"Matt was her *life.*"

"Matt was her life." He took in the jury, then went back to the witness. "She loved her son?"

"Completely. Oh, God, yes."

"Did you ever see any sign at all that she ever mistreated him, abused him, anything like that?"

"No, nothing. If anything, I thought she was a little overprotective. Maybe spoiled him more than I would have. But I understood where that came from."

"And where was that?"

"Well, what she'd seen. Her father and me. Larry was the same way, overprotective. They just didn't want anything bad to happen to Matt."

This was good. It put Larry and Jennifer on the same side. Back at the defense table, Jennifer was staring straight ahead, crying without a sound.

"Nancy," Hardy said abruptly, "could your daughter have killed Matt, her son, even by mistake?" He held his breath, waiting.

She shook her head. "*No.* If she did, even by accident like you say, she would have killed herself."

Powell got up slowly. He knew this was emotional testimony and he didn't want to appear callous himself, but he felt he had to object to the speculation. Villars sustained him.

But Hardy at least had what he wanted. He went on to his last prepared questions, and to the answer he expected but that he believed was genuine. "What are your feelings for your daughter now?"

"I love her," she said. "She's all I have left."

Powell knew he had his work cut out for him, especially since Villars had denied a recess before his cross. Here was an emotionally charged, physically abused woman, and his job was to discredit her, take her apart. If he was going to be effective, it had to be a slow dance.

He smiled, breaking the ice. He had no doubt that she remembered him from the previous night in the homicide detail, but he had no choice — he couldn't come out swinging. He was going to be her friend, just clarifying a few little things. Her shoulders were forward, hunched, defensive, but she gave him a tentative smile. It was a start.

"Mrs. DiStephano, you and your late husband also have a son, don't you?"

This, from out of left field, put her off balance. "Yes. Tom."

"And was Tom ever the victim of your husband's abuse?"

"Phil hit Tom a few times when he was younger, but it was more like just spankings. He never hurt him."

"And how are the two men now? Are they close?"

Hardy stood up. "Your Honor, if it please the court, Mr. Powell knows full well that Mr. Di-Stephano is deceased."

It was casual, and Hardy's phrasing of the objection side-stepped the overt admission that Nancy had killed him, if anyone didn't already know. Powell gestured apologetically. "Did Tom ever witness your husband beating you?"

"Yes."

"Just like Jennifer did?"

"Yes. I mean until later."

"What happened later?"

"Well, later, when Tom got older, he'd, like, he tried to protect me. So Phil would make sure Tom wasn't around."

"But that wasn't the case with Jennifer?"

"I'm sorry. What wasn't?"

"Your late husband, Phil, would hit you even if Jennifer was around?"

"Sometimes."

"And she didn't try to stop it?"

"She couldn't stop my husband. I couldn't . . ." She stopped, realizing that finally she had done just that. "He was too strong. Jennifer just hid, I think."

"So Jennifer hid and watched her father beat you without trying to help you in any way. But your son Tom tried to step in. How do you feel

about your son now?"
"Tom? He's a good boy."
"You love him?"
"Of course. He's my son."
"And of course mothers love their sons."
"Yes."
Powell let that sink in. "And yet you testified that Jennifer was all you had left?"
Nancy glanced in panic around the room, then looked at Hardy. He nodded. It was okay. She was doing fine.
"That was a figure of speech," she said. "She's the only daughter I have left."
"And you are close to her?"
"Yes. Very close."
"You're very close. I see. Can you tell the jury roughly how many times, in the past year before your daughter was arrested, that you visited her at her house?"
Hardy put a hand to his forehead. The trap was going to spring here. Jennifer had her hand on his arm.
Nancy hesitated, sitting back now for the first time. Seconds crept by.
"Mrs. DiStephano," Villars prodded, "please answer the question."
Powell waited some more. He wasn't pressing — it was an obvious and simple question, hanging in the room. No one, least of all Nancy, was apt to have forgotten it. "Not last year," she said at last.
"You didn't visit your daughter's home during the last year?"
"No."

"How about visits to your home? Did she come and visit you?"

"No."

"Not at all?"

"No."

Powell did a three-sixty, his expressive face showing every nuance of his deep surprise. "Well, how about the year before that?"

Nancy started to sound a little snappish. "No, we didn't see them very much. Larry was . . . Larry didn't want us to."

"Larry didn't want you to." Powell, sparing Nancy's feelings, a good guy, tried to find a way out for her. "Then, with your very close relationship, you and Jennifer must have spoken on the phone quite a lot?"

She looked down. "She was very busy."

"Your daughter was busy. Did she have a job?"

"*I* had a job, I have a job."

"Which left nights and weekends, is that right?"

Hardy stood up. "Your Honor, this is badgering."

"Overruled."

Powell asked again. "Just approximately, Mrs. DiStephano, how often did you and your daughter speak?"

Nancy kept her eyes down.

"Every week? Once a month?"

"She always called on my birthday. I always called on hers."

Powell let the words speak for themselves. He nodded, then walked back to the prosecution table. "I'd like to explore one last point — you've told us, Mrs. DiStephano, that Matt was Jennifer's life, that she even spoiled him. I wonder if you could be more specific."

Again, the eyes came to Hardy, pleading for help. "What do you mean?"

"I mean, if you didn't see much of Jennifer and Matt, which you've just told us, how do you know how she felt about him or how she treated him?"

"Well, when he was younger, when he was a baby —"

"Matt was Jennifer's life then?"

"Yes."

"And now?"

"Yes."

Powell was still trying to seem gentle, generous. He came close to the witness box, speaking softly. "Mrs. DiStephano, I just don't see how you can know. Please help me here."

Nancy sat quietly for an hour's worth of fifteen seconds. Finally Hardy stood and asked if a question had been asked. Powell gave it some more time, then sighed, saying he supposed not. Mrs. DiStephano could sit down.

49

Finally, after lunch, the defendant took the stand.

She wore a taupe-colored suit with a bright multi-colored scarf. Hardy wasn't sure how he felt about the outfit — it gave out conflicting messages. On the one hand, it cut Jennifer away even further from the common thread shared by the rest of the people on the jury, which was not good. She needed their empathy, not their envy. But he had to admit, and statistics supported it, that there was a subtle dynamic at work in death-penalty cases. A natural reaction, he guessed, although not a particularly noble one. A jury would only be likely to vote for the death penalty if it had become convinced that the defendant was, in some tangible way, a kind of monster, a deformity cut off from the bonds of humanity. To avoid this impression — shallow as it might be — Jennifer's clothes would help. Looking as she did, dressed as she was, she was very much a *human* presence, not a non-person, certainly not a monster. More than that, there was something in her physical beauty and carriage that was generally highly valued in America. Hardy hoped the jury — especially the men — would not be inclined to vote to turn this suffering beauty into a corpse.

Of course, his fear in calling her to the stand was that by opening her mouth she would break the spell cast by her appearance. And Hardy well knew that from behind that appearance might erupt someone to turn off even the most predisposed in her favor.

They had discussed the format for this testimony, and had decided that Jennifer should say what she had to in her most modulated voice. She would be her best self. The risk would come with Powell's cross-examination. Meanwhile, Hardy tread lightly.

"Jennifer, you're up here today to argue for your very life. Is there anything you would like the jury, and the judge, to know?"

She turned to them. "I know that you have found that the evidence was enough to convict me." Swallowing, nervous, she looked at Hardy, who nodded. "I'm really not here to make an argument for my life, as Mr. Hardy says. I'm here to tell you that I did not do any of this. I did not kill my husband. I certainly did not kill my son." She swallowed again. "I admit I may not have been the greatest mom in the world, but I loved Matt . . ." Again, she stopped, bit down on her lower lip. Gathering herself, she forced a weak smile. "I guess that's all."

Powell was scribbling furiously — about what?

Hardy had intended to question her some about Larry, but this statement was so clean that he was tempted to stop right there. The jury now had heard her deny the killings with her own voice — it just might be all he needed, or at least the best he was going to get.

But on the other side, the jury might feel it was too easy to fake something so short. He felt he had to bring her out a little more — as Freeman had said, life was a risk.

"Do you want to tell us about the morning of December 28?"

Powell stood up. "Your Honor, this testimony belonged in the guilt phase of this trial."

Hardy had to get in a word before Villars ruled. "This is Jennifer Witt's story and the jury deserves to hear it, Your Honor."

The judge frowned as she always did when counsel went at each other, then she agreed with Hardy. Turning to Jennifer, she said, "Tell us about that morning, Mrs. Witt."

Jennifer nodded. "I got up early because we'd had dinner late and I hadn't done the dishes from the night before. And Larry was going to be home all day, all week really, so I wanted to be sure the house was perfect. I wanted to go jogging later, which I usually did, so I just put on my running clothes and went downstairs.

"It got pretty late, maybe eight-thirty, but it was Larry's vacation and I thought he should be able to sleep in if he wanted. Then finally he came down. Matt was still sleeping, he was a good sleeper."

Nice touch, Hardy thought shamelessly.

"Anyway, Larry reads the paper in the morning with his breakfast. It's just something he always does . . ." She paused, collecting herself. "I mean he always did. But this morning he came down angry."

"Over what?" Hardy said.

She swallowed hard. "I wasn't dressed right."

"Didn't you say you were in your running clothes?"

She nodded. "But that wasn't going to be for an hour or so, you see? I guess I still looked kind of like I just rolled out of bed. I mean my hair and no make-up."

"But hadn't you just been up for a while cleaning house, doing the dishes?"

Jennifer might not want to talk about Larry beating her, but this was good stuff for her. Saint Larry was taking a few hits and Hardy was trying to keep Jennifer swinging. "Well, yes, but . . . he just didn't like it."

"Did he yell at you?"

"No. I could just tell he was upset. You know?"

"I think so, Jennifer." Hardy included the jury. "And then what happened?"

"Well, I got his coffee and then I tried to rub his shoulders, which he liked when he was tense about something, but he shrugged me off."

"He shrugged you off? You mean he physically moved you away?" Powell seemed willing to let him lead the witness and Hardy would use a leash if he had to.

But Jennifer wouldn't go along. "No. You know, he just didn't want me to look this way. So I told him I'd go upstairs to change if he wanted me to . . ."

"Even though you were still going running in an hour?"

She nodded. "If he wanted. It wasn't a big deal to me. But then he told me not to bother, he said he'd been awake for an hour upstairs, going over our bills. He was worried about money. Christmas, you know, that sort of thing?"

"And what happened then?"

"It got to be a family budget argument." Jennifer was facing the jury. "You know, everybody has them."

"All right, and then what?"

"Then Matt came down, rubbing his eyes, like he did when he woke up . . . I didn't like to have Matt hear us arguing and yelling so I stopped and went into the kitchen and made him some French toast, which was his favorite. Then I went upstairs to make the beds. I thought maybe it would all blow over."

"And did it blow over?"

"No . . . When I came down Larry started in again on how I looked. He thought I'd gone upstairs to change into something decent. I told him I was going running now, but he was still mad about the other . . . about everything. So we had more words and Matt was crying. I thought I could make it stop if I left, so I did."

"You went out running?"

"Yes."

"And what time did you leave the house?"

"I don't know. I walked down a couple of blocks, which is what I always do to warm up, then I started running."

She told it well . . . the stop at the bank, her return to the house, the inventory where she didn't list the gun as missing because she hadn't gone back into the bedroom. Hardy was coming to the opinion that in his fear over Jennifer's abrasive personality, Freeman had badly erred in not putting her on the stand. She had a consistent story to tell and she told it well, her voice gaining in confidence as she went on until her direct testimony came to an end just before they broke for lunch.

If only she could stand up as well to Powell's cross-examination.

"I'd like to start by asking you to clarify something for me. Is that all right?"

During lunch in the "suite," Hardy had let her savor her partial victory for a few moments, and then thought he'd best begin to prepare her for Powell's expected onslaught. Perhaps it would work — she was facing Powell calmly now, her eyes clear as she nodded.

"You've said, and I quote: 'I didn't kill my husband. I *certainly* did not kill my son.' Do you mean that you're not as certain that you didn't kill Larry?"

This was a get-your-goat question and as such, Hardy thought, it was good strategy. But he wasn't about to let Powell get away with it. "Argumentative, Your Honor. What's the substance of that question?"

Villars agreed. Jennifer did not have to answer, but Hardy could see that the question had rattled her, already chipped at her reserve. He caught her eye and half-lifted a palm — keep cool, Jennifer, don't let it get to you.

Powell smiled at the defendant and started again. "If you don't mind, Mrs. Witt, I'd like to clear up one part of your story I still don't understand. You've testified that when you came back downstairs after making the beds and so on, that you and your husband started fighting again."

"Larry started yelling again, yes."

"And Matt started crying?"

"Yes."

"And as a mother, your response to your son's crying was to leave the house?"

"I tried to stop it by leaving."

"Yes, I see that, but how did you try to comfort your son? Did you hug him? Tell him you loved him?"

"No, not then. I thought when the fight between Larry and me stopped, he'd stop —"

"And that was the point, wasn't it? To get him to stop?"

"Well, no. I mean, he would."

"So you just walked out on him?"

Hardy stood up. "Asked and answered, Your Honor." Disastrously.

Powell withdrew the question before Hardy could be sustained. He stepped closer to the witness box. "All right, Mrs. Witt. On another subject — you've mentioned that you and your husband had this fight about money — family budgets, the kind we all have, is that right?"

"Yes."

"And your husband, Dr. Witt . . . was looking over your family budget before coming down to breakfast?"

"Yes."

Powell had something, Hardy realized. Relaxed, taking his time, he went back to the prosecution table and took a document from Morehouse. He walked back to the center of the courtroom. "Your

Honor, I have here a copy of a statement of an account of Mrs. Witt's from Pioneer's Bank. I'd like to introduce it into evidence as People's 14." Jennifer visibly tensed.

Hardy's stomach tightened. As Powell came over to his table to show him the bank statement, he decided to buy her some time. "Your Honor, sidebar?"

The judge, scowling, motioned Powell and Hardy forward. "What is it now, Mr. Hardy?"

"Your Honor, this document wasn't on the People's evidence list." During discovery, counsel for both sides were supposed to present the other side with complete lists of witnesses they intended to call, and physical evidence they intended to present. Neither witnesses nor evidence had to be used, but if they were not listed beforehand they normally could not be used. In theory, at least, the courtroom was not a place to spring surprises — in practice, attorneys loved it when it worked out that way. "I object to its introduction now," Hardy said.

"Counsel is mistaken, Your Honor." Prepared for this, Powell motioned Morehouse up to bench. The young assistant gathered a thick stack of papers and brought them forward, handing them to Powell, who in turn passed copies to Hardy and to Villars. "Line eighteen, page one of the evidence list, Your Honor."

Hardy read it. It said: "Financial papers."

Powell was now holding up the thick sheaf. "These are the papers, a complete copy of which we presented to defense counsel on" — he paused, checking another page — "August 1."

Hardy and Freeman had, of course, received this package. It was undoubtedly somewhere in Hardy's office among the seven book boxes filled with statements, interviews, police reports. Because Powell hadn't seen fit to introduce it in the guilt phase, Hardy had allowed himself the faint hope that Powell hadn't noticed it in the mass of documents. No such luck.

The financial package Powell now held was three-and-a-half inches thick and contained nearly five-hundred pages of the Witts' past tax statements, insurance forms, bank accounts, IRAs, stock records, copies of canceled checks, receipts for most of their household items. None of it was in any order and there was no index — a ton of camouflage for the one thing that was going to hurt Jennifer — the one-page statement revealing the existence of her secret account. Powell was flipping through the pages upon pages of photocopied copies of canceled checks until he found it, hidden among them. "Here it is, Your Honor."

Villars leaned over, adjusted her reading glasses, nodded. "There it is, Mr. Hardy."

It was entered into evidence and Powell descended on Jennifer. "Now, Mrs. Witt, take a look at People's 14 here. Is this your account?"

The clear look in her eyes was gone. Panic had taken up residence there. And Hardy was not much help — he felt it himself. Jennifer nodded. "Yes, that's my account."

"Did your husband know about this account?"

Jennifer swallowed. "Yes, of course."

Hardy knew that perjury wasn't much compared to murder, but he hated to hear the lie, anyway, even though he understood why she told it.

"Mrs. Witt, would you read to the jury the address on that statement?"

Jennifer glanced at the copy she held. "P.O. Box 33449, San Francisco, California."

"A post office box? Statements from this account weren't sent to your home?"

"No."

"And why was that, Mrs. Witt?"

Wide-eyed, Jennifer turned to Hardy. "I don't know."

"You don't know!" Powell's voice rose and grew deeper. "You don't know?" he repeated. "Isn't it true, Mrs. Witt, that your husband had no knowledge of this account?"

"No —"

". . . and that he had discovered that something was wrong with your family budget. What he'd discovered was that you had been lying to him about money."

"No, that's not true —"

But as Hardy knew, it was true.

And Powell wasn't finished. He backed up a step, lowered his voice again, came at her from another direction. "Mrs. Witt, have you received any money yet from your late husband's insurance?"

Thrown by the change in tack, Jennifer might have thought for a moment that Powell was easing off. She said she hadn't.

"Did you and Larry have a large savings account?"

"No, not really. I think about twenty thousand, something like that."

Powell turned to the jury. "Some people might call that large, Mrs. Witt, but I'll take your word for it."

"Then we had Matt's college fund." Jennifer, not knowing where he was going, was trying to be helpful. "That was about another twenty."

"And what about the house?"

Hardy jumped up. "Your Honor, where is this going?"

Powell turned to him, then back. "I'll tell you where it's going, Your Honor. It clearly demonstrates that these murders happened because of *greed.*" He held up the Pioneer's Bank statement again. Wound up now, Powell turned back to Jennifer. "Mrs. Witt, this account of yours that got mailed to a post office box, how much money did it contain when you were arrested for these murders?"

Jennifer studied her hands.

"I'll tell you how much it contained if you don't remember. It's here in these statements. It's a little over three-hundred-thousand dollars, Mrs. Witt. Money you had been stealing from your husband for almost seven years. Money you embezzled from your own household!"

Jennifer lost it, voice shrill. "We *never* went out! Don't you understand that? He *never* let me do anything. You don't know what it was like, what *he* was like. He never even missed it —"

"But he did that morning, didn't he, Mrs. Witt? And your beloved Matt was in the way, too —"

"Objection!"

"You didn't grab the gun in the heat of the fight — you had *planned* the basics for some time —"

"Your Honor, *objection.*"

"You went upstairs to get the gun —"

"Objection." Hardy's voice had gone up several octaves. Villars banged her gavel. Powell rolled over both of them, at the top of his voice, moving closer to Jennifer.

"Now suddenly, this became the moment when you must act. He said he was *taking* his money back, *isn't that it?*" Finally, in her face — *"Isn't that why you killed him?"*

Exploding out of the witness chair, nearly knocking it over, Jennifer lunged at Powell, her face distorted. *"No. I didn't kill him, you son of a bitch!"*

"Sit down, all of you. Mr. Powell . . ." Villars slammed her gavel.

Jennifer, out of control, was screaming.

"Order! Order! Bailiffs!"

But even the bailiffs stood back, letting Jennifer wind down until, spent, she pulled the chair upright again and lowered herself into it.

Powell stared at her. His shoulders sagged. "I just don't understand why you had to kill Matt," he whispered. Turning, he said he had no further questions.

It took the jury two ballots, two hours and seventeen minutes. It was, as the law prescribed it had to be, unanimous. And it was for the penalty of death.

PART FIVE

50

Hardy woke up sweating, gasping for air, the green room closing in around him as the almond-scented, corrosive gas burned its way down his windpipe, into his lungs, exploding them inward, leaving him in mute agony — in his dream, the scream woke him. In life, in this style of death, the scream would be silent, choked off the instant it was born.

It was all right. He was in his bedroom, Frannie curled in sleep next to him. The clock next to the bed said it was a little after three o'clock — he'd been asleep almost two hours.

He got up and went naked into the bathroom to throw water on his face. He'd been sweating — his hair was stuck to the side of his head. Gulping water and aspirin, he pulled at the skin around his eyes — the blackened circles under them didn't smudge away.

At the front of his house, still undressed, he sat in his armchair. It was cold, colder than it ever got. After a couple of minutes he heard footsteps, and Frannie was next to him.

"Bad dream?" She sat on his lap, her arms around his neck. "You're all clammy," she said.

He couldn't talk. Her hands moved over his

head, smoothing his hair. He had his arms around her and held her tight against him.

"I'm going to get a blanket."

When she got back he was shivering. He couldn't stop. She put the blanket over him, then went to get another comforter. When she returned he was out again, breathing heavily. She tucked the extra blanket around him, rubbed a hand across his damp and burning forehead and lay down in the windowseat under an afghan, her head on a sitting pillow near her husband's knees.

He woke up again. It seemed to be a long time before dawn.

Still in the chair, he listened in the darkness, trying to hear something beyond the sounds of his quiet house — Frannie breathing on the windowseat beside him, the aquarium gurgling way in the back, in their bedroom.

Something — he thought it might have been a noise — had gotten into his consciousness.

A chill shook him, bringing with it a sudden jolt of fear. If he was on to what he thought he was, suppose there was someone trying to make it impossible for him to tell what he might know?

He didn't remember getting into bed. He didn't remember getting to this chair, or why Frannie was here. Throwing off the blanket, he realized he must have come in, taken off his shoes and collapsed.

His guns!

His guns from his cop days were locked in his safe. When Rebecca had moved into what had been his office he had moved the safe out behind the kitchen, on the top shelf over his workbench. Now, woozy and stumbling, he forced himself up, back through the house, turning on lights as he went.

The safe was untouched.

He opened it. The guns were still there. He really was losing it. No one was coming for him. Not here. Not at his home.

And then it occurred to him that maybe Larry Witt had thought the same thing. And so had Simpson Crane. And both had been shot with their own weapons in their own houses —

Ridiculous.

The .380 in his hand, shivering, he decided he'd finish making sure. There wasn't much of the house left to check. Vincent's room, Rebecca's, his own bedroom. He passed back through the kitchen, dining room, living room, back up the long hallway, turning lights off behind him. Nothing. He was crazy.

He looked at the loaded gun in his hand, knowing that this was how domestic accidents occurred. A half-dark house, a wife or child walking in unexpectedly while the husband holds a loaded weapon, thinking he's heard somebody break in, that somebody might have a reason to.

He went back to the work room. As he was putting the damn thing back in the safe, it came to him suddenly. His legs went mushy on him. No, it was too grotesque to consider. He had to sit.

Larry had finally hit Matt. And more than once. Maybe Matt had come in during the fight and taken sides with his mother, pulling at his dad to leave his mom alone, and Larry had lost it entirely with the boy, smashing the gun he was holding into the side of his face. And then realizing what he'd done, that this couldn't be covered up or undone. The boy, maybe with a broken jaw, a living indictment of what Larry had become, of who he really was. His career would be over, his carefully ordered, totally controlled life . . . And in a beat, as Matt lay on the floor by the bathroom and Jennifer begged him to stop, the only solution had come to him. Destroy the evidence of what he'd done. A bullet would erase any sign that he'd ever hit his son. They could never say *that*.

And then there would be nothing left, no point in continuing your life, so you turn the gun on yourself.

But before he does, he turns to Jennifer and says, "This is all your fault." And, being who she is, she at that moment, and beyond, *believes* him.

Hardy, on the floor in the workroom, followed it through to the end. But of course it couldn't have happened that way. The gun being gone eliminated that possibility.

Except if Jennifer, blaming herself as she always did for the fight and everything it precipitated, removed the gun herself, took it to the dumpster? That way it wouldn't be Larry's fault. The precious reputation of Dr. Larry Witt would be saved. And she — Jennifer — she'd get what she deserved for having started it, for being who she was.

It was too twisted. It couldn't have been that.

And yet some of it did fit — Jennifer's unyielding denial that she had killed her son and husband.

And, more chillingly, he thought, it fit her profile — self-hatred, guilt, the need to be punished. Because, in fact, her immediate feeling when it was done was her guilty joy that Larry was dead. She'd hated him, hated everything he'd done. Though she almost couldn't physically bear the loss of Matt, it didn't — in that first instant flush — diminish her overriding happiness that *Larry* was gone. That she was free of him at last.

And if she could feel that way right after losing her son, then she had to feel she truly was without a soul and deserved whatever punishment society gave her. In fact, she would help it. She *had* helped it. She was doing this to herself.

Hardy leaned back against the wall, feverish. This wasn't what happened. It couldn't have been what happened. He had other ideas he had to explore and they made a lot more sense. He was delirious.

"You can't do it today."

Hardy's fever had leveled at 101, which was also the age he felt. He was on his third cup of black coffee, having forced himself to down some hash, toast and orange juice. "The appointment's at nine. I've got to go. I've only got three days."

Three days until Villars, the thirteenth juror, gave the final ruling on the verdict — Tuesday at 9:30 A.M. Hardy had his automatic motion to set aside the verdict due at that time and, in spite of everything, thought he still at least had a chance to reduce the sentence to life in prison. If only he could find something to bring Villars to it, something she could find admissible.

After the verdict he had spent half the night with Jennifer talking about options. He held back his trump — on his own he had decided that he would at least lay out the battered-woman issue to Villars if it was the only thing that could mitigate death. But in the meanwhile, he had filled Jennifer in on the YBMG situation and she had authorized him to go wherever he had to and do whatever was needed to get any proof he could. At least she now wanted to live.

His first step — at eight on a Friday night — had been calling the chairman of YBMG. Dr. Clarence Stone lived in San Francisco, and, persuaded by Hardy's urgency, had cleared an hour in his home on a Saturday morning for him. So flu or no, Hardy had to go.

Rebecca and Vincent were playing with Leggo's in the nursery. Frannie said, "Look, you're sick. You've been working around the clock. You haven't been home in a month. You've got to take care of yourself."

He tried to smile through the haze. "That's my plan. I will. Soon. Promise."

Vincent let out a wail and Frannie rushed to the back of the house. Hardy slowly got up and, more slowly, grabbing handholds as he passed them so he wouldn't fall down, made his way to the nursery door. Vincent had caught his finger in one of the joints of the stroller and Rebecca had sent up a sympathetic wail. Turning his head away from her, he picked her up and bounced her in his arms.

In a minute or so, the kids in their arms, they bundled back to the kitchen. Frannie, holding Vincent, was getting a piece of ice from the freezer to put on the pinch. "Can't you just appeal like everyone else?" she said.

"Peel what?" Rebecca asked. "Banana peel?"

Vincent looked over Frannie's shoulder for the banana peel, repeating it. They started to chant. "Banana peel, banana peel." It continued, getting louder. His kids were some comedians. It was great that they loved each other, had the same sense of humor. This banana peel game was funny funny funny, a real laugh riot.

Hardy thought his head was going to levitate without him attached. Now, of course, the kids wanted bananas and, predictably, they were out of bananas.

"You feel good enough to go out, why don't you take them to the store and buy some?" He knew she was justified to some degree in feeling this way, but that didn't make him appreciate her at the moment. "Both of them," she continued. "Mommy needs a break."

Clarence Stone lived in a mansion in the Seacliff area, geographically less than a mile from Hardy's house and psychologically in another galaxy. The short walk from the head of the circular drive to the front door wiped Hardy out. He took nearly a minute getting his breath before he rang the doorbell.

A bona fide butler admitted him and they walked a long hallway, their footfalls swallowed by the thick Oriental runner. The butler ushered him into a library/office, where a white-haired man with a clipped mustache sat at a desk that rivaled the one in Freeman's office for expanse. He wore a maroon silk robe and was writing with a fountain pen. When Hardy was introduced he finished writing, put down the pen, stood — he was wearing black slacks under the robe — came around the desk and offered his hand.

"You don't look good, son."

Hardy didn't doubt it — he also didn't feel good. He'd had chills driving over. The thick fog seemed to insulate against any warmth or even light. The heater in the car had been turned up high, blasting him, but it hadn't helped.

"Touch of the flu," Hardy said. "That's all."

Stone the doctor told his butler to bring in some tea with lots of lemon and honey. He had Hardy sit down on a club chair and remove his coat. He asked his permission to look him over. No charge.

"You getting much sleep? You ought to stay in bed with this, you know?"

Through his chattering teeth, Hardy laughed weakly. "I got my eight hours this week. I'm fine."

Stone had an old-fashioned black doctor's satchel and he set it on the floor now, taking out some instruments. He listened to Hardy's chest, stuck an instant-read thermometer into his ear, looked in his ears and at his throat. "Yep, you've got the flu."

The tea arrived and Stone prepared a couple of glasses. "This must be important," he said. "You really shouldn't be out walking around."

"It is important," Hardy said. He had his coat back on and pulled it close around him.

Stone sat kitty-corner to him, turned in. "Last night you said it concerned YBMG?"

Assuming Stone was familiar with the background, Hardy gave him the short version, concluding with Larry Witt's concern over the timing and tone of the offering circular.

When he had finished, Stone did not answer immediately. "You know many doctors, Mr. Hardy?"

Hardy nodded. "Some."

"You know how many people try to sell them things?" He held up his hand. "No, I'll tell you. Not a day goes by that the average successful doctor doesn't get ten stock brochures, two or three credit-card applications, offers of lines-of-credit, you name it. Even if you go to the trouble of trying to get the post office to eliminate all this solicitation mail, you're inundated. Believe me, I've tried. It's out of control."

"All right."

"All right. But you seem to think a flashy presentation, high-profile sales pitch is going to matter. It is not. We get them every day. In fact, the Board specifically decided to issue a low-key circular rather than a sensational one. We didn't want to raise hopes in the Group's future success after it went for-profit. It was entirely within the realm of the possible that we could have gone under altogether. No one — certainly no one on the Board — anticipated PacRim's interest, or the windfall."

"What about the short turnaround time you gave everyone?"

"It wasn't that short." Stone sat back, apparently relaxed, and crossed his legs. "Doctors tend to be fairly literate people, Mr. Hardy. They can read. But like everybody else, often they don't act until they have to. So you give people a deadline, it moves things along. Besides, remember that this was a twenty-dollar investment at most. Twenty dollars. Not the kind of decision you'd have to discuss with your wife or lawyer. It was straightforward and everybody had an opportunity."

"But not everybody bought."

Stone shrugged, nodded. "If you see a conspiracy in that, I'm afraid we have to part company there."

It would have been easier if Stone had shown the slightest sign of defensiveness, but he was sitting so comfortably, speaking so moderately, and, worst of all, making such perfect sense.

Hardy leaned forward. "Ali Singh said only thirty doctors bought."

Stone agreed. "Perhaps forty. I'm not exactly sure. Certainly less than wish they had now." He spread his arms, palms up, apologetic. "But that's the nature of these things. Who doesn't wish they'd bought Apple when it opened, or even McDonald's?"

"But Dr. Witt complained even before the windfall."

"Do you know that he complained? Who did he complain to? Maybe he just wanted to ask for an extension. Maybe he had a quick question. Maybe anything. I didn't know Dr. Witt personally, so I have no idea."

This interview was taking on a sense of déjà vu — Villars had had the same objections. Hardy just didn't know. He was surmising and hoping but he didn't have a fact. Another wave of nausea hit him and he leaned back against the seat and closed his eyes.

"Mr. Hardy?"

"I'd better be going," he said. "Thank you. You've been very helpful."

Taking Hardy's arm, Stone walked with him across the room, through the door to the hallway. "You know," Hardy said, "I've got one more question if you don't mind . . . What happened to the shares no one bought?"

This was just another administrative detail, and Stone was forthcoming about it. "Some of them are in an escrow account, part of the Group's assets. Others we gave as bonuses. Some we traded for services."

"Such as legal fees?"

Stone smiled. "As a matter of fact, yes. Mr. Bachman pulled quite a coup on that. And we thought we were getting a very good deal, an incredible deal, in fact."

They had come to the door. Stone was still enjoying Bachman's cleverness. "Crane normally hits us for two-fifty an hour, and Bachman suggested he handle the paperwork on the turnaround for fifty thousand shares. We figured it would be a hundred hours of legal work and the shares were worth twenty-five-hundred dollars — at the time. It was a steal. So the Board took it. And actually it turned out to be more like three hundred hours, so we thought we'd done very well indeed."

"Fifty thousand shares?"

"At a nickel a share, remember. It was peanuts. Of course, now . . ."

Hardy waited.

"Well, we all made out well, I shouldn't begrudge Mr. Bachman. He put in a lot of work and he's made us all much wealthier. Is that a sin?"

"How much did he wind up getting?"

Stone pursed his lips, smiled. "I suppose it's in the public record. I can tell you — a little over seven million dollars."

Hardy repeated the number. Slowly. Out loud.

Stone agreed it was a great deal. "Now you'd better get home and get in bed. Take aspirin every four hours."

"Drink lots of liquids," Hardy said.

The doctor smiled. "Right. Then send me fifty dollars." The smile broke into a wide grin. "Sorry, forget the fifty dollars. Force of habit."

But he didn't go home.

David Freeman was up and about, conducting a classical concert — Hardy wasn't familiar with the piece — in his living room. Hardy threw his briefcase onto the floor and sank heavily onto Freeman's couch, pulled a couple of stuffed pillows over him for warmth, and watched Freeman — baton in hand — direct his symphony.

He dozed.

When he woke up the fog still clung to the windows. Freeman had thrown a blanket over him. It was quiet and the older man was working over his kitchen table, reading a file, taking notes.

"What time is it?" Hardy's bones were too heavy to lift his wrist.

Freeman looked up. "After two. I usually get

sick after a trial, too."

"I can't be sick." Hardy tried to straighten up. He wasn't entirely successful. "Why did I come here?" he asked, half to himself.

"Why are we here? What is life? The great questions. That's why I like you. You feel like lunch? I'm starving."

"I don't think I can eat."

"Okay." Freeman, however, went to the refrigerator and started rummaging around.

"I remember." This time Hardy got himself pulled up. He wrapped the blanket around him. "Jody Bachman made seven million dollars."

The sound of rummaging stopped.

"Fifty thousand shares," Hardy said.

Freeman's head appeared above the refrigerator door. "Which was it?" he asked.

"It was both."

"You mean he got seven million dollars *plus* fifty thousand shares of stock?" He shook his head. "We're in the wrong business."

"No, he got fifty thousand shares of stock, which turned out to be worth seven million dollars."

Abandoning his foraging efforts, Freeman crossed the small living room and sat at the end of the couch. His face was suddenly troubled. He scratched at his stubble. "He took stock as payment? Is he the managing partner down there?"

"Yes, he took stock. No, he's not the managing partner. Why?"

Freeman sat back. "What were the shares worth?"

"A nickel each," Hardy said. "What are you thinking?"

"I'm thinking maybe you've found something."

"I thought that, too." Hardy knew exactly what he thought but he wanted corroboration. He'd flown off too many times without getting his facts nailed down. It wasn't going to happen again. "I'm not sure I know what it is, though," he waited.

The thought, the argument, seemed to be blossoming in Freeman's head. He stood up and went to the window, studied the fog. Hardy rode out another bout of the shakes, then realized he'd broken a sweat. He threw off the blanket but then the chills started again.

Turning around, Freeman's face showed distaste. "You look like hell." That said, he moved right on, coming back to the couch, sitting close to Hardy, and explained his reasoning.

Large corporate firms like Crane & Crane did not usually allow associates and junior partners to trade essentially worthless stocks for eminently liquid billable hours. Jody Bachman, young and ambitious, had somehow put together a deal with PacRim, or knew PacRim might be a viable marriage with YBMG. Freeman said he wasn't sure of the details — who could be? — but Bachman then sold his contingency stock idea to the Group.

All of which might have been fine except for Simpson Crane, the managing partner of Crane & Crane. Bachman was putting in hundreds of hours of billable time and not bringing in a dime for his efforts. His utilization stunk. Simpson might have called him on it, or Bachman might have gone to Simpson and asked permission for the contingency. But if Simpson Crane made a habit of accepting stock with a maximum face value of twenty-five *hundred* dollars in lieu of a guaranteed fee of seventy-five *thousand* dollars in cash, he wouldn't have a law firm for long.

He would have said no. And that would have ruined Jody's plans — both for his advancement in the firm and for his own fortune. It might have even jeopardized his engagement to his millionaire socialite girlfriend Margaret Morency.

If Simpson Crane were the only thing standing in the way between Bachman and everything he'd worked for and wanted in his professional and personal life, and if Simpson had threatened to pull the rug, might that be worth killing for? Simpson might even have threatened to fire him outright. Freeman certainly would have.

"So. There it is," Freeman concluded. "How do you like it?"

Hardy's eyes were burning now and his mouth was parched, but he had been paying attention throughout the recital. It was close enough to the scenario he had imagined. Now all he had to do was prove it.

"I give it a nine," he said. "My girlfriend can dance to it."

Freeman looked at him as though he were a Martian. Hardy was getting delirious and Freeman told him he'd call a cab to take him home. He left him sitting on the couch and went to the kitchen to make the call.

In spite of everyone's well-meaning advice, there were no odds in going home. He didn't have time to go home. He was seeing Villars on Tuesday morning and if this didn't work out, he had to spend Monday getting his last-ditch motion prepared.

But this was his best chance. This might work.

He called Frannie from the San Francisco airport and endured the expected anger. She had every right to be angry. He hadn't been much of a father or husband in the past months. But he was going to make it up to her, to the kids. This trial had taught him something. A lot. It was an insane life and he had fallen into it. But he was going to get out. Do something else, or do this some other way. As soon as this was done.

First, though, he was going to finish this.

When she cooled off she'd understand. She wouldn't, in fact, expect any less — she was the one, after all, who had insisted he do all he could to find the truth behind Larry Witt's murder. And Matt's. For Jennifer's sake. And now, sick or not, unless he died trying, that's just what he was going to do.

51

The plane was scheduled to land in Burbank an hour before dusk. He was sleeping in a window seat, covered with a blanket, when the pilot came on announcing their descent. He opened his eyes, taking in the view. Two or three times its normal size, the sun shimmered through a red haze out over the ocean. Looking down, Hardy picked up the maze of freeways winding through the Valley, the Hollywood jammed even now on an early Saturday evening, the Golden State also packed heading downtown. The Pasadena wasn't yet a parking lot, at least not from the air.

Feeling wasted with fatigue and fever, he closed his eyes again until they came to the famous complete stop at the gate.

This, he told himself as he tried not to stagger walking to the nearest rent-a-car booth, was a dumb idea.

But somehow he made it to Pasadena. He had taken a couple of DA training classes at an Embassy Suites there and had a vague memory of where he was going. Within an hour of landing, he had registered, showered, left a message for Frannie that he'd made it and passed out under the covers.

He slept fourteen hours and woke up in soaked sheets feeling he had a chance to survive. It was close to noon, Sunday, October 24. After another shower, still shaky, he called home again, and again no one answered. He left another message. He was feeling better, which wasn't saying much. He'd try again tonight.

Restoffer picked up after three rings. The greeting was cordial enough, but when Hardy started to brief him on why he had come down here, he hadn't gotten out two sentences when he sensed a change, an almost ominous reserve.

Restoffer interrupted him. "You gotta leave this. Or at least leave me out of it."

An unwelcome surprise. Last time they'd talked, Restoffer had told him he'd be around if he was needed. Now he was backing out.

"Did something else happen?"

"Nothing else happened except your prosecutor called my chief."

Silence. But nothing else needed to be said. Hardy had made some serious problems for Floyd Restoffer in the months before his pension was going to kick in. He didn't want any more. "I've got to go."

The line went dead.

Hardy squeezed the receiver. "Now we're having fun," he said to no one. He went into the bathroom and took three more aspirin, catching a glimpse of himself in the mirror. "Nice eyes." Backing up a step, he realized the rest of him matched his eyes — he needed a shave, clean clothes, another fourteen hours of sleep. He didn't have the courage to take his temperature.

After pacing the room for fifteen minutes, he ordered breakfast from room service, then called Restoffer again. "Margaret Morency is engaged to Jody Bachman, you know that?" There was a long silence and Hardy said: "I've got to start somewhere, Floyd. I'm down here. I need a little help. Please?"

Restoffer's breath echoed on the line. Hardy waited. "Believe it or not, Morency is in the book. I checked." After another moment the cop said, "San Marino," and hung up.

Hardy left a message for Jody Bachman at Crane & Crane. He was sure it was just an oversight because he was so busy, but Bachman had never gotten back to him on the Larry Witt matter. Now he was down in LA today and tomorrow. Maybe they could get together sometime, perhaps for lunch. He left the number of his hotel if Bachman wanted to call him back. Also his room number.

His luck ran out. Yes, Clarence Stone had been able to see him. Freeman had come up with pretty much the same conclusion. The plane had had an open seat, the hotel a vacant room.

That was it — that had been the run of it.

Now Restoffer wouldn't talk to him, Frannie wasn't home, Bachman wasn't at work on a Sunday and Margaret Morency's phone apparently didn't even have an answering machine.

Steeling himself for the shock, Hardy drew the shades back. The San Gabriel mountains rose sparkling in front of him. Closer in, squatting along the Rose Bowl parade route on Colorado Boulevard, he noticed the low buildings were waging a losing fight with graffiti. He pushed open his window. The air was fragrant and warm with a late-summer softness to it.

A new rush of dizziness came over him and he was tempted to yield to the inertia, to lie down, call it a mistake and fly home this afternoon when he woke up. Sitting on the bed, he flopped onto his back, closed his heavy eyes.

Suddenly, anger forced him up. He was disgusted with himself, with his weakness, with being sick. If he was going to sleep fourteen hours he could have done it at home. He hadn't come all the way down here to catch up on his sleep, to let a run of bad luck do him in.

The sitting up cost him another hit of dizziness. He knew the fever hadn't broken but he'd done a lot yesterday feeling even worse. He picked up his shirt, soggy and wrinkled. It wouldn't do. He had to get some clothes. He had to keep moving . . .

Clarence Stone's home in Seacliff had been a nice, human-scaled, run-of-the-mill mansion. Margaret Morency's place in San Marino put things in perspective. Hardy was getting a lesson in the investment community — there were the very comfortable, then the rich, and then there were the people who had houses that weren't visible from the road. The drive, through the double iron gates, wound back into a forest of scrub oak up over the crest of a small knoll and disappeared.

It hadn't been as hard to find as he had expected. The Huntington Library was open on Sundays (after noon) and they carried back issues of the city's weekly society sheet. In the past year there had been several charity events at Margaret Morency's.

Pastille was on Swan Court. Pastille was the name of her place. After those French breath candies. Maybe that's how Ms. Morency thought of her home — a trifle, a confection to soothe the spirit.

Hardy pulled his rent-a-car up to the gates. He had to get out of the car to ring the bell. No one had answered the last time he'd tried the telephone but that had been nearly an hour before. Something might have changed. If it hadn't, he'd try Bachman again, then come back here. Something.

A deep young female voice spoke through the box.

"Yes."

"Ms. Morency?"

"Yes."

He didn't feel he could launch into a long story. He had to see her. "I couldn't reach you on the phone," he said.

She laughed. "I know. I just let it ring. I don't know why I keep the thing. Who is this?"

Hardy took a gamble. He was an acquaintance of Jody's.

"Oh, just a minute." There was a whirring sound and the gates began to open. "I'm back by the pool. You'll find it."

"I give the staff Sundays off."

They sat on thick-cushioned picnic chairs under an umbrella. Two sweating pitchers — iced tea and lemonade — sat on a serving platter on the table. She had taken crystal glasses from the bar at the gazebo near the head of the pool and poured lemonade for them.

It was crude, he knew, but Hardy's first reaction, shaking her hand, was that he had seen better heads on beer. Orange Court debutante or not, she had one of those faces that didn't quite work — a jaw that was almost merely strong, but it jutted. A trace too much down clouding her cheeks. Her forehead reached her hairline a half-inch too soon. Being mega-rich could cover a multitude of sins.

She had also apparently perfected the art of diverting attention from her face. Blonde hair hung shining to her shoulders. She wore black bikini bottoms and a white top tied halter-fashion over her breasts. The top was diaphanous. A gold chain hugged her flat, tan waist. She was barefoot with long, tapered legs; another discreet chain encircled one ankle. Hardy noticed the top of the bathing suit draped over some flagstones by the flower bed on the opposite side of the pool. She had obviously been swimming, lounging, topless.

"I like being here alone."

They were certainly alone. No other houses were visible. Only trees, the pool, the manicured garden and rolling lawn beyond, the mansion behind them, the perfect blue sky. A jet flew high overhead.

"How do you know Jody?" she asked.

Hardy's every bone ached. He could feel sweat

gathering between his shoulder blades as the fever began to spike again. He sipped the lemonade and smiled weakly. "I'm afraid I'm another lawyer."

She had, he thought, a great laugh — deep, full-throated, uninhibited. She threw her head back, seemingly delighted. "Lawyers aren't afraid of anything," she said. "That's what Jody tells me."

"This lawyer is."

"What are you afraid of, Mr. Hardy?" She looked directly at him, her deep eyes a shade too dark. "You look pretty much able to take care of yourself."

"Right at this moment, I'm fighting a cold. I feel like an eight-year-old could take me down without too much trouble."

She looked another question at him. Had she been coming on? Had he just turned her down? Whatever, it didn't seem to bother her. She seemed to think it was interesting. It was such a different league here. There must be different rules and maybe he didn't know them.

"So where were we?" she asked.

"How I knew Jody. I don't."

For a moment her eyes registered something. Fear? Annoyance? "You're not a policeman, are you?"

"Why? Is Jody in trouble with the police?"

"There's no reason he should be. And you didn't answer me."

"I told you. I'm a lawyer. I'm not a cop."

She sat back and crossed her arms under her halter. Her face remained impassive. "What do you people think he did? You ought to leave him alone."

Hardy nodded. "Yes. That's what Mr. Kelso told Inspector Restoffer. But I'm on my own. I'm not with him and I'm trying to save my client's life." He gave her Jennifer's story in a nutshell. By the time he finished, she had uncrossed her arms. She took a long drink of lemonade.

"But Jody didn't call Frank — Mr. Kelso. I did. Jody knew nothing about it, probably still doesn't."

"Why did you call him?"

"Because, Mr. Hardy"— she leaned forward again — "because Jody doesn't need this. He's very sensitive and he hasn't done anything wrong. And then suddenly out of nowhere this Restoffer person starts questioning him as if he were a criminal. These accusations were tearing him apart and it was ridiculous. Do you know who Jody is?"

"I know he's your fiancé. That's about it."

"He's a one-in-a-million person, that's who he is. He spends half his life helping people. He came from nowhere and now he's moving into the city's elite, he raises money for twenty causes — that's where he is now, at a charity golf function. He's a partner at his firm and he makes a good living. He's engaged to me, so as you can see money will not be an issue. He doesn't need to do anything criminal. Money just doesn't drive him."

If Jody were so wonderful, Hardy wanted to ask her, why did she give the impression she would have taken him to bed, maybe still would. It could be that all his goodness didn't satisfy her, which, of course, didn't mean it wasn't there.

It could also be that one-in-a-million Jody didn't

love her, didn't find her desirable, had arranged for himself a convenient marriage that would give him still more money, more power. But maybe, in this strata of society, marriages more resembled strategic alliances than love affairs. Connections and loyalty might count for more than sexual attraction. He just didn't know, he was out of his league.

And he was almost out of steam. "Did Jody tell you that Restoffer had accused him of anything?"

"Not specifically, but it became obvious that he thought Jody might have had something to do with Simpson Crane's death, which is simply absurd. Simpson Crane was like his father. He cried when Simpson was killed — I was with him and I saw it. That's not something you fake, Mr. Hardy."

It's been known to happen, Hardy thought.

"Besides," she continued, "everybody knows who killed Simpson. It was the damn union. He was, I guess everybody knows, a union buster. He believed unions were ruining the country — and by the way he was *right* — so he went after them. He was just too good at it. And one of them killed him, or had him killed. That's just the kind of people they are."

Hardy wanted to ask her if she had ever had a meaningful conversation with a working person but thought he'd save his breath. That wasn't his fight, he wasn't about to become a life influence on Ms. Morency.

Suddenly she pushed herself up from her chair and crossed the flagstones. At the gazebo she grabbed a towel and draped it over her shoulders, covering the halter. It hadn't gotten any cooler — the implied invitation, if that's what it had been, was withdrawn.

Hardy stood up. "I appreciate you seeing me."

She came up to him and laid a hand on his arm. "I really wish you would leave Jody alone," she said. "He doesn't need this."

"Thanks for your time," he said. "I'll find my way out."

The phone was ringing. It was six-thirty on the clock next to the bed, and at first Hardy didn't know where he was, then whether it was morning or night. The last time he had fallen asleep during daylight he'd slept through the dark, and for a moment there he wondered if he'd done it again.

He picked up the telephone. It was Jody Bachman, personable Jody Bachman. "Margaret said you came by. I'm sorry I missed you. Also, listen, the other thing — never calling you back. What can I say? I got busy again. It's been really crazy. So I got your message at the office checking in, but I was late for this event. You know how it is. You want to get together?"

"Tonight's out. I'm fighting a cold here."

"Okay, how about tomorrow? You still in town? If you're free for lunch I've got a table at the City Club. Great food. Better view. Noon okay?"

"Noon's fine," Hardy answered.

"Noon then. You know where it is?"

Hardy said he'd find it. Bachman said he'd see him there.

He collapsed back down on the bed. When he

closed his eyes he had a sensation of motion, of the room spinning around him. He forced himself up to a sitting position.

He was forgetting something. It seemed important, maybe crucial, but he couldn't put his finger on it. And the effort at thought was so tiring. Minutes passed. He started to doze sitting up. The telephone rang again.

"Are you still sick?"

"I'm still sick."

Frannie's earlier anger had given way to concern. "Why don't you come home, Dismas? You ought to see a doctor."

He told her about his scheduled meeting the next day with Bachman. One way or the other, that would be the end of it. He had to stay until then.

She stopped pushing. Okay, if that's what he was going to do. The kids, she said, were fine. Rebecca was really missing him — that wasn't a guilt trip, just a fact. She, Frannie — his wife, remember? — missed him, too. Would he please try to take care of himself, be careful?

He told her he would. He didn't have much choice. He wasn't going anywhere feeling like he did. Hermetically sealed in his hotel room, he was going to sleep right now for the night. He'd see her tomorrow.

In the bathroom he took some more aspirin, drank two glasses of water. His face in the mirror was drawn and sallow. Everything ached. He crossed to the window to pull the shade closed. A purple dusk lay on the city streets. Further off, Mount Wilson, up on the crest of the San Gabriels, glowed vermilion, diamond glints of the gasping sunlight sparkling out of the rocky brush. He put an arm up against the window and leaned heavily against it.

Below him in the parking lot a lone man got out of his car, closed the door and went to his trunk. He took out a small carrying case, looked around the lot, closed the trunk, then quickly, without wasted motion, bypassed the lobby entrance and walked directly underneath into Hardy's wing of the building.

It was just the way he had felt at home. Paranoid. Stupid.

But knowing that didn't help. Suddenly he knew he had to get out of here. He had given Jody Bachman his room number, told him he'd be staying in all night.

Jody Bachman, who by Hardy's scenario had hired someone to kill Simpson Crane, Crane's wife, Larry and Matthew Witt. And now Hardy was the only one standing between him and his seven million dollars . . .

There wasn't much to pack. He gathered his old clothes, still wearing his new ones. There was no one in the hallway when he stepped into it.

The elevator opened and he was facing a thin dark well-dressed man. The man carried the small carrying case he'd seen earlier, or one very much like it. Hardy stepped by him into the elevator as the man got out. He was looking for room numbers as the door closed.

52

Jody Bachman was twenty minutes late, and if he was surprised to see Hardy sitting alive at the table he had reserved, he showed no sign.

The fever had broken after another twelve hours of heavy sleep in a motel just outside of Glendale. Hardy, in new loafers, slacks, an indigo sports coat and regimental tie, still hurt. His muscles still ached.

He had given himself a couple of minutes of feeling like an idiot when he woke up. But, after all, he *had* woken up and that was some consolation, maybe even justification. It had probably been fatigue and fever. Absolutely nothing to it. But it was done. He had changed hotels. In all likelihood it had been foolish and unnecessary. He could live with that. Had, in fact.

He knew who Bachman was before he got to the table. Entering the room as though he owned it, he was one of those southern California ex-surfers whose aging process didn't seem to run on the same battery pack as that of mere mortals. He had to be thirty-five or so if he was a partner at Crane, but he looked ten years younger — chiseled cheeks, a cleft in his chin, not a worry line anywhere. The hair, which would have been peroxide blond fifteen years before, was now a light chestnut and fell forward in a Kennedy lock. He either used a tanning salon or spent a lot of time at Margaret Morency's pool.

There was no question — it was a power room. Bachman's first stop was where the mayor of Los Angeles sat at a table for six, at least one of whom Hardy recognized as a prominent and much photographed state legislator.

As Bachman worked the room, winding his way back to the window seat, Hardy sipped his club soda. There was no smog. Los Angeles south of downtown sprawled over some warehouses, then expanded to a horizon of oil derricks, rail yards, power lines, freeways, gypsum quarries. It was a view for those who favored expanse over anything pleasant to look at — there were no bridges, islands, bodies of water, distinctive buildings, hills or green patches. Maybe Bachman didn't yet rate the better window tables, where the mayor and the congressman and whomever they ate with could glimpse the ocean, the glittering and verdant west side, the San Gabriels.

"Sorry I'm late. Jody Bachman." Bachman mouthed another greeting to someone he had missed on his first pass through the room, then — finally — sat. "I can't seem to catch up." He laughed. "It never ends. You having a drink?"

Hardy tipped the glass. "Club soda."

"Me, too. How guys have a martini or even a beer in the middle of the day . . ." He shook his head. "It wipes me out. I might as well take a sleeping pill. So what can I do for you?"

"I'm trying to get to the end of something myself. My client got sentenced to death on Friday."

Bachman, sipping his water, stopped it halfway to his mouth. "Jesus," he said, putting the glass down, "that's a different breed of law."

"It's not exactly boardrooms and bylaws."

"Death, huh? Witt's wife, right?"

"That's right. Jennifer."

Bachman whistled soundlessly. The waiter arrived. He wore a tuxedo and placed a glass of what looked like cranberry juice on the table. "Just the special, Klaus, for me. Whatever it is." He included Hardy.

"Sounds fine." When Klaus was gone, he said, "I'm trying to get the judge to lower it to life."

"I thought you appealed. Forever."

"Eventually," Hardy said. "If it comes to that." He didn't intend to explain the protocol. "Jennifer says she's innocent and" — Hardy allowed a bemused grin for Bachman's benefit — "I'm still tempted to believe her. So what I've got to do is give the judge some doubt. Doesn't have to be much . . ."

"And you think Witt's call to me . . . ."

"I don't know, Mr. Bachman. It's the only unturned stone at this point."

Another power broker passed the table, giving Bachman a friendly shake of the shoulder. He nodded absently, then sat back in his chair, reaching for his juice. "If this is your best bet . . ." He took in the view for a minute. "After we talked, I tried to check the logs last night but I couldn't get into the computer until this morning."

Hardy waited.

Bachman reached into his coat pocket and extracted two pages, stapled and folded. He opened them, handing them across to Hardy. "I went ahead and copied my original timesheet on the back — sometimes they get my writing wrong."

The first page was a section of typed summary of Bachman's billable time. On December 23, beginning at 6:10 P.M., he had billed .20 to YBMG. Under desc./svs. was typed: "Tcon w/Witt. ???."

Bachman translated. "It was just a call to answer some questions. I guess I got about ten or so and Witt was one of them."

"Do you remember what his question was?"

"Not a clue. I billed it to the Group, so it must have been something to do with the offering, but it's gone. Sorry."

Hardy looked again at the bill. "But the call lasted twenty minutes? Isn't that a long time to have no memory of at all?"

For the first time Bachman showed an edge of pique — the pleasant smile faded for an instant. He pursed his lips, then drank some juice. By the time he put the glass down he had recovered. "You've got it wrong, .20 isn't twenty minutes. In its wisdom, the firm's billing is done in tenths of an hour. Two tenths is twelve minutes." He leaned forward, confiding in Hardy. "And even one second more than six minutes counts as twelve — we round off. The call itself might easily have been less than five minutes . . ." His smile held no warmth now. "But I really don't remember. What more can I say?"

Hardy flipped to the original timesheet on the back. Whatever had been written after "Tcon w/Witt" — about two lines worth — had been scratched out.

"I know." Bachman, seeing Hardy on that page, answered before Hardy could put the question. "And the answer is I don't know. Maybe my pen ran, maybe I just wrote an unnecessarily long description. They ask us to keep it simple. You should meet my secretary — she flays me if I get redundant or wordy."

Hardy stared at the scratching for another useless moment. He'd love to get his hands on the original, see if some expert could get something to come up. But even then, what? Whatever Bachman had originally written, it couldn't have been so incriminating that, by itself, it would help Jennifer now.

He looked up. Bachman was studying him. "You know, I'm happy to help you if I can, and I think I've been pretty forthcoming. But I have to wonder when this YBMG inquisition is going to stop. It gets old. I mean, is this what happens when you close a deal? Everybody wants a piece of it."

"I don't want a piece of it."

"Well, I know, that's not what I meant. But all these questions . . ."

"I've got a young woman who's got a good chance of getting executed unless I can prove somebody else killed her husband. To me, I'm sorry, but that's worth a couple of questions."

Klaus returned with lunch — an avocado stuffed with baby shrimp, three pieces of high-end lettuce, a wedge of pumpernickel bread.

Bachman pushed the lettuce around. "That's

understandable," he said. "But what does Dr. Witt's phone call to me have to do with his death? You're not suggesting that somebody with YBMG killed him, are you?"

"I didn't know. It was a question that wasn't answered. I knew that Witt had called you, and his lawyer in San Francisco told me he was upset about the circular. I wondered if he threatened you somehow —"

"And then I killed him? For what? You just can't be serious."

"Hypothetically, if you're interested, I can explain it." The shrimp, all two ounces of them, were sweet.

Hardy thought it would be instructive to watch Bachman's reaction. He ran it all down to him — from the phone call to Simpson Crane to Restoffer getting called off.

When he had finished, Bachman nodded, his smile a distant memory. "A lot of lawyers are writing novels these days, Mr. Hardy. Maybe you ought to try your hand at it."

Hardy spread his palms. "This is non-fiction."

"Yes, and so is the fact that nobody is hiding anything here. Everything is completely out in the open."

"Simpson Crane let you trade out your hours for stock?"

This stopped him, momentarily. "Sure."

"Your firm does that often? Takes that kind of risk?"

This had moved nicely from the hypothetical. Bachman rubbed a hand over his upper lip. Maybe he was starting to sweat. "Hey, in these times you take whatever business you can get. It's a buyer's market out there."

"And Simpson had no problem with that?"

Thinking fast, Bachman said, "Of course not. Simpson and I were friends. I wouldn't have done anything to hurt Simpson." Hardy realized he had never directly accused him of that. "We talked about it, of course. At length. We figured there was a more than reasonable chance of downstream recovery. Which, I might add, has materialized. The firm has made two million dollars on my time. It took a risk, sure, but I'd say it was worth it. Wouldn't you?"

Bachman's hand seemed unsteady as he picked up his water glass.

Hardy nodded. "What about the other five million?"

He stopped the glass midway to his mouth, then drank, nearly slamming it back down. "There is no other five million."

Finally, Hardy felt he had forced Bachman into an outright lie. Time to call him on it. "Clarence Stone said the Group paid you fifty thousand shares. That's several million dollars. If two went to your firm, where's the other five?"

Bachman swallowed. "That was a personal bonus," he said.

"You just said there wasn't any other five million."

"I mean for the *firm*. To the firm."

"So there is another five million?"

"How was everything? Are you gentlemen finished?" It was Klaus. "Perhaps a little dessert?

Some cappucino, espresso? We've got a marvelous *tiramisu.*"

Bachman had pushed himself back from the table. "Nothing," he said. It was a dismissal. Klaus did not even look at Hardy.

The interruption had given Bachman enough time. He had not gotten to where he was by giving in to panic. This was another hurdle, an obstacle to overcome. "Yes, I made a bundle," he said. "And the last time I looked, *that* was not a crime."

Hardy leaned forward, trying to regain his momentum. "Witt threatened to call all the other doctors, didn't he? He would've blown the deal."

Bachman's smile returned. "If you're going to be making those kinds of accusations, Mr. Hardy, you'd better have some proof. There are libel and slander laws in this state that could make you a poor man in a heartbeat. You should know that."

"Who did you hire?"

Bachman shook his head, not amused. "I didn't, Mr. Hardy. But if I did, would I be so foolish as to leave a trail? Do you think I might have written the person a check? Now, if you'll excuse me" — he pushed his chair back, standing — "I've got a one o'clock I'm running late for." He nodded one last time, caught Klaus' eye and told him to put lunch on his bill.

53

Whatever he found out or thought he had uncovered in Los Angeles, the unpalatable truth remained that he still couldn't prove a goddamned word of it. In the plane he scribbled notes on courses of action he ought to take — he would call the FBI and try to have them pursue their RICO investigation into Simpson's death. He thought it might be possible to trace a withdrawal of funds from one of Bachman's accounts if he could get some federal agent interested in his theory.

A big if.

Another possible avenue was getting through to Todd Crane, Simpson's son, now the managing partner. Maybe he'd be interested to learn that Jody Bachman had turned over to them only fifteen thousand or so of the fifty thousand shares he had earned.

Or did Todd already know it? Maybe he was plain thrilled and delighted with two million against seventy-five thousand in billables. It was, Hardy realized, only his personal fantasy — unverifiable, as fantasies tended to be — that Bachman would have traded *all* of his fifty thousand shares against his time. Who said he would have to do that?

If those two approaches failed, maybe Restoffer . . . ? No, not realistic — Restoffer was out of it.

It was down to Judge Villars, sitting as the thirteenth juror — down to what he could make her believe.

His own theories didn't matter. He couldn't prove them. They weren't going to do Jennifer any good. He had to go another way. He had to be lawyer and make an argument out of whole cloth if need be, even if he hated what he had to do.

But — to be fair — it *wasn't* whole cloth. At least he'd be starting with one truth, the one that had been denied throughout and yet had remained constant — Jennifer had been battered.

Overriding Jennifer's objections — he wouldn't even ask her again — he was going to lay it out for Villars — Jennifer's intractability, the Freeman affidavit, the defense decisions.

The irony did not escape him. He could not use anything he knew about Jody Bachman and YBMG. And what he could introduce probably had no direct bearing on what had happened in the Witts' bedroom on December 28.

The plane nosed down over the Bay. It was almost four o'clock and he was to face Villars tomorrow morning at nine-thirty.

He was down to his last dart.

"Of course, I'll do anything."

Dr. Lightner sat framed by the glass in his office. His secretary had gone home. The eucalyptus grove behind him was dark, in shadow.

"Good. I want you to tell the judge about Larry beating her."

Lightner sat forward, ramrod stiff at the proposal.

Hardy leaned forward, almost pleading now. "I know what I'm asking, Doctor, but it's really Jennifer's only hope. You've stood by her so long in all this."

But standing by someone and revealing their privileged communications were very different matters.

After a couple of seconds Lightner stood up. He turned his back to Hardy and looked out into the grove. "I can't believe it's come to this."

Hardy came up next to him. "After Larry died, when you were seeing her, she never . . . ?"

Lightner was already shaking his head. "She wouldn't talk about it."

He felt a sudden sinking in his gut, a vertigo. For an instant he thought it was the flu again. Unbidden, the awful thought reoccurred — had she done it, after all? *Stop it.*

Lightner walked back to the window, put an arm against the door jamb, looking out. "This is priest and confession, isn't it?"

Hardy couldn't put a lighter face on it. "Yes, it is."

"Betray the privilege. Betray her trust."

"Save her life."

Lightner turned and faced Hardy, the ruddy face pale and drawn under the beard. "What about the doctors I gave you? Couldn't they help?"

"What are they going to say? Where is their proof?" At this stage statements about her bruises and abrasions weren't enough. He needed her therapist's confirmation.

Lightner turned back toward the grove, opened the door and stepped outside. Hardy followed, and they walked a hundred feet over the duff.

"What do you think happened that morning?"

Lightner let out a long breath. There were muffled sounds of traffic on 19th Avenue. The doctor stared through the trees. "I think it was pretty much the way she told it, except she left out the physical part."

"The physical part?"

"Larry hitting her."

"He hit her that morning?"

Lightner turned to him. "Let's say I saw the bruises the next time I saw her, which was two days later. I think he hit Matt too. I'm not saying he did, I'm saying it could have happened —"

"Matt didn't have any bruises."

Lightner shook his head, unable to get it out. "Matt's head . . ." he began. And Hardy saw what he meant. If Larry had struck Matt in the head, the bullet would have destroyed any sign of it. It evoked his own delirious scenario of a few nights before.

"I don't know what happened," Lightner repeated.

"What do you *think* happened, Doctor? This is Jennifer's life here. I've got to make Villars see it."

Lightner was trying to walk a line, trying to stay on the angel's side of privilege. "All right, this is what I believe happened."

Lightner faced him, the last low rays of the sun

striking the red in his beard. Worn down by the tension, by the moral and professional dilemma, at last he appeared to have made up his mind. "She was leaving him, taking Matt with her. That was the fight. He had beaten her, badly, on Christmas Eve. She called and told me."

"And what did you do?"

"I told her to leave, to get out. She said she was afraid Larry would kill her. She told me about the gun. It was in the headboard. He would use it. I told her to take it and get out. Obviously, she didn't."

"Then what?"

"On Monday it started again." And he began to develop a scenario with chilling plausibility. Hardy could scarcely breathe as he listened. "He hits her and she says she's really going, leaving for good. She starts yelling for Matt, who is nowhere to be found. Maybe he's hiding somewhere. In any event, suddenly Larry, who's been after her, apparently decides he has had enough. He runs upstairs. Knowing what he's doing — going for the gun — Jennifer starts running up after him to get him to stop, to plead — anything. By now she is screaming, hysterical, just like that woman from next door said.

"But Larry isn't in the bedroom. And the gun is. She grabs it, hears a noise behind her, turns. There is another gun! Coming out of the bathroom door — he's gone in there. She fires. It's Matt. She has hit Matt, who has been hiding in the bathroom all this time with his new Christmas present. A toy gun from his grandparents.

"And then suddenly Larry is out, rushing her,

his hands raised to strike. She fires once, point blank . . ." Blinking now, as though coming back to himself from a place removed, Lightner turned to Hardy. "It was over," he said. "Later she tried to cover up. But she had no choice. Larry would have killed her . . ."

Hardy stood a long moment. The sound of traffic was gone. The sun was down, a chill coming up off the leaves. It was a great defense, if it were true.

"*That's* how I *believe* it may have happened. Larry went upstairs for the gun. There was no premeditation. All Jennifer wanted to do was get out, get away from him. She should have done it long ago. It was self-defense, I'm convinced . . ."

"Will you testify to that tomorrow? If I have an affidavit for you, will you sign it?"

"To what? There's no evidence there. Even I know that."

Hardy knew it, too. But he needed Lightner there, needed his story, a story but a highly educated one, for his own ends. "Let me worry about that. My question is, can I count on you? Will you at least tell the judge what you have just told me?"

Slowly, sighing with the weight of it, Lightner nodded at last. "All right. If she'll let me."

Rebecca had missed her daddy.

He was lying on the rug in front of the fireplace snuggling with her. She hadn't let him get up, wrestling him back down to the ground, both of them laughing and talking their own language. Rebecca had given Hardy ten minutes of unsullied joy with her repertoire of kisses — rabbit kisses, nose to nose; butterfly kisses, eyelashes against Hardy's cheek; heart kisses, which Rebecca had invented herself, where she kissed her hand, held it to her heart, then pressed it to Hardy's and held it there.

It was past the children's bedtime, dark out, lights off inside, but the family was together again. The fire crackled. Vincent fell asleep and Frannie laid him down on the couch. She came down to the floor and rested her head on Hardy's stomach. Rebecca lay heavily across his chest — her breathing became regular.

"Are you coming to bed? Isn't tomorrow it?"

"In a minute."

"Dismas." Her eyes were soft, worried. She crossed over to him and put a hand on his shoulder. "Hon, it's eleven o'clock."

Hardy sat behind the manual typewriter at the kitchen table, his forehead in his hands, sick with exhaustion, his brain a buzzsaw. He could not stop thinking. He had been writing for three hours. First, touching up Lightner's carefully worded affidavit. Then he had reviewed his motion under California Penal Code Section 190.4(e) to modify the sentence down to life without parole, which was within the judge's absolute discretion.

The second brief was trickier because he knew he could not hope to prevail unless he had legitimate grounds to demand a new trial. To this end he had two arguments: The first one was that the packaging of the Ned Hollis murder count with those of Larry and Matt had fatally prejudiced the jury as a matter of law.

True, both Freeman and Jennifer had personally waived this issue on the record, but that could be dealt with. Hardy argued that no *competent* lawyer could have ever declined a mistrial under those circumstances, and that Jennifer's acquiescence was the result of incompetent advice.

(He knew Freeman wouldn't bat an eye at such a tactic, and in fact would have pointed it out to him if Hardy hadn't thought of it himself. The idea was to keep your client alive, not to stroke egos.)

This was a reasonable point, although — again — Villars had already ruled on it and was unlikely to change her mind.

His second argument was his last best hope — evidence on Jennifer as a battered wife had been suppressed . . . and Hardy knew that here, legally, things got shaky because who, after all, suppressed the evidence but Jennifer herself? He would need to try to explain why.

He was trying to bring up an argument for life in prison rather than death, under guidelines outlined in the penal code. The argument, technically, at this point could only be used in mitigation, not in overturning the guilty verdict. It was probably inadmissible under the other section as grounds for a new trial.

If he dared hope for a new trial, then Villars would have to make the connection, and the leap. And she would have to go out on a judicial limb to do it. He had no idea if she would.

But he had no choice — his eggs had to go into

this basket — he had to rely on Villars being interested in justice, in the truth, as she thought she was. She had told him she agonized over the death penalty, that the responsibility staggered her. But even so, he would be asking her to reverse herself on rulings she had already made during the trials. If she wavered at all here, Powell would scream. And Powell was going to be the state's Attorney General. He would not be a good enemy for Villars to acquire just now . . .

Part of Hardy knew that he was kidding himself. He knew that, in practice, reversals at this stage didn't happen. The final administrative motions might be dressed up as the defendant's last stand, but their true intent was to give the judge a chance to save herself from the stigma of reversible error. Only on paper *might* this last hurdle have an effect on fairer application of the death penalty — in practice, historically, it rarely made any difference.

After he had gone over his motions, he spent the rest of the night triple-checking the evidence folders and reviewing the interviews from the beginning. His notes on Tom DiStephano. What the physicians had told him about Jennifer's "accidents," her bruises. Freeman's affidavit about Jennifer's forbidding the battered-wife defense. The abortions. The dentist Harlan Poole's first testimony.

And thank God he had spoken up back then, insisted it go on the record.

He thought that Villars would give him an opportunity — he would probably be allowed to start.

But his leeway would be severely constrained — if it wasn't on the record she wasn't going to let him bring anything up for the first time tomorrow, that was for sure.

Frannie kissed the top of his head and went to the bedroom. He noticed the light going off. She had wisely given up on him for tonight.

He stood up and grabbed the telephone, pulling it around the corner into the work area off the kitchen. He closed the connecting door behind him.

A phone rang five times before a weary voice answered.

"Nancy, I'm sorry to wake you up, but there's one last thing I need to know."

54

He was at the Hall of Justice by seven-thirty. Even at that time reporters were beginning to swarm. This was judgment day, and it attracted them like clover drew bees. There were three minicams parked outside on Bryant and a couple of knots of news professionals sipped coffee from Styrofoam and ate danish.

As Hardy approached the Hall, one of the stringers recognized him and trotted over, asking for a statement. Hardy stopped, his insides churning. He wanted to avoid all of this. It might jinx him. "What do you want to say? It hasn't happened yet. The verdict isn't verified." Chew on that, he thought.

Others followed:

"Do you have new evidence?"

"What do you think of Dean Powell as Attorney General?"

Hardy had to laugh. "Let's say I'd rather have him in Sacramento than in my courtroom."

"Do you think Jennifer Witt will be executed?"

This sobered them all. This was reality. Hardy didn't want to prejudice things at this point. Villars had warned them all about talking to the media, and it would be unconscionable if he made a convincing case this morning in court only to have Villars see him posturing on television, like Powell or Freeman, while she was considering her decision.

He started moving again. He was sorry, he couldn't comment. Through the press he spotted David Freeman as his colleague turned from 7th onto Bryant. It should have been a surprising relief — an ally to talk to — but he had lost his stomach for Freeman, too. Still, it was good of the old man to come down, put on a show of solidarity, talk to the media if he got the chance, and Hardy would see to it that he did. "Here comes David Freeman," he said, pointing.

The swarm moved to the next field of clover and Hardy escaped up the wide and grimy steps into the lobby, past the metal detector, to an empty elevator, down to the evidence lockers, finally taking refuge in a deserted jury-selection room on the third floor.

It was power-suit day. Both attorneys were dressed identically — dark charcoal suits, white shirts, red ties. Hardy's tie featured a nearly invisible pattern of tiny blue diamonds. Wild flamboyance.

They had gathered in the courtroom. Coming up the aisle, Hardy exchanged greetings with Freeman and Lightner, who were sitting next to one another. He handed Lightner the affidavit he had prepared for him and waited, making small talk with Freeman, until the psychiatrist had read it, scratched corrections in a few places and signed it.

Hardy nodded at Powell, who was leaning over his table, alone this morning. His assistant, Morehouse, didn't need to be here, he must have figured. This wasn't going to take long.

Now Jennifer came through the doors. She had dressed simply — dark flat shoes and a blue skirt, a white blouse with a small collar. No makeup. No jewelry. As the bailiff left her, she turned around and looked at the gallery, raising a hand. Hardy saw Lightner nod. Jennifer's face brightened slightly. "My mom's here," she said. "And Tom."

It was true. Nancy had just come in. Her son held her arm. Last night she had told him they had the funeral for Phil over the weekend. She hadn't been able to get back in to visit Jennifer, but Tom and she had reconnected. He was her good boy again. She was getting her children back. What a place to do it, Hardy thought.

The bailiff announced that the Superior Court of the State of California, City and County of San Francisco, was now in session, Judge Joan Villars presiding.

The judge sat at the bench, her familiar gray helmet of hair perfectly in place over the perennially stern visage. She wore her reading glasses. The court reporter, Adrienne, had her machine set up and was waiting.

"All right," the judge began, adjusting her robes. "Good morning. Mr. Powell, do you have a statement?"

"No, Your Honor. The jury has spoken loud and clear on this. Submitted by the prosecution." He looked at his watch. He obviously did not expect this to take long. He sat back in his chair. "Mr. Hardy?"

Hardy stood and handed his papers to the judge. "Your Honor, I have two motions. Under Sections 1179-1181 of the Penal Code of the State of California I am presenting to the court a motion to grant a new trial. Concurrently, under Section 190.4(e) I have prepared a motion for the court to mitigate Mrs. Witt's sentence to life in prison without the possibility of parole."

Villars nodded. This was expected. "Have you new evidence to present at this time in support of these motions?"

"Yes, Your Honor, I do."

Powell straightened up and looked across at him.

He continued. "I have two affidavits, Your Honor. If I may." He approached the bench again and handed them to the judge, who took a long moment looking them over. Pulling her glasses forward and peering over them, she looked down at Hardy. Then: "Mr. Powell." Her little finger ordered him to approach. When he got next to Hardy she stood. "Chambers," she said. Then, to the room at large: "Court will recess for ten minutes."

Villars had moved ahead of them and seated herself behind her desk. Hardy and Powell had gone for their chairs and pulled them forward. She sat glaring into space while Powell read the affidavits. Finishing, he placed them on the desk in front of her. "I'm not going to accept either of your arguments on your motion for a new trial, Mr. Hardy," Villars said. "I've ruled on these issues repeatedly during this trial, and I'm certain the appeals court is going to uphold me."

Slowly, Hardy let out a breath, preparing himself for the worst. Next to him, he could sense Powell's excitement, his elation. Villars held the papers open before her, her eyes scanning them again, frowning, perhaps, Hardy hoped, searching for something else she had overlooked. Finally she asked, "Lightner is the psychiatrist she was sleeping with?"

Was this an opening? Hardy jumped in. "That was never established, Your Honor."

Powell came up halfway out of his chair. "What do you mean it was never established? Your Honor, these affidavits should have been presented days ago so we could look into these matters . . ."

"Mr. Powell, please. I'm asking the questions here. Mr. Hardy?"

"The affidavit speaks for itself, Your Honor. Dr. Lightner says he has previously undisclosed information regarding Jennifer's situation on the morning of the murders. Her husband was beating her. If she killed him, it was to save her own life, right then, that morning. There was *no* premeditation —"

"Your Honor, please!" Powell wasn't having this, not at the eleventh hour.

"Self-defense is a justification for homicide, Mr. Hardy. If that was your defense, you and Mr. Freeman had every opportunity to bring it up earlier."

Hardy had known this was coming and was prepared. "That point is addressed in the other affidavit, Your Honor. David Freeman's. I did not have the opportunity. Mr. Freeman did. He chose not to do it. I was not Mrs. Witt's attorney in the guilt phase. My client shouldn't be penalized now because of Mr. Freeman's strategy." Hardy knew this was a reach . . . he and Freeman had been acting as a team, and Villars knew it as well as Powell. Still, technically at least, he wasn't wrong.

Villars sat, her face a mask.

"Your *Honor,*" Powell said, "this battered woman question has never been introduced. It's not part of the record."

Hardy started to answer but Villars stopped him. "I know, Mr. Hardy, you don't have to remind me." She gestured with her palm. "You'll recall, Mr. Powell, that it was explicitly included in the record by Mr. Hardy himself."

"But that was during the Hollis phase of the trial. It has no bearing on what Jennifer Witt was convicted of."

Villars did not see it that way. "It was your decision to combine the counts in this trial, Mr. Powell. It's your problem if something leaks over. But" — she turned back to Hardy — "this affidavit does not say what Lightner's evidence is."

Hardy knew that. He had no immediate answer for it. "It will come out in his testimony."

"Oh for the love of God . . ."

Villars pointed at Powell. "Watch your language, Mr. Powell. This court will not tolerate blasphemy."

"I'm sorry, Your Honor, but I fail to see what we're trying to get to here. You've already said you're not allowing Mr. Hardy's so-called evidence —"

"On the motion for a new trial." Villars didn't like it but she understood her duty. If there was a reason that Jennifer should not be sentenced to death she *had* to consider it. "On the motion to mitigate, I think I should listen to what Dr. Lightner has to say. *If it's a fact,* if Mr. Hardy can prove by Dr. Lightner's testimony, that Mrs. Witt had been psychologically and physically abused, she deserves consideration of that fact before I sentence her."

"If it's a fact at all, Your Honor. Mr. Hardy gives no indication that he's got any facts."

Villars pondered that. "Mr. Hardy, can you tell us anything of the substance of Dr. Lightner's proposed testimony?"

This was Hardy's hand and he had to play it. "I'm sorry, Your Honor. You can read Dr. Lightner's affidavit — I'm reluctant to try to paraphrase his testimony in any more detail . . . I might inadvertently misinform the court."

This was something they all understood. Hardy wasn't sure how much he could get out of Lightner but he couldn't say that.

Villars rubbed the papers between her fingers, the sound dull yet somehow insistent. "I'll let Dr. Lightner begin, Mr. Hardy," she said at last. "But I warn you . . ."

Hardy knew.

"What is he going to say?" Jennifer whispered to Hardy, grabbing his arm. "He thinks I'm guilty."

Hardy had to admire it — she wasn't budging on her story. There hadn't been the slightest slip or deviation from it in all these months. She flat did not do it. Of course, she would not be the first killer to deny it to the death.

He leaned over, urgent. "Trust me here. Don't interrupt. I believe you." It was his turn to squeeze *her* arm. He pulled her toward him. "Do you hear me? I believe you."

Villars was now looking down on Lightner. "Doctor," she began, "I want to be clear here. Your testimony today will not be admissible regarding the guilt or innocence of Mrs. Witt. That has already been decided. However, the court understands that you have information that might have some influence in mitigating the death penalty that the jury has recommended."

Lightner swallowed.

"Is that so?"

The doctor shrugged, looking to Hardy for help. "Yes, Your Honor, I believe so."

Villars nodded. "Okay. Mr. Hardy?"

Hardy rose slowly. "Dr. Lightner, what is your relationship with the defendant?"

"I am her friend and her psychiatrist."

"How long have you been her psychiatrist?"

"About four years."

"And her friend?"

"I've considered her my friend all along."

"And in your role as friend, doctor, have you seen Mrs. Witt other than in circumstances that might be described as professional? Lunches, dinners, that sort of thing."

He was fishing, but regardless of the answer he

was also giving Lightner a big hole to skate through. He could tell from Lightner's posture, his eyes, that he understood what was being offered. "Yes."

What Lightner did not realize was the price Hardy would have to exact.

"Many times?"

"Several. Yes."

Then Hardy dropped his bomb. "Dr. Lightner, at the time of Larry and Matt Witt's death, were you Jennifer's lover?"

Lightner, apparently stunned, sat back in the witness chair, then turned to the judge. "Your Honor . . . ?"

Villars shook her head no. "Answer the question, Doctor." Although he already had.

Hardy reminded him that he was under oath. He cast a helpless glance across the room at the defense table, at Jennifer. "Yes," he whispered.

Powell exploded. "Your Honor, this witness has already testified, under oath, that he and Mrs. Witt were not intimate."

Villars leaned over. "You're admitting to perjury here, Doctor. Do you realize that?"

Soberly, Lightner nodded, answered yes.

There was a ripple of noise in the courtroom and Villars hit her gavel once. She motioned the lawyers to the front of the bench. "This is your friendly witness?" she asked, but it called for no answer.

Hardy turned to check on his client. Jennifer was a statue, her teeth over her lower lip, biting. He had told her to trust him, that he believed her. He had to let her know.

Stepping back in front of Lightner, Hardy asked, "Doctor, did you ever hypnotize the defendant?"

"Yes."

"Did you tell her, under hypnosis, that she should deny having this affair with you?"

Lightner gulped some air, swallowed. "I thought it would hurt her defense. Compromise her somehow. She was having trouble enough handling what was happening to her."

"You mean the deaths of Larry and Matt?"

"Yes."

Hardy took a moment, stepped toward the jury box, gathering his thoughts, then turned again. "Because you were, in fact, having an affair with Jennifer, some of your time with her, therefore, was not related to your practice? Or her psychiatric condition?"

"That's right."

This was the point, and Lightner understood it. If Jennifer was to have a chance at life, though it cast her and Lightner in a negative light, the affair had to come out, as he would try to demonstrate.

"Did you see Jennifer, either professionally or personally, after December 28 of last year."

"Yes, of course. I've told you. Almost every day. She was devastated by the death of her son. She blamed herself." There was another buzz, short-lived, behind them. "But Jennifer blames herself for everything."

"And yet she denies killing her husband and her son."

"That's correct."

This wasn't a question, but Powell didn't object

and Villars said nothing, so Hardy took a deep breath and continued. "Doctor Lightner, did Jennifer tell you about any decisions she had reached before December 28?"

"Yes. She was leaving her husband. She called me on the telephone on Christmas Eve."

"As a friend, not as a psychiatrist."

"Yes."

Hardy began to lead him up through it, slowly, with a rhythm. The fact that Larry had threatened to kill her if she left. The gun by the bed. The increasing tension in the household. He had to keep the story flowing, slipping back and forth from conjecture to fact, slowly working his way — details, details — until they got to Monday morning.

"Now, Dr. Lightner, Jennifer has never admitted to you that she shot Larry or Matt. Correct?"

"Yes. Correct."

"Nevertheless, based on your training and experience, and sitting through this trial, have you formed an opinion as to Mrs. Witt's state of mind at the time of the killing?"

"Yes, I have."

"Incidentally, Doctor, all the information that you have received about this case has come from either Mrs. Witt or from this trial."

"That is correct."

"No one has provided you with any police reports, photographs or information out of court?"

"That's true."

"Tell us then, Doctor, your professional opinion as to Mrs. Witt's state of mind."

"Basically, she was in a panicked state due to

battered-wife syndrome. Her husband had beaten her repeatedly. They had just argued. He was running upstairs after her. She was in terror . . ."

Hardy picked up the pace, keeping the rhythm, setting the stage, bringing Lightner along with him. Larry was running upstairs . . .

"And what did she do then?"

"She grabbed the gun from the headboard," he said.

"And what did she do then, Doctor?"

Turning, Matt with the toy gun — the new Christmas present — in the bathroom door . . .

"And then?"

Matt. Larry's screaming rush toward her. The single shot at point-blank range . . .

The courtroom was silent. Perhaps ten seconds elapsed without a sound.

"Now, of course, Dr. Lightner, as you've told us, Mrs. Witt categorically and consistently denies any part in these killings. So this is your own reconstruction of events?"

"Yes, sir, it is."

"Entirely?"

"Yes, of course."

Hardy let it go until it had sunk in, then stepped closer to the witness box. "Dr. Lightner," he said, "how do you know about the toy gun Matt was holding?"

The silence grew. Lightner, telling his story, had gotten caught up in the emotion of it. Now, drained, he slumped slightly. Finally, he spoke. "I beg your pardon."

Hardy repeated the question. How did he know about the toy gun?

Lightner blinked. "I'm not sure."

"But this situation you've just described to us. Jennifer didn't describe it that way to you, did she?"

Powell stood up. "Your Honor . . ."

Villars did not hesitate. "Overruled. I'd like the doctor to answer."

"I must have seen it in the photographs, then. The ones at the trial here."

"Jennifer didn't tell you about it? She told me Matt didn't have any guns. Wasn't allowed to have them."

Powell stood again. Villars shook her head.

"No, that's right. She must not have. It must have been the photographs."

Hardy, nodding, walked back to his table and picked up the thick envelope containing all the forensic and murder-scene shots. "I'd like you to go through these photographs and point out this toy gun if you can find it."

Lightner took the envelope and began slowly turning the pages. Standing over him, Hardy waited. Villars was a sphinx. Halfway through, Lightner suddenly looked up. "But that was just a story. There might not have been a gun. That's just what I *thought* had happened. It's informed conjecture."

"But, Dr. Lightner, it is far more than conjecture."

Hardy again walked to the desk. He reached down into his briefcase and removed a large ziploc plastic evidence bag. Back at the witness box, he opened it and removed Terrell's "mistake" — the realistic toy gun that had been found in the same dumpster as the murder weapon. "This is the gun, is it not, doctor? This is the gun Matt was holding, is it not? The gun that you thought was real. The gun that provoked you to shoot him —"

"God!" Hardy heard Jennifer behind him. *"Ken?"*

Hardy did not trust himself to move but he could still talk. "This was the FedEx package — a Christmas present from Nancy, Matt's grandmother. How did you know, in your story, that it was a Christmas present? It didn't get to the house until 9:30, after Jennifer had left to go running. You had removed it with the murder weapon by the time she got back. Jennifer never knew it had been there. *Did she?*"

Lightner shifted on the seat, eyes on Hardy, then around the courtroom, as though looking for help. Finally turning to Villars. "I don't have to answer this, do I? I can take the Fifth Amendment."

Villars nodded. "If you believe your answer will tend to incriminate you."

He rubbed his hands on his pants legs. He looked at Jennifer, then Hardy. "I'm going to take the Fifth Amendment," he told Villars. "I'm not saying anything else without an attorney."

It was his only chance, his last chance.

She had called as she increasingly did when they had been fighting. Larry was beating her.

Why wouldn't she leave him? It wouldn't get any better. All the literature, and the facts, agreed on that. He had told her. And still she wouldn't leave him. She believed she had to keep trying.

So he'd listened. And counseled her. And, yes, made love to her.

He lied to Hardy and the court about that, but he'd told the truth to Hardy about his caring for her. Caring? That was putting it mildly. Yes, she loved him, more than transference, he told himself. But she had her family. She just wasn't leaving them. Which meant he could never really have her. The call on Christmas Eve wasn't that she had decided to leave. It was another fight, another beating, another call for help. He had responded, as he always did, and then she went back for more.

And now, again, here Monday morning. Another call, more terrible damage. It had to stop. It was his only chance, her only chance. He could save her and . . . have her . . . he would do anything for her. Anything . . .

Olympia Way. Her beautiful house. The street empty, dead, silent under a cold brittle morning sun. It took him ten minutes, perhaps less. Jennifer was going jogging. There was enough time. She'd be gone . . .

No one on the street.

He had been here. Three times in the afternoons, Matt and Larry gone, Jennifer meeting him. He knew his way around there. He knew where the gun was. Not that he was really planning on using it. Was he? No. It would never come to that. He would talk to the husband, tell him what he had done, what he was doing, to Jennifer. Now that he was here, it seemed —

"What is it?"

"Dr. Witt? We've got to talk. May I come in,

please? It's about your wife."

The guilty eyes narrowing. "Who the hell are you?"

"Her psychiatrist." Looking around, scanning the deserted street. "You know what it is, it's confidential."

No other sounds. They were alone in the house, the two of them.

"All right, just what is this about?"

"She needs me, Dr. Witt. She called. Is she upstairs?"

"She doesn't need you. What do you mean, she called? When? What are you talking about?"

"She told me she would be here. You were hitting her again. I'm taking her out —"

"You're not taking anything. She's not here."

"If I leave I'm calling the police. I'm calling them immediately."

"What the hell . . . what do you want?"

"I want to see Jennifer. I want her out of here. She's my patient. You should understand that, Doctor."

"She's not here, I told you she's not here."

"I need to see that for myself. I swear to God, I'm calling the police directly. I cannot let her stay here like this —"

"You want some proof? You need the goddamn grand tour." Less confident now, he thought.

Upstairs, at last, in the bedroom.

"There, satisfied? I told you, she's out. Now you get the hell out of my house!"

The gun right where she said he kept it — in the headboard. "I don't think so." He didn't need to think about it. Events were taking over.

"What are you doing with that? Goddamnit . . ."

Coming toward him, the noise, the other sound . . . maybe there all along, subliminal . . . water running into a sink? He hadn't even heard it. No. The noise stopped. That was it. It was the noise stopping. Somebody was in there.

"Don't move." To Witt, stopping him. The blood rushing now.

"What the hell do you think you're doing?"

"Who's in there?"

Witt yelling over his shoulder. "Matt, stay in there!" Half-turning, trying to fake him — "Don't come out!" — just as the other gun appeared . . . a blur really . . . in the bathroom doorway. Somebody shooting at him! But no one there. Nothing now but panic. A shadow. Things moving too fast.

Witt begins to lunge. But something else, too, at the same instant, off to the side, in the bathroom door. In his peripheral vision there is another gun. God! Somebody else is here, a witness. More, a threat.

He doesn't have a second. No time for more than a glance at his side. It's a gun — but something's wrong, it's too low to the ground, someone crouching? It pops, the gun pops . . .

He has no choice, he spins, points, squeezes the trigger just as he sees . . .

. . . the boy in a crouch stepping out, holding a gun, pointing it? It pops again. It can't be. It can't be Matt, he's at school. It's a school day and the father is at home alone . . .

He has to stop! He must! But his hand has already squeezed too far. His gun kicks, exploding in the room with the sound of a bomb, and the bathroom mirror splinters in a haze of sickly bright red.

No stopping now. Only an instant to move while Witt is struck dumb, immobilized by the explosion, by what he's seen, his eyes on the splayed body of his son . . .

A beat while the horror sinks in, but it is enough. Lightner yanks the gun back on Witt, now coming with a choking scream, hands raised. The face, eyes, a wild man closing in.

Impossible not to fire. Impossible to miss . . .

The reporters were rushing to telephones and minicams as Hardy turned back away from the witness stand. In a daze, he was aware of Villars using her gavel and of Powell standing at his table, mute. Of Nancy standing in the gallery. Nancy had confirmed in the call last night that she had sent the toy gun to Matt.

Lightner slumped in the witness chair. Hardy sat down next to his client, who turned her face against him, crying out of control.

Powell had Terrell take Lightner into custody on the perjury charge. Villars retired to her chambers alone.

A half hour later she returned to the bench. Hardy and Jennifer remained at the defense table, holding hands the whole time. Nancy and Tom were in the front row and Freeman had come inside the rail. Powell was across the room, slumped in his hard chair, pretending to study some papers. His face was set.

Villars' face was flushed, her mouth a thin line. She looked below her, over her reading glasses, at Hardy and Jennifer, then to Powell.

She spoke clearly, formally. "This court grants defendant's motion for a new trial under Penal Code Section 1181."

Hardy finally let himself lean back in his chair. Granting the motion for a new trial was a legal formality — Villars was ruling on Hardy's first motion, and that was all she was doing. It was clear there was not going to be any new trial for Jennifer Witt. As she had maintained all along, she had not killed either her husband or her son and, at last, everyone in the courtroom knew it.

"Further," the judge continued, "it is the decision of this court under California Code of Civil Procedure Section 657.6 that the verdict of the jury in *The People vs. Jennifer Lee Witt* be set aside — it is the judgment of this court that the evidence received is lacking in probative force to establish the proposition of fact to which it is addressed.

"Mr. Powell, I cannot imagine you would oppose a motion for release of the defendant on her own recognizance at this time." It was not a question. "Mr. Hardy, would you care to approach."

55

After the trial Hardy had built a new brick border to enclose Frannie's roses by the fence in his backyard. He had his foot on it now, looking back toward the house. Isaac Glitsky, Abe's oldest, was taking his job very seriously — he lifted the top of the barbecue, poked the turkey in the thigh with the long fork. "It's still a little pink," he said.

Abe, finally, on Thanksgiving, holding what Hardy thought was his first beer of the year, spoke patiently, gently, the voice nothing like the one he used in his police life. "Just close it up, Ike, it'll get done."

The boy did, then went to join his brothers playing with Hardy's kids up under the overhang by the house.

It was unseasonably warm, sunny, with a westerly breeze. Moses and his pregnant bride Susan were expected soon, and Frannie and Flo were inside cutting things up, setting up condiment trays, cooking side dishes.

Hardy was having what he called the traditional Thanksgiving Old Fashioned — bourbon and soda and sugar and bitters and oranges and cherries and God knew what else. He wanted to enjoy it before Moses, the purist, arrived and tried to ruin it for him. He sat on his new low wall, taking in his world.

"This works," he said. He smelled the turkey smoke, the newly mown grass. Then: "You'll never believe who called me yesterday."

Glitsky looked over at him. "Orlando Cepeda?"

Hardy shook his head.

"Michael Jordan?"

"Not a sports figure."

"I know it wasn't Clinton. I'm sure he would've mentioned it when I talked to him."

Hardy sipped his drink. "Jennifer Witt."

The warm breeze came up again for a moment. Isaac was back at the barbecue and Abe told him to leave it. "And turn that hat around, son. We've talked about that."

Isaac was wearing his Giants hat backward. His homicide-inspector father agreed that while it was probably a harmless fashion, he wasn't going to allow his son to affect even the smallest trademark of gang affiliation. No baggy clothes, Raiders jackets, turned-around baseball caps for Abe Glitsky's sons.

Isaac flipped the cap around and Abe shrugged at Hardy. "I'm turning into a conservative. It's kind of sad."

"Let's see," he said. "A conservative in San Francisco would still leave you just to the left of Lenin, right?"

The scar lightened slightly — Abe's not-quite-beaming smile. "So how's Mrs. Witt?"

"She's rich. Really rich."

"This soon. They paid?"

"They had to. She didn't do it."

The shade from the house had reached them and Glitsky moved down a bit on the brick. "I've been meaning to ask."

Hardy nodded. "There were no prints at all on the toy gun."

"And this means something?"

"To a trained investigator like yourself, I'd think so."

Glitsky gave it a minute. He actually took a sip of his beer. "It was wiped. If some kid had ever played with it, it would have had his prints on it."

"See? I knew you'd get it. Anyway, there was so much other stuff, I just missed it. Something, as they say, was nagging at me, but I couldn't get it into the picture until Lightner slipped up. It should have had some prints, some partial prints, some smudges at least."

"But why did Lightner frame Jennifer if he loved her?"

"He didn't start out to. He must have convinced himself she wouldn't get nailed for it. He was so confident he confided to me he was afraid she did it, but only to save herself from Larry.

"I hear even shrinks can get caught up in believing what they want to believe. Just like 'real' people."

"He should have stolen something," Abe said. "Made it look like a botched burglary."

"Of course, with your years of experience, that's easy for you to say. In any event, Jennifer getting arrested screwed up everything. He hoped with Larry gone, she'd eventually marry him, her rod and her staff and her comforter. He said the obsession neurosis, whatever, was hers. It seems it was the other way around. He also didn't figure on Matt being home. Christmas vacation. He forgot about the boy."

"Why did he come just then?"

"I asked Jennifer the same thing. How did he know? She had called him when Larry started beating her up that morning. I suppose she blames herself for that, too. Anyway, obviously he'd been thinking about it. Jennifer at some point had told him about the gun, where it was. And now he thought with Larry gone . . . Anyway, Jennifer told me she called him when she ran upstairs in the middle of the fight. He told her to get out. He must have figured it was the right time, told his trusty secretary he was in conference, closed the door and walked out through the patio. It's not ten minutes to Jennifer's house from his office."

Glitsky drank again. "And Terrell gave him his alibi."

Hardy nodded. "I'm sure he'll work out fine in his new position." Terrell's job change to the DA's office had been finalized the previous week. "Lightner's secretary said he was there all morning and that's what Terrell wanted to hear . . ."

"It fit his theory."

"Except now the secretary isn't so sure. Funny, huh?"

"Hysterical. Unprecedented. And Lightner's going down?"

"It looks like it. He gets to have his own trial, anyway."

"He should have split when they charged her."

Hardy gave him the eye. "How could he without pointing the finger directly at himself? No, he thought he had an alibi. He *had* to stay around to watch Jennifer's defense. He couldn't leave me alone. He had to push the battered-wife defense. It was the only way to get Jennifer off that didn't put it back on him. And if that didn't work, well, everything had been for nothing. And remember, he really was, and is obsessed with her."

"But her husband did beat her, didn't he?"

Hardy nodded. "But Jennifer was always telling the truth about that — she didn't kill him *period.* She might have been full of guilt and other hang-ups, but she'd be damned if she'd put up a defense for something she *didn't* do. Her big problem was getting people, including her lawyers, to believe her."

The back door opened and Moses McGuire started down the steps. Hardy polished off his drink, chewed the cherry and dropped the orange slice into the dirt behind him, covering it. He and Glitsky stood up.

"Ike, want to check the bird?" Abe said.

Moses was shaking hands, his Scotch in the other hand. "This is my first one. You guys ahead of me? What are you drinking, Diz?"

Hardy held up his empty glass. "Bushmills, straight up, no ice."

"My man," Moses said. Then, turning to Glitsky, "So how's the murder business? Still booming?"

On Saturday, December 11, Hardy's wash-out "other dude," Jody Bachman, and Margaret Morency exchanged vows in a ceremony at Ms. Morency's estate in San Marino. As one of the biggest society weddings of the year, the event made the "Living Section" of the Sunday *Chronicle.*

Over three hundred guests had been in attendance. Among the stars and celebrities listed, Hardy noted both the mayor and the police chief of Los Angeles. Frank Kelso was also there, along with a host of other supervisors, state legislators, civic leaders, philanthropists.

Jody and Margaret smiled out at Hardy from the photograph. On Jody's right was Todd Crane, his best man, managing partner of Crane & Crane.

The couple was planning an extended honeymoon in the South of France.

It was a small house — three bedrooms, two baths — on a cul-de-sac in Belmont, twenty-two miles south of San Francisco. The people who had lived there before had kept it up beautifully — in the backyard the grass was trimmed and green. Just off the new deck some stone benches surrounded a small fountain. On the periphery, the fence was bordered by fruit trees — two bearing oranges, a lemon, a cherry and two plums, though now in the middle of January the cherry and plum trees were bare, leafless.

Jennifer Witt had gotten up at dawn and run three miles down Ralston and back up behind the college. She had not had a cigarette since the trial. Sitting in the breakfast nook, the window open a crack, she drank coffee and ate a plain croissant from the good bakery down the street. It was an overcast day, but still, outside, she could hear the sounds of birds and the fountain.

It was the first day of the spring semester and she had showered and gotten dressed by eight. Her first class was at nine. She did not have to declare her major for two years, but she knew it was going to be psychology. She wanted, finally, to understand herself, and thought that might be a good place to start.

When she finished she put her dishes in the sink. Wrapping a sweater around her shoulders, she walked back into the house and pushed open a door.

Her mother was still sleeping. She crossed the room and kissed her on the forehead. "I'm off," she said. "You want to meet for lunch?"

Her mother had been sleeping a lot since they had moved. Now she stretched and put an arm around her daughter's neck. "You have lunch," Nancy said, "make some friends. Stay at school."

"What about you?"

Her mother pulled herself up. "Don't worry about me."

"But I do." Jennifer sat on the bed and her mother smoothed her daughter's hair.

"This is the best it's ever been," Nancy said. "For me, at least."

Jennifer nodded. Her hand rested on her mother's. "I know. I guess I just never wanted to get here this way."

Nancy smiled. "At least we're here. I think it's where we take it that matters now."

"I know that." She squeezed her mother's hand and stood up. "I know. It's just kind of hard."

Nancy didn't let go of her. She looked up. "Okay, how about if, just today, I come down and have lunch? One time. Get you over the hump. Get me out of the house, too. I think I'm getting ready for that. Maybe I'll even call Tom."

Jennifer thought about that. "That'd be good, Mom. I'd like that."

The last school color picture of Matt was blown-up to eight-by-ten and framed on a small table by the front door. On her way out, Jennifer stopped, as she always did. This time, she picked it up, holding it in front of her. A gap-toothed Matt smiled at her. She kissed the glass.

Putting the frame back in its place, she opened the door, took in a deep breath and walked out into the morning.

The employees of G.K. HALL hope you have enjoyed this Large Print book. All our Large Print titles are designed for easy reading, and all our books are made to last. Other G.K. Hall Large Print books are available at your library, through selected bookstores, or directly from us. For more information about current and upcoming titles, please call or mail your name and address to: